Tony Park was born in 1964 and grew up in the western suburbs of Sydney. He has worked as a reporter, a press secretary, a PR consultant and a freelance writer. He is also a major in the Australian Army Reserve and served as a public affairs officer in Afghanistan in 2002. He and his wife, Nicola, divide their time equally between Australia and southern Africa. He is the author of twelve other novels.

Barbara,

Hope you like this!

Love, Cathy

TONY PARK
Red Earth

MACMILLAN
Pan Macmillan Australia

First published 2016 in Macmillan by Pan Macmillan Australia Pty Ltd
1 Market Street, Sydney, New South Wales, Australia, 2000

Cataloguing-in-Publication entry is available
from the National Library of Australia
http://catalogue.nla.gov.au

Typeset in 12/15 Birka by Post Pre-press Group, Brisbane
Printed by McPherson's Printing Group

Cartographic art by Laurie Whiddon, Map Illustrations

For Nicola

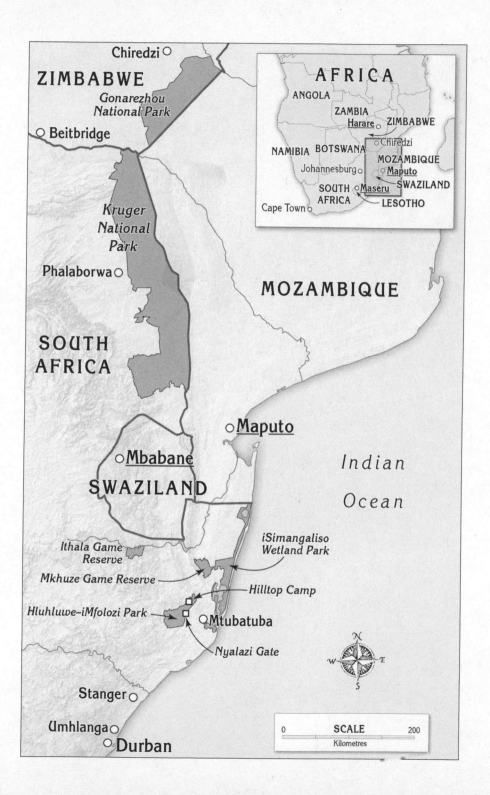

PART 1

They called him Inqe and he flew all over southern Africa, searching, always searching.

The sky was clear, the day warm, perfect weather for flying though summer's storms would soon be on their way. The golden grasslands and crops passed below him. Inqe was heading for the rolling hills and coastal wetlands of KwaZulu-Natal, nearly seven hundred kilometres south of his base in the Kruger National Park. He wasn't alone; his wingmen were either side of him.

They crossed the monumentally scaly back of the dragon, the Drakensberg Mountains, and the greener, lusher land opened out beneath them. Specks in the distant sky caught Inqe's eye and he changed direction to head towards them. As he flew closer he could see the fliers were in a landing pattern, each holding in perfect formation until it was his or her turn to land. Inqe joined the circuit, as did his wingmen.

As he orbited, waiting for his chance to touch down, Inqe saw there was yet more traffic in the air. Over King Shaka International Airport, a Boeing was on its final approach, and a small helicopter was coming towards them, low, fast, hellbent on a mission of some sort.

He returned his attention to the others immediately around him, and their target on the ground below. Those that had landed were already hard at work. He hoped he wouldn't be too late. On the thermals rising from the sun-warmed African grasslands he smelled the sweet scent that had brought the other fliers, and which had lured Inqe and his wingmen to Zululand.

Death.

Chapter 1

'ZAP-Wing, this is Tracker,' Nia Carras said into the boom microphone attached to her headphones. 'I've located your target.'

She adjusted her course slightly and pushed her Robinson R44 helicopter into a wide turn to stay clear of what looked like a swirling tornado of black dots against the blue sky. 'It's a kill all right, over.'

'Roger that, Tracker,' said Simon, the operations officer on duty at ZAP-Wing, the Zululand Anti-Poaching Wing, a force of air assets patrolling twenty-four game reserves in KwaZulu-Natal Province. 'Can you confirm it's a rhino, over?'

Nia keyed the microphone switch on the stick. 'Moving in closer, ZAP-Wing, but I'm taking it easy. There are vultures everywhere here.'

Nia tightened her orbit and, checking to either side and above her, brought the R44 lower. The carcass of the dead animal below was rippling with the bobbing heads and beating wings of scores of vultures, all fighting for the tastiest morsels of their lifeless prey. The noise of the approaching helicopter startled some of the birds, which began the ungainly process of taking off. Each vulture's wingspan was up to two metres wide.

'Getting visual now,' Nia said into her radio. She was used to continually scanning the sky around her, and her instruments; her eyes rested momentarily on the satellite navigation system in the cockpit. 'Hey, ZAP-Wing, you do know this kill is outside the park, right? Over.'

Nia peered through the rising curtain of birds, trying to catch sight of something that would identify the animal they were feasting on. The most prevalent and serious big game targets of poachers in the province were rhinos.

'Negative, Tracker,' said Simon. 'We received a report on the hotline from someone who thought the kill was inside the park, over.'

'Well, they got that wrong. It's just outside, in the communal lands.' A white-backed vulture, startled by the noise of Nia's engine, alighted from the head of the dead beast. 'Wait, ZAP-Wing. I see a horn and it's not of the rhino variety. It's a dead nguni, over.'

'A cow?'

'Affirmative. Something odd there, too. I'm going down for a closer look.'

'Your call, Tracker, we appreciate you going out of your way in any case.'

Nia could hear the diminishing interest in Simon's voice. If it wasn't a dead rhino in the Hluhluwe–iMfolozi Park then there would be no need to call in the police or national parks anti-poaching teams. The Hluhluwe Game Reserve and the adjoining iMfolozi Game Reserve, now designated as one park, were home to large numbers of black and white rhino. The cow had probably been hit by a car or a truck; it was close to the main tar road that ran between the two reserves, towards Mtubatuba.

She should really have been heading back to her base at Virginia

Airport on the coast just north of Durban, but she had some fuel left and it was a beautiful day for flying. It had been a good morning, even if it hadn't started out too well. She'd received a call-out early, just before six, from the control room of Motor Track, the vehicle tracking company that Coastal Choppers, her employer, was contracted to. A Volkswagen Jetta had been stolen from outside a pub in Ballito and was last seen heading for the N2. Her tracker, John Buttenshaw, who normally flew with her, had received the call at the same time. At that time of day Nia had made it to Virginia from her home in Umhlanga Rocks in nine minutes, but when she'd arrived at the gate to Coastal Choppers it was still locked and the lights were off in the office. Nia's cell phone had rung just then.

'John?' she'd asked as she saw his number flash on the screen. 'What's wrong?' John, who was a trainee helicopter pilot trying to get his hours up in his spare time, lived much closer to the airport, just a kilometre away, and by the time Nia arrived he'd normally be there getting everything ready. Together, they would push the Robinson R44 outside and she would start it up.

'Sheesh, you won't believe it,' John said, sounding stressed. 'I pulled out of my house and this drunk guy came screaming round the corner and T-boned me.'

Nia had checked that John was OK – he was – but the drunk had cracked his head on his windscreen and John was waiting with him for an ambulance. It wasn't ideal for her to fly a tracking mission by herself, but John would be tied up for an hour or more, so she'd wheeled the R44 out by herself, grabbed John's tracking pack from the office, and taken off alone to find the stolen Jetta.

It had been a pretty uneventful mission. She'd picked up the signal from the radio tracking device hidden in the car north of the town of Hluhluwe and found the vehicle abandoned on the side of the N2. The Motor Track ground crew, her boyfriend,

Angus Greiner, and his partner Sipho Baloyi, had arrived about twenty minutes after her while Nia orbited the vehicle. She'd done a low-level fly past and Banger – Angus's nickname – had blown her a kiss. Over the radio they'd confirmed the car was fine – luckily for the owner he or she had neglected to fill the fuel tank lately and the Jetta had run out of fuel.

'Probably some *okes* just looking for a quick ride home from the pub,' Banger had theorised over the radio. 'We'll put some fuel in it and I'll take it to the owner. Sipho will follow me. Catch you later, babe.'

Some of the vehicles they tracked were stolen for parts; others were destined to be resprayed and smuggled across the nearby border into Mozambique; some were taken to be used in a robbery; and others, like the Jetta, were taken because they provided a quick, easy ride home. This had been a good morning, Nia told herself. The vehicle had been recovered, no one had been held up or shot and no other crime committed, and Banger and Sipho had not had to face down a gunman or two. She worried about him constantly. Like the other ground crews, Banger and Sipho were always spoiling for action and were sometimes brave to the point of being stupid. But Nia acknowledged that Banger's recklessness was part of the attraction she felt for him.

Nia flew a slow orbit around the dead cow, keeping a careful watch out for flying vultures – a hit from one of those massive birds could bring her down. Through the Perspex windshield Nia could see several birds, maybe a dozen or more, still on the ground around the carcass, most of them with their wings outstretched as though they were sunning themselves. The majority of the vultures, however, had taken flight. She brought the helicopter in as close as she dared.

'ZAP-Wing, there's a problem here,' she said as she settled into a hover.

'What is it, Tracker?' Simon said.

The vultures on the ground were not moving at all. All the birds that were able had taken off. The bones of the cow's rib cage had been stripped clean and were shining bright white against the dun-coloured grass and the red gore of what was left of the animal.

Nia keyed the radio switch. 'Better call your vulture guy, ZAP-Wing. There's a span of dead birds on the ground here.'

*

Suzanne Fessey closed the door of the house in Hillcrest she and her husband had been renting for the last six months. She picked up her baby and took him to the Toyota Fortuner.

She felt mixed emotions about leaving the house, about taking the baby when she would never see her husband again. They hadn't been ready for a child, hadn't expected or wanted one, but they had decided to go through with the pregnancy.

Suzanne had cleaned the house from end to end, vacuuming, scrubbing and wiping down everything. There was no trace of her left there. She unlocked the Fortuner and put the child in his car seat, squeezed in among her possessions. He wriggled and gurgled as she fitted his restraints – he was active and adventurous and she knew he would be walking soon. She wasn't taking a lot with her, but it was surprising how much stuff one accumulated.

With her son securely belted in, Suzanne reversed out of the driveway and drove out of the small walled estate's gates. She turned right and headed down the street to the on ramp to the N3, heading towards Durban. It was a warm day and she turned up the air conditioner and switched on East Coast Radio.

She caught the tail end of the news. The Sharks had beaten the Stormers on the weekend. The recap of the news was about more load shedding and a corrupt local politician. Nothing out of the ordinary there, she thought to herself.

Suzanne turned off the radio before the music began again. She checked the clock on the dashboard. If she didn't take too many breaks she would be in Mozambique in a bungalow on the Indian Ocean by four that afternoon, after which the rest of her life would begin.

She skirted Durban and took the N2 north. Suzanne had deliberately left late to miss the peak-hour traffic and the motorway was flowing well. Soon she was clear of the city. In just under an hour she would check the news again. She turned and looked back at her son. 'Not long now.'

Emerald-green sugar cane fields lined the road and off to her right she could see how the sky turned a deeper shade of blue where it met the sea, which was out of sight, but not out of reach. As she crossed a bridge a long-crested eagle took flight from its perch on the railing. Suzanne watched it fly off into the clear sky. She remembered another time, another life, when she was a child and her parents used to take her into Hluhluwe–iMfolozi to see the animals. Her father was interested in birds, but Suzanne wasn't; she hated anything her father liked. She had left home at seventeen, lived on the streets, and the nightmare that was her life, not eased by the *dagga* or the *tic*, or even the heroin, had been almost as bad as her time at home. But she had turned her life around, with the help of a good but weak man. And he had given her a child. Suzanne had realised two things late in life – she was a fighter, and she was a survivor. She would find a better place.

Coughing, spluttering and an awful smell from the back made her turn. 'Oh, no!'

Her son had vomited, all down his front. The stench made her gag. Suzanne banged the steering wheel in anger. 'Shit, shit, shit!'

Up ahead, beside a bus stop layby, was a small caravan. Suzanne saw two cars there, one a beaten-up *bakkie* attached to the caravan, the other a red Volkswagen Golf. As she drew closer she saw that the trailer was a mobile *boerewors* roll stand. It was as good a place as any to stop and clean the baby with some wet wipes; as tough as she was she couldn't stand the smell. She slowed down and pulled over.

*

Shadrack Mduli looked in the wing mirror of the Golf and saw the white Fortuner indicating left to pull over at the caravan. He nudged his partner, Joseph Ndlovu, in the ribs.

'Can you believe this shit? It's like home delivery,' Shadrack said.

Joseph stretched and yawned. 'What, brother? I was sleeping. What are you talking about?'

Shadrack pointed over his shoulder with a thumb. 'Check. Late model Fortuner, white, single woman driving. Our luck has changed. She's coming right to us.'

This, Shadrack realised, would be even easier than he thought. The woman was pulling over a good fifty metres away from the caravan selling *wors* rolls. He checked the mobile eatery and could not even see the cook inside. If he couldn't see the chef, then the chef couldn't see them.

The woman got out of her car, clearly looking flustered, and walked around to the rear door. 'Let's go,' Shadrack said. Joseph unfolded his lanky frame from the small Golf.

Shadrack pulled the nine-millimetre pistol from the waistband of his low-slung jeans. With Joseph following he raised the gun and strode up to the woman. 'Give me your keys, now!'

She turned to him. Shadrack closed the gap between them and pointed the gun at her face, just centimetres away. 'Now! I said give me your keys or I'll blow your head off.'

The woman glared back at him. Shadrack was used to his victims screaming or crying or madly scrambling for their keys to give to him, not just staring back at him. He had never killed a person during a robbery, but he fully believed he could do so.

This woman mocked him with her stare. Well, she would be his first. He tightened his finger on the trigger, hoping the muscle action would still the slight tremor he felt in his hands. 'Last chance. Don't just stand there.'

'Shad . . . brother,' Joseph called behind him.

Shadrack risked a quick sideways glance and saw that Joseph was at the driver's side door.

'The keys are in the ignition,' Joseph said.

Shadrack saw the movement in his peripheral vision but he was too slow to move. He felt the blow on his wrist at the same moment and pulled the trigger, instinctively. His shot went wide. The stupid woman had hit him – no one had ever defied him like that. Her other hand was moving as well. He swung his gun hand back towards her, but before he could fire he was on his back, on the ground, his ears ringing from the blast of another gunshot. How could that be? he wondered. He was sure he hadn't fired again.

Shadrack tried to raise his hand to aim his pistol, but he felt too weak to do so. He looked down and saw red blossoming across his chest, soaking the fabric of his white T-shirt. He saw the woman's feet step over him, heard the crunch of her shoes on the gravel of the layby. The Fortuner's engine roared to life and the wheels spun on the loose surface.

'My baby!' The woman turned and punctuated her cry with two shots at the escaping vehicle.

The pain hit Shadrack as the numbness from the shock of the bullet's impact wore off. He screamed with the effort of rolling over. His eyes were clouding and the effort it took to stretch out his right arm and hand nearly made him black out. It was worth the pain, though. The woman was a blurry target beyond the tip of the barrel. Curse her. He pulled the trigger, once, twice, three times, and had the satisfaction of seeing her stumble before his world ended.

Chapter 2

Themba Nyathi felt ill.

Health-wise, he knew he was perfectly fine. He had checked his pulse rate against the second hand of his cheap Chinese watch, and had inspected the inside of his mouth and throat in the cracked mirror in the school bathroom. He'd even had his friend, Bongi, hold the back of his hand against his forehead to see if he had a temperature.

'You're fine.' Bongi had laughed at him, good-naturedly. 'Maybe you've got something else on your mind.'

Themba had frowned in the hallway as they bustled their way out into the hot, humid Zululand morning. It was always hot in Mtubatuba. It was hot and dry during the winter, and hot and wet in the summer. But the sun and water brought life and it sprang up everywhere, in the rich green grasses, in the sugar cane in the fields, in the trees in the bush and the animals who chose the lush, wet summer to give birth.

Themba was more aware of the world around him than he'd been at any other point in his seventeen years, and he had good reason to appreciate the natural environment. It may very well have saved his life. He'd explained this theory to Lerato, the new girl at school, how his recently discovered love of the bush had helped him come to terms with some terrible things that had happened in his life. He had neglected, however, to tell Lerato that some of those bad experiences were of his own making. This omission, he was now sure, was what was making him feel sick.

'Hey, you're always reading that book between classes, Themba,' she had said to him during the morning break.

Themba had looked up. Lerato Dlamini was the talk of the school. She was beautiful, intelligent, and the word was that her father was very wealthy, a former ANC member of parliament who owned a trucking company and two cane farms.

The smart guys, the bad guys, the football players, every boy in school in fact, were all vying for Lerato's attention, but she affected a haughty air. Themba liked the word 'haughty', having recently discovered it, and tried to use it whenever possible. It made her seem unattainable, and that only increased her attraction.

Themba blinked. 'Excuse, me?' His two words were punctuated with a cough as though his response threatened to choke him.

Lerato looked down at him, like a giraffe whose attention has been piqued by some little creature below her. 'That book. Animals. Why are you so interested in that stuff?'

Themba had licked his lips and then looked at the cover of his book, as if only just now discovering what it was about. 'It's . . . it's not only animals. It's . . . it's birds and snakes, and, and, even some trees and plants.'

Lerato had laughed out loud, for real. 'Oh, well *that* makes it all right then. I just *love* snakes and trees.'

Themba did not know why she was teasing him, but all of a sudden it didn't matter. The important thing was that she knew he existed and, even better, she was talking to him – even if she was ridiculing him. 'Did you know *Inkwazi*, the African fish eagle, mates for life?'

Her eyes widened.

Idiot, Themba said to himself. He'd regurgitated the last piece of information he'd read from his field guide and the implications of what he'd said pumped through his body like a black mamba's venom. He felt his body start to stiffen with paralysis.

'That's really nice.' Lerato set her rucksack full of books on the ground and sat down on the wooden bench next to him. 'I never thought of birds falling in love and getting married.'

Themba had been bracing himself for another jibe. Perhaps as a defence mechanism his ears were shutting down, because Lerato sounded like she was talking to him underwater. But he picked up something of what she said. 'Nice?' he croaked.

'Yes, nice.'

He had dared to turn his head a little, to look at her beautiful face, and to his surprise he saw she was smiling at him, but not in a mocking way. She had said something about love, hadn't she?

Themba felt blood forcing its way past the coma-inducing poison in his veins. Feeling returned to his fingertips – he wiggled them surreptitiously to make sure he was still alive – and a switch tripped in his brain. 'When it comes to animals, birds and other wildlife, we have to be careful of anthropomorphism, which means –'

'Ascribing human qualities to animals – I've heard the word before,' Lerato said.

'Sorry.' He was impressed. Like 'haughty', he'd thought of 'anthropomorphism' as one of his personal words. He was happy to share it with Lerato, though, more than happy. 'But, yes, it is "nice" to think of two creatures spending their whole lives together, and if the fish eagles were human we'd probably put that down to love.'

She laughed again. 'You're funny.'

He felt the paralysis creeping back. Even if she was just making fun of him, he didn't want her to leave. 'Male and female steenboks, little antelope, also sort of live together, sharing the same territory.'

'Serious? I didn't know there was this much monogamy in the world.'

Just watching her lips move as she formed the words, and catching sight of her perfect, even white teeth when she smiled, brought the life back to him, made him glad to be alive. Now all he had to do was think of something witty to say, to keep her there, next to him. But he couldn't.

'What about lions?' Lerato had asked, filling the chasm of silence that had opened between them in just three seconds.

Themba exhaled, then closed his mouth, not wanting her to notice his relief. 'Oh, no, lions don't mate for life, far from it. Lionesses will mate with several different males during the course of their lives, depending on which males have taken over the pride. Males come and go. As they get older they're challenged by young males for control of the pride.'

Lerato laughed again. She laughed a lot. 'Gangsta.'

Themba felt like she might be mocking him again, but to his surprise, Lerato reached out and put a hand on his forearm. It felt like an electric shock. 'You've seen lions for real, right? In the wild, not in a zoo?'

He'd nodded his head. 'Yes, in the Hluhluwe–iMfolozi Park. It was during my training as a youth rhino guard.'

'I remember, you went and lived there, in the bush, for a month.' Lerato couldn't hide her incredulity. 'Are you mad?'

It had been Themba's turn to laugh. 'Yes, it was a month, how did you know?'

'I was at the talk you gave to the school a few weeks ago.'

Themba felt an acute flush of hot embarrassment. 'You listened to my talk.'

She rocked her head from side to side. 'Well, a little bit of it.'

Themba had been encouraged by Mike Dunn, the coordinator

of the month-long course, to find a forum where he could address people about what he'd learned, and Themba had reluctantly asked the school principal for permission. To Themba's horror, the head of the school had agreed and he'd found himself addressing more than four hundred students one sweltering Monday morning. He had stumbled through his written speech and been angered to see some of the older boys and girls talking while he delivered it. The younger students, however, had seemed interested in his stories, particularly the one about the lion.

'You were in a tent, I remember you saying,' said Lerato, 'and you could hear two lions walking around you in the middle of the night. You said it sounded like they were purring, but, like, really loud. You must have been *terrified*.'

She remembered! Themba felt his heart swell. 'It wasn't that bad. The main thing our instructors drilled into us was to keep our tents zipped up and to stay very quiet. It wasn't easy.' In truth, Themba had been shaking in his sleeping bag, absolutely petrified once his tent-mate, Julius, peeked out the window of the tent and saw the outlines of the two massive lionesses. Themba had thought he would die for sure. Julius had suggested they make a run for it, to a minibus van parked at the campsite; this had galvanised Themba into action, hissing furiously to his friend not to even think of doing something so stupid.

'Serious?' said Lerato.

'You have to remember that lions hunt by sight and sound, not smell. They're like house cats chasing a mouse or a gecko. If their prey is running, then they will chase it, and there is no way a human can outrun a lion.'

Lerato sagged a little. 'I've never seen a lion, not even in a zoo.'

'I'll show you one.' The words had tumbled out of Themba's mouth before he'd even thought about how he might do that. He had no car, no money, and no means of getting Lerato to the national park.

'Oh yeah? How are you going to do that?' She had seen right through him.

'I'll find a way.'

'Well, good luck with that. My dad wouldn't let me go anywhere with you anyway – not with any boy, I mean.' At that moment Lerato's phone had begun to play a rap tune. 'Speaking of my dad, just let me get this. I called him to see if he can come pick me up now.'

It was an odd day at school. Their teachers had just called an impromptu strike over wages and school was finishing before lunch. Themba walked to and from school, seven kilometres each way, but Lerato's dad dropped her at school every morning and collected her each afternoon, in a shiny new black BMW.

She had answered the phone, stood and walked away to talk to her father. Themba had felt like a piece of him had been chopped off as she left, even though she was standing just a few metres away.

'What? No, I understand. OK. There's someone who can help. He's a good guy, Dad, honest. No, Dad, he's not like other boys, he's kinda nice. He's totally not the sort of guy who would try anything, trust me, please. Here, you can talk to him.'

Themba looked up at Lerato as she returned to his side. He didn't know if he'd heard right. 'What is it?' he mouthed to her.

She lowered her phone. 'My dad can't come pick me up or send his driver because he has some business meeting he needs to attend. It's urgent and he can't get out of it. He's very protective of me. I have to get a taxi home, but he's paranoid something will happen to me. Here.' She thrust the phone into his hand.

'Hello?' Themba had said tentatively.

'My daughter says you can be trusted, is that correct?' the deep voice on the phone said, no preamble, no greeting.

'Um. Yes. Yes, sir.'

'Listen carefully to me, boy. Do you know who I am?'

Themba swallowed. 'Yes, sir. Mr Bandile Dlamini.' He wasn't sure what else to say, so added, 'a very important man.'

'I don't need your flattery, I need your help. If my daughter is harmed in any way, trips over, stubs her toe or has a hair out of place, I will make it my business to hurt you. Do you understand me?'

Themba understood the soft, menacing tone perfectly. 'Yes, sir.'

'Put my daughter back on the line.'

Lerato had reassured her father that all would be fine, and that Themba would see her home safe. Lerato's mathematics teacher was the last to leave the school and she had stayed back to explain something to Lerato, her favourite student. Now Themba was waiting, feeling sick to his stomach with apprehension, and maybe something else.

'I'm not hanging around any longer,' Bongi said.

'OK, fine. See you tomorrow,' Themba replied.

Bongi punched him in the arm. 'Man, you've got it bad.'

'I do not.' Even as he said the words, Themba knew they were a lie.

Bongi walked away, waving his hand in the air without looking back. Themba looked at his shoes. The toes were scuffed. He licked a finger and wiped them, then rubbed each on the backs of his trouser legs. The shoes didn't look much better; there was no disguising the fact that he was poor. He sighed. Lerato's father might be happy for him to shepherd his daughter home, but he would never allow Themba to take her out on a date or anything like that.

'Hi. I'm done.'

Lerato's voice was more melodious than any bushveld bird he had heard. His heart felt like there was an invisible hand wrapped around it, squeezing.

'OK,' he croaked. 'Let's go.'

As he walked out the gates to the road to where they would pick up a minibus taxi, with the prettiest girl in school by his side, Themba felt like the luckiest boy alive. Part of him felt a little miffed that Lerato had told her father he could be trusted because he was some kind of harmless nerd, as opposed to the other boys who strutted loud and proud in front of her to try and gain her attention. But he consoled himself with the fact that she hadn't suggested anyone else to escort her. His days of pretending to be a tough guy were through. Even though the taxi would be packed with a dozen or more people it would be like a limousine compared to his normal daily commute. He looked up to the sky to say a quick, quiet prayer of thanks, and noticed a helicopter.

*

Bandile Dlamini hoped his daughter would be all right. Since his wife, Siphokazi, had died in a car crash two years earlier, he had been paranoid about Lerato's safety. They had wanted more children, but Siphokazi had been unable.

'Mona market,' he said to his driver.

'Yes, boss. The deal is on?'

'Yes.'

Located near Hlabisa, to the west of Hluhluwe–iMfolozi Park, the Mona market was a place where animal products and various other sources of *muti* – traditional medicines – were traded, legally and illegally.

In the boot of the BMW was a bag full of several hundred thousand rand. He wiped his palms on the fabric of his tailored suit pants. He wasn't really going to a business meeting, as he had told his daughter.

He was going to the market to buy three rhino horns taken from animals illegally poached in KwaZulu-Natal's national parks.

Chapter 3

Mike Dunn stopped his Land Rover Defender on the side of the road. He reached into the back and took the gun case from the floor, unzipped it and removed his .375 hunting rifle.

His office was the bush and much of his time was spent in Big Five country, among lion, leopard, buffalo, rhino and elephant. He carried the Brno rifle for protection, and while he was outside the nearby Hluhluwe–iMfolozi Park he didn't dare leave the rifle in the truck while he was gone from it. No one would be mad enough to steal a Defender, but a heavy-bore hunting rifle was highly sought after by rhino poachers or the criminal gun dealers who supplied them.

Mike smelled the carcass before he saw it. The sky was clear and there was no noise around him save for the *swish-swish* of his canvas gaiters, a protection against ticks, as he strode through the long grass of the uncultivated field. Not a breath of wind blew. His khaki shirt was soon sticking to him.

He was ready for the sight that would match the terrible smell. The stench was like an invisible wall, one he couldn't pass through.

With each step he moved deeper into it, became part of it. Mike was no stranger to death. He could see it now, a trident of white ribs sticking up above the grass, and sound had come to the scene in the form of the hum of gorging blowflies.

Mike wiped sweat from his eyes. He knew what he was walking into, the terrible sight that awaited him, but knowing, preparing, was not the same as armouring.

At first he thought all the birds were dead, but a strangled squawking noise attracted his attention. He jogged to a white-backed vulture that was somehow still alive. Seeing him it tried to hop away, but it had lost its sense of balance and stumbled over its talons and fell, its giant wings sprawling outwards. It was gagging and convulsing, trying to regurgitate the poisoned meat. Its head was drawn back, its neck bent as the painful process of dying continued.

Mike worked the oiled bolt of the Brno, chambering a round. He knew from bitter experience there was nothing he could do for this magnificent creature. He took aim and the gunshot echoed across the veldt.

He walked back to the carcass and felt anger displace the sadness when he saw the first body. As he knelt beside the vulture he indulged himself in a brief fantasy of what he might do if he caught the people responsible for this in the act. If one of them was armed and raised a gun to him, he would be within his rights to . . .

No. It didn't help talking about shooting poachers, nor the people who used the end products. It was the same with the current epidemic of rhino poaching; hunting poachers, arresting them, or even killing them if they opened fire on the national parks and security forces was only one part of the fight. It was Mike's view, stated ad infinitum at conferences, in media interviews, and around the fire at *braais*, that the war on poaching could not be won in the African bush; it had to be fought and settled in the mind.

It was easier said than done, however, the business of convincing a Vietnamese businessman that rhino horn was not a fitting status symbol or a cure for cancer, or persuading an aspirational African believer in traditional medicine that sleeping with a vulture's head under his pillow would not guarantee him success at a job interview or a win on the national lottery numbers.

Mike went to another dead bird – he estimated there had to be at least two score of them. His shoulders sagged and his heart hurt. He dropped to one knee, the butt of his rifle resting in the yellow grass. This one, and ten others in close proximity, had been beheaded, probably just before the helicopter arrived overhead. Blood from the magnificent creature's neck mixed with the red earth of Zululand. It was ever thus. Mike looked up and scanned the grassland around him. He saw no movement, but when he took another look at the lifeless birds scattered around the remains of the cow he saw that several, a dozen or more, still had their heads on.

'Where are you?' he said, addressing the heat haze at the edge of the clearing. Whoever had done this, whoever had killed this cow or, more likely, dragged the roadkill from the tar to the grass then laced it with Carbofuran or some similar poison, was probably not far away. Mike's fingers tightened around the oiled wooden stock of the rifle until his knuckles showed white through his deeply tanned, sun-creased skin.

He stood and scanned the tree line, but there was no sign of movement. Mike walked to the hollowed-out remains of the cow. The vultures had gutted and stripped it with their trademark frenzied efficiency. He knelt again to examine it more closely, and his eyes locked onto a few purple granules. It was definitely Carbofuran. The poison was used by farmers to combat pests and aphids, but it was also harmful to birds and animals. It was deadly enough to take down a lion – farmers in Kenya had been using it against predators, illegally, for years. The poison even had a nickname among poachers, 'two-step' – the distance a victim would cover before succumbing to the deadly substance.

Mike took out a plastic zip-lock bag from the back pocket of his shorts and a pen from his shirt. He used the pen to scoop some of the poison into the bag. With luck a lab might be able to trace its exact make and source.

The Zulu called vultures Inqe, which meant the one that purifies the land. They did nature's dirty work, clearing up the remains of kills that had provided nourishment for others. They prevented the spread of disease and did not prey on live, healthy animals or people. In short, they did nothing wrong, and a hell of a lot of good. Man repaid the good work Inqe did by vilifying and poisoning them.

Mike felt angry, sad, dejected, and, at the same time, galvanised. He walked around the scene of death, eyes down, looking for spoor. He'd tried calling his contact at Mtubatuba police station, Sergeant Lindiwe Khumalo, but couldn't even get through to the switchboard. Mike had heard on the news that there'd been a bomb blast in Durban. He cared little for international politics or politicians, and while he was saddened by the loss of the American ambassador and her bodyguards, his war was here, in the blood-spattered grass, not in the global war against terrorism, or a clash of religions.

There were parallels, though, he mused as he checked the ground for footprints, tyre tracks and other signs of the people who had committed this mass killing. The poachers killed animals and birds in order to prey on the unproven beliefs of their customers; terrorists invoked religious beliefs to encourage young men and women to die for something ethereal, a promise of a better life after death. It was all crazy.

He had learned to track as a youngster from his father, who had hunted, although Mike himself had never had an interest in hunting beyond shooting a couple of impala for the pot. From an early age he'd set his sights on a career with the old Natal Parks Board. He'd managed it, and had thought he'd have a job for life in the bush. But change had come to South Africa in 1994 with the end of apartheid and the election of Nelson Mandela. Mike had known, like the overwhelming majority of his peers, that their lives would change.

Unlike some, he hadn't been bitter when the axe fell. He was one of the lucky ones, who had completed a university education in the pursuit of his love of wildlife. When he was made redundant, eventually, from the renamed Ezemvelo KZN Wildlife, he left as one of the country's foremost experts on birds of prey, especially vultures. He had found a job with an NGO; money from foreign donors and South African businesses with a conscience kept him in work, but did little to stem the bloodshed. As depressing as his work often was he appreciated the benefits that came with it. He travelled southern Africa, working with various national parks services, counting nests and tracking birds with GPS devices. He trained police and parks officers in what to look for at the scenes of vulture killings and sometimes accompanied them on operations. He gave lectures and media interviews and worked with other researchers and volunteers. He was his own boss and his funders were grateful for the publicity his work generated.

He would need to collect the birds that had not yet been beheaded. Mike scanned the tree line again. He was sure that whoever was responsible for this barbaric crime was nearby, probably watching him, waiting for him to leave.

He stopped at another dead vulture. This one was a lappet-faced, bigger and more powerful than the white-backed vultures around it. With its wickedly curved beak and strength it was the 'can-opener', capable of opening the toughest skin. It fed first and, in this case, had probably been one of the first to die. He stroked its pinkish neck. His student volunteers were usually surprised at how soft yet strong that skin was. He rarely saw a nick or a scar despite the fierce competition of sharp beaks on a kill.

Mike raised the rifle again and started to walk towards the bushes, his senses ratcheted up a few levels, the hairs on his arms prickling. He'd taken no more than a dozen steps when his phone vibrated in his pocket.

He stopped and thought for a moment. If there was a poacher there, and he was armed, he should at least tell someone what he was doing. He pulled out his phone. He didn't immediately recognise the number, but hoped it might be the police. 'Mike Dunn.'

'Mr Mike, it's Solly.'

Solomon Radebe was a sixty-something-year-old ex national parks ranger from Mtubatuba. He had been invalided out of the parks service after a buffalo had charged him and trampled his right leg, breaking it in several places. He walked with a limp. A lifelong protector of wildlife, and as straight as they came, Solly had worked with Mike before his retirement and still kept in touch; he had tipped Mike off in the past about the illegal trade in vulture heads.

'Howzit, Solly?'

'Fine, and you?' he replied.

'I'm fine,' Mike said, and with the protocol out of the way it was safe to say, 'what can I do for you, Solly?'

'There is something going on at the Mona market today, right now. This is important, Mr Mike. There is a big man here, fancy car, bodyguards. Something is about to happen.'

Mike had never had reason to question Solly's instincts or his information. Solly had noticed that the buffalo that had charged him was about to attack, and had put himself between another trails guide and their party of tourists to protect them from the charge he saw coming. He'd shot the buffalo, fatally wounding it, but the momentum of its charge had carried it onwards and over Solly's body. He'd received a commendation for bravery.

'Something like what, Solly?'

'A big deal. I have seen this man before; he's an ex-politician. I think he is here to buy or sell something very valuable.'

'How valuable?'

'Enough to warrant him bringing a bodyguard as well as a driver.'

'You're watching them?'

'I am, Mr Mike. I don't want to approach them myself.'

Mike wanted to spend more time at the cow carcass, collecting evidence and photographing the scene. However, Solly's instincts were good and he was fearless. Mike had the option of preserving the scene of one wildlife crime or preventing another.

He went back to his truck and from the rear he took an anemometer, a cigarette lighter and a five-litre can of fuel he kept for cases like this. With the rifle slung over his shoulder he jogged back to the carcass. He held up the wind-measuring device and checked that the direction and speed were in his favour. They were; the wind was blowing back towards the road, and the breeze was only a couple of knots. Even better, the grass on the other side of the road had been recently burned.

Mike set down the device, fuel and his rifle and set to work dragging the dead vultures back to the carcass that had killed them, piling dead upon dead. When he was done, his clothes soaked with sweat, he splashed half the container of fuel over the grisly mound. He lit a handful of dry grass and tossed it; the pyre erupted with a *whoof*. Ideally, he would have had people here to watch that the blaze didn't get out of hand, but at this time of day he was sure the wind wouldn't change. The grass would catch, but the fire would stop at the roadside and burn itself out. Mike spared a look back to the trees and hoped the bastards who had done this were watching the rest of their profits go up in smoke. He gathered his things and jogged back to the Land Rover.

It wasn't far to the Mona market and he pushed his Land Rover as close to the speed limit as it would let him. Villages and bare, overgrazed hills flashed by. When he came within sight of the stalls, but not too close, he pulled off the road and parked. Solly walked down the road to meet him.

The market itself ran along both sides of a back road, a linear collection of ramshackle stalls and huts made of timber, corrugated iron and other cast-off building materials. Here and there were a few more substantial shelters of mud brick. Some sellers plied their wares on makeshift shelves in the open. Side alleys had sprawled from the main road and Mike knew it was usually in these back lanes that the illegal products were to be found. Solly led him to the rear of a brick building, a shebeen, a local bar.

The market was quiet now; the end of month rush, when people were paid, had just passed and many of the stalls were closed, wrapped shut against the elements with fraying canvas and plastic sheeting. A dog, all ribs and mange, trotted down the street searching for scraps. A woman selling tomatoes and cabbages cursed it in Zulu.

After they'd exchanged greetings and shaken hands, Solly said: 'I got closer to them, and I recognised the big man, the one who is obviously in charge. He was wearing dark glasses, so I couldn't be sure from a distance.'

'Who is he?'

'Bandile Dlamini.'

Mike swore quietly. 'The former politician turned entrepreneur?'

Solly looked left and right. 'Yes. He talks a good deal about protecting wildlife and the fight against rhino poaching.'

'Then what's he doing here?'

Solly shrugged. 'I don't think it's a photo opportunity for the local media, or a campaign rally. He's gone back to his car now. He has a driver and one other man, who looks like a bodyguard.'

'Why does a businessman need a bodyguard?' Mike asked. 'It's not like he's a government minister who'd warrant protection.'

Again Solly looked around, checking no one had moved into earshot. 'I've heard talk about him. Before he got into politics, back in the days of the struggle, he moved guns and explosives for the ANC, but people said he also supplied criminal gangs. They say he was involved in car hijackings as well, not stealing the vehicles himself, but running garages where stolen vehicles were stripped and resprayed. But this was years ago.'

Mike had read Dlamini's tough talk in the newspapers, and had met him once at a conference on rhino poaching, but he hadn't had time or the opportunity to form his own opinion of the man. 'Let's take a look around.'

They walked out from behind the shebeen onto the dusty road that ran the length of the market.

Most of the people selling goods greeted them both, but every few stalls someone would retreat further into the shadows at the rear of their tin hut, avoiding eye contact with Mike, perhaps thinking he was police or national parks – or they recognised old Solly. As they passed one stall Mike glimpsed a giraffe skull with dried skin still stretched across the bone, and a set of hippo tusks beside it. The seller tossed a blanket over his wares, but Mike didn't care about him right now.

Solly put a hand on Mike's forearm and pointed down the street. Mike saw the black late model BMW sedan with the tinted windows, a heavy-set man in a leather bomber jacket and sunglasses leaning against the bonnet.

'That man is the driver,' Solly said.

The rear door on their side opened and a man got out.

'That's not Dlamini,' Mike said.

'The bodyguard,' said Solly. 'Dlamini is inside in the back seat.'

The driver pulled the keys from his pocket and pressed the boot release on the remote. The boot popped open and the bodyguard,

29

dressed in jeans and a grey hoodie, took out a hessian bag before closing it again.

Mike and Solly moved between two stalls, where they were out of plain sight but could still track the man with the bag. He crossed the road and came their way, to a small shack about a hundred metres up the street.

'Let us go behind the stores,' Solly said.

Solly led them to the rear and they moved cautiously but quickly along the line of stalls. Away from the street chickens foraged in garbage, women cooked pots of *pap* over small fires, and young men brought more stock for the various sellers.

'It is this one,' Solly said, then put his finger to his lips. He and Mike moved quietly to the rear of the stall.

Mike let Solly translate, though his Zulu was almost as good as the old ranger's.

'The man with the bag is selling something,' Solly said. 'The other man is asking what it is.'

'Inqe,' Mike whispered, before Solly could translate the next sentence. 'Vulture heads.'

Mike took a deep breath to try and still himself. He wanted to kick the ramshackle back door of the hut in and grab the man with the bag and throw him to the ground. He would probably be armed, but Mike had a gun as well.

Solly put his hand on Mike's arm again. 'We must wait.'

Mike exhaled. 'You're right. Listen.' Mike put his finger to his lips to tell Solly he could understand what the men said and didn't need any further translation.

The bodyguard was saying the vulture heads were fresh, not yet even dried. The stallholder asked how many he had. '*Ishumi nanye.*'

Eleven. Mike remembered the headless birds he had found at the site just outside of Hluhluwe–iMfolozi, where the cow had been poisoned – the exact same number. If it hadn't been for the helicopter tracker scaring away many birds with the helicopter, there would have been more. It was no coincidence; these had to be the heads of the birds he had burned.

The men argued over the price, with the stallholder eventually offering an amount acceptable to the seller. It was a tidy sum, but Mike thought about Dlamini, in his big black sedan waiting across the road. Vulture heads were worth good money, but good enough for a high-profile man such as Dlamini to risk hanging around in public while his minion did the trade?

Inside the shack the stallholder told the bodyguard that he needed to go fetch the cash from elsewhere; it made sense the man would not keep a stockpile of money in his stall or on himself, in case of theft. Solly and Mike backed up between the shop and its neighbour, as they heard the rear door creak open.

Mike reached behind his back and drew his pistol. As the stallholder came into view he took three steps forward, wrapped his hand around the man's mouth from behind and rammed his pistol into the man's temple.

The stallholder was wide-eyed, but didn't struggle.

Solly unthreaded the belt from his trousers and, with Mike keeping the gun on the man and his finger on his own lips to warn him to continue to be quiet, Solly trussed the stallholder's hands behind his back. Mike took a cleaning rag that was hanging on a wire fence between the huts to dry and stuffed it in the man's mouth. They lowered him to the ground, on his knees. Solly produced a knife from inside his threadbare suit jacket and held it to the man's neck. Mike returned to the rear of the shack.

He cocked his head, moving along the wall of the shack to the back door. There was movement inside. Mike paused, felt the tension and adrenaline firing up his nerve endings. The man Solly was holding a knife to had been about to commit a crime, but he had not handed over any money. Mike wondered if they had gone too far too soon, but the thought of those eleven headless vultures, and the other birds he'd seen slaughtered and nests destroyed enraged him. This, he was sure, went beyond the killing of birds for traditional medicine. This deal was a curtain raiser.

Mike glanced back at the bound man. He looked terrified. He would not be a dealer in rhino horn; his market was local people who wanted a talisman or a potion to improve their lot in life, not Vietnamese businessmen half a world away who wanted to avoid hangovers or impress their commercial contacts.

The back door of the shack creaked as it swung open.

Mike moved to where Dlamini's bodyguard was exiting, probably looking to see where the stallholder was, and noticed him reaching under his hoodie. From a shoulder holster under his left arm, the man drew a black pistol. He had his back to Mike, who moved forward, raised his arm and smashed the butt of his own gun down on the back of the man's head. The bodyguard crumpled to the ground. Mike straddled the man and reached down, snatching the pistol from his hand and putting it in his pocket.

The man moaned and writhed on the ground at the rear of the stall, not out cold, but stunned. Mike bent down again and snatched up the hessian bag the bodyguard had dropped beside him. Inside he saw the pinkish-grey heads, the glassy eyes, the hooked beaks. Mike gave the man a kick.

'Who are you?' the man croaked.

'Shut up.' Mike pointed his gun at him. 'What's your boss doing here?'

'Who?'

Mike kicked the henchman again. 'Dlamini. Don't tell me he's here just to oversee the sale of some vulture heads.'

The man spat. 'I don't know what you're talking about, and if you're not police then get off me.'

'You'll wish I was the police once I finish with you.'

'Hey,' Solly called, 'let's just wait for the police.'

Solly was right, but Mike was angry. The bag of vulture heads had incensed him. 'There's more to this than just the heads.'

'I agree,' Solly said, 'but we are not the law.'

Mike ignored the older man's words of caution and addressed the henchman. 'If you're delivering the vulture heads for Bandile Dlamini then you're just a courier, not a serious criminal. Tell me where you got them from and I'll put in a good word for you when the police arrive.'

The man spat blood. 'I'll tell the police what you did to me and I'll charge you with assault, white man. Go fuck yourself.'

It wasn't in Mike to torture the man any further, beyond the kicking he'd given him, but he needed him to talk. He picked him up by the hood of his top and pushed him around the corner of the stall to where the stallholder was sitting, bound and gagged. 'OK, how about I let you go free. I'll take the heads, and this guy,' he gestured to the stallholder with his pistol, 'can tell the cops how he was never going to buy any vulture heads and instead cooperated fully with the police and national parks officers. You get to go back to Dlamini and tell him you lost the heads and didn't get the cash. How about that?'

The man's eyes darted from the stallholder back to Mike, and then to Solly. Seeing he'd get no sympathy from the old ranger he looked at Mike again. 'What do you want?'

'I asked you already,' Mike said. 'Who's your boss?'

'Those vulture heads weren't mine. I was just making a delivery.'

'A delivery for who?' Mike replied.

'Fuck you. I want a lawyer.'

Mike leaned over the man and again pressed the pistol to his head. 'You think I won't shoot, right?'

The man glared back at him. 'I know you won't, and I'm going to see that you're charged.'

Mike looked to Solly. 'Take the stallholder away, out of sight. You don't need to see this.'

Solly hesitated. 'Mr Mike . . .'

'Go. No one will miss this piece of shit, certainly not his boss, since he lost both the goods and the money. Leave me to finish this. He is no use to us any longer and it's time I sent him on his way.' Mike took his captive's pistol from his pocket and passed it to Solly.

Solly took the firearm, lifted the stallholder up by his bound wrists and pushed him towards the street.

'Please,' the man at Mike's feet said. Mike had never had any intention of executing him, but he had the satisfaction of seeing the fear in his face.

Solly, who seemed unable to tell if Mike was bluffing or not, gave him a worried look. 'What do you want me to do?'

'Keep that guy under wraps somewhere. Call the police. They're busy with a load of other *kak*, but they'll get here eventually. Don't let Dlamini see you've got our shopkeeper here, or he might drive off. We want him as well.'

'You've got this all wrong,' the captive said.

The man cast his eyes towards Solly, but the ex-ranger had turned his back on them, probably with a measure of disgust for both of them.

'Solly can't help you, only I can.' Mike raised the pistol so it was pointed between the man's eyes. 'And right now, we could be the only two people left in the world. Say a prayer.'

The man licked his lips, quick, like a snake. 'Wait. There's more at stake here than the heads.'

Mike looked over the barrel of the gun. 'Like what?'

'Bigger stuff than vulture heads.'

'Tell me.'

'Bandile Dlamini's not involved.'

Mike rolled his eyes. 'Whatever. Tell me what you know.' The man hesitated, as though wondering if he should continue. Mike pressed the pistol into the gap between his eyebrows. 'Tell me.'

'All right. Chill. Lose the psycho act.'

'You've got one minute to give me something useful or I'll kill you.'

The man sighed. 'Yeah, well, you would have done that by now if you were going to.'

Mike clenched his jaw then forced himself to breathe. 'I'm handing you over to the cops whatever happens, and if you don't give me something I can use then you'll be the man who was responsible for Bandile going to prison as well.'

'You have to let us get away.'

'I what?'

The man nodded his head vigorously. 'Yes, I mean it. I didn't want to be part of this deal.'

'What deal?' Mike was losing his patience.

'There is a man coming here.'

'What man?'

'An *umlungu*.'

'So what?' Mike said. 'A white man. What does he want?'

'He wants to sell three rhino horns.'

Mike whistled through his teeth. 'Bandile's trading rhino horn?'

'I did not say that,' the man said. 'Bandile Dlamini is an honest man. He fights for the rhino. He heard about this deal and he is setting up an operation to capture this criminal.'

Mike scoffed. 'Right. OK, I'll play along.'

'It is no game.'

'Tell me what you know.'

'A man is bringing the rhino horns and Bandile will offer to pay him for it, then, when inspecting the horns, some police, from Durban, will arrest the man.'

'Where are these police now?'

The man shrugged.

The plan sounded too far-fetched. If Bandile Dlamini really was part of a sting operation then the police would have already been there, in position, undercover. Also, they would not have countenanced this man doing a deal with vulture heads on the side, nor Mike getting the jump on him. The man was doing his best to extricate his influential boss from an ambush. He probably figured that the loss of the rhino horn would be outweighed by none of them going to prison.

'Who's the white man Dlamini's meeting?' Mike asked. 'What's his name?'

Solly had darted between the neighbouring shacks until he could see up the road again to where Bandile Dlamini's car was still parked. Mike looked away from his captive and saw a car flash past, driving fast up the street.

'Did you get the make of that car?' Mike asked Solly.

'An Audi Q5. It's pulling up near Dlamini's BMW. A white man has just got out of the car and now the Audi is leaving.'

'Shit,' said Mike.

Chapter 4

Nia Carras had landed her helicopter at the quiet airstrip at Mtubatuba. After tracking the stolen vehicle earlier in the day and chasing the vultures off the carcass she had stopped to use the bathroom and get a Coke from the vending machine.

She was heading back to Virginia Airport now, looking forward to a surf and a cool drink, when her phone rang. It was connected to the helicopter's on-board communications system via bluetooth, and John Buttenshaw's name showed.

'John, howzit? Everything OK?'

''Fine, well, not fine. The guy who hit my *bakkie* wasn't insured. I've been chilling in the office all morning. Nia, we've got another call-out. There's just been a hijacking on the N2 near Stanger and get this – there's a baby on board.'

Nia swore. 'No way. OK, give me the details.'

John read out the information the control room had taken from the vehicle's owner, a woman who had called the Motor Track emergency line. Her vehicle was a white Toyota Fortuner, a very common vehicle and a popular target for thieves. Its engine

and gearbox were a perfect match for a minibus taxi and unscru-
pulous taxi operators sometimes upgraded their vehicles with
stolen parts. 'It's got a sunroof, Nia, and a half-length roof rack.
Last seen heading north.'

'That's good, John, thanks.' The extra details about the sunroof
and rack were a bonus, as they'd help her differentiate the stolen
vehicle from the other Toyotas she was bound to fly over.

'OK, I'm on it. Where's Banger?' Nia brought the R44 around
and pointed her nose down to pick up airspeed. Even while
turning she was switching on the tracking device again. Any
thoughts of a relaxing afternoon surf fled Nia's mind.

'I've called him and sent him a WhatsApp. Just waiting to hear
back from him.'

'OK. We found that car we went looking for this morning –
abandoned and out of fuel. Banger and Sipho had fuel with them
and Banger was going to drive it back to the owner. He should
have been done by now.' Banger and Sipho were good operators,
but Nia knew that once a job was done they sometimes took their
time heading back to Durban. They both had huge appetites so
she wouldn't be surprised if they'd found a Steers or a Wimpy
somewhere for lunch. It would be irresponsible for them to stop
somewhere with no phone signal, but Banger's stomach, like
another part of his body, sometimes overruled his brain.

If John were with her he would be holding the antenna of his
tracker, which looked like a small version of an old-fashioned
television antenna, and swinging it left to right to try and pick up
the radio signal from the tracking device hidden in the Toyota.
Nia couldn't do that while flying so, instead, she positioned the
antenna on the co-pilot's seat and turned the helicopter to the left
and right, flying in an 'S' formation, to simulate John swinging
the tracking device.

Attached to the antenna was the tracker itself, and this was
fed into her headphones. Next to the antenna was her iPad, onto

which she had loaded a satellite navigation app. At first she heard only static, but as she headed east from Hluhluwe towards the N2, Nia started to pick up a scratchy *tich, tich, tich* signal in her headphones.

She made a turn north, to the left, and the noise died out, then brought the Robinson around a hundred and eighty degrees. The signal returned and intensified to a clearer, stronger, repetitive *tick*.

'Yes!'

Nia settled above the N2 at 1000 feet and reduced her speed. She checked her fuel. Hanging around the vultures had burned her supply, but the increasing volume and frequency of the signal in her headphones told her the Fortuner was coming towards her, so she could ease off and save fuel. Now all she needed was for Banger to get here, and he shouldn't be far away.

She keyed her radio. 'Ground crew, ground crew, ground crew, this is chopper.'

There was no answer. Normally once a call was received Nia would only stay in contact with Banger, or whoever was on duty as the ground crew. They, in turn, would receive updates from the Motor Track control room, thus freeing up her and John to fly and track. But today, clearly, was not a normal day. She tapped the screen of her iPad to mark her current position. The GPS coordinates flashed up.

Nia picked up her cell phone and selected John's number from the top of the recent calls list.

'Hi, Nia.'

She dispensed with the civilities. 'Any word from Banger? I can't raise him on the radio.'

'He must be in a dead spot. I can't reach him either.'

'Shit,' Nia said. 'I'm picking up a strong signal on the Fortuner. They're heading north on the N2.' Nia read out the GPS coordinates to John. 'Give that to Banger when you get hold of him. Hey . . . wait a minute, I think I see it.'

Below her Nia saw a white Fortuner, with half roof rack and sunroof, barrelling down the motorway, passing a line of traffic and just swinging back into the left-hand lane as a truck came towards it, narrowly avoiding a head-on.

'Got him, John. I'm in pursuit. Get Banger, now!'

'OK, I'm trying.'

Nia ended the call and turned the chopper around so she was headed north, behind and above the speeding stolen vehicle. Through the Perspex she could see flashing blue lights ahead, but they were coming towards her. 'Where are you guys going in one hell of a hurry?' she asked herself.

Nia pressed the speed dial and called John again. 'Hey,' she said when he answered, 'I've just seen three cop cars pass underneath me heading south towards Durbs. What's happening? Are the cops looking for this guy because there's a baby on board?'

Nia didn't carry a weapon of any kind in the air and she was not permitted to try and stop a fleeing car thief by landing. Safety was of paramount concern in her line of work. Her job was to find a stolen vehicle, keep it in sight, and report its position to her ground crew – wherever they were.

She kept her eyes on the road below, not losing track of the Fortuner. It was moving like a cheetah chasing lunch. Nia knew the tracking signal still ticking strongly in her ears could drop out at any time; car hijackers usually worked in pairs and while one was driving the other would be frantically ripping off door panels, pulling up carpet and ransacking the dashboard in search of the vehicle's tracking device. Once they found it, they'd throw it out the window or, if they could stop somewhere, such as a service station, they might try and plant it on another vehicle.

'Control room's called the cops,' John said, 'but I've got no word back on whether they're in pursuit or not. In fact, I doubt it.'

'Why?' It wasn't unusual for Nia, Banger and Sipho to be first on the scene, or for them to find a stolen car and for the ground crew to make an arrest; in fact, it was the norm, as the tracking companies were better set up to respond faster than the police. Nia did think, however, that a case involving a baby would have stirred the police into action.

'There's been an explosion in Durban, Nia.' The words tumbled out of his mouth. 'The cops are going crazy, the police frequency's hectic. It sounds like the American ambassador to South Africa's been blown up.' John paused for a breath.

'A bomb? In Durban?' For all of South Africa's problems it wasn't a terrorist target. She was gaining on the Fortuner so she backed off a little, making sure the driver wouldn't be able to spot her in his mirrors or by looking straight up through the sunroof. Another police car whizzed under her skids, siren flashing as it raced towards the provincial capital. Nia could imagine the police radios were choked, stressed dispatchers taking calls from units all over the city and beyond. The car thief must have panicked when he'd seen the first police car pass him, but now he'd be high-fiving himself or his partner.

'Yip. They're saying the ambassador, Anita someone, was visiting an AIDS hospice and was then on her way to the harbour to check a visiting US warship. What are we going to do about the missing kid, though?'

'I'm trying to think, John.' She hoped the baby was all right. She couldn't imagine what state the mother was in. Nia was thirty-one and had never been married. After university she had travelled much of the world, partly as a backpacker and in later years as an itinerant pilot. She liked the idea of having a child, but hadn't yet met the man she was sure she wanted to start a family with. Banger was a fun guy, but she had a hard time picturing him as a dad.

One thing Nia really couldn't imagine was having a baby and then losing it, especially to a random act of violent crime.

From her relative airspeed Nia reckoned the *tsotsi* in the Fortuner was sitting on about 140 kilometres per hour.

Nia switched frequencies to the police emergency channel. Predictably there was plenty of chatter following the bomb blast. She still couldn't quite get her head around what had happened. American embassies had been attacked in other parts of Africa, but how could something like this have happened in her South Africa?

'John, maybe call another ground crew, Peter and Chris; even though they're not on duty maybe they're sober and can get up here. It'll take a while to get from Durban, but someone's got to take this situation seriously, no matter what's happened in the city.'

'OK, Nia. I'm on it.'

'Wait, John. Call the control room. Banger should be passing on information to them, but God knows where he is. Let control know I'm following the Fortuner and I won't let it out of my sight. The mother must be going crazy. Someone's got to give her some news.'

'Right, will do.' John sounded almost relieved that she had given him something straightforward and achievable to do, even if it was just calling for help. She had loaded the poor guy up with instructions, but there was nothing more she could think of doing. The Toyota was still in sight and as long as she had fuel in her tanks that fucker down there would not get away from her.

This was crazy. Car hijackings had decreased in South Africa in recent years. Some of the older pilots she knew talked of daily call-outs to track stolen vehicles, sometimes multiple missions in a day. In the past, pilots had carried guns and transported armed-response security officers and helped with the arrest of armed thieves. There had been shootouts, but these days there were more rules and the job was more about tracking and observation than being an airborne cavalry unit.

The sky around her was clear, the day still perfect. There was little she could do for now other than keep trying for a response and keep the Fortuner in view. That was easy enough while the vehicle stayed on the motorway.

*

'Shut up!' Joseph yelled again at the screaming child in the back seat. The Fortuner smelled of baby vomit and Joseph gagged.

He gripped the steering wheel so hard his hands hurt. He continued to look in the rear view mirror, but there were no police following him. Another cop car flew past him, heading in the opposite direction, its siren blaring and blue lights flashing. When he'd seen the first three cars he'd thought they were going turn around and chase him for sure. Something big was happening somewhere, though, and so far the police were ignoring him.

But Joseph couldn't ignore his situation, or pretend that everything was OK. It wasn't. Shadrack was down, maybe dead, and he had a baby in the back of this truck. He looked back at it again; it was still crying. What to do? he wondered.

He needed to get off the motorway as quick as possible, before the police did pick him up, but he was a long way from home. No, wait, he told himself, he didn't want to go home. If Shadrack was alive and gave him up to the police then they would go to his mother's place. He thought hard. A sign to Mtubatuba flashed past. He had relatives between there and the Hluhluwe–iMfolozi Park, near the mining town of Somkhele. They would look after him and he could hide the car there.

Part of him wanted to just stop and abandon the Fortuner and the baby and make a run for it, but more of him wanted to see this job through. As well as the baby the Toyota was loaded with high-end stuff. It looked like the woman had been moving house. He'd noticed a flat-screen TV, a couple of laptops, a wardrobe's worth of clothes, and the handbag on the seat next to him had contained two new iPhones, an iPad and a wad of cash. He had already pocketed the money – US dollars and rand – and the phones, but he could make a fortune fencing all this gear.

The baby. He thought about what he should do with it. It yelled and it screamed and there was not only the smell of sick to contend with. Joseph had little pity for the child. He didn't really care what happened to it, as long as he didn't have to do anything with it.

He shook his head. This was madness. He had done more than steal a car, he had kidnapped the child. The newspapers and television would be going crazy. He was probably already making the news. He turned on the car radio, and although it was not on the hour or half hour, a newsreader was speaking. His heart hammered in his chest.

'*. . . and to repeat that breaking news, the US Ambassador to South Africa, Anita Rosenfeld, and two of her bodyguards have been confirmed killed in a bomb blast that rocked downtown Durban this morning. The South African National Defence Force has been deployed on the streets and the city is in lock-down. As yet, no group has claimed responsibility.*

'*Ambassador Rosenfeld was supposed to visit a hospice and attend a cocktail party on board a visiting US warship today, along with unspecified South African government representa-tives. It's no secret that the US is keen to engage South Africa in its war on terror in other parts of the continent, but experts are already saying today's attack, believed to have been carried out by a suicide bomber, means closer cooperation with America will make South Africa a target.*'

It wasn't him. Joseph exhaled long and hard through his nostrils as he tried to calm himself. The police he had passed were going to Durban. A bomb would keep them busy, but eventually someone would come looking for the child, if not the Fortuner.

He needed to get rid of both of them. He toyed with the idea of driving to the nearest police station – the cops would not expect that – and offloading the baby on the street.

No, he reconsidered, too risky.

The vehicle itself he would stash at his cousin's place. Themba Nyathi would not be happy to see Joseph, but if Themba complained or threatened to go to the police then Joseph would soon shut the sanctimonious young swot up.

Chapter 5

Egil Paulsen got out of the Audi and the vehicle, with his three men still on board, did a U-turn and drove off. Egil stood on the opposite side of the street from the man he knew as Bandile Dlamini. He had seen the former politician's picture on the internet in dozens of online articles about the man's political and business careers.

He was not the only serving or ex-politician to be involved in a corrupt deal. The problem with this deal, however, was that Egil was coming to it as the vendor, but he had nothing to sell.

Ideally he would have had his men with him, but Egil had sent Bilal, Ibrahim and Djuma to find the stolen Fortuner with a baby on board. Paulsen wasn't worried about the imbalance in firepower, though – if his soon-to-be business partner had ever killed in the line of his dealings, Egil was sure it would not have been nearly as many men and women as he.

Egil took a few seconds to size up Dlamini. Egil was as white as Bandile was black, yet he considered himself just as African. He had been born in Port Shepstone, 120 kilometres south of Durban; his Norwegian forebears had come to South Africa in the 1880s, lured by the offer of land in the British colony of Natal. They had settled mostly around Egil's birthplace.

He had grown up not in the cold, clean crispness of Scandinavian Europe, but amid the wild game and blood-red earth of Africa and its politics of hate. Egil's grandfather had served with the South African Army in Italy during the Second World War, and his father had fought in South West Africa, now Namibia, and the early battles in Angola.

South Africa's border war had ended too soon for newly conscripted Egil to see wartime service, but as a young soldier he had been deployed on township duties. He had seen the beatings and machete wounds inflicted by Zulu against Xhosa, people burned to death with necklaces of fuel-filled tyres. He had fired, first tear gas then bullets, into rioting youngsters, and he had killed.

He'd loved army life, while so many of his surfer and *dagga*-smoking comrades had hated it. But he'd felt cheated of real action and disillusioned by the direction South Africa was heading in. His parents, while not Afrikaners, were conservative supporters of the apartheid regime. When his military service was up Egil travelled to Europe, to see distant relatives in Norway, and in a bar got to drinking with some Norwegian conscript soldiers who were talking about travelling to Bosnia in the former Yugoslavia to fight Serbian aggression.

In Bosnia he'd joined the mujahideen, fighters from around the world aiding the Bosnian Muslims. Here he had tested himself in real combat, against armed men, and had become addicted to a life lived on the edge and converted to Islam. His faith had taken him to other war zones, to Chechnya where he had killed Russians, and Afghanistan where he had fought America and her allies and narrowly escaped capture in the Tora Bora mountains.

Egil walked towards the shebeen and Dlamini ambled slowly across the road in the same direction. The big man's driver was in tow, carrying a green canvas safari travel bag in one hand.

Although he had no rhino horn Egil had no intention of leaving without the money the driver was carrying in that bag, nor without another car so that he could catch up with his men.

The two Zulu men had entered the bar first. It was the most substantial structure in the market, constructed of brick and rendered with rough plaster and whitewash on the outside. The Starlight Lounge advertised cold Castle Lite and 'fun times'. Inside, Egil knew, were two rooms, one with a cement-topped bar and the other with a pool table covered in ripped felt. In the rear, in a separate building, were five rooms side by side where the resident prostitutes plied their trade.

Egil closed one eye as he approached. Even before he entered, the smell of stale beer, disinfectant and vestiges of urine and vomit assaulted his senses and sensibilities. He drew a breath.

As he entered the room he noted Dlamini had taken up position with his back to the wall at a table beyond the pool table. A girl in a tight red dress darted out through the rear door and a man who had been about to take a stroke put the cue down on the torn felt of the table. He and his friend moved to the bar room. The music blaring from the speaker on the wall offended Egil almost as much as the smells and Dlamini, perhaps seeing him wince, called to the barman in Zulu. The music died.

Dlamini had told Egil he would be bringing two men, but there was no sign of the second. Egil wondered if he was hiding somewhere, waiting to spring a trap.

'You're empty-handed. Where did your car just go? Where is the stuff?' Dlamini said without preamble. The driver stood behind his boss, the bag in his hand.

'I don't have it.'

'You what?'

'It was stolen.'

Dlamini's hands, visible and resting on the scarred and cigarette-burned plastic tabletop, curled into fists. He looked at his watch. 'You have wasted my time and I urgently need to be somewhere else. Tell me what happened, quickly.'

'The vehicle carrying the stuff was stolen. It's South Africa, it happens.'

'I know what goes on in my own country. Where was it stolen?'

Egil considered the question a fair one. Who knew, perhaps Dlamini did, as some old reports had suggested, have a finger in car theft – perhaps he could reach out to some contacts. 'On the N2, north of Durban. I have information that it may be headed this way, in fact. I have my men looking for it. The car's owner has been in touch with the tracking company. Where's your other man?'

'Around. Watching us.'

Egil noted how Dlamini had looked up, briefly. Perhaps he didn't know where his bodyguard was. 'I need the money your driver has in that bag. I will deliver the horn to you once my men and I find it.'

Dlamini laughed. 'You're joking, of course.'

Dlamini glanced back and spoke softly in Zulu to his driver. What Bandile Dlamini didn't realise was that Egil Paulsen had been raised in no small part by a Zulu *gogo*, a nanny who had been loving where his parents had been cold and cruel, and who had spoken to him in Zulu from the day he was born to the day he left home.

'Take him,' was what Dlamini had said to the driver.

Egil's reflexes had been honed and tested on the bloodiest battlefields of his time. He had passed every one of those tests, won every one of those competitions to see who was quickest, the most accurate, the most ruthless. In one movement he drew the pistol from his belt and fired.

The first bullet caught the driver in the chest, the second his face. The money bag slipped from the driver's fingers as he tumbled backwards.

Even as he fired, Egil was dropping to one knee, to make himself a smaller target. Dlamini was pushing his big frame back from the table. Egil didn't know whether the businessman was armed, but he didn't want to wait to find out. He got one shot off, hitting the man in the right shoulder, but before he could put a second round into him a figure blocked the light from the back door of the shebeen. Egil dived and rolled behind the pool table, crawled two metres then popped up and put two rounds towards the door.

*

Mike Dunn ducked back out of the doorway. He moved just in time, as two shots punched the air where he had just been. The man with the white hair was too quick for him.

Mike tried to process the big picture while at the same time figuring out how not to get killed. It wasn't easy. Mike heard a yelp of pain from inside.

'Don't come in here after me. I've got a hostage,' said a voice from inside.

Mike had seen Dlamini take a bullet and clutch at his shoulder, so he assumed the white-haired man had him. Mike backed around the shebeen into the laneway again. He moved to the front of the bar and peeked around the corner.

The white man was crossing the road, walking backwards with one arm around Dlamini's neck. The driver's canvas bag, presumably full of cash, was slung from its long carry strap around the white man's torso. Dlamini had his hand pressed to the bleeding hole in his shoulder.

The man with the white hair paused in the middle of the dirt road. People scattered to the shelter of the various stalls. He pressed the pistol harder into Dlamini's head.

Mike looked behind him; Solly had sat Dlamini's remaining man down in the alley. Mike had roughed him up, but had probably saved the man's life.

'Get ready to cover me,' Mike said to Solly.

'Aren't we better just to sit tight? Not even a rhino horn deal is worth dying for.'

'You're right about that,' Mike said, 'besides, I want Dlamini alive, and if we don't do anything the white-haired man will kill him as soon as he's clear of town. He's only keeping him alive now as a human shield because he must know Dlamini has a second man.'

Mike left Solly and the captured man and ran behind the row of market stalls. He glanced between the stands and stopped when he was opposite Dlamini's car. The white-haired man, with Dlamini clenched in one arm, was moving more slowly now. Mike took a deep breath and raised his pistol, steadying it against the tin wall of a shack.

The man reached Dlamini's car and backed up against it. He said something that Mike couldn't hear.

'Lawrence, come out,' Dlamini called.

No chance, Mike thought to himself. Lawrence was presumably the man Solly was holding.

White-hair was smiling as he shoved Dlamini in the back. 'Get down on your knees, hands behind your back. Keys.'

Dlamini did as ordered and took his keys from his pocket. The man snatched them. Mike steadied himself. Dlamini lowered his bulk down, slowly, and the man reached behind him and opened the driver's side door of the car.

Mike took aim high, at the blond man's chest. For a moment he wavered, wondering if he could shoot a man like this, in cold blood. Just then, his target forced his hand, by raising his own and pointing his pistol at the back of Dlamini's head.

Mike squeezed the trigger. The white man's body jerked, but a fraction of a second after he was hit he also fired, and Bandile Dlamini pitched face forward in the dirt. Mike fired again, but the man, who had dropped to one knee, was able to hoist himself up into the car. Mike couldn't tell if he'd hit him or a near-miss had caused him to flinch.

Mike ducked back into the shadows as four or five rounds headed his way. Whether he had been hit or not, the man was still a danger.

More gunfire came from where Mike had left Solly and the fleeing man had to return the exchange in that direction as well. The engine on the BMW purred to life and the man floored the accelerator.

Mike looked around the corner of the shack and fired again. He saw two of Solly's shots hit the car's windscreen and he put another two shots into the passenger-side window. The black sedan fish-tailed on the dirt road and raced through the market place.

'Dammit.' With the car accelerating away, Mike strode out into the middle of the dirt road and, seeing no innocents in front of him, he emptied his magazine at the disappearing BMW.

Mike nodded grimly. They went to where Dlamini was lying in the middle of the road. Curious stallholders were now starting to venture out of their hiding places and onto the street.

A man had his phone out and was taking a photo. 'You,' Mike called to him, 'call an ambulance.'

Mike dropped to his knee next to Dlamini, who groaned and held a hand to his shoulder. Blood seeped between his fingers. 'You were lucky.'

Dlamini coughed and winced. 'I don't feel lucky. But he missed with his second shot, so thank you for that. I fell forward to make him think he had hit me.'

'Find me something I can use to stop the bleeding,' Mike said to Solly. 'One of the *sangomas* should be able to help.' Solly nodded and jogged to the nearest stall in search of a traditional healer.

'I need a car,' Dlamini said.

Mike took out his handkerchief and pressed it against the wound in Dlamini's shoulder. 'You're not going anywhere until the police have finished with you. What was your business with that man?'

Dlamini looked into his eyes. 'None of your business.'

'Then let me help refresh your memory. He was the *oke* that was about to shoot you in the head before I winged him. He was the one you came here to buy rhino horn from.'

'I came here to investigate a tip-off that a white man was selling rhino horn. I'm working with the police.'

'There are no police here, and I busted your man with the vulture heads. That alone is enough to get you locked up.'

'I know nothing about any vulture heads.'

Solly came to them with a couple of bandages and a compress made of some plant materials. 'The *sangoma* says this will slow the bleeding.'

Mike tore away some of Dlamini's tailored shirt and told the man to be still as he dressed the wound. 'You can talk now or talk later, Mr Dlamini. Why were you buying rhino horn from him?'

'I wasn't buying anything. He had nothing to sell, but he robbed me.'

'You're selling out our country's national heritage. I should kill you myself.'

'Lies. I've been on the record opposing poaching. Anyway, the important thing now is that I get to my daughter.'

'What about the money in the bag the man took?' Mike asked.

'The money was real, but that man was never supposed to get away with it. I was here to pretend to buy rhino horn from him and my men were going to catch him in the act.'

'Interesting story, but why did you go ahead with your so-called sting when the police clearly haven't pitched?'

'It is no story. It is the truth. I wanted to catch a rhino horn trader. Please, you must help me. I have no car now and I need to get home to my daughter.'

'Tell me, where did my bullet hit him?'

'I'm not sure it did,' Dlamini said. 'Please, I need a car.'

'Where's your phone?' Mike asked him.

'He frisked me after he'd shot me. He stomped on my phone, destroyed it. Call her for me, take me to her.'

'What's your daughter's name?'

'Lerato.'

'Give me her phone number.' As Dlamini dictated the number, Mike punched it into the contacts section of his phone. When he was done he called to Solly.

'Please . . .'

Mike looked down. Dlamini's head dropped to the ground and he closed his eyes. He put his fingers on the man's neck; he had a pulse but his breathing was shallow.

'Ambulance is coming,' Solly said.

Mike's phone vibrated in his hand. He didn't recognise the number, but it had been a day of surprises. 'Mike Dunn.'

'Mike, howzit, my name's John Buttenshaw from Coastal Choppers at Virginia Airport – we do the airborne tracking for Motor Track, the car monitoring people.'

Mike thought for a moment. 'Oh, right. Your people passed on the information about the vultures. I appreciate it, but I'm busy with something else right now.'

'No, no, wait, this is urgent! Did you go there, to the carcass and the dead vultures?'

'Yes, I did. Tell your pilot thanks for his work.'

'Her work. The carcass; it's a crime scene, right?'

The man sounded young, panicked, his words fighting each other to escape his mouth. 'Yes, at least it was before I burned it. Vultures are protected under law, and by the Zulu king. Technically it's a capital offence under tribal law to kill a vulture – not that it means anything.'

'Right, good, terrific,' John said. 'Mike, I need to talk to whatever police are with you now. This is really, really important.'

Mike sighed. 'I'm not at the carcass any more. I'm at the Mona market, my second crime scene of the day, as it happens, but there are no police here, either. I haven't been able to get through to them. All the numbers are busy or the cops I know are tied up in Durban because of the bomb. You heard about the bomb, right?'

'Yes, of course. Damn. I really need to talk to some cops.'

'So do I. What's up?' Mike squeezed the bridge of his nose with his thumb and forefinger as John explained about the stolen car and the missing baby. Only in Africa.

'Our pilot's getting low on fuel,' John added. 'She's the one who found your carcass and the vultures; she burned a lot of gas keeping the birds away from the poison. But the Fortuner's still on the move. It's not far from you.'

'All right. I'm going. Give me five minutes then call or SMS me your radio frequency. Talk me in to where your pilot is.'

'No, man,' John said, 'you're a civilian. I'm not asking you to go catch the dude, just to please flag down a policeman, or tell them to contact me if one comes to your location. These guys were armed when they took the car and . . .'

The adrenaline was still fuelling Mike's senses. He was a 'civilian' now, as John had said, but once he'd been a foot-soldier in the war on wildlife poaching, not simply a researcher. He was once more relying on the instincts he had honed as a warrior. A child was at risk and that stirred a barely suppressed, painful memory – something that still haunted him. He'd tried to atone, by helping troubled youngsters in South Africa set a new course in their lives through working in the bush, in conservation and the rhino guards program, but it never felt like it was enough. It was impossible for him to redeem himself, but he never wanted to stop trying. The woman who had saved so many vultures today was now trying to rescue a baby and the police weren't helping. 'Your pilot helped me out, so I'll return the favour. Put me in touch with her.' He jogged back to the Defender.

Chapter 6

Nia Carras was having a hard time keeping a lid on her anxiety. The Fortuner had turned left off the N2, heading northwest towards Hluhluwe–iMfolozi.

The Fortuner raced past the Somkhele coalmine, crazily overtaking every car it came to, and narrowly avoiding a head-on as it crested a rise. The signal from the tracking device was still loud and clear which told her the man was either alone or his accomplice had failed to find the tracker. The Fortuner slowed and took another left, this time onto a dirt road that led into a rural area dotted with huts. Cows and goats fed on the sparse covering of dry grass that barely masked the red earth.

'Getting close to home?' she asked the driver, rhetorically, as he skidded through a bend, the rear of the Fortuner fish-tailing.

Her phone rang. It was John. 'Please tell me the cavalry is on its way.'

'Well, kind of,' John said.

'I don't have time for games, John. Who's coming?'

'You know those dead vultures you found this morning?'

'Yes, John.'

'Well, the vulture guy who went to check out the carcass – his name is Mike – is now on his way to you.'

Nia rolled her eyes. 'Some bird hugger? That's my ground crew?'

'Afraid so. I asked him to find some cops, but he insisted on going Chuck Norris. He'll be in touch with you soon. Maybe he can just follow the Fortuner from a distance.'

Nia wondered what good a nerdy researcher could do. He was probably some PhD student with no friends. Whoever he was, though, he was the only person who had responded to John's call, and she was fast running out of options. As it was she did not have enough fuel to return to Virginia and had spent the time waiting for John's last message contacting other airfields, and even King Shaka Airport, seeking approval for an emergency landing.

'OK, John. Give him this location.' Nia tapped the iPad and read off the coordinates of the intersection where the SUV had left the tar road. 'The Fortuner's moving slower now, into the rural areas, heading northwest up into the hills towards the game reserve. Give the guy my number and tell him to call me. If we're lucky they'll hide the Toyota somewhere or start stripping it and maybe this vulture guy can find somewhere to keep it under observation while I land and refuel.'

'Sounds like a plan,' John said, then hung up.

Nia banked sharply to the left when she saw that the dust cloud behind the Fortuner had stopped moving. The driver had pulled up next to a cluster of three shabby-looking huts.

Her phone rang, but she couldn't answer it as she was too busy flying. She backed off away from the *kraal*, and went into an orbit. She hit the number on her phone to redial.

'Howzit, it's Mike Dunn here.'

'Vulture guy?'

'Yes, vulture guy. I hear you have a situation.'

'You could say that.'

'I've got your coordinates and I've been trying to visualise exactly where you are since I spoke to your guy. Is there a blue rondavel perched on top of a hill, probably to the east of where you are right now?'

Nia was impressed. 'Yes, there is. How did you know that?'

'I know some people there. I spend a lot of time in the communities around the national park.'

'OK, whatever. You think you can get here soon and keep the place under surveillance until the cops arrive?'

'I think I can manage that.'

His voice was deep, and his tone calm. Nia was doing her best to sound professional and cool, but wasn't sure she was pulling it off. This guy sounded like she'd just asked him if he could go to the bar and buy her a beer.

'Don't do anything stupid,' she warned him. 'There's a baby in this car.' As she spoke she saw some movement below. 'OK, wait. Driver's out of the car. He's taking a break for something, maybe to try and find the tracking device and get rid of it. Doesn't know I'm here. This is your chance to put foot and catch up.'

'All right. I'll be there soon.'

'Quick as you can. I can't stay here much more than ten minutes or I'm going to have to put down where I am. I don't want to lose this kid.'

'Understood.'

Nia ended the call. She didn't want to risk getting closer to the Fortuner and being spotted, but she also wanted to keep the thief in sight, to see what he did with the child. From the corner of her eye she picked up movement and for a second she thought it might be the vulture man, here already. Unfortunately it was a white van, a minibus taxi. The driver of the Fortuner was pulling stuff out of the back of the vehicle and dropping the various articles on the ground. She could see his bottom protruding from the vehicle's boot.

The minibus taxi slowed, perhaps out of curiosity, and came to a stop.

*

Warrant Officer Vusi Matsebula had been sleeping pleasantly in the back seat of the crowded taxi, until it lurched to a halt. He was jerked awake. He vaguely recalled a thud, as though the taxi had hit something. That was the last thing he needed. He rubbed his red eyes.

Vusi looked past the pregnant woman next to him out the window of the taxi, and saw a white Fortuner parked at an oblique angle.

'What happened?' he asked the woman.

She shook her head and tutted. 'Some crazy young man is throwing things out of that car and something hit the taxi. The driver is not impressed.'

A surge of adrenaline roused him. There was a young man standing by the driver's side of the vehicle. He wore low-slung jeans, his underpants showing above the waistband. He moved his right hand behind his back and Vusi saw the guy pull out a gun. Vusi stood in the cramped cab of the taxi.

'Hey, watch what you're doing,' said the man in the suit in front of him as Vusi bumped him as he drew his Z88 police-issue nine-millimetre pistol.

'Quiet, keep your heads down.'

'He's got a gun,' said a woman on Vusi's left, pointing to his pistol.

'Shush. I'm police,' Vusi hissed.

The driver of the taxi was out of the van, hitching up his trousers and then stabbing a finger towards the young man. Vusi could see the man by the Fortuner was still hiding his gun behind his back, but the driver obviously hadn't seen the firearm.

'Hey, you, what are you doing throwing stuff at my taxi?' the driver yelled in Zulu.

The young man raised his arm, pointing his gun at the driver. 'Back off, old man.'

'Shit,' Vusi whispered. 'Everyone, take cover.' Vusi nudged his way to the door of the taxi, his pistol held down by his right leg and out of sight. The young man had his eyes locked on the driver, who was not backing down.

'What's going on?' a girl in school uniform with a boy next to her said in a quavering voice.

'It's OK,' Vusi quickly assured the girl. 'Just stay low.' The girl lowered her head and the boy, maybe seventeen, put his hand on her back and then covered her with his body. Vusi took a moment to squeeze the boy's shoulder.

The driver wagged his finger. 'You back off, and you put that gun away or . . .'

'Joseph, no!'

Vusi looked back at the seat he had just passed. The schoolboy who was comforting the girl had slid open his window and called to the gunman. Vusi rolled his eyes. This day was fast deteriorating. He thought of his wife and child, waiting for him just a few kilometres down the road. He'd been lucky to be allowed to leave at the end of his shift, given the storm that had erupted over Durban that morning, and now he was being sucked into his own personal nightmare. Vusi took a deep breath.

'Themba,' called the man with the gun. He looked to the bus. 'Damn, get off the bus, I was looking for you. Why didn't you just stop the bus and get off here at your home?'

Vusi swivelled his eyes to look at the schoolboy, Themba.

'I've got stuff to do, Joseph. Hey, cousin, just put the gun down. Chill, man.'

'Don't tell me what to do, Themba. Get off the taxi now. Come, I need help.'

'I can't do that, Joseph,' Themba replied.

Vusi crouched lower in the taxi and whispered: 'Themba.'

The boy glanced down.

'Don't look at me, Themba,' Vusi said. The youth looked back outside the taxi. 'I need you to keep talking to that guy. Who is he?'

'My cousin, Joseph,' Themba said out of the side of his mouth.

'Will he use that gun?' Vusi asked. Themba's silence told Vusi all he needed to know.

Themba took a deep breath. 'Joseph, lower your gun, please, let the driver get back in the taxi. Mister Driver, please, let's just keep going.'

Both the driver and Joseph were looking at Themba. Vusi crawled along the floor of the van. He slid between the two front seats like a python and rolled out of the taxi onto the grass, on the opposite side to where Joseph swung his gun from the driver to the bus and its passengers. Vusi stood in a crouch and, his back to the vehicle, edged slowly around the front. His pistol was cocked and ready.

'Themba, get off the bus, now. I need your help, cousin.'

'I'm not doing that, Joseph.'

Joseph aimed his pistol at the driver's head. 'Get off that taxi or I'll shoot the fat man.'

A woman started screaming on board the taxi. Vusi saw a piece of door trim on the ground. It was clear Joseph had been stripping the inside of the vehicle. There was another noise above the commotion. It was a baby crying, but Vusi could not recall seeing an infant or even a young child on board the taxi. He swore quietly in Zulu.

Vusi drew a deep breath. He could not shoot Joseph outright without first identifying himself. Also, the taxi driver was between him and the car thief, partially blocking his view. Added to his difficulties, he was terrified. Vusi worked in community relations and had not been on the streets, dealing with criminals, in more than fifteen years. He was overweight and he needed a new pair of glasses. He gripped his Z88 harder to try and stop his hands from shaking, but the effort made it worse.

'Police . . .' he began to yell, but as he stood straight and extended his pistol the driver, seeing that Joseph's attention was again on Themba, reached behind his back and pulled out his own pistol. 'Down!'

Vusi ran out from his position of cover at the front of the van. Joseph turned and fired a snap shot that caught the taxi driver in the chest and poleaxed the big man. Vusi fired twice. His first shot missed, but his second seemed to catch Joseph in his left shoulder. The younger man's body twisted sideways, which meant Vusi's next shot whizzed by him.

Joseph, however, still had his gun hand up and he blasted away. Vusi had to sidestep to avoid being hit by the falling driver, and the fraction of a second this took gave Joseph the chance to steady his aim. He fired again.

*

Nia watched the scene unfolding below her in horror. It was over in a matter of seconds.

She saw the fat man fall, then another middle-aged man with a gun emerged from his hiding spot at the front of the taxi. He, too, fell in the exchange of gunfire and lay as still as the driver in the blood-stained grass.

Nia hit the redial button on her phone, which was connected to her Bose headset via bluetooth.

'I'm about ten minutes away,' the vulture man said without preamble.

'Hurry, there are people shooting at each other here.'

'You OK?'

'No, I'm not *OK*. There are two men down here. A taxi pulled up next to the Fortuner. The hijacker got spooked or something. This is out of control.'

'I'm coming as fast as I can.'

'Can you make a call for me?'

'Yes.'

'Call for an ambulance. Two people down, and it's not over.'

The gunman backed away from the minibus, towards the Toyota. A younger man, no more than a gangly boy in a school uniform, Nia saw, climbed out of the taxi and ran past the gunman to the Fortuner. She had to do something to stop more bloodshed below.

Nia lowered the collective, pushing the Robinson into a fast dive. She banked hard to the right and used the pedal to pull the tail around in a tight descending turn, keeping the crime scene on her right. The fuel warning light flashed on and off. That was the effect of the aviation gas sloshing in the tanks. When she levelled out the light went out, but she was dangerously close to minimum fuel. The gunman was not threatening the schoolboy; in fact, he was turning his attention and anger on her – he had spotted the chopper.

The gunman looked up at her and she could see the wild look in his eyes. The man raised his pistol and Nia saw it buck in his hand. Metal pinged on metal somewhere on the helicopter. Nia climbed out of the turn and the warning light flashed again.

Orbiting out of pistol range she saw the gunman run back to the taxi. He was yelling something back over his shoulder, apparently telling the boy to rip some possessions from the back seat of the Fortuner, which he began to do. Nia saw household goods, an iron, a cardboard box of plates and other crockery that fell apart and spilled its contents on the grass, blankets and clothes on hangers.

Nia tightened her turn, raising the collective lever to increase the power and use the torque of the main rotor to help her around. She was acutely aware of the risk of the engine flaming out because of a lack of fuel and started mentally preparing herself for a low level auto-rotation, an emergency landing.

The next time she saw the boy in the school uniform he had a military-style rifle in his hands with a curved magazine – she recognised it immediately as an AK-47.

She knew of pilots who'd been shot at, but she could hardly believe it had just happened to her. Her heart had begun to beat painfully in her chest. If it wasn't for the child in the Fortuner she would have been long gone from here.

The man with the pistol climbed into the taxi again and this time emerged with a teenage girl in a school uniform. She struggled against him, but he grabbed her and frogmarched her to the Toyota, holding the pistol up to her head, high enough for Nia to see.

The gunman appeared to order the girl and boy into the front of the Toyota while he took the cleared seat in the rear, and the doors slammed.

At the same time, someone inside the minibus taxi had taken the driver's seat and the bus was backing down the red earth road at high speed, jinking left and right as the driver fought to keep control.

Nia flicked the radio to the police emergency frequency again and broadcast what she had seen, and the fact that she had been shot at. As she did so, she thought that even if the police couldn't respond immediately at least members of the news media, who monitored the police channel, might pick up the story and this would put pressure on the police to devote some resources to saving the kids. To her it seemed that the gunman had taken the schoolgirl as his hostage as he had kept the gun on her and not on the boy, who was armed with an AK-47. He could have been threatening the boy in some other way, but something about the way they had interacted made Nia think the two young men knew each other. Her phone rang.

'Five minutes away,' the vulture man said.

'Hurry, but be careful. Sheesh, I don't know. Maybe don't come at all, there are people killing each other down there!'

'OK, keep the phone line open.'

The passenger behind the wheel of the taxi had turned the bus around and it was disappearing back towards Mtubatuba. Nia saw the Fortuner start to move. She followed it, bringing the R44 down low, closer than she had ever come to a moving vehicle. Slowly, she pulled ahead of the Toyota. The boy at the wheel accelerated to ninety kilometres an hour.

She thought of the boy and wondered how skilled he was at driving. He hadn't looked more than sixteen or seventeen. Nia thought she might be able to slow him down, but she was acutely aware of the girl and the baby in the car. The last thing she wanted was for the guy to crash and injure the innocents on board.

Nia was terrified of engine failure, but she had to try something. She eased sideways with the pedal, trying to keep the aircraft level to avoid sloshing the fuel. She was as low as she dared, her skids at windscreen height as she tracked right just ahead of the stolen car. The driver braked, but rather than giving up, as Nia had hoped, he turned off the narrow gravel road and into the veldt.

'I see you on the horizon. Nearly there. What's the status?' asked the vulture man.

Nia spoke into the headset. 'The status is, this is fucked. I'm in pursuit, but I have to land ASAP, I'm nearly out of fuel. The kid driving has just gone into the veldt. That's slowed him down. If you hurry you might be able to catch him.'

'All right. I'm just coming to the *kraal*. I see the two men down. I called the ambulance like you asked but it looks as if it's too late and . . . wait a minute.'

Hurry up, Nia urged the man silently.

'One of these guys is still alive. I have to stop and help him.'

Nia exhaled, puffing her cheeks. This was crazy. 'There's a baby and a kidnapped schoolgirl in the car ahead of me.' Nia waited for a reply, then tried again. Nothing. She wheeled the helicopter in a wide climbing turn, keeping the bank angle as shallow as possible to keep the remaining fuel in her tanks steady. She looked down helplessly at the vehicle ploughing through the grass. The boy was driving fast, competently, heading for the trees. She saw what he was doing now. He was going to drive amid the thorny acacias, where he would know she couldn't land to block him, and then cut back out onto the road on the other side of the hill.

The low-fuel light glared solid now, demanding that she put down. Reluctantly she turned back to the *kraal*. Running on vapours, she set down about five metres from the side of the road, near a Land Rover Defender with pictures of vultures on the doors. A man was kneeling over one of the shooting victims, covering the wounded man with his body to protect him from Nia's rotor wash. Nia closed her eyes and permitted herself a short sigh. She had been closer than she'd ever come in her flying career to having to make a forced landing. She tugged on the rotor brake handle, attached to a short chain hanging from the cockpit ceiling, unbuckled, took off her headset, unplugged her phone and jumped down.

Her phone chirped and she accepted the call, too frazzled to even check the screen. 'It's Nia.'

'Babe, it's me.'

Nia slumped against the helicopter. 'Sheesh, Banger, it's good to hear your voice.' Her relief turned quickly to anger. 'Where the hell have you been?'

'I got a missed call from you but couldn't get through. Damned network's been clogged because of the bomb in Durbs. I finally got hold of Virginia and John told me where you're at. Give me your exact position.'

She'd been worried about him, but at least he was safe. She described where she'd landed. 'Hey, if you can get through to John, can you tell him I need fuel?'

'OK, I can pass on the message, but I *am* close. You're between Mtubes and iMfolozi, correct?'

'Yes, that's right. I wish I could have got through to you earlier. There was this hijacking, but they took a baby, and there was shooting, and . . .' Nia fought back a rising tide of tears.

'Sheesh, babes. Stay right there, I'm coming. Just tell me your GPS coordinates, or if you need a minute, SMS them to me. I picked up your earlier locstat from John. See you soon, OK?'

Nia sniffed. The reality of what she had just been through was only just starting to hit her.

Chapter 7

Mike had seen a few gunshot wounds in his life; this one was bad.

The man he was working on was a police officer. Vusi had been able to tell him his name and his rank. Mike had ripped open the warrant officer's shirt to find a hole in his belly from which blood was welling and pouring out over the man's side. Mike took off his own shirt, balled it and had Vusi hold it against the wound while he unzipped the first aid kit he always carried with him.

'Shit. How is he?'

Mike looked up, into the sun, and saw the silhouetted face of a woman. It was hard to make out her features, beyond the initial impression that she was attractive, and angry.

'Not good. Who knows how long it will take the ambulance to get here.' Mike lowered his voice. 'He would have bled out if I hadn't stopped.'

The woman ran a hand through her untidy hair. 'This is a mess.'

'Want to pass me that bottle of saline from the first aid kit?' he said.

She dropped to her knees and passed him the small plastic one-use container. 'Sorry. I'm Nia.'

'Mike. Help me.' As Mike removed his shirt from Vusi's wound blood pumped out. He bit the end off the saline bottle and squirted the liquid all over and around the bullet hole, then pressed the pad of a wound dressing over it. 'We need to roll him.'

'No exit wound,' Nia said.

He nodded. She seemed to have some idea of what was going on, and with her help they turned Vusi, passed the tapes of the dressing around his back and tied it tightly. 'He's lost a lot of blood. If that ambulance doesn't get here soon, can you fly him to Durbs?'

Nia shook her head. 'That was the last of my fuel. I'm stuck here until my guys can bring me a resupply.' She took the policeman's hand and looked into his eyes. 'You hang in there, man, we're going to get you help. You'll be fine.'

Mike wasn't so sure, but Nia had dropped her surly attitude and was reassuring the patient, which was sometimes all you could do in this kind of situation. 'Thanks. The car you were chasing; tell me what you saw.'

Nia took a breath and ran through the shooting of the taxi driver and the policeman, the schoolboy seeming to help the car thief and the girl being forced into the Fortuner. She put a hand to her head. 'I think I screwed things up, though.'

'How?' She really was very pretty, he decided, now that he could see her properly. Her black hair was cut in a short, practical bob and her skin had an even, mellow, Mediterranean colouring. Her fingers had left a smudge of Vusi's blood on her forehead.

'The hijacker hadn't seen me until that point; I was standing off and he was too busy. I went in closer and he panicked. He shot at me and that's when things started kicking off. Vusi was shot; the taxi driver was killed. The gunman decided to take a hostage – another one – a schoolgirl in addition to the baby. Shit.' She looked to the driver, whose body lay motionless in the grass.

'Don't blame yourself, blame the shooter,' Mike said. 'I don't think me getting here sooner would have helped you. I've got guns, but by the sound of it, this gunfight was all over in seconds.'

She blinked a few times and Mike had the feeling she was fighting back tears, though something about her no-nonsense manner told him that she was not the sort to show weakness.

'You might have been able to stop them,' she said.

Mike shrugged. 'They were already mobile; if I'd opened up on the Toyota I might have hit the baby, or the girl. I'm an OK shot, but to take out the shooter from another moving vehicle with a rifle is just about impossible.'

'Yes, yes, yes. I know about guns.' She waved her free hand dismissively, then looked at him. 'You said on the radio you know this area.'

He nodded.

Nia gestured with her thumb past her helicopter, in the direction in which the Fortuner had disappeared. 'Where does that road lead?'

'Either back to the N2 or, eventually, to Hluhluwe–iMfolozi.'

Nia looked up the road, then back at him. 'So if we can get a police roadblock on the motorway on ramp then we can bottle them up.'

'Good luck finding a policeman today,' Mike said. 'You heard about the bomb?'

'Yes. Are there any other villages between here and the national park?'

'A few small *kraals*. Your hijacker had to know someone out here. It's not the sort of place he could easily disappear into.'

Nia looked around them. 'Why would he stop here, of all places?'

'Funny,' Mike said, following her gaze.

'What's funny, I need a laugh.' Nia tended to Vusi, mopping his brow with Mike's bloodied shirt.

'I know a young guy who lives around here.'

'I didn't see anyone in the *kraal*, just a few goats.'

Mike could feel the sun stinging his bare back, but he didn't relish the idea of asking Nia for his shirt back and feeling Vusi's blood stick to his skin. He had an old one in the back of the Land Rover which he used when he had to get under the old bus and see to something. He would get it once the ambulance arrived – *if* it arrived. 'You've heard of child-headed households?'

Nia nodded. 'Mom and Dad die of AIDS and the eldest kid is left to run the family.'

'Well, the kid who lives in that rondavel over there,' Mike pointed to a mud-brick circular hut with a thatched roof, '*is* the family. His parents are dead, his one older brother got the virus as well and is gone, and his younger sister was raped by their uncle, their only surviving close relative. The little girl's in care, in a foster home.'

'Sheesh,' Nia said. 'They didn't take the boy into care as well?'

Mike shook his head. 'He went into juvenile detention; he got busted stealing a car with his cousin, the uncle's son. He was going to sell it to make money for their school fees and food. While he was inside he left his sister with the uncle.'

Nia looked heavenwards, then back to Mike. 'And the uncle?'

'Dead. Shot out the back of a local shebeen.'

'Good riddance. Is the kid out of detention now?'

'Yes,' Mike said.

'You think there might be a connection between today's hijacking and the kid? Think maybe it was him who stole the Fortuner? The guy who shot at me wasn't old; maybe early twenties.'

Mike looked out over the rolling hills to the line that marked the division between marginal farmland and the wild bush; Hluhluwe–iMfolozi was as close as it got to heaven on earth.

It was a place of sanctuary, and, perhaps by extension, a place of refuge for a troubled soul. 'I hope to God it wasn't.'

*

Themba drove like he hadn't driven in two years. It was scary, not only because Joseph kept waving his pistol around, and now had the AK-47 resting across his lap, and not only because Lerato had been crying. It was scary because Themba had almost forgotten what a rush it was to drive fast with someone in pursuit.

Themba had found the AK in the Fortuner and had considered shooting his cousin, but he couldn't do it. Joseph had ripped the rifle from his hands then ordered him to drive. Mostly, he felt shame. There was a baby in the back of this stolen car and that, even to Themba, who had experience in driving stolen cars, was just not right.

'What are you thinking, cousin?' Joseph mocked him from the back seat.

Themba glanced in the rear view mirror and saw that Joseph's face was going grey. He had picked a piece of clothing from the pile in the back of the vehicle and balled it and tied it, with a belt, around his injured shoulder. The clumsy bandage had slowed the flow of blood, but Joseph's heavy lids belied his crazy grin.

'I asked what's on your mind?'

'Why did you have to involve me in this, Joseph? That is what I am thinking. And what are you doing with a baby in this car? Are you crazy?'

'Turn around, bitch, don't look back at me,' Joseph said to Lerato, who wiped her eyes and looked ahead again.

'Leave her alone, Joseph,' Themba said, looking in the mirror. 'And please answer my question. Why?'

'I wasn't planning on coming to you, all right? I had . . . problems. I needed help.'

Themba knew that stealing a car these days was not a one-man job. Too much could go wrong. Joseph would have had a partner, someone to drive while he searched for the tracking device, or vice versa. 'Why are you working solo?'

Joseph stared out the window for two seconds, then snapped his head back around. 'None of your damn business. Just drive. We need to find somewhere to hide up while I contact the buyer. I'll get him to come to us.'

Themba shook his head. 'You know the buyer won't do that. Too risky, man. I've got a better idea. Why don't I take you to the nearest clinic, drop you out the front and the baby nearby where someone will find it, and then I'll go burn this ride. No one will be any the wiser. You just tell the doctors you got caught up in a robbery.'

'No. I'm not letting you or your little girlfriend here out of my sight until I've got my money for this piece of shit white man's car. Who is she, anyway?'

Themba looked to Lerato then glanced back at his cousin. 'No one, she was just on the bus. We should let her go, Joseph.'

'You shouldn't have used my name, now she knows it. What's your name, sexy?'

Lerato folded her arms and stared resolutely out of the windscreen. Joseph leaned forward between the seats and pressed the end of the barrel of his pistol against her temple.

'I said, what's your name, sweet girl?'

'Joseph, leave her alone!'

She swallowed hard. 'Lerato.'

'*Le-ra-to*, nice name. Rolls off the *tongue* nicely. You and me going to be friends, Lerato?' He pressed the pistol harder.

'Please don't hurt me. Can't you just let me and Themba go?'

'Aha,' said Joseph. 'So you and my cousin *do* know each other. It figures, same school uniform and all.'

'My father,' Lerato breathed, 'he's a big man, wealthy, with connections to the government. You don't want to upset him. Please, just let me go and I'll say nothing.'

Joseph grinned. '*Wealthy*, you say? Well then maybe he'll pay me to get you back, *Le-ra-to*. What do you think, cousin, will Lerato's daddy shell out some coin to get his baby girl back in one piece?'

Themba glared at his cousin. 'You *do not* involve her in this, Joseph. I'm going to stop and let her out as soon as I find somewhere safe.'

Joseph tapped the barrel of the pistol against Themba's head. 'You *do not* give me orders, cousin; you know that's not how it works. While I've got the guns, I'm the one in charge here.'

Themba drove on, regularly checking the rear view mirror in search of someone following them. He wondered why the helicopter had given up on them. He also kept an eye on the baby which, surprisingly, had drifted off to sleep. He tried easing off the accelerator, but Joseph jabbed him again in the back of the neck and told him to speed up. He was a little scared, but mostly he was angry at his cousin. Joseph had never pointed a gun at him, let alone stuck one to his head. Also, he didn't like the way Joseph kept leering at Lerato. 'Joseph, please, you don't need us. You know I won't tell the cops anything and I'll make sure Lerato doesn't, either. Right?'

She looked back at him, her beautiful big eyes now all red-rimmed and misty. She sniffed. 'Yes, right. I won't say a thing.'

Joseph laughed from the back seat, then winced. Themba looked at his cousin again in the mirror and saw Joseph's lids slowly dropping. The wound must be worse than he was letting on, Themba thought. He didn't want to think of his cousin dying, but after the way he'd been acting today it was hard to feel pity for him.

'Don't slow down again.' Joseph lifted his head up and opened his eyes. 'We have to find somewhere to stop so you can strip this car. In fact, pull over now.'

Themba frowned. He considered telling Joseph to go to hell, but then his cousin leaned across to Lerato. She screamed as he put the gun to her head.

'OK, OK.' Themba pulled over and stopped the car.

'Get out.' Joseph motioned to Lerato. Joseph slung the AK-47 over his good shoulder. 'Over here, get on your knees.'

Themba got out, holding his arms loosely at his sides, clenching and unclenching his fists.

'Don't look at me like that, cousin.' Lerato knelt in front of Joseph, who kept the gun pointed at her. 'If you don't find it in ten minutes I'm going to see how good this little playmate of yours is with her mouth.'

'Don't even think of it.'

'OK, I'll just kill her now, then. You're right, I don't need either of you as hostages, and she knows too much about me, about you, now.' He straightened his arm and touched the barrel between Lerato's eyes. 'On three. One, two . . .'

Themba threw up his hands. 'All right, all right. Enough. I'm doing it.'

Themba set to work, checking under the seat and carpets. He opened boot and started dragging out more household goods.

'Faster, Themba, I'm getting bored here,' Joseph wheezed.

'I need tools. Where are they?'

Joseph shrugged. 'How should I know? Maybe with the spare?'

Themba cursed and tossed out a DVD player and a plastic bin bag that split and disgorged half a dozen pairs of women's shoes onto the grass. He saw a red metal box. He grabbed the handle and it was reassuringly heavy. He opened the cantilevered lid. 'Tools.'

'Get on with it,' Joseph snapped.

The tool box was comprehensive. There was a good deal of electrical gear – a soldering iron, solder, different grades of insulated wires, a multimeter – but Themba dug deeper until he found a cordless drill. He pulled the trigger; it was charged. Finding a pack of drill bits and screwdriver tips he fitted one and pocketed another couple. Themba went to the front of the Fortuner and started stripping out the door trim panels.

Sweat formed under his arms as he worked, and he wiped it away from his brow and upper lip. He worked methodically, running his hands inside the doors, under the carpets, as he moved around the vehicle. When he reached the side that Joseph and Lerato were on, he saw her staring at him.

'Wondering what your boyfriend's doing, Lerato?' Joseph asked his captive.

She said nothing, but Themba felt his embarrassment rise as he worked to the whine of the drill. He wanted them to be moving again. If the law was still tracking this vehicle they would find them soon, and he didn't want Lerato being hurt in a shootout. He saw the face of the woman behind the controls of the helicopter again; she had seen him while he was waving the AK-47 around. *Dammit, I should have just shot Joseph.*

No. That was the old him talking inside his head. But then again, this was the old him methodically stripping the inside of the Fortuner.

'He's one of the best, your boyfriend,' Joseph said mockingly to Lerato. 'He's looking for the hidden tracking device; the thing that almost got us caught by the helicopter. That pilot, she chased us a long way, but no one's going to be bothering us once we get the tracker out. Right, Themba?'

Themba said nothing, he was too busy. He removed the last screw in the internal side panel in the right rear of the Toyota's luggage area. Themba had a feeling – the same one he'd experienced when being an assistant car thief had been more or less his fulltime job – that he would find something there. He did.

'What have you found, Themba?'

Themba could feel fabric behind the panel. He pulled the whole piece out and looked into the cavity. There was a canvas bag, about the size of a school satchel. It wasn't a tracking device, but someone had hidden it there for some reason. He undid the drawstring at the top of the bag.

'Themba?'

'Um, I thought I'd found it, but it's not there. Still looking,' he called back. Themba opened the bag and peered into it. He whistled under his breath. Inside were three long objects, each ranging in length between the tip of his fingers and the crook of his elbow. They were curved and smooth, though not man-made. *Rhino horn.* Themba did the calculation in his head; each horn, he had learned, could weigh two to three kilograms. If there were, say, eight kilograms of horn, at roughly 65,000 US dollars a kilogram, then the bag contained millions of rand or more than half a million dollars' worth.

He rummaged quickly in the bag; it also contained three rhino tails. Themba was sickened by the discovery. Although the tails had no direct value themselves he knew that they were proof that these horns had come from three different rhinos. The wealthy businessmen in Vietnam and the organised criminals who supplied them wanted proof from poachers that the horn they were supplying came from wild, free-roaming rhinos, and not from some vault where horns from animals who had died from natural causes were stored.

At the bottom of the bag were two spare magazines of ammunition for the AK-47. Finally, his fingers closed around something smooth, round and heavy, about the size of a cricket ball. He drew the object out and when he looked at it he could hardly believe it; it was something he'd only ever seen in the movies.

'No, nothing here, my mistake,' Themba said to Joseph. He slipped the orb into the pocket of his school blazer. His heart was beating even faster as he started work on the opposite side panel, the drill buzzing in his hand. Joseph had made him leave the radio on while he had been driving and music had been playing in the background while he worked, but he had been too worried and too preoccupied to pay it any mind. Now the news came on and led with a story about a bomb going off in downtown Durban and killing the US ambassador. Most of the bulletin was devoted to speculation about the attack, and the chaos that had ensued. Themba tuned out as he worked, but the next item on the news made him stop the drill. The announcement said police were hunting for car thieves who had stolen a vehicle with a baby on board.

'Police say a taxi driver was killed and a police officer wounded when they tried to stop the thieves. Two males and a female have been seen in the stolen Toyota Fortuner and both men in the car reportedly fired gunshots at a vehicle-tracking helicopter that was following them. The unidentified female is dressed in a school uniform and it's unknown if she is part of the gang or, like the child, an innocent victim.'

Themba slammed the drill down. 'She's innocent, we're both innocent,' he whispered to the radio. 'And I didn't shoot at anyone.'

'What are you saying? Was that the news I could just hear?' Joseph called.

Themba ran his hand along the inside of the off-side rear compartment he had just exposed. 'Nothing.'

Finally, his fingers brushed over the small bump. Someone who didn't know what they were doing, someone who hadn't searched a score of Toyota Fortuners, might have assumed it was just another part of the bodywork. 'Got it.' He wrenched the bug free, got out, and tossed it so that it landed at Joseph's feet.

'All right, cousin, good work.'

'You can go now, Joseph. No one will find you. Leave us. You know me, I won't tell. The radio news was just on. It was all about a bomb in Durban. No one knows about you yet.' The baby started crying again.

Joseph appeared to consider the proposition for a couple of seconds, then looked at the child.

'Leave the kid with us,' Themba said. 'You don't want to get caught with it. We'll leave it somewhere safe, anonymously, like at a hospital or a church.'

Joseph said nothing, but moved his hand from where he had held it at his shoulder. When he looked at his palm it was slick with bright blood. He lowered his gun hand and stared at Themba.

'Joseph? Come on, man, leave us.'

Themba heard the noise of a vehicle engine coming from the direction they were headed in. They all turned to face the sound.

Chapter 8

Themba watched the black Audi Q5 accelerate towards them, a fantail of red dust trailing in its wake.

Joseph took a couple of steps towards the car. Themba motioned to Lerato to come to him. Her face was contorted in fear. His heart lurched in his chest.

As the vehicle came closer Themba saw the blue light flashing through the windscreen. He sighed and looked to the sky and thanked God. He again looked to Lerato, who had taken the child from its car seat and was holding it to her, murmuring over and over that everything would be all right. Themba wondered whether she was trying to soothe the baby or herself.

'It's over, Joseph.'

His cousin looked at him blankly and swayed. The pistol hung loosely at his side. Joseph coughed and blood welled at his lips.

'They'll take you to a hospital.'

There was no siren, but Themba thought the cops might be detectives, hence the unmarked Audi and the portable light placed on the dashboard. The Audi stopped a hundred metres down the road from them.

'Thank God,' Lerato said, echoing Themba.

'Joseph, put the guns down,' Themba said.

Joseph looked from the car back to Themba. His eyes were glazing over.

The doors of the Audi opened and three men got out and took up firing positions behind their respective doors. Themba noted that they all had rifles, military-style R5s. These men meant business.

'Police! Put down your weapons, put your hands on your heads and move slowly into the open. Leave the child in the car.'

The man calling the orders was coffee-coloured, as was one of the others, while the third gunman was African. There would be explaining to do, but Themba was sure when they heard his story he would be fine. The cops would see that Joseph had the AK-47, not him. The woman on the radio had said he had fired on the helicopter, which was not correct. Themba raised his hands.

'He said put the baby down,' Themba said to Lerato.

She nodded, and started walking back to the car.

Joseph stepped out from behind the Toyota and held his arms out to the side, his pistol dangling harmlessly from his finger by the trigger guard.

The men from the Audi moved cautiously forward, rifles up. 'Drop your guns, both of them,' the man called.

Lerato was soothing the baby as she put it back in its car seat and buckled it in.

Joseph let the pistol slide from his finger and it fell to the grass, then he unslung the rifle and lay it down. Themba followed his cousin, moving from the rear of the Fortuner to the front, where Joseph stood, unsteadily. Themba kept his arms raised. He was so pleased Joseph had not decided to go out fighting, like some gangster.

'Clear,' said the man who had done the talking so far. One word.

The first two gunshots, fired in quick succession by the man who was giving the orders, punched Joseph in the chest, but before he'd even hit the ground more rounds were plucking pieces off him.

'No!' Themba felt something tug at his blazer as a bullet passed through the heavy fabric. Something burned the side of his chest. He tripped over his own overly large feet as he tried to run, and his stumble probably saved his life. He fell behind the car.

Themba's brain couldn't process what he'd seen. Joseph had dropped his gun and both he and Themba were clearly no threat to the three police detectives.

Lerato crawled to him. 'Themba? Themba, what's happening?'

'I don't know!'

'Forward,' called one of the men. 'Finish them. Mind the child.'

Themba looked at his cousin Joseph, staring up at the blue Zululand sky. His people were the children of heaven, the literal meaning of the word 'Zulu'. Themba was sure Joseph was not headed there, but he hadn't deserved to die this way.

Lerato got to her feet and waved a hand in the air. 'Don't shoot, I was a hostage. Don't –'

Themba heard the gunfire and grabbed Lerato's other arm and dragged her back to the ground. Peering under the Toyota's chassis he could see the three pairs of legs moving through the grass, closing on them.

'They tried to *kill* me,' Lerato hissed.

'They're not cops,' Themba said.

'You think? But what are they after, why are they trying to kill us?'

In Themba's mind the pieces slotted together, just like a jigsaw puzzle. The rhino horn, the AK-47 hidden underneath all the clothes and possessions. Whoever owned the vehicle Joseph had stolen was on the run, moving house, maybe moving country, with a load of cargo worth millions of rand and an AK for protection. These *tsotsis* wanted what was in the car and would not want to leave witnesses, but they also wanted the baby alive. Maybe they were crooked cops. Maybe, Themba thought, the child belonged to one of them.

Themba crawled to where Joseph had fallen.

'What are you doing, Themba?'

'They're not going to let us live. They're gangsters, Lerato. They're after the rhino horn.'

'What horn?'

Themba could hear the rising panic in Lerato's voice but he didn't have time to explain. He took the discarded AK-47, lay on his belly and aimed the rifle under the car. He saw the legs getting closer. Themba flicked the safety catch to automatic, lay the assault rifle on its side and pulled the trigger. The AK bucked and he could barely control it. He heard a man scream and saw a couple of pairs of legs go sideways as men hit the deck. The baby began wailing in the back of the Fortuner. Themba had no more moving targets he could see, so he swung the rifle towards the parked Audi. He held it as steady as he could, then pulled the butt tight into his shoulder and fired again, leaving his finger depressed until the magazine was empty. When the cordite smoke wafted away on the warm breeze he had the satisfaction of seeing steam hiss from a punctured radiator and the Audi settling onto four flat tyres.

'Up!' called the man to his comrades.

'Get in the car and lie down on the floor in the back,' Themba said to Lerato. 'Get the baby, cover it.'

'I'm scared, Themba!'

'Me too, but we can't stay here.'

'You're out of bullets.'

'Get in,' he said again.

Lerato pulled herself up and crawled into the back of the Fortuner. The baby was screaming, its pink mouth wide and its fat cheeks red.

Themba reached into the pocket of his school blazer and pulled out the hand grenade he had discovered in the bag of rhino horn.

He waited until Lerato was in the back of the Fortuner. His heart swelled when he saw how she took the child out of its seat and placed it under her torso; she was shielding it. How had this happened? He pulled the pin out of the grenade.

'Outflank him,' called one of the men.

Themba knew he had to do it now, before they split up. He stood and immediately heard the whizz of a bullet past his face and the *thunk* and *ping* as another ricocheted off the Toyota, leaving a silver gash of bare metal on the roof a metre from him. He saw that the men were already moving apart so he lobbed the grenade towards the two closest to each other. He dropped.

'Can't see the girl, she must be in the truck,' one of the men called. The shooting stopped.

'Grenade!' yelled another.

They would be hitting the deck, Themba told himself. He hauled himself up and into the front of the vehicle. He doubled over in the driver's seat and turned the key, put the car into gear and floored the accelerator. A noise like a shower of hailstones sounded along the right-hand side of the four-by-four and the window behind him shattered. Lerato screamed. Themba glanced around and saw a plume of smoke. Two of the men were already getting up, but one was still on the ground writhing in pain. Themba saw smoke rising from his body, which had been peppered with shrapnel.

'Stay down,' Themba called back to Lerato. The baby was screaming hysterically. He looked in the rear view mirror and saw that the two able-bodied men were aiming their rifles at him still, but there was no fusillade of fire. He did hear a bullet hit somewhere in the rear. They were taking carefully aimed shots, he realised. They did not want to hit the baby; they must be aiming for his tyres.

Themba hauled on the steering wheel and the Toyota jinked left, and then he turned right again, zigzagging away. He wouldn't give them an easy target to hit. Again, though, he heard a round thud its way into the bodywork. 'Are you OK?'

'I'm still alive, if that's what you mean,' Lerato said.

They crested a hill and in the dip on the other side they were momentarily out of sight of the crazy men who had tried to kill them. Themba spied a rough dirt track off to the left, more of a cattle trail than a road. He turned onto it.

He reckoned he had disabled the Audi, but he wasn't slowing down for anyone. He pushed the vehicle onwards, ignoring Lerato's yelps from the rear as she and the baby bounced up and down over the rough terrain.

Lerato poked her head up and looked out the rear window, then met Themba's eyes in the rear view mirror. 'Where are we going, Themba?' She picked the baby up and, cursing as she was rocked to her side again, put it in its car seat.

Themba held her gaze for a second before returning his eyes to the rutted track. 'I have no idea.'

Chapter 9

Banger arrived in his security patrol car, alone, just as the paramedics were loading the wounded policeman into the ambulance. There were still no police in attendance.

'Babes, thank God you're safe. I'm sorry I'm late. I dropped Sipho at his home and I couldn't get a phone signal for ages.' He ran to her and hugged her, then held her at arm's length. 'Sheesh, are you sure you're all right? All this blood . . .'

Nia nodded towards the departing ambulance. 'It's his. I'm fine. Sort of.'

He clasped her tightly again and she let herself melt into him, or get as close as she could, given he was wearing a bulletproof vest and had a nine-millimetre pistol in a holster velcroed to his chest. He smelled of sweat and gun oil. She looked up into his eyes and he kissed her and ran his fingers through her hair, gently massaging her scalp at the same time. He knew how to soothe her.

Nia just wanted to go home and get into a bath, but there was unfinished business here, plenty of it. Reluctantly, she broke the embrace. The vulture man had disappeared into the nearby hut and *kraal*. He was walking back to them now, wiping his bloodied hands with a fistful of grass. 'Banger, this is . . .'

'Mike Dunn.' He came to them and held out a closed fist. 'Don't want to get blood all over you.'

'Angus Greiner. Everyone calls me Banger.' He bumped fists with the older man then looked from Dunn to Nia. 'So, someone tell me what's going on here.'

Nia ran through the series of events and as she spoke the emotion welled up from deep inside her. By the time she got to the part where she was being shot at she could barely form her words. She fought to remain controlled.

'It's OK, babe.' He patted her shoulder. 'Have the police been and gone already?'

'No, they haven't got here yet. It's this bomb in Durban or whatever,' she said.

'But I heard, on the radio news, that a tracker helicopter had been fired on and that the police were investigating,' Banger said.

Nia shook her head. 'No, I told John that a kid had pointed an AK-47 at me and told him to pass that onto the police. It must have got lost in translation.'

Banger nodded. 'It sure got my attention; when I spoke to John he told me it was you in pursuit. I want to get these bastards.'

'We should wait for the police, Banger,' Nia said.

Mike looked up the dirt road, in the direction the Fortuner had headed, then back at the *kraal*. 'The kid I was telling you about, his name's Themba . . .'

Nia nodded.

'Just as I thought, that's his home over there. I found a couple of his school books in there with his name on them. I knew he lived around here somewhere, just not where exactly.'

'You think he's one of the car thieves, that he's gone back to his old ways?'

'Who is this?' Banger interrupted.

Nia brought him up to speed.

'We don't know he's a criminal,' Mike said. 'You said he was wearing a school uniform?'

Nia put her hands on her hips. 'Yes, he was. Maybe the hijacker brought the Fortuner here to hide it. He certainly left with the kid.'

'And a girl. You think she's in on it?'

Nia shrugged. 'Who knows? All we do know is they're gone and they've got a child with them.'

'All right, I've got to go and get those kids,' Banger said.

Nia turned from him and walked to her helicopter. A flush of anger burned her cheeks. It was irrational to be mad, she knew, but it really irked her that Banger had no sooner showed up than he was going again. Behind her, she heard Mike saying something; it was hard to hear exactly what it was that he muttered, in his deep voice, but she thought she heard him say, 'go to her'. That riled her even more.

'Babe?'

She recoiled at her pet name but didn't look back at him. Instead she went to the chopper, opened her door and climbed into the pilot's seat.

Banger came to her. He looked down at her with his pale green eyes. His colouring was odd, exotic, a legacy of his Hungarian father and Irish mother, he'd told her. His parents had come to South Africa in the seventies and Angus had been born in Durban, like her. They'd met at Joe Cools on the beach.

'Babe, I'm sorry. The old dude, he says I should stay here with you.'

Nia snorted. She hadn't really thought of Mike as an 'old dude'. She looked over to where he was reaching into his Land Rover, through the right rear door. He was tall, rangy, with dark hair turning to grey. He pulled out a gun case, unzipped it, and extracted what looked like a heavy-bore hunting rifle. He placed the rifle down and then found a leather cartridge belt in the vehicle which he buckled on. He had the air about him of a man who knew what he was doing. His face was longish, angular, sort of handsome. She wondered, indeed, how old he was. Maybe mid-forties, she thought, perhaps fifteen years her senior, but to Banger, who was two years younger than her, that would qualify as 'old'.

She looked back to Banger. Like her, he surfed and worked out in the gym. He was tanned and ripped and could have been on the cover of a fitness magazine. 'I'm fine.'

'Yeah? You don't really look it. What are you going to do?'

'I have to wait here until the company can send some fuel. God knows how long that will take. I'm worried about the baby, Angus.'

He nodded. 'Me too. And I'm worried about you. You put your life at risk today.'

She felt the anger rise in her again. 'You put your life at risk *every day*. I know how many security guys get shot in this country. You were probably safer when you were in Afghanistan.'

He grinned. 'Probably.'

Banger had been a policeman but had left the service after being passed over for promotion to detective. Like many South Africans with police or military experience he'd gone to Afghanistan to work as a civilian security contractor, providing protection to VIPs and riding shotgun on convoys out of Pakistan for the American and NATO war machine. When the war had de-escalated he'd come home.

'We should wait here for the cops,' Nia said.

Mike was walking over to the helicopter. 'You're right, we should,' he said, breaking into their conversation. 'But there are kids in trouble in that car. We can't just wait. I'm going to pick up their trail, see if I can get eyes on them.'

'You won't try and stop them, do something silly, will you?' Nia felt a rush of concern for the man, perhaps because he had been the only person to come to her assistance when she needed someone.

'I can back you up,' Banger said.

Mike looked to Banger's little hatchback car. 'Not in that. The road just goes from bad to worse up here. If they've headed into the hills, rather than down to the motorway, you won't get more than another kilometre.'

'Dude's got an AK, *bru*, and it's two against one. You sure you're up for those odds?'

'I'm going to find them, not start a gunfight,' Mike said.

Nia folded her arms. 'Well, there's nothing I can do. When I've refuelled I can go have a look for the Fortuner. Until then, you two sort this out between yourselves.'

Banger looked into her eyes. 'Are you OK, seriously?'

'I'm fine.'

'I'm going,' said Mike.

Banger went to his patrol car, reached under the front seat and pulled out a .38 special revolver. He brought it to Nia.

'What's this?' she asked him.

'My back-up weapon.'

'Legal?'

Banger's mouth crinkled into a half-grin. 'Ish.'

She took the pistol. 'I hope I don't have to use it.'

Banger kissed her.

Mike was already in the Land Rover, starting the engine. Banger jogged around to the passenger side and climbed in. He blew Nia another kiss and she smiled back at him.

*

Mike drove as fast as he dared on the corrugated red earth road. After a couple of kilometres, though, he saw a stationary car, an Audi, with three doors open. He slowed. It had been a black Q5 that had dropped the white man at the Mona market.

Banger was texting on his phone, smiling to himself. Mike guessed he was communicating with the helicopter pilot. *Lucky guy*, he thought. She'd been gutsy to stay close to the hijacked Toyota when people were shooting at her. 'Check this out,' he said.

Banger looked up, put away the phone and drew the nine-millimetre from his chest holster and cocked it. 'Look how that car's sitting low. Its tyres have been shot out. Take it easy, man.'

Mike nodded. As he came closer he saw the bullet holes and the bare metal scratches where bullets had scored the paintwork. He stopped the Land Rover and got out, taking his rifle with him.

Banger approached the Audi with his pistol up, his left hand wrapped around his right. Mike could hear a hiss, like a snake, and saw the puddle that darkened the earth under the radiator. He sniffed the air.

'Explosives,' Banger said, then pointed to a patch of burnt grass and disturbed dirt. 'Grenade.'

'You get many grenade attacks in your line of work?' Mike asked.

'I did in Afghanistan.'

Mike nodded. The kid was brash, cocky, and pumped up from long hours at the gym, maybe steroids, but he did have some experience. Mike scanned the ground and started in a circle around the car, while Banger checked the vehicle itself.

'Nothing inside,' Banger said.

Mike dropped to one knee and ran his pinched thumb and forefinger along a stem of flattened grass. He held his hand up to Banger when the security man came over to him.

'Blood.'

Mike touched his fingers together a few times. 'Fresh.' He stood, placing himself so the tracks were between him and the sun. 'One man, dragging a leg, headed that way.'

'Back towards the chopper, where we just came from?'

Mike looked back up the road, thinking the same thing as Banger. 'We didn't see him.'

'Shit, he could be headed for Nia. If we didn't see him he must have been hiding from us.'

Mike continued his circuit, moving faster now, and found the tracks of two other men. He followed them, tracing the course of the battle. He stopped and bent to pick up a couple of bullet casings. '5.56-mil. R5s, fired in three-round bursts. These guys meant business. I was at a rhino horn deal that went wrong at the Mona market this morning. There was an Audi like this one on the scene. These could be poachers.'

Banger followed in his wake. 'This is hectic. I'm getting a bad feeling about it.'

'I agree.' Mike found the tread patterns of the Toyota Fortuner, the copper-coloured casings of Russian ammunition, from an AK-47, the same weapon Nia had seen pointed at her.

Then he saw the body.

'Sure,' said Banger, coming up next to him. 'Someone wanted this *oke* gone.'

The man had been stitched by an R5, maybe two judging by the number of bullet holes. Mike knelt by him and placed a hand on his throat. The skin was already cool. The man was in his early twenties and he looked familiar. Mike searched his pockets and noticed, while doing so, a wound in his shoulder, and a balled, blood-soaked T-shirt. He found a wallet and a driver's licence. 'Joseph Ndlovu. He was the car thief.'

'How do you know that?' Banger asked.

'I know his cousin, the kid who lives back at the hut where the shooting was. I was at a court case his cousin attended. Joseph's a career hijacker and he might have come here looking for help. Themba, what have you done?' he whispered to himself.

Banger looked at the car tracks that led towards the distant hills. 'So the kid, the one in the school uniform, was the apprentice.

Looks like he got away with the wheels, as well as the kidnapped baby and a schoolgirl.'

Mike didn't want to think that Themba had turned bad again, but he had to admit it was a possibility. But where had he – or Joseph – got a hand grenade, and who were the men who had been shooting at them? Maybe the grenade was theirs and one of them got shot while trying to throw it? Mike cast about further and saw two sets of tracks heading to the hills. 'Two guys went after the Fortuner on foot.'

'That's crazy.'

Mike stood and looked around him. Yes, it was crazy, like so much that went on in this country, this world.

Banger looked back down the road. 'I'm worried about Nia. If some wounded guy with an assault rifle was headed her way and decided to hide from us instead of seeking help, then she's in danger.'

Mike didn't know if that was the case or not. He didn't know what to think about this day or this scene. There was no sound of police sirens on the wind, so for now they were on their own. If he went after the Fortuner in his Land Rover he would soon encounter two armed men on foot. They would, he presumed, take his vehicle by force.

'Take the Land Rover back to the chopper,' Mike said.

'What? Why? No, man, we stick together.'

'Go check on your girlfriend, make sure she's safe. Tell her to leave her chopper; it's got no fuel so even if someone knew how to fly it they couldn't steal it. Fetch her, then come back for me. I'm going forward, on foot.'

Banger pulled his shoulders back, squaring up to him, as if he was going to argue some more. They stared each other down, but Banger broke eye contact first, looking back the way they had come, then once more to Mike. 'You're not just a bird researcher, are you?'

'Let's just say you're not the only one here who's been in combat. Go to her.'

Banger nodded and went to the Land Rover and started it. 'Good luck,' he called.

'Be careful,' said Mike. 'Remember that other guy's still out there somewhere.'

Mike watched the Land Rover disappear over the hill, then turned his eyes back to the tracks. He set off at a slow jog, rifle at the ready.

*

'Help me, please,' the man called.

Nia licked her lips and climbed out of the pilot's seat of her helicopter. She had seen the man coming, and it was clear even before his plaintive call that he was in trouble. He was nursing his left arm with his other hand and dragging his left leg. Nia opened the rear of the chopper and unfastened the first aid kit from its place on the bulkhead.

She started walking towards him, the first aid kit in her left hand, but the fingers of her right, in her pocket, closed around the grip of the .38 revolver Banger had left with her. As the distance between them closed she could see that the left side of his face, and his clothing on that side, were blackened as though they'd been burned. His face was streaked red.

'Help me,' he said again.

'Who are you?'

'My name is Ibrahim. I was driving down the road when this madman in a Fortuner hit my car, trying to get past me.'

'I was following a stolen Fortuner. A white one?'

The man nodded. They met and he staggered; Nia took her right hand out of the pocket of her flight suit and put an arm around him to support him.

'There was a young man, a boy really, and a girl in school uniform, and they had a child with them,' the man croaked.

'Yes, that's them, for sure,' Nia said. 'Here, sit down. Let me look at you.'

'I'm fine. Can we get to a hospital, though? Perhaps you could fly your helicopter?'

'You don't look fine to me at all. Besides, my chopper's out of fuel. I'm waiting for a resupply. I'm hoping the police will be here soon as well. You can tell your story to them. What else happened to you? Have you been burned?'

'The police are coming?' he asked.

Nia shrugged. 'Today, with what's happened in Durban? Who knows? But they know where I am, and an ambulance showed up at least to take away an off-duty policeman who was here, so someone's got to make a report some time.'

She looked him up and down. This Ibrahim, with his designer stubble, looked like a nightclub bouncer or someone's hired muscle. He wore a gold chain over a black T-shirt and black jeans. Unusually, for the weather, he wore a charcoal sports coat, the left side of which was peppered with tiny holes. When his coat flapped open a little she saw that his side was not only burned, but his shirt was sticky with blood.

'That car,' he pointed to Banger's security company vehicle, 'where is its owner?'

Nia took a step back. There was something in his eyes or, more to the point, nothing in them. They were dark, empty, and at the same time calculating as he looked around him, through her. 'Nearby. He'll be back any minute.'

'I need to get going.' He eyed the car again.

'Wait,' she said. 'Let me see to your injuries at least. You nearly fell a minute ago.'

'No, it's fine.'

He turned his back on her. A chill passed through her, raising tiny hairs on her arms and the back of her neck. This guy had not simply been in a car accident, and he was avoiding her questions.

'Stay right where you are.' Ibrahim flicked his head around and looked back over his shoulder. She saw his eyes go to her hand, which was reaching into the pocket of her flight suit.

His right hand was a blur as it arced through the air and Nia's head rocked from the closed-fist blow to the side of her face. The next thing she knew she was on her backside and Ibrahim was standing over her, a pistol pointed down at her, between her eyes.

'If that's a gun in your pocket, take it out, very slowly, finger-tips on the handgrip.'

Nia took a deep breath to stop from letting out a sob and did as he told her, reaching slowly into the pocket of her flight suit and drawing out the pistol.

'Good, now toss it to my feet.' She threw the gun and he ordered her to put her hands on her head. 'So, you're out of fuel?'

She blinked and nodded.

'You're waiting for a resupply?'

'Yes.'

'Good, then we will wait together. I will be inside the heli-copter, with a gun pointed at you. When the driver arrives with the fuel you will tell him you are taking me to hospital. You will not give him any signal that anything is wrong, or I will kill you and the driver. I would like to have you fly me in this helicopter, but I can make do with a truck. The choice is yours, either to save your life and the life of an innocent man driving a truck, or for you and him to die at the same time. Do you understand?'

Nia gave another brief nod.

The man coughed and winced at the pain the action produced. 'If the man who drives this security car comes back you will say nothing to him, nor give him any sign that anything is wrong here, or I will kill you both before he has time to draw his gun.'

'Who are you?' she asked him.

'I am a man seeking to reclaim something that was stolen, that is all. I have no need to hurt you, but you made a mistake by asking too many questions and trying to pull a gun on me. I acted in self-defence.'

Nia scoffed at that. 'I don't know what you're up to, but you should know that there really are police on the way here. They'll be here any minute, probably before my fuel, which has to come all the way from Durban. The cops will be coming from Mtubatuba. There's already been a policeman shot here and you know how cops get when one of their own is injured.'

The man seemed to weigh up her words, rocking his head slightly from side to side as he absorbed the news. 'I believe you.'

'Good.'

He smiled. 'No, not so good. I think I'll have to kill you now, before the police arrive.'

Nia heard the clatter of a diesel engine. Ibrahim picked up the pistol from the ground and tucked it in his trousers, then knocked her hands from her head and lifted her to her feet by grabbing a handful of her hair. He pressed his pistol into her back and retreated to the helicopter, taking cover behind it.

The white Land Rover, Mike the vulture man's vehicle, crested the hill. Nia could see only one face through the windscreen – Banger's. Her relief turned quickly to dread. This maniac would kill Banger, and her, in a heartbeat.

Ibrahim climbed into the rear of the helicopter, awkwardly squeezing into the cramped rear seat until he was lying on it, facing her. He pulled the door closed, but left it slightly ajar. 'If he stops, tell him to be on his way. Don't give him any signal that you're in danger. Same deal as before: I'll kill you both.'

She nodded. Banger drove off the road and parked a few metres from the helicopter. Nia started to walk towards him.

'Stop,' Ibrahim hissed. She complied. 'Don't walk any further from me or I'll shoot you in the back. If you try anything I will kill him and then come for you.'

Nia gave an almost imperceptible nod. 'Hi there, no need to worry about me, man, I'm fine, don't need any help,' she called to Banger as he climbed out of the Land Rover. She didn't want Angus running to her and throwing his arms around her.

He stopped and looked at her, momentarily puzzled. 'What's up?'

'My chopper's run out of fuel and I'm just waiting for a delivery here. But like I say, everything is totally fine.'

'Really?' He raised an eyebrow.

'Hundred per cent. No problem at all, whatsoever. Just another ordinary day at the office.'

'Serious?' Nia saw Banger's eye drop to the first aid kit that she'd taken from the helicopter then dropped on the ground.

'Yes, man, very serious.'

'Do you want me to take you back towards town?'

Nia shook her head. 'No, I'd be killed for sure if I left this chopper alone.'

Banger moistened his lips with his tongue. She could see he was flexing his fingers, the rage building inside him. As well as being impetuous he had a temper, but he could control it when he had to. When he made love to her it was with a barely constrained passion, a kind of animalistic savagery.

'I'm fine,' she repeated.

'All right, then, I guess I'll be on my way,' Banger said.

'You'd better be quick then, cowboy,' she said. Angus liked to pretend he was a cowboy, sometimes, when they were fooling around at home. He would practise drawing his pistol from his holster in front of the mirror, and he'd tell her he was the quickest draw on the wild east coast. His terrible American accent always made her laugh.

'Yes, ma'am,' he said, with the slightest of drawls. He had got her message; now was the time for him to be quick on the draw for real.

Banger turned, as if to leave, and Nia saw his right hand go up. They had only one chance. The man in the back of the helicopter was going to kill her, if not now, then later. He wouldn't be the kind to want witnesses around. She still had no idea what, if any, connection he had with the stolen Fortuner, but it was becoming clear this was more than just an ordinary car hijacking.

Nia dived to the ground and rolled left, under the nose of the helicopter. Even as she started to fall she heard the first shots from behind her, a deafening double bang, and felt the displacement of air close by her as a bullet passed her, missing her by millimetres.

Angus was firing as well and Nia heard the *thunk* of his rounds passing through the skin of her chopper. She kept rolling, staying low so as not to get hit. Banger yelled and she screamed.

Nia scrambled away on her hands and knees then pulled herself to her feet. There was nothing she could do. She had no weapon and she would have to cross open ground to get to the Land Rover. She screamed in frustration, but when she finished she stood there, in the dry grass, alone. Around her was silence, then a few seconds later a groan of pain.

She jogged back to the helicopter and gingerly peered around the nose. A brown hand protruded from the gap where the rear door had been left open. Blood dripped from the fingers. Nia drew a deep breath, summoning the last of her reserves of courage and composure, and pulled open the door. She had to step back as Ibrahim's body tumbled to the ground.

Seeing the danger was gone she went to Angus, who was lying on his back, and crumpled to her knees beside him. Nia cradled his head on one arm and with her other hand searched him for the wound that had felled him.

Banger coughed and Nia feared she would see blood coming from his mouth, but there was none.

'Shit,' he said.

'Banger, where are you hit?'

He coughed, then started to laugh. 'Took one in the vest. Damn, I fell backwards and winded myself and landed on my arse bone.'

He was alive. She wiped away a tear and collapsed into him. At long last she heard the wail of a police siren.

Chapter 10

Mike Dunn dropped to the grass as he approached the crest of the next hill. This was open country and he would be easily spotted if he allowed himself to be silhouetted against the sky.

He crawled forward and pulled a pair of compact Zeiss binoculars from the pocket of his bush shirt. He rested himself on his elbows and scanned the valley ahead. About four hundred metres distant were the two men he had been tracking, one African, one brown.

He put the binoculars back and took out his cell phone. He checked its screen; no signal. *Who are these guys?*

They had made short work of Joseph the car thief, and if they were police, then at least one of them would have been left behind, or reinforcements would already have arrived. They were heading towards the game reserve and if it was, in fact, Themba driving the car with the schoolgirl and the baby on board, that might make sense. The young man would see Hluhluwe–iMfolozi as a kind of sanctuary. Mike knew this because he'd described the national park in exactly those terms to Themba.

He ran his hand through his hair. He was tired, but he could carry on. The question was, however, what to do when he caught up with the men. He checked his watch. Angus, the security man, would have had plenty of time to get back to the chopper by now, pick up Nia and get back to him. But there was no sound of his Land Rover's engine.

Mike stood and was about to carry on his pursuit of the two men, in the hope he could get closer to them while staying out of their sight, when he heard faint gunshots coming from the direction in which the helicopter was parked.

He stopped. Mike was worried about Themba and the other kids, but this was a job for the police. Concerned that the missing wounded man had got the drop on Angus and Nia, he turned and started jogging back the way he'd come.

Mike thought about Themba as he ran. He hoped the boy would be safe. Mike had seen too many young kids from bad backgrounds fail in their attempts to lift themselves out of the gutter, but he just couldn't believe he was wrong about Themba. Life wasn't fair. Africa wasn't fair, but Themba had a strength that had been lacking in too many of the young men Mike had tried to help.

From a distance he could see flashing blue lights at the spot where Joseph had been killed. As Mike approached the police car he held his rifle up high above his head.

The two uniformed police officers, a man and a woman, pulled their guns as soon as they saw him.

'Coming in,' he called out to them. 'Don't shoot.'

When he came closer to them he recognised the woman. 'Sergeant Khumalo.' That was a relief. She was based in Mtubatuba and they had worked together in the past. Mike had supplied her with information about *muti* deals in the past and, unlike some of her colleagues in other towns and villages, Lindiwe had come through and busted a few sellers.

Lindiwe and her partner lowered their weapons. 'Hey, Mister Vulture Man, how are you? What are you doing here?'

Mike gestured to Joseph's body. 'I'm fine, Lindiwe. I heard gunshots.'

The male police officer pointed back down the hill to where the helicopter had landed. 'Shootout between a security guy and one of the occupants of this Audi.'

'Are they OK?'

'The pilot and the security man, yes,' Lindiwe Khumalo said. 'Who are these people, Mike?'

'No idea, but they're packing R5s and dressed like gangsters. I've just been following two of them.'

'*Umlungu?*'

'No, I didn't see a white man, just one African and one coloured or Indian. However, there was a shootout at the Mona market earlier today and a white man was one of the perpetrators. He was dropped at the market by a black Audi Q5.'

'I heard about that gunfight on the radio,' she said. 'You've had a busy day. We all have. You didn't see the registration of the Audi at Mona?'

Mike shook his head. 'No, but the guy who was dropped off was supposed to be selling rhino horn, to none other than Bandile Dlamini.'

'*Yebo,*' Lindiwe said. 'He's in hospital, but no one that side is telling me what's happening with him.'

'Those men I was following,' Mike said. 'They were with your other dead man in the Audi, and he was wounded before Banger – the security man – shot him. Grenade fragments.'

Lindiwe narrowed her eyes. 'How did you know that?'

Mike gestured to the scorched earth. 'Crater's over there, and you'll see the Audi has been peppered with shrapnel.'

'These guys are armed like rhino poachers. I'm calling for back-up before we go after them.'

Mike nodded. 'Good idea.'

'What is going on here?' the sergeant asked no one in particular.

'Good question,' Mike said. 'There are plenty of 5.56-millimetre casings here, also some 7.62-millimetre from an AK.'

Lindiwe narrowed her eyes. 'For a man who researches vultures you know a lot about weapons.'

'I come across a lot of poaching carcasses and work with the crime scene teams sometimes.' He didn't want to go into more detail about how he knew about assault rifles.

'Call for back-up, Elphes,' she told her partner. The policeman headed back to the car. 'What is this, I wonder? A business deal gone wrong? And what are these people doing with hand grenades?'

Mike had wondered the same things. 'I've heard of rhino poachers with grenades; they've been known to pull the pin on one and leave it under a dead rhino so when the police or rangers get there and try to move the carcass the grenade goes off.'

Lindiwe tutted and shook her head. She called to her partner: 'Hey, ask base what information they have about this missing Fortuner.'

Mike thought out loud. 'So we've got two, formerly three, guys trying to get back a stolen Toyota that's now transporting a baby, two teenagers and an AK-47.'

Lindiwe pulled out her notebook, flipped over a couple of pages and made some new jottings. When she was done she looked up. 'I knew this dead man, Joseph. He was small-time, not even a good thief. According to the report the car-tracking service received, the woman driver almost got the better of him. She killed his partner.'

'Really? How is she?' Mike asked. 'If she's the baby's mother she must be going crazy.'

Lindiwe clicked her tongue a few times and drew a breath. 'There is the problem. I can't find a record of this woman making a call to the police.'

'Really?'

'For sure it's been a crazy day, with the bomb in Durban, and the emergency number was almost overloaded with the number of calls that came in afterwards, but according to Nia Carras and the tracking service, they got the call about the stolen Fortuner half an hour *before* the bomb exploded. I checked with the call centre – no hijackings or car thefts reported in the Durban area this morning.'

'So she called her car-tracking service direct before, or instead of, calling the cops?'

Lindiwe nodded. 'I don't like to say it, but you're probably thinking what that woman was thinking: that it would be quicker for her to find her child by using a private security company with a helicopter on call.'

The thought had crossed Mike's mind. 'But surely she would have followed it up with a call to the police.'

'The guy who took the call from the tracking company says he told the woman to call the police emergency number as well.'

'You get a number for her?'

Lindiwe rocked her head from side to side. 'I've probably talked enough about this case with you, Mike.'

He liked her, and he hoped she felt the same way about him. Lindiwe was intelligent and honest.

She hesitated, but then continued anyway. '*Yebo*, I got her cell number off the car-tracking company, but it's out of service. I'm getting a trace done to find out what number she called the company from, but as you can imagine there are lots of people tracing calls today and a car theft is way down the list of priorities compared to a major terrorist attack.'

'Even though there's a baby missing?'

'A baby who's missing, but whose mom hasn't bothered reporting it to the police yet.'

'The road the Fortuner was on leads to the border with Mozambique, or Swaziland. Maybe Mom was heading for the border and Dad didn't know?' Mike thought about his own daughter. Debbie was sixteen and he'd taken her to Mauritius for a week last year. He'd been surprised when his ex-wife, Tracy, had told him about the rigmarole he would have to go through. The government was trying to cut down on child trafficking by tightening the rules allowing children to leave the country with only one parent. He'd needed to get a certified copy of Debbie's unabridged birth certificate and a letter of permission from Tracy.

'I'd already thought about that,' Lindiwe said quickly. 'And, for your information, there's some evidence to back up that theory. The helicopter pilot saw the younger guy, the one in the school uniform, pulling out all sorts of stuff from the back of the Fortuner to make room for him and the girl, apparently. I took a look at what was lying around – blankets, pots, pans, an iron, a couple of bags of clothes – it looks like she was moving house, or maybe running away.'

'So who are our three killers who showed up looking for the car?'

Lindiwe sighed. 'That's what I intend on finding out when my back-up arrives. Maybe they're friends or relatives of the mom and she trusts them, over us, to get her kid and her car back?'

'Or maybe it goes further than Mom running away from the father – if she doesn't want to involve the police, maybe she's on the wrong side of the law herself,' Mike said.

Lindiwe nodded. 'I'm way ahead of you. I got the location of where the hijack went down, from the tracking company; it's out of my jurisdiction, closer to Durbs, and I think I'm going to have a hell of a time trying to get some detectives to go and check it out.'

'What about the guys following the kids?'

She called to her partner and asked for an update.

'No helicopter available,' Elphes said. 'Any spare manpower's been called to Durban or put on roadblocks to catch the people who blew up the ambassador. It's chaos, Sergeant. They say we might have to wait a few hours.'

Mike looked to the sun. 'Getting late. It'll be dark before your back-up arrives. You sure you don't want me to drive you up into the hills in my Land Rover?'

Lindiwe seemed to consider his offer. 'No, this is a police matter now, Mike. Thank you for your help today, but I think you should go see how the pilot and the security man are, and if you can help them. He took a bullet in his body armour vest.'

'All right,' he said, 'but let me know if I can help.'

'I will. The way things are going, I may well need you again in some capacity,' she said. 'Before you go, is there anything you can tell me about this business with Bandile Dlamini today?'

'Dlamini and one of his men claimed they were there on police business, part of a sting to catch a rhino horn trader. Did you know about it?'

She shook her head. '*Aikona*. Not any of our people. Could be the Hawks, from Durban, or the rhino task force, but if so, no one bothered to tell me about it. I'll send my one spare man to the hospital, though, to interview Dlamini, to see if he got the registration number of the Audi that dropped off the white guy.'

'This shootout here, these armed men chasing the Fortuner, it smacks of organised crime,' Mike said.

'I agree. But it's time for you to get back to Durban and back to your vultures, Mike.'

He would have liked to turn his back on this day of killing, but Mike got the feeling that was wishful thinking.

*

When John Buttenshaw arrived with a *bakkie* loaded with jerry cans of fuel, Nia sent Banger on his way back to Durban. She and John refilled her chopper, and she flew back to Virginia Airport in the dark.

She wasn't home much before Banger as she had to secure the helicopter by herself. John was driving back to Durban; it had been a long day for all of them.

In her flat she took off her hiking boots and socks, poured herself a gin and tonic and turned on the television. The assassination of the ambassador and speculation of who was behind it and what it signified was all over BBC and CNN.

Banger opened the door and she stood and went to him. He enfolded her in his big arms and squeezed her in a bear hug. Tears welled up and he kissed them away.

'I'm here. I'm always here for you, babes,' he said. 'You were amazing today, so strong.'

She kissed him again, tenderness melting into passion. 'I need you. Turn me on, please,' she whispered into his ear.

He dropped to his knees in front of her and slowly unzipped her flight suit. He kissed his way down between her breasts to her belly.

'I stink.'

'I love the smell of you,' he whispered, and kissed her soft, springy hair through the fabric of her pants.

Banger helped her out of her flight suit and quickly shed his body armour and weapons. He went to the bathroom and ran the bath while she took off her underwear. He picked her up, in his arms, as though carrying her across the threshold, and she giggled.

While they waited for the bath to fill he sat her on the vanity unit. It was cold on her bum, but that made her hotter, as did his kisses. She could feel him through his uniform trousers and he pressed against her, still dressed, rubbing slowly.

He motioned for her to get into the bath while he undressed. Nia added bubble bath before turning off the tap and climbing in. She sank down in the water, letting the steam and the scent and the hot water relax her while, at the same time, the sight of his body made her heart beat a little faster. Banger knelt by the bath, took a flannel and soap and started to wash her. She loved it when he did that. The angry purple bruise on his chest, where the bullet had struck his vest, reminded her of the day's horrors.

He slipped one hand under the water and Nia closed her eyes and arched her back as he touched her the way she liked it. When she was breathing faster he got to his feet beside the tub and she sat up and ran her soapy, slick hand up and down the length of him. Then it was his turn to close his eyes and she grabbed him more forcefully. He needed no encouraging.

Banger got into the bath with her and they moved so that he was on his back and she was lying with her spine along his chest. He played with her some more and she lifted her hips out of the water. When she almost couldn't take any more she moved again, foamy water slopping over the edge onto the tiles as she presented herself to him, knees in the water, hands on the edge.

He positioned himself behind her and slowly entered her. She loved that moment, the first push as she closed around him, gripping him, feeling his need to tease and his desire to be part of her, completely.

They moved slowly, in unison, both getting closer, savouring the moment that felt like it could, should, last forever. They were well suited when it came to lovemaking, each seeking the right mix of tenderness and force.

'Yes,' she said, as he quickened the tempo.

Water broke like waves over the back of her thighs and more was spilled, but she didn't care. She was lost in this basic, primal act. He could do this so very well, take her to another place, and she ached for the sound of his exertions, his grunting.

When he had finished they washed and dried each other and he led her to the bed. It was bliss to climb between the cool white sheets. Banger rolled over onto his back and within a few moments he was snoring softly.

Nia was so exhausted sleep eluded her. She was still wired. She closed her eyes and slowly, so as not to disturb Banger, moved her hand between her thighs. She closed her eyes, thinking about him and their sex in the bathtub. In time she tensed as her body went rigid and the little tremors overtook her.

Sated, Nia relaxed and finally drifted to sleep, but woke a few hours later, having dreamed of a baby lost in the wilderness.

Chapter 11

Themba woke up cold and confused.

The moon was setting, and the night was entering the darkest, coldest hour, just before the dawn. He wished he had taken another blanket from the car. He had given his to Lerato and she was cocooned inside it, plus she had the blanket she'd taken for herself. In addition, she had the baby for warmth.

The Fortuner had run out of fuel, its tank holed by a bullet. By that time they were close to the fence of the Hluhluwe–iMfolozi Park. Themba had been heading for the reserve, hoping it would be easier to lose the men there than staying on foot outside. Animals were a risk, but he had learned a good deal from Mike Dunn and others about staying safe in the wild. He had found a spot where a warthog had dug under the fence, so he scraped out more loose earth and rocks with his hands and shimmied underneath. Lerato had handed him the baby and then she, clearly nervous, had reluctantly followed.

The baby, a boy, as they had established after the first nappy change, had cried for his mother for the first couple of hours, as dusk had turned to dark. He had calmed a little when they fed him some mashed banana from the stock of food they had found in the Fortuner. Themba had brought a wrap from the vehicle and Lerato had fastened the baby on her back after he had finished his food. The warmth of her back and the beating of her heart had soothed the child to sleep. He had cried again for a while after they set up camp, but Lerato had fed him again and held him close to her chest. She had looked at Themba, her eyes communicating the silent worry that he also felt, that the child might give them away to their pursuers. He had shrugged. What more could they do? They couldn't abandon him in the bush for a hyena to finish him off.

The little fellow with the light caramel-coloured skin and silky soft black curls had started to reveal something of his personality to them. They learned quickly that as soon as they set him down in the grass, if he was awake, he would start crawling away from them. He was an explorer. He picked up rocks and tasted them and at one point Lerato had shrieked and snatched away a big beetle he was about to eat. If they hadn't been so scared, the child's antics would have made them laugh. Even as it was the little one gave them something other than their fear to concentrate on.

Themba had found a good place for them to sleep while he thought about their next move. It was near the top of a kopje, a granite-studded hill with a slight overhang of rock to give them shelter.

'I wonder if people slept here in the old days,' Lerato had said in a thick voice, trying not to let her fear and exhaustion show as she rocked the little boy in her arms.

He looked down at Lerato now. She was even more beautiful asleep, her face serene, her skin flawless. The baby gurgled a bit, but stayed asleep.

Themba shivered and wrapped his arms around himself. He thought about making a fire, but, again, the fear of giving away their position made him reject the idea. He had no clue if the men from the Audi had moved through the night. He had pushed Lerato onwards until it had become too dangerous for them to continue, lest they fall or drop the child. The last sign he'd seen of their pursuers was a glow in the west and a pall of dark smoke. Themba had seen enough car fires to know that they had found the Fortuner and torched it. That told him the men following them didn't want the police taking a close look at the car, which was not surprising given what he had found inside it.

Themba knew he had to get somewhere safe where they could explain everything that had gone on, but in order to do that they had to stay ahead of whoever these crazy guys were that were following them.

Themba's eyes were drawn to the tote bag into which he'd stuffed the rhino horn. It made him sick and scared just to look at the package. He tried hard not to think about what he could do with the money the horn was worth, but he failed. In his mind's eye he saw himself and Lerato in a big house, maybe a lodge on a game farm, with a black Range Rover out the front for him and a BMW for Lerato. They wore fine clothes and his belly was full of good food.

Lerato had been horrified when he had shown her the rhino horn and she had argued that he should just dump it. She had told him of her father's outspoken stance against poaching. 'You're not going to sell it yourself, I hope!'

'No,' he had told her. Themba had given up on crime. He'd been convinced that he could make it through life without hurting people, without stealing from them, and without needlessly killing animals. He looked up at the sky, which was still studded with stars but showing the first, almost imperceptible traces of lightening. He remembered his first night out in the bush.

He had been terrified.

'What are you scared of?' Mike Dunn had asked when he had locked eyes with Themba across the campfire.

Themba, full of anger, hatred and resentment, had stared the man down through the smoke and flames. 'Nothing.'

'You are.'

Eventually he had broken, looking away. 'It's just not natural,' Themba had replied, almost immediately realising how stupid his reply had been. 'I mean, people have moved on, in the world, we live in houses, towns, cities, we drive cars. We don't need to live like this in the bush.'

Mike had nodded. 'I get that.'

'You *get* it? If you really did, we wouldn't be here.'

'Then where would we be?'

Themba had felt the anger well up in him. 'We wouldn't be poor, we wouldn't be sleeping in tents; we'd have parents, jobs, futures . . .'

'Or you'd be in prison.'

Themba had hated Mike back then. Others in the group had looked at him, and he'd felt singled out, belittled. The fact was that he was on the wildlife ambassador and future rhino guards' camp because of the man staring him down across the fire, and because he'd been arrested for, and convicted of, being an accessory to a car theft, thanks to his cousin. Joseph himself had escaped when he had crashed the car that they'd been driving. He had abandoned Themba to face the music. This man thought he was doing Themba a favour, or perhaps he was just trying to unburden himself of his English-speaking white South African liberal guilt. Either way, Themba had felt like leaving then.

'This is what it's all about,' Mike had said. 'The bush. We all make mistakes in life but out here, it doesn't matter who you are, what you've done – right or wrong – what you're worth, or how useless you are. Here we're in our natural state, and the fact is that without our cars, our guns, our houses, our lies, our money, or our pride, we're at the bottom of the food chain. Just about anything that wants to can kill us. All we have is one thing.'

Themba had let the words sink in but the proposition unnerved him. The man was right; Themba felt more scared now, out here in the bush, than he had ever felt riding in a stolen car with Joseph, being shot at, or jumping fences to get away from the police. Here he felt . . . naked. Out of his depth. Close to panic.

'OK,' Themba conceded. 'What do we have?'

'Choice.'

It wasn't the answer he'd expected. 'What do you mean?'

The man was tall, skinny, not muscled, but his eyes were hard, much harder than his body. 'I mean you can choose to be a *tsotsi*, a criminal, or you can choose to work.'

'Yeah, right.' This was more familiar territory.

'I don't mean you choose to get a job,' the man had said.

'Then what do you mean?' Themba said, challenging him.

He had taken a sip of his brandy and Coke. Themba had felt no respect for the man at that point. He was just another old man from a lost, forgotten tribe, trying to curry favour with the new administration by helping disaffected young people. It was laughable.

'You choose whether to be a man or not.'

Themba had rolled his eyes towards the moon. 'Who says I'm not a man?' he'd asked.

'The wife of the man whose car you and your cousin stole; their children, the ones who cry themselves to sleep remembering the horror of the man with the gun. Your mother, if she was still here, would weep with shame for what you've become. Look at yourself. You are nothing.'

Themba had stared back at him, open-mouthed now, full of hatred. It wasn't right for this old man to talk to him in such an insulting way. He'd felt his hands ball into fists at his side.

'You call yourself a man, but you inflict pain on people for what, a few thousand rand? You're nothing. You probably carry a gun, but you're not man enough to fight for your country, South Africa.'

Back then Themba hadn't known that Mike Dunn had been in gunfights in the defence of wildlife, and had killed. Mike had changed his own life. Themba had joked with some of the other boys on the course about what it would be like to learn from a weedy wimp who spent his time with birds. But no, Mike was a warrior, and Themba had felt nervous anxiety as the older man had stared him down. He had relaxed his hands, partly because he'd wanted to hear what the man had to say, and partly because he'd feared that if he did take a swing at the old man he would be *bliksem*ed by him.

'Do you know where we are, right now?' Mike had asked him, across the fire.

'The middle of nowhere.' A couple of the others had laughed in the darkness and Themba had felt emboldened.

Mike had slowly shaken his head. 'No, not nowhere. This is hallowed ground, royal land. Did you know that this park, Hluhluwe–iMfolozi, was once the private hunting ground of the king of the Zulus?'

Themba had not known that. He'd thought of national parks as places reserved for whites in the old days, and still largely visited by them these days. This was land whose resources were fenced off, denied to the rightful owners, who lived outside the reserves. He had shrugged.

'This is your land, my China,' Mike had said. 'Being here is your birthright. A hundred and fifty years ago you would have done anything to be here, to take part in one of the king's hunts, to corner a lion or a buffalo on foot and bring it down with your *assegai*. You would have been prepared to *die* to prove your manhood and impress the king – and maybe even be rewarded with a young woman or two.

'And today, how do you prove your manhood? By stealing cars and pointing guns at helpless old ladies.'

Themba had seethed. 'Why are you singling me out, old man? There are others here for the same reasons as me. You are being racist.'

Mike had snorted at the suggestion. 'You think I'm singling you out? You think I *care* about you?'

Themba stood up. 'I've had enough of this bullshit. I'm leaving.'

Mike had nodded. 'Fine. Head due south. You'll come to the tar road in about five kilometres – that's if you make it that far.'

'You think I'm too scared to walk at night.'

'No, just stupid to walk here at night without a firearm.'

Mike had reached behind the log he was sitting on and picked up a big-bore hunting rifle, bolt action. He'd hefted it, one handed, and held it out towards the fire, towards Themba. 'Take this.'

'You're kidding, right?'

'You want to be a man. You want to carry a gun. I don't want to be responsible for a dead runaway child.'

'I am not a *child*.'

'You're acting like one.'

Themba was tiring of the old man's jokes, but he was ready to call his bluff and make the old man look stupid in front of the others, to undermine him and his stupid do-gooder program. He walked around the fire, slowly, and held out his hands. Mike let him hold the rifle, but did not let go of it.

'If you take this, you'll never come back here.'

Themba had nodded.

'If the recoil doesn't knock you on your arse, and if your night vision is good enough, you might be able to take out a buffalo, perhaps a lion. If it's a hungry pride you won't stand a chance, though. You probably won't see an elephant before you bump into him. A white rhino you could kill, comparatively easily, if you're quiet, but if you come across a black rhino he'll try his hardest to kill you. A leopard . . . if there's an old or hungry or sick one it will be eating you before you even know it's there. Still want to go?'

Themba did not let go of the rifle. 'You want me to become a criminal, to die a criminal?'

Mike had shrugged. 'I don't care. You're already a criminal, Themba. Like I say, the choice is yours. I'll get my gun back, whatever you decide.'

'What's the other option? To become one of your *rhino guards*? To inform on my brothers, on my community, to do your job, to find the poachers where you can't?'

Mike nodded. 'That's part of the job, but not all. We can't stop poachers just by arresting people or shooting them dead. We have to educate people, the old and the young. That requires young men and women who are not afraid of change, who are brave enough to take a stand, and to take on traditional beliefs, and even their elders. Are you brave enough to do that?'

Themba had still held the rifle, but the words had resonated with him. He had done things he regretted because of beliefs that had been instilled in him by others. He had taken *muti*, medicine, to protect him from bullets, yet he had a friend who had been shot dead by the police after taking the same potion. He'd seen his sister, Nandi, raped by their *uncle* because he believed having sex with her would cure his disease.

Themba vowed to himself that if he survived this mess he had fallen into that he would fulfil the promise he'd made to her when she had been taken away, that he would build a life for them and come for her. The thought of her with strangers still burned his soul, even though he knew she was with a good family.

Themba wondered if he could create that new life by working in conservation, if he would be able to live in a proper house one day, and care for Nandi. Mike Dunn had held out that hope to him.

'There is more. We hope that some of the rhino guards will use the knowledge they gain to better themselves, to find jobs as rangers, or researchers or in other fields of conservation,' Mike had said.

Themba knew he could make more money stealing cars than he could working for the Ezemvelo KZN parks board, but he was also more likely to die or go to prison if he did. There was also a chance he could die protecting wild animals; rangers had been killed by wild animals while on patrol and the rhino poachers they fought were usually armed with AK-47s.

'There's a war going on here,' Mike had continued, as everyone around the fire sat silently, transfixed. 'You guys becoming rhino guards won't win it. If you do your job we might stop one poacher, one gang, but it won't win the war. The only way we win this war is if we all come together, like an army. And these days, make no mistake, armies don't just employ people to pull triggers. We need teachers and public relations people and lawyers and doctors and cooks and mechanics and we even have people undercover, in your communities, infiltrating gangs. We all work together here in the game parks. We look after each other and we watch each other's back. It never ends, and it may not be winnable, but without you,' Mike cast his gaze away from Themba for the first time in a while, to make eye contact with every young person around the fire, 'we will not win, and there is no point in trying.'

'Without me?' Themba had asked. At that moment, Mike had relinquished control of the rifle. Themba had felt its weight and for a second thought he might drop it. His heart had lurched as he stopped the weapon from falling to the ground. He'd looked at it.

'Yes,' Mike said. 'Without you and everyone else here, there is no point to any of this. Do you want to leave?'

Themba looked up and saw that the question was once again addressed to him, directly. 'I don't want to go back to the life I had.'

'Then where do you want to go?' Mike asked.

Themba had glanced down at the rifle again, felt its smooth, oiled wood against his fingertips. He held the rifle away from him, back towards the older man. 'I don't know, but I don't want this to take me there.'

'Don't want to be a ranger on anti-poaching patrol, hunting poachers?'

Themba shook his head. 'No. I want to be a warrior, but I don't want to kill. I've seen enough death.'

He had looked into Mike's eyes then, ready to stare him down, and he had seen the white man blink, twice, then look away. Mike had started to say something, but the words had caught in his throat. Themba thought the man looked different now, and Themba had wondered, just then, if Mike was there because he had problems as well.

'You don't have to kill to be a warrior, Themba,' Mike had said.

'I want to learn how to survive out here, in the bush.'

'You will,' Mike said. 'But your first job is to be an ambassador for the rhino, to spread the word in your schools and communities that these animals are valuable to you, the local people. Tourists come from all over South Africa and around the world to see our parks and our animals. They bring money that should go towards making your lives better.'

'*Should*, but doesn't,' Themba said, regaining some of his defiance.

'*Yebo*. Yes, I agree, Themba,' Mike said. 'Not nearly enough benefit comes through to the surrounding areas from our country's national parks. But you people are the next generation. If you are in the system, working with national parks people, perhaps in the organisation, or if you're in business or politics, then in the future you will find ways to involve the local communities more in the business of wildlife and the business of conservation.'

Themba had extended the rifle, one handed, trying hard to still the tremor in his skinny arm – he was no longer that weak, for he had spent the past year exercising his body as well as his brain. 'Take this back.'

Mike had stood again, held out his two hands and taken the weapon. 'Thank you. One day this will be yours.'

*

Lerato stirred, woke and rubbed her eyes. She was shivering and it took her a moment to realise where she was. When she did, she felt like crying.

The baby gave its first small cry of the day as the sun crested the ridge towards the coast, a fingernail of red visible through the dust that hung low over the hills. Themba, she saw, was looking in the same direction.

She could not believe she was here, in the middle of the bush, a fugitive. She had thought Themba was a smart, quiet guy, and kind of cute in a slightly dorky way, but she'd had no idea he would be related to a car thief or seemed to know how to find a tracking device in a stolen vehicle. She wondered what other secrets he was hiding from her. He must have sensed that she was awake because he stood and came to her, offering a biscuit and jam for her and a jar of baby food.

'I'm not his mother.' The baby grizzled. At least he had kept her warm.

'I'm sorry,' Themba said. 'I'll feed him if you like.'

'No, I will. I'm cold. Freezing.' She nuzzled the baby into her breast, silencing him for the moment, clinging to his warmth. She felt her tears well as she pressed her face to him, but then he started to cry. She sniffed. Lerato knew she must feed the child.

Themba took the binoculars they had found in the Fortuner and scanned the hills and valleys for signs of movement. 'I can see a giraffe.'

Lerato sighed as she wrenched the lid off the jar of baby food. '*Enough* with the animals. We're not on a sightseeing trip, Themba!'

'No sign of the men who were following us, which is good.'

Lerato spooned some food into the baby who, at first, seemed hungry enough to appreciate it, but he soon started wriggling against her and closing his mouth so that the food smeared on his grubby little face. She wanted to scream in frustration. 'Eat.'

She set the food and the baby down. He started to crawl towards Themba. She switched on her cell phone. 'Still no signal. And my battery is nearly dead.'

'We need to get moving soon. They could still be looking for us.'

She pulled a frown. 'This is *so* not right, Themba. I'm cold, I'm scared and I'm filthy. I am *not* spending another night in the bush. I need to call my father. He'll be going crazy.'

'I know. I understand. There is a main road that comes into the national park, north of here, from the Nyalazi Gate. We can flag down a car and ask them to take you to Hilltop Camp, the main camp in Hluhluwe, or if they're going the other way, then out to the gate and the nearest police station.'

'What about you?'

'I can't risk it, Lerato. The police think I'm involved in the car theft.'

'That's crazy, Themba. Look, my dad's rich, right? I'll get him to get you a lawyer. We can go to the police together. I'll tell the cops you had nothing to do with the car theft.'

He seemed to ignore her words. 'I need to find a guy, a man called Mike Dunn. I trust him. He will take me to the police, or, better, to the national parks security people. He knows them all. When I bring the rhino horn with me Mike will know I didn't kill the animals it came from, and it will help with my story, show that I am not a criminal.'

Lerato thought about the words Themba's horrible cousin Joseph had said before he died, about Themba being 'good' at what he was doing, looking for the tracking device in the stolen

Toyota. Try as she might, though, she couldn't picture him as a dangerous boy, even if he had a chequered past. 'Themba, no matter what you've done in life, you're *not* a criminal now. You spend your life with your nose in a book, you're a model student. Why would anyone even think you were anything other than an innocent victim of a crime?'

He stood and raised the binoculars to his eyes and looked south again, for the men who would still be following them.

'Themba?'

He said nothing and couldn't look at her.

She felt the dread flooding through her body. 'Themba, you're not in trouble with the law, are you?'

He drew a deep breath. 'Lerato, I'm sorry. I am a criminal.' He told her of his history with Joseph and of the charges and the commuted sentence that had led to him getting involved with the rhino guards, and Mike Dunn. He looked away from her and went back to scanning the bush with the binoculars.

Lerato didn't know what to say. She watched the baby. The little one seemed to prefer crawling around in the red earth putting dirt and bugs in his mouth to eating proper food, though he spat out more than he took in.

'I don't know how to do this,' Lerato said at last, and she felt the tears start to run down her cheeks again.

Themba lowered the binoculars and turned to her.

She sniffed. 'I don't know if I can trust you any more.'

PART 2

PART 2

Inqe had returned from Hluhluwe to his home in the Kruger National Park, but he could not rest.

There was a hungry chick squawking in the nest he and his partner had made. It was a fine construction of sticks lined with soft grasses atop a grand leadwood tree that had stood near the Sabie River for eight hundred years.

His kind had been in Africa for millennia, but they were disappearing. Each year more and more died, electrocuted by high-voltage powerlines and poisoned by farmers and poachers. It had taken nearly two months for their single chick to hatch, and by the time he fledged they would have been feeding him for four months.

His partner dropped a skerrick of rotten meat into the chick's ever-hungry mouth. Their future and that of their offspring was anything but certain.

So he flew, again, this time to the north and the east across the border with Mozambique. Game was starting to cross back into the vast tracts of the Great Limpopo Transfrontier Park, which until a few years ago had been the preserve of hunters and poachers. That journey, however, was as risky for the land dwellers as it was for vultures.

Below him, in the dry bed of the Shingwedzi River, others had found a hearty meal, the carcass of a slain elephant. Inqe joined the flock and descended. The kill was fresh, and just one tusk had been removed from the old bull.

The sound of gunfire startled Inqe and the other birds, who rose in panic and temporarily sought refuge in the nearest trees. When the shooting stopped it was followed by the sound of vehicle engines.

Men arrived to inspect the dead elephant. It was a bittersweet moment, as battle often was. An elephant had been killed, but the arrival of the first of the vultures had alerted a national parks patrol to the presence of a kill. The rangers had investigated, disturbing the poachers before they could remove both tusks and poison the carcass. A chase had ensued.

In the back of the patrol's Land Cruiser was the body of a poacher, and in the following vehicle were another two in handcuffs.

When the men departed, Inqe and his kind set about cleaning the elephant. When he was done, his belly full of food to be regurgitated for his hungry chick, Inqe took off, and headed for his nest.

Chapter 12

Nia stood on the balcony of her flat, watching the sun rise over the Indian Ocean. It was a beautiful morning. Banger was on his back, snoring. She would have to wake him soon.

The sheet was half covering him, his smooth chest bare, marred only by the bruise, the skin turning gold in the first rays of light. He was built like a god but had the face of a boy.

The kettle started boiling so she went inside and poured herself coffee, black and instant. She came from a wealthy family, but prided herself on not depending on them – the beachside apartment was one privilege she was willing to bear, though. Taking her mug she went back to the balcony and sat down on one of the chairs, the bare metal cold on her thighs under one of Banger's T-shirts. It smelled of him, and she liked that.

Nia held the cup in her two hands, blew on the coffee and took a sip. She was restless. She stood again and went back to the bedroom, where she looked down at Banger. He really was beautiful. Perhaps sensing her there, he blinked a couple of times, then focused on her and smiled. He looked over at the digital clock on the bedside table. 'Come back to bed, we've still got half an hour before we have to get up.'

'And good morning to you, too.' She sipped some more coffee. 'You've got a one-track mind.'

He grinned, then gave that dirty little sneer that she usually liked so much. 'You weren't complaining last night.' He ran a hand through his thick hair. 'That was wild.'

The image of the man Banger had shot, his face in death, her feeling of terror, suddenly flooded her mind again. The coffee cup began to shake in her hand, and when she saw the brown droplets staining the pure white duvet she felt the tears well up in her again. She shut her eyes tightly to try and force away the images of the dead taxi driver, the wounded policeman, the boy with the AK-47. Banger had saved her life.

He took the cup from her and set it down on the side table. She kept her eyes closed, just wanting to forget again. She felt his arms around her as he rose up on his knees on the mattress and enfolded her. She melted into his naked body and buried her face in the crook of his neck. His big arms were squeezing her and his lips were kissing the tears from her eyes. 'It's OK, babes. I'm here. I'm sorry.'

Shit happens, she told herself as she let him draw her down with him back to the warmth of the bed, as his tongue probed her mouth, as his hands moved down her body.

Banger rolled on top of her, his hand under the T-shirt, feeling for her breast. She had to leave to go to work soon, but his touch was dispelling the horrific images.

She felt her body start to respond to him and shifted in the bed, opening herself to him again. He brushed against her thigh and she felt him, ready for action as always; it aroused her further. Nia reached for him and closed her hand around him. He gave a small moan and she liked how that made her feel.

Her phone rang.

'Leave it,' Banger mumbled into the skin of her inner thigh; he had already made his way down over her body.

'Could be work,' she said.

'If it's a call-out they would have rung me first.'

It was too late. The whistling birdcall of her phone, a woodland kingfisher, had broken the moment. 'It might be about yesterday.'

He slapped the bed sheet with a palm. 'Leave it.'

Don't tell me what to do, she thought. Nia pushed Banger off her and he rolled onto his back, letting out an exasperated sigh. She didn't recognise the number, but answered it.

'Howzit,' said the man's voice on the other end of the line. 'It's Mike.'

'Mike?' It took her a moment to recognise him. 'Oh, vulture Mike.'

'Yes, vulture Mike. Sorry to call so early. Can you talk?' Nia glanced at Angus, who raised an eyebrow. She waved dismissively, got up, and went back out onto the balcony. The sun was warm on her face. 'Sure.'

'I've been thinking about those kids, on the run.'

'So have I. Is there anything in the paper today?'

'No, the *Mercury*'s all about the bomb; same with radio and TV. There's nothing about the hijacking or the missing baby. I spoke to Lindiwe, the policewoman on the scene, and she's going to try to track down the mother today, but the hijacking happened a long way out of her jurisdiction, and apparently the woman lived in Hillcrest.'

'So?'

'So, it's going to be one policewoman and her partner trying to work a case that should be assigned a task force of detectives. The mother of the child hasn't called the police at all, as far as Lindiwe's been able to ascertain, but things are crazy in Durban right now.'

Nia shared Mike's concerns. She'd spoken to John on her flight back the previous evening and had him call the tracking company control room and ask them for more information or contact details for the woman. The message had come back, via John, that the company had repeatedly tried to call the woman, but there had been no answer.

'What are you going to do?' she asked him.

'Lindiwe's going to try and get down to Hillcrest today to check the woman's house; see if she's there or if there's any other way to contact her. It'll take her a few hours to get here, but I just got a call from a friend of mine at the vehicle licensing office in Durban. He ran the woman's plate, from the Fortuner.'

'That's illegal,' Nia said.

'He owed me a favour.'

'What are you, a vulture researcher or some sort of private investigator?'

He ignored the question. 'She lives in Hillcrest, not far from where I am. I'm going to her place now, to see if she's there, maybe save Lindiwe some time.'

'Does your policewoman know what you're up to?'

'No, and if she did, she'd tell me I have no authority to be there, which is why I'm not telling her.'

Nia went back into the bedroom and picked up her coffee, then returned to the balcony again. 'So why are you telling me?'

'So someone knows where I've gone. You saw what went down yesterday. There were people there prepared to kill to get to that car, or what was in it. If something happens to me, if you don't hear from me by, say, ten, do me a favour please and call Lindiwe. I'll SMS you her number.'

Nia felt uncomfortable. She *was* worried about the missing child, and the mother who seemed to have disappeared, but she didn't like the way Mike was drawing her into his shady unauthorised investigation. 'What else?'

'What do you mean, "what else"?' he asked.

'You must have other friends you can call to let your cop friend know if you disappear, so why else did you call me?'

'You have a helicopter. We need to start searching for those kids and I'm worried it will take the police too long to get their arses into gear. Lindiwe Khumalo is a straight shooter but the whole police service seems to be fixated on the explosion in Durban.'

Nia scoffed. 'Hey, mister, for a start it's not *my* helicopter; it belongs to Coastal Choppers, and they're not about to let me go off on some wild goose chase after what happened yesterday. Do you have any idea how much it costs to keep a chopper in the air, let alone search an entire national park? Also, there's the small matter of the law that bans flying over parks – they're controlled airspace.'

She remembered the look of him, the khaki bush shirt with the frayed collar, the old *veldskoen* bush shoes that had clearly been restitched, the gaiters and faded shorts, the battered older model Land Rover. 'We're talking *thousands* of rand per hour to charter a chopper from us. Plus, like I said, I'm not allowed to take joy flights over Hluhluwe–iMfolozi.'

'I know the parks people and the ZAP-Wing guys who fly anti-poaching patrols over the park. I'll get a clearance; I'll say I'm looking for the guys who poisoned all the vultures yesterday.'

'Then why not fly with the ZAP-Wing guys?'

'Because you know, and I know, that I'm not actually looking for poachers. Plus, if they spot a kid with an AK-47 they're going to scramble their Rhino Reaction Force, and before you know it Themba will be locked up in prison. No matter what he did or didn't do, it's an offence for him to be in the national park, and carrying a weapon.'

Patience was not one of Nia's virtues. Her anger thermostat shot to near boiling. 'For goodness sake, aren't you being naive?

Don't you think that boy with the gun, your *friend* Themba, could be part of the theft?'

'You're jumping to conclusions.'

'Yes,' she said loudly into the phone, 'you're jumping to a conclusion that this kid is actually some poor misunderstood youth instead of a car thief and a kidnapper.'

'Calm down.'

'Don't you tell me to calm down! Why are you doing this, Mike Dunn? We're all worried about the baby but why are you on some one-man mission to look after a possibly delinquent teenager?'

'It's complicated.'

'That's it? You want me to go to my boss with "it's complicated"? You said yourself the policewoman in charge is competent. Why go to all this trouble for the boy? What does he mean to you?'

He drew a long breath, audibly. 'I'll tell you as soon as I get a chance. Just let me say I can't see another sixteen or seventeen-year-old kid gunned down by mistake. Themba's on the run in the bush because I taught him to survive there. He's relying on me. I need to find him and I need your help to do that.'

Banger walked out onto the balcony, a pair of running shorts barely covering his erection. He held up his hands and mouthed 'what's up'? Again she waved him off and he went inside to the bathroom.

Nia felt like she was being backed into a corner, but she was worried about the missing baby and schoolgirl, even if the jury was out on the teenage boy. 'All right. The truth is my boss is overseas. I'll fly a search for the cops, and if I don't hear from you by ten I'll call in the cavalry.'

'Good, thanks.'

He hung up without saying anything else, not even goodbye. Nia wondered who Mike Dunn was. Maybe he was just bush crazy, having spent too long with vultures and not enough time with people, and there was all that other angst about a dead teenager. He didn't wear a wedding ring and she couldn't picture him with a happy wife and children.

'Babes?' Banger called from the bathroom. 'What did that guy want?'

She went back inside and Banger came out, freshly showered, with a towel around his waist.

'He wants me to go back to the park, to help him search for those kids.'

'I'll come with. Me and Sipho will be on standby for you if you find them.'

Nia shook her head and went to the bathroom while Banger started putting on his uniform. She turned on the taps and stepped under the shower. He followed her in, buttoning up his dark blue shirt. 'You're on call. I don't need your protection, Banger. I'll be fine. I'll let you know how it goes. If we find those kids in the park, or the guys who were following them, then it will be a job for the national parks rangers or the police, not you.'

'I'm worried about you. You sure you're OK after all that shit that happened yesterday?'

Nia massaged shampoo into her hair and closed her eyes. 'I'm sure.'

*

Mike cooked himself a fried egg on toast and ate it at the kitchen table. He spent as little time as he could in the three-bedroom house he'd bought with his share of the divorce settlement.

He'd been happy to let Tracy take the good furniture; he'd been left with a favourite, if cracked, leather armchair that she'd always hated. He'd had it since he was a bachelor, first time around. The secondhand two-seater in the lounge room was a reminder of the time he'd thought of taking in a room-mate to help pay the bills and to have someone look after the house while he was away in the bush. It hadn't happened though. He was happy being alone. If the house was burgled while he was away, which so far it hadn't been, there was little worth stealing. His television was near its planned obsolescence date and his sound system was a cheap portable one. He carried his cash and his guns with him when he travelled.

Mike washed his plate and knife and fork, finished his coffee and rinsed the cup. He hadn't unpacked his camping gear from the Landy as he had planned to drive to Mkhuze Game Reserve, north of Hluhluwe–iMfolozi, today, to check on vulture nests. He had, however, brought his weapons inside with him. He took the rifle from the large locker in his wardrobe, and the nine-millimetre from where he kept it under his mattress.

Hillcrest was only a few minutes' drive from his place, but a major step up the property ladder. The address he had for the owner of the Fortuner, a Suzanne Fessey, was in a complex. Mike pulled up fifty metres from the entry gate and contemplated his first challenge – it was a secure estate with a high wall topped with an electric fence. The gate needed a remote control to open it, or for someone inside to push a button.

He got out and walked to the gate and pressed the buzzer for number three, which was Suzanne's house. He pressed once, twice, three times, but there was no answer. Mike heard foot-steps and turned.

A man with fair hair and beard turning to grey, maybe late forties or early fifties, stood there, a newspaper under his arm. 'Can I help?'

'I've got to drop something off for a friend who lives here. It's too big for the post box. I thought she'd be here, but she's not answering. Strange.'

'Really? I live here. What's your friend's name?'

Mike couldn't quite place the man's accent. He wasn't South African, but he'd been here a while. He looked fit, and wore a Cape Union Mart checked shirt loose over tan chinos. 'Suzanne Fessey.'

'Oh, Suzanne, right. Number two?'

'Number three,' said Mike.

'Yeah, right. Number three.'

'Did I pass the test?' Mike asked.

The man smiled. 'With flying colours. I'll let you in.' The man took a remote from his pocket and pressed it. The gates opened and he walked in. 'I'll hold the gate for you while you bring your truck in.'

Mike went back to the Land Rover, started it and drove in. The bearded man waved and smiled as Mike went past him. Mike found the third house and got out. From the rear of the Land Rover he took a cardboard box in which he'd packed some food, emptied it, and carried the box to the house. The man was watching him, so he called out: 'I'll just take it around the back.'

'Go right ahead.'

Mike found his way around the side of the house to the rear. He thought about the man who had let him into the complex. He'd seemed friendly enough, but Mike thought it unusual that he'd been so accommodating to a stranger. He peered through the first window he came to. He could see into the living room of the house; it was empty.

Further along he came to an open window. Mike looked around in case the bearded man or a neighbour was watching, then peered in. This was the kitchen. There was nothing on the bench tops and the doors of a couple of cupboards were open. He could see inside one and it was empty. It looked, so far, like no one lived here, certainly not a woman with a child if the state of his place when he was married was anything to go by. There had been food, plates, toys and stuff lying around all the time, even when they'd had a maid.

Mike tried the back door. It was locked. He returned to the open window, grabbed the sill and boosted himself up and in.

He hauled himself across a counter and then dropped down onto the tiled floor of the kitchen.

There had been a pile of household goods at the *kraal*, where the action had gone down the day before, and Nia had spoken of seeing the car thief and his possible accomplice – who Mike thought might very well be Themba Nyathi – pulling stuff out of the Fortuner.

Mike moved quietly from the kitchen to the bare living room. The place spooked him and he drew the nine-millimetre from the holster clipped to his pants, under his shirt. He cocked the weapon, and the noise sounded deafening in the uninhabited home. He moved to the stairs and took them, slowly, his gun hand outstretched.

Too much of this didn't add up. This woman, Suzanne Fessey, had left here, of that he was sure. The kitchen, he had noted, had smelled of cleaning products, and the surfaces looked polished. The carpet, too, was clean and white. She hadn't run out of here in a hurry, she had taken her time to spruce the place up. That made her a good tenant, but what else? he wondered.

At the top of the stairs he came to the open door of a bathroom. It, too, smelled freshly scrubbed, but there was nothing in it, not even a roll of toilet paper. In the master bedroom there was a wooden bed, but no mattress. That would have been hard to fit into a Fortuner, along with all her other possessions and a child.

Mike sniffed and caught the scent of cleaning products and air freshener, not of perfume or a man's sweat or cologne. He went into the bedroom and checked the wardrobes. Again, they were bare.

He stepped back into the corridor and walked along it, checking the second bedroom, also empty. The door to what he imagined was a third bedroom was closed.

Mike heard a creak behind him and instead he spun and dropped in one fluid motion. He raised his gun hand and saw the dark face of a man also pointing a gun, his torso just coming into view at the top of the stairs.

'Drop your gun!' the man yelled.

Mike fired and the man ducked. He hadn't identified himself as a police officer. If he had, Mike would have done as he had ordered. He began to turn, to make it to the third bedroom and hopefully climb out a window, but as he did he saw a blur out of the corner of his eye and felt a painful thud at the base of his skull.

He passed out.

Chapter 13

Sergeant Lindiwe Khumalo was about to walk out of the Mtubatuba police station to make the long drive to Durban when her landline rang.

'Sergeant Khumalo.'

'Sergeant, a woman calling for you. She says it's about the stolen car you investigated yesterday, and a missing child.'

'OK, put her through,' Lindiwe said to the desk officer. She lowered herself back into her chair. 'Hello?'

'Is that Sergeant Khumalo?'

Lindiwe took out her notebook and pen. 'It is.'

'Howzit, my name's Suzanne Fessey. My car, a Toyota Fortuner, was stolen yesterday and my baby son was on board. I've been calling around and I hear you're the investigating officer, is that right?'

The woman was speaking fast and sounded agitated, which was understandable. 'Yes, I am. There was a shootout. A taxi driver and the man we believe was the car thief were killed, and a police officer was wounded. We have been looking for you, Mrs Fessey. Why didn't you contact the police after you called your car-tracking company?'

'I was shot, Sergeant. I was able to call Motor Track then passed out before I could call the police. Have you found my baby? Is he safe?'

Lindiwe sucked a breath in through her teeth. 'I'm sorry to say your baby is gone. Apparently two teenagers, a boy and a girl, have him. We're looking for them right now. Are you all right?'

'I'm hurting, but I'm being discharged from hospital later this morning. I was knocked unconscious – one of the bullets creased my skull. I was lucky.' The woman started to sniff. 'And now you tell me my baby is still missing.'

'I'm sorry, Mrs Fessey. Can I come to you? What hospital are you in?'

'No. I want to come to you. I need to find my baby. I'll drive to Mtubatuba as soon as I get out of here. Can I meet you somewhere? You said men were killed, hurt. Where is my car?'

Lindiwe thought it a bit odd that Suzanne was worried about her car all of a sudden, when clearly she would have been going crazy about what had happened to her son. Still, now that she didn't have to go to Durban to meet Suzanne, the next logical place to pick up the search was where the Fortuner had been found late last night, burned and abandoned near the border of Hluhluwe–iMfolozi. Lindiwe had put in a request for a police helicopter to look for the missing suspects and the baby, but she had been told all air assets were still on security missions over Durban following yesterday's bomb blast. Mike Dunn had said he would talk to Nia Carras or the ZAP-Wing anti-poaching air operations outfit, to try and organise a search aircraft, so she would check on his progress next. 'Your car was burned out, it's near the iMfolozi Game Reserve,' she told Suzanne.

'I can be there in about an hour,' Suzanne said.

'You're not in hospital in Durban?'

'Um, no, north of the city. I'm not far from you. I'm signing out of the hospital now. Please, I need you to find my baby.'

'We will. All right, I'll see you soon.' Lindiwe gave the woman directions to where the car was. A flat-bed tow truck was due to pick it up later in the day, so Suzanne's timing was good. Also, some of her clothes and other possessions that had been thrown out of the car by the thief or thieves had been recovered and bagged. Lindiwe went to the evidence room, unlocked the door and retrieved the bags, which she put in her car.

She set off immediately, deciding to take a look in and around the burnt Fortuner with the benefit of the morning sun. On the way, she used her hands-free in the car to call Mike Dunn. His phone went through to voicemail.

'Mike, it's Sergeant Khumalo. When you get this, call me, please. I'm not coming to Durban now because I've found Suzanne Fessey, the owner of the car, or rather, she's found me. I'm meeting her at the burnt-out Fortuner. I hope you had some luck organising your aerial search, because I can't get a police helicopter. Maybe with Suzanne's help I can pressure our guys into starting a proper search. Call me.' She ended the call.

Lindiwe drove past Somkhele mine and then turned left up into the hills towards iMfolozi. When she reached the spot where the Fortuner had been abandoned, she got out and scanned the ground as she walked to the blackened hulk of the vehicle, thinking about Suzanne Fessey as she did so. Suzanne had sounded concerned about her child, but not freaked out, as Lindiwe would have if one of her three children had gone missing. There was a calmness about Suzanne despite her rapid-fire speech. It was almost as though she was being businesslike rather than emotional. However, Lindiwe also wondered if that was just a manifestation of shock, or perhaps she was medicated as a result of her gunshot wound.

In any case, Suzanne was lucky to be discharging herself out of hospital just a day after being shot. At least the wound explained why Suzanne hadn't contacted the police herself. Lindiwe wondered who had taken her to hospital, and made a mental note to ask her more about what had happened when Suzanne arrived. She would need to be formally interviewed, in any case. Lindiwe had taken a picture of the dead car thief's face with her phone and she would need to show the image to Suzanne to find out if the dead man was the one who had shot her.

The grass had burned in a radius of about fifty metres around the Toyota so there were no footprints or other evidence of use in the immediate vicinity of the SUV. Lindiwe cast her net further afield, following the path the fleeing teenagers had taken with the baby while being pursued by the two mystery men.

The body of the man who had taken Nia Carras hostage and then been killed by Angus Greiner had been of Middle Eastern appearance. Lindiwe thought of the bomb that had gone off in Durban; so-called terrorism experts were already all over the media speculating that Islamic extremists had been behind the plot to assassinate the American ambassador.

South African soldiers had been involved in fighting against the Séléka rebels in the Central African Republic, and while this mostly Muslim force had committed atrocities against Christians in that country it was not as organised and fundamentalist as, say, Boko Haram in Nigeria. South Africa had been free, so far, of the terrorist acts that had rocked Kenya and other parts of Africa, but the Americans wanted more support in the south of the continent and many Islamist groups clearly didn't want that happening. Suzanne Fessey didn't strike her as the name of a jihadist, but Lindiwe reminded herself not to fall prey to racial or ethnic stereotyping. Many Westerners, and quite a few South Africans, had been lured to Syria to fight for the Islamic State, and not all of them came from Muslim backgrounds.

Lindiwe looked to the wooded hills in the distance that marked the end of the communal grazing lands and the beginning of the protected national park. It was forbidding country for a couple of young people on foot carrying a small child. It was dangerous, too, with healthy populations of lion, leopard, buffalo and hyena. Lindiwe wouldn't want to be in the park on foot without a ranger for protection. She had been there recently to investigate a rhino poaching incident and even with a guide she'd been quietly terrified of encountering a wild animal.

It was eerily quiet, and the night-time cool hadn't been entirely banished yet by the morning sun and clear blue sky. A light breeze still carried a trace of chill. She heard a vehicle and turned to see a late model black BMW sedan trundling towards her on the rutted red road.

A woman with a blonde bobbed haircut got out. She wore jeans and a black T-shirt and had a scar on her upper left cheek. 'Sergeant Khumalo?'

'Yes, Suzanne? Hello. How are you?'

'I'm fine,' said the woman, smiling.

Exactly, Lindiwe thought. She had the sudden, grave thought that she ought not to have come out here alone. Suzanne Fessey had supposedly been grazed by a bullet, but was walking fine and there was no bandage, not even a sticky plaster, on her head. And her child was missing, but she was grinning.

The pieces of the puzzle started spinning and aligning, like the old Rubik's Cube her eldest son used to play with. Suzanne Fessey was fine; she had reported her car stolen to the tracking company rather than the police; it appeared she had the help of three armed men, one of whom had died trying to hijack a helicopter, to find her missing son. Suzanne Fessey didn't need the police.

Lindiwe moved her hand slowly to the pistol on her hip.

Suzanne stopped, two metres away from her. 'Is there a problem, Sergeant?'

'Who are you?'

'You know who I am. All I want is to find my son, and to get back some property that belongs to me. The kidnappers took it.'

Lindiwe drew a breath. Suzanne Fessey didn't *want* the police involved in this either, because whatever it was, it was illegal. Lindiwe started to draw her pistol. 'I'm going to have to ask you some questions.'

Suzanne held her smile and shook her head, slowly, three times.

A gunshot echoed over the rolling hills and Lindiwe Khumalo toppled sideways. The bullet had passed through her neck. Lindiwe looked up and saw the blonde hair, haloed by the sun behind it.

Lindiwe tried to breathe, and now felt the pain. Coppery-tasting liquid bubbled up in her mouth. 'Why?' she gurgled.

Suzanne kneeled and started undoing the buttons of Lindiwe's uniform shirt. 'Shush, shush, Sergeant. Let me help you.'

Lindiwe coughed blood and screamed as Suzanne rolled her to one side and pulled her shirt off. Suzanne lay Lindiwe back down in the grass and took the garment and held it up. 'Not too bad.'

'Why?' Lindiwe asked again, though she wasn't even sure the word came out.

Suzanne tossed the shirt to one side and reached behind her back. From a holster she drew a nine-millimetre Glock 17 pistol. She held it up and aimed it at a spot between Lindiwe's eyes. 'Because you're too clever, Sergeant.'

*

Suzanne pulled the trigger and it was over. She began changing into the dead woman's uniform.

Egil Paulsen came out from behind the BMW. He had been hiding on the floor of the back seat when the car had driven up. Egil had picked Suzanne up yesterday after stealing the money and the car from that crooked businessman, Bandile Dlamini.

'We were lucky she came alone,' Paulsen said. 'Made it easier.'

Suzanne buttoned the blue shirt. 'First piece of luck we've had so far.'

'Now that we have a police vehicle we'll easily be able to establish a roadblock in the national park. The kids will not have reached the tar access road through Hluhluwe–iMfolozi yet. There's a road that runs through the iMfolozi half of the park, from Mpila Camp to Nyalazi Gate. They'll hit that first and either try to flag down a lift or, if they see us, hopefully surrender themselves to the police.'

Suzanne turned her back to him and Egil did the same as she unzipped her jeans and swapped them for Khumalo's trousers. The fit was not bad. She took the policewoman's gun and phone also. 'Agreed. I didn't really expect Bilal and Djuma to catch them. They don't know Zululand like we do. I'm sure they'll be pleased to be picked up.'

Paulsen turned back to her. 'All that remains to be seen is how quickly the Americans can get their shit together.'

'Well, we've got our shit ready for them.' Prior to meeting the police sergeant Suzanne and Egil had driven to a remote site in the bush not far from the N2 and uncovered a cache of extra weapons and ammunition that she had buried two years ago, in a waterproof plastic bin, for just such an emergency.

'We could just head for the border. We can be in Mozambique in a few hours,' Paulsen said.

'Not without my baby.'

*

Nia checked her watch again as she sat in her boss's office at the small Coastal Choppers headquarters at Virginia Airport. It was now ten minutes after ten and Mike still hadn't called. She had phoned him three times and been put through to voicemail on each call.

Nia called the number Mike had given her for Sergeant Khumalo. The woman answered, but Nia could barely hear her. 'Hello? Sorry, you're breaking up.'

'Hold, please,' said the woman faintly.

Nia waited. 'Hello, who is this?' asked a woman, who sounded like a white English-speaking South African.

'My name is Nia Carras. Who are you?'

'I'm Sergeant Munro, Sergeant Khumalo's partner; she's busy and asked me to take this call. Can I help?'

'Um, I guess so,' Nia said. One cop was the same as the next. 'I'm the helicopter pilot Sergeant Khumalo met yesterday when we were chasing a stolen Toyota Fortuner.'

'One second please.'

Nia held.

'OK, Sergeant Khumalo asks what can we do for you?'

'Well, there was another guy at the scene yesterday, his name is Mike Dunn. He went to look for the owner of the stolen car today, a woman called Suzanne Fessey, at her house in Durban.'

'Yes?'

'Well, it's weird, but Mike asked me to call Sergeant Khumalo if he didn't get in touch with me by ten, and, well, he hasn't. This could be a bit paranoid, but as the other sergeant knows, there were these armed dudes chasing the people who stole the car and it was pretty crazy.'

'So I've heard. OK, I'll pass the news on to Sergeant Khumalo, thanks for that. By the way, Suzanne Fessey is here and she's fine.'

'She is? Wow, that's good to hear. And how about her child?'

'Well,' said the woman, 'naturally Suzanne's frantic, but there is a search under way for the child. Hang on –' another pause, '– Sergeant Khumalo is saying we need to see you, to get an official statement about yesterday. Sergeant Khumalo and I need to interview you, that is.'

'Sure, no problem. Hey, Mike Dunn has booked my chopper to search for the missing child and the young people who have him this afternoon. But I guess you've got a police chopper now, right?'

There was a moment's silence on the other end of the line. 'Well, actually, no. With the bomb going off in Durban yesterday all our police helicopters are tied up on security operations. Is there any chance you could still come up here and help us? We'll send some officers to check on Mr Dunn, by the way.'

Nia didn't know what to do. She wouldn't know where to start searching for the missing child.

'I can get authorisation from national parks to overfly Hluhluwe–iMfolozi, and I can fly with you to direct the search,' said Sergeant Munro, reading Nia's mind. 'This is really important. Shame, it's a missing child, after all.'

'OK,' Nia said. 'I'll be on my way soon. But please do check on Mike. He was really worried. I'm not sure what's going on.'

'Leave it to us,' Sergeant Munro said. 'Ever since those terrorists killed the ambassador the cell phone signal has been regularly clogged. You're lucky you even got through to me.'

'Well, my call got through to his number, too, it's just that he didn't answer.'

'No problem,' the woman said. 'We'll send someone to check the Fessey household. If you do hear from Mr Dunn, please let me know, and bring him with you in your helicopter. Sergeant Khumalo and I would like to interview both of you. Call me when you're getting close. I'm going into the national park now so I'll let you know where I am.'

'All right,' Nia said, then ended the call.

John was in the office next door. Nia walked in and found him reading an aviation magazine. 'I've got to fly up to Hluhluwe again. If Mike Dunn calls, could you tell him I've gone searching for the missing kid? Also, call me and let me know if he does get in touch.'

'Will do.'

Nia went outside and did her pre-flight checks. Although she had called the police like Mike had asked her to, and the sergeant had said she would send officers to look for Mike, she felt a knot of worry begin to form in her stomach.

'It's nothing,' she said aloud to herself as she started the engine.

*

Themba walked down the grassy hill, the child warm and sleeping – at last – against his back. It felt weird, having another person attached to him. Carrying infants was the work of women and girls, but Themba had to admit the weight and warmth of the child was oddly comforting. In his hands he carried the AK-47 he had taken from the Fortuner. He had reloaded it with one of the spare magazines.

He glanced over his shoulder. Lerato trudged along about thirty metres behind him, eyes downcast. She was not happy, but there was nothing he could do for her right now. Just as it was a relief that the little one had stopped crying, it was good, in a way, that Lerato was silent. She had been berating him most of the morning, telling him they should give themselves up, but so far they hadn't come across another soul.

In the distance a glint of light caught Themba's eye and he could hear, far off, a low rumbling. He lost sight and sound of the apparition as they descended to a river. As was now his custom, he tuned his senses to full alert. The vegetation along the river was much thicker and greener than on the slopes; perfect habitat for predators and other big, dangerous game to be seeking shelter from the sun.

Themba slowed and checked behind him again. Lerato had stopped, not wanting to close the gap between them.

'You must stick close to me,' he called back to her.

'Don't yell at me.'

He had deliberately raised his voice, to let any animal that might be waiting in the jungle-like fringe know that there were humans coming into their territory. In response a turaco squawked and flew out of the threes. Themba saw Lerato flinch.

'It's all right. Just stay close to me when we go through thick bush. I don't want to lose you.'

She blinked a couple of times and Themba thought for a moment she was going to start crying again, and that brought on a sudden feeling of sadness and helplessness in his own heart. He swallowed hard and told himself to be brave, to be a man, for all of their sakes.

'It will be fine,' he said, 'but in this, you must stick with me.'

Lerato gave the slightest of nods and started to make her way towards him. He told himself to remember that she was a city girl, spoiled and not used to life in the bush, let alone sleeping outdoors and being on the run with a criminal. Themba sighed. He had made a mess of this from start to finish. When it was over, however it ended, Lerato would never want to see him again. He sagged under the weight of the child, which suddenly felt unbearable.

'Let me take him.'

Themba turned. 'It's all right. He's not a problem.'

Lerato shook her head. 'His poor little legs are probably in agony from being splayed across your big back.'

The child stirred and started to grizzle. 'OK,' Themba said. He put the rifle down in the grass and unfastened the wrap tied across his chest.

Lerato eased the little boy from Themba's back. Themba felt the immediate relief from the removal of the weight and the cool of the breeze on his back through his shirt. How did people do this every day? he wondered. 'Thank you.' He picked up the AK-47.

She scowled. 'Don't thank me for anything. You got us into this mess and soon I'll be getting us out of it. But in the meantime you need to get us to civilisation and we need to make sure this little man is not harmed.'

Themba took a deep breath. 'You are right. About everything.'

Lerato flicked him a glance as she hoisted the child onto her back and tied the wrap around him and her, as though she'd been doing it all her life and not just the last twenty-four hours. 'How do you mean?'

'We – I mean I – should turn myself in. We need to find the police or someone who will take us to them.'

The relief was plain in Lerato's sigh. 'Yes, Themba. You have nothing to worry about, you know? You're a good guy.'

He felt, again, though for different reasons, as though his heart might break. 'I'm not, but thank you. We haven't done anything really wrong, have we?'

She shook her head. 'No. My father will help us. He is well connected in the ruling party. He can talk to the police. I'll put in a good word for you. And that will be that.'

Themba felt the sadness creep back into his soul. He had been right; whatever happened, Lerato would never speak to him again after this. She would wash her hands of him. He would have a hard time talking his way out of this situation and she would go back to her big house and her pampered life. He was crazy to have thought it would end any other way.

'I'm sorry I put you through all this, Lerato.'

She stopped walking. 'I won't lie, Themba, I'm tired and I'm filthy and I'm scared, but you did save my life. I'm sorry I haven't thanked you properly for that.'

Themba smiled. 'I would do it again.'

'Well, you're not going to get the chance, hopefully. Promise me we'll stop as soon as we see a car, people, whatever.'

Themba nodded. He didn't want to spoil this moment of forgiveness. He led off again, focusing on the ground ahead. As he approached the river he slowed, then stopped and listened.

'What is it?' Lerato asked.

Themba held up a hand to silence her, and sensed her resentment without even looking back at her. He turned his head slightly and heard it again, a snort. 'Go back.'

'What?'

'Back up,' he said to her.

He started to move and then saw the dark brown shape emerge from the reeds, trotting up the bank of the river towards him. Themba drew breath. 'Stop.'

Lerato exhaled. 'First you tell me to back up, then you tell me . . .'

'*Shush.*' Themba held his hand up again, then pointed. 'Look.'

The rhinoceros took two more steps, climbing up onto the top of the rise. It looked at him with its little eyes, sniffing the air as its ears rotated. Themba could tell immediately from the way it held its head up, and from its hooked, pointed upper lip, that it was a black rhino, and that was bad news. Unlike the relatively placid grass grazing white rhino, the black had a justified reputation for being aggressive and quick to charge.

Themba looked around. 'Dead tree, on the left,' he whispered. Slowly, so as not to provoke the animal, he began to unsling the AK-47, moving it from where it had rested on his back around to his front.

'I see it,' Lerato said quietly.

Themba almost had the rifle off his body. The rhino snorted, then charged.

'Run!'

Themba glanced left and saw Lerato heading for the tree, so he headed right, waving his hands in the air. 'Hah!'

The rhino followed his shout. That was what Themba wanted, but even so he was filled with terror. He could hear the animal's feet pounding the ground behind him, carving great divots from the dry ground as it clawed for purchase. Themba's arms were pumping. The rifle bounced against his side but he'd also been carrying his blanket roll on his other shoulder and the AK's sling was tangled in it. He imagined the point of a horn hooking him and tossing him high in the air then trampling his broken body to death.

Themba was running, instinctively, away from the river, but something in his brain told him to break left and head back to the watercourse. Even though other dangers might lurk there he knew he couldn't outrun the horned freight train behind him.

Directly ahead of him was a bend in the river. On the opposite side was a sandy deposit on the point. Themba had no idea of how high the drop would be on his side, but the drumming noise in his ears told him he had no choice. He sucked air into his lungs, pumped his arms and pushed his legs to run faster than he ever had in his life.

Themba could hear the huffing and puffing of the rhino behind him and almost feel its hot breath on his neck and legs. Themba glanced over his shoulder and saw the rhino sweep its head up in an attempt to gore him. Instead, the wickedly pointed horn hooked the blanket roll bouncing on his back. Themba screamed, fell and somersaulted as his bedding was ripped from him. He was vaguely aware of the rifle coming untangled and falling free from his body.

The ground beneath him disappeared and Themba flailed his arms and legs as he tumbled through the air. The next thing he knew he was on his face in the water. He had landed hard in the shallows. He looked up, fearing the rhino was going to come flying over the precipice and land on him. It had, however, stopped short, its malevolent face staring down at him. It snorted its contempt for him and shook its head.

Themba coughed muddy water. At least he was safe for the moment, and he hoped Lerato had the good sense to stay in whatever tree she had found until he could get back to her and the child.

The rhino lifted its head high, sniffed again and then turned and trotted away from the bank. Themba went to stand, but his foot slipped on a rock and he fell backwards into a deeper pool of the river. He came up snorting water and coughing again.

His body ached in various places but he realised he'd been lucky not to break a bone. He had only just escaped with his life.

'Themba!'

He stood and held his hand up to his eyes to shield them from the glare. Lerato was standing on the bank above him, the baby still tied to her back, holding the AK-47 which she must have found on the ground where it fell.

'Get back in the tree. The rhino could still be around,' he called to her.

'Themba, look out! Behind you.' Lerato raised the rifle. 'Get down!'

Themba turned and ducked at the same time, and felt his stomach churn as he saw the scaly ridge of the crocodile's tail and its evil eyes bearing down on him through the water. Lerato pulled the trigger and a burst of bullets sent geysers of river water rising around him.

Chapter 14

Mike Dunn came to with a slap in the face. He blinked. The man in front of him hit him again.

'Who are you?' the man asked.

Mike focused, which wasn't easy, and saw that the man had his wallet. 'You've got my driver's licence, so you've got my name.'

'Don't be a smart-ass. Who are you, Michael Dunn, and why are you here?' The man was black and spoke with an American accent.

'I could ask you the same thing.'

The man raised his hand to strike him again, but then another man came into focus. He was fair haired, with a blond beard flecked with grey. He put a hand between Mike and the other man. 'Leave him be.'

'Dude nearly killed me,' said the African American.

'We all just need to cool it,' said the fair-haired man with the beard. Mike recognised him; he was the man who had let him into the estate through the security gate. He had been set up. The man's accent was no longer disguised; it was pure American.

Mike raised a hand, slowly, and felt the lump on the back of his head. 'Yeah, cool it like nearly caving my skull in.'

'Well,' said Blondie, 'you did take a shot at my partner here.'

'You're police? What, FBI?'

'Something like that,' said the bearded man. 'Now, you tell us what *you're* doing here.'

'You first.'

The black man laughed. 'I say we water-board him.'

'CIA?' Mike said.

'Enough,' said Blondie. 'Michael, I'm going to level with you. My name's Jed Banks and my partner here is Franklin Washington. We're looking for Suzanne Fessey, the woman who lived here, until recently. How do you know her?'

Mike touched his lump again and winced. 'I don't. Her car was stolen yesterday and I ended up helping a woman who was trying to get it back.'

'What woman?' Jed asked.

'Helicopter pilot. She works for a car-tracking company. I was nearby and she couldn't get police assistance, on account of your ambassador being assassinated. You got anything to do with that?'

'What makes you ask that?' Franklin said.

'Well, we don't get too many CIA agents breaking into houses in Durban.'

'Who said anything about the CIA?' Jed asked.

Mike shook his head, and the act hurt. 'If you were police or FBI, you would have identified yourself. If you're plain old criminals – maybe burglars on a safari holiday – you probably would have killed me after I opened fire on you.'

'You a cop, Michael?'

'I'm a zoologist.'

Franklin snorted. 'Dr Doolittle? With a nine-mill?'

'And a .375 rifle behind the front seats of his Defender out there.'

'The police are on their way, so we can all have a chat with them soon,' Mike said. 'I'll start with getting them to charge you with breaking into my Land Rover.'

'That's an old trick,' Jed said.

'Old, but true. I left a message with a friend to call the police-woman investigating the theft of Suzanne Fessey's car if she hadn't heard from me by ten.'

Jed reached into the side pocket of the lightweight jacket he was wearing. Mike glimpsed the shoulder holster and the big old-fashioned Colt automatic inside. Jed pulled out a phone – Mike's phone. He dialled the message bank and put the phone on speaker.

'*Mike, it's Nia Carras,*' the recording began. '*I hope you're OK. I called Sergeant Khumalo but her partner, Sergeant Munro, told me Suzanne Fessey is with them. I'm going up there to help her with the search. Please call me and let me know you're fine.*'

'There were a few more missed calls. Where's "there"?' Jed asked.

Mike wondered what the Americans wanted with Suzanne Fessey in the wake of the assassination of their ambassador. Were the armed men following the Fortuner CIA agents?

'Nia Carras is your helicopter pilot friend. We've already got a line on her,' Jed said.

'Then you'll know where she's headed.'

'The guy who answered the phone at the chopper company wouldn't tell us, but we'll find out. You can save us all some time, Michael, and do some good as well.'

'Good?'

'We're the good guys, Michael,' Franklin said. 'In case you couldn't tell already.'

They both had that bulked-up US military look about them, Mike thought, though that didn't mean they were 'good', even if they were CIA, or FBI, or whatever.

'We can wait for your police to get here,' Jed said, 'but that will cost us time.'

Mike thought about the situation. Jed and Franklin, whoever they were, knew about Nia, and probably more about Suzanne Fessey than they were going to let on. It wouldn't take them long to find out where Nia was headed if they really were with a security service of some kind. He replayed the message from Nia in his mind.

'Why are you looking for Suzanne Fessey?' Mike asked them again.

Jed and Franklin looked at each other. Jed raised his eyebrows and Franklin shrugged his shoulders.

'She's important to us, Michael. Very important,' Jed said.

'Which is why you are in her house, with guns, snooping around and waiting to see who turned up. How long was I out for?'

'A while,' Franklin said. 'We can't wait around here all day. You going to help us or not?'

'Why should I?' Mike asked.

'Because we didn't kill you – even though you took a shot at Franklin – and we didn't water-board you.'

Mike looked Jed in his blue eyes and the American held his gaze.

'I can't tell you everything, Michael, but if Suzanne is where your chopper pilot lady friend is going then you should be concerned for Nia's safety.'

'Let me call her,' Mike said.

Jed held up the phone again. 'Tried that, while you were out cold. We got sick of waiting for you to wake up. But when we did try her phone was out of range, probably because of where she's flying. Want to tell us now where that is?'

Mike was having a little trouble collecting his thoughts after the bump on his head, but he realised what it was, now, that he'd thought odd about the message from Nia. 'There's no Sergeant Munro that I know of at Mtubatuba police station, where Sergeant Khumalo works.'

'Could be an outsider,' Franklin said, looking to Jed.

'Maybe,' Jed said. 'Nia said she was going to help "her" with the search. She could have been referring to Sergeant Khumalo, or maybe this Sergeant Munro is a woman as well.'

'Is Suzanne Fessey a criminal; is she wanted for something?' Mike asked both men.

They looked at each other again, then Jed turned back to Mike. 'I'll know soon enough if you're involved in this or not. I've already phoned your driver's licence details and ID number through to the South African police.'

Mike felt his anger rise; now he was not only worried about Themba, but also Nia, as he had dragged her into this. 'I'm not *involved* in anything. I'm only trying to help. Just tell me, is Nia flying into trouble? Is this Suzanne dangerous?'

'Well,' Jed said, stroking his beard, 'either you do know and you're not letting on, or you've really just stumbled in on this. In any case, you need to know that Suzanne Fessey could just be the most dangerous woman in Africa at the moment.'

Mike looked to Franklin. 'I'm sorry for taking a shot at you.'

Franklin shrugged. 'Only would have been a problem if you'd hit me. Many scientists pack Glocks here?' he pressed.

'Not unusual,' Jed weighed in.

The blond, Mike realised, was the good cop in this show.

'Are you *okes* going to kill me?'

Jed looked to Franklin, who shrugged. Jed turned back to Mike. 'Probably not.'

'Then let's get to where Nia is going to meet Sergeant Khumalo and this Sergeant Munro, and Suzanne Fessey.'

'Where are we going?' Jed asked.

'Zululand, up near the iMfolozi Game Reserve. Few hours' drive. Tell me, did you send three men, armed with assault rifles, after Suzanne's stolen car and her baby?'

'Nope, but we know about them.' He turned to Franklin. 'Get the chopper organised.'

'You have a helicopter?' Mike said.

'Michael –'

'Mike.'

'Mike, we have the United States Army, Navy, Air Force and Marine Corps if we need them.'

'You think we might need all of them?' Mike asked.

Jed stroked his beard again. 'Maybe.'

*

Lerato held out a hand and Themba grasped it. She helped pull him onto the sandy riverbank. Behind him, the crocodile floated dead on its back. The baby was wailing.

'Thank you,' Themba said.

Lerato yelled, 'Don't thank me, get us out of here!'

'OK.'

Lerato unfastened the child from her back and rocked him in her arms to try to soothe him. 'Now look what's happened, he's going crazy. *I'm* going crazy. I don't want to be out here any more. And if I put this kid down for two minutes he tries to crawl away into the bush.'

'I know,' Themba said. For the first time in a long time he was beginning to feel the same way she did. He did not live in comfort, but right now his modest shack and single bed with the moth-eaten blanket seemed like a king's castle.

Themba was soaked but fortunately it was a warm sunny day. He first walked fifty metres in each direction along the riverbank, satisfying himself that the rhino wasn't circling back to have another try at killing them, then sat down on a rock and unlaced his shoes. He wrung out his socks then took off his shirt and squeezed most of the water out of it.

Lerato was jiggling the baby, trying a variety of cooing noises to calm it. 'He's hungry, I think,' she said.

'We're almost out of baby food.'

'I *know*. We can't let this child die of starvation, Themba.'

He stood up and went back to the water's edge.

'Where are you going?'

Themba shielded his eyes against the glare on the water then waded into the river again. 'We need food.'

'You're going to get yourself killed, like you nearly did just now.'

'Then cover me with the rifle.' Themba grabbed the crocodile by its tail, giving it a shake first to confirm it really was dead. When he dragged it up onto the bank he saw it was about a metre and a half long.

'You can't be serious.'

He went through the pack and pulled out a Leatherman tool he'd taken from the Fortuner. 'We have to eat.'

'Crocodile?'

'People say it tastes like chicken.'

'Um, Themba, people say anything gross tastes like chicken. Personally I'd rather have KFC.'

Themba shook his head and went back to the carcass. He knelt beside it and lowered his head. He heard the crunch of footsteps behind him.

'What are you doing now?'

'It gave its life to feed us,' he said. 'I'm saying a prayer of thanks.'

He looked up at her. She had the baby on her back again and her hands on her hips. 'You can thank *me*. I'm the one who killed it.'

'Thank you.'

It was funny, he thought. She was frightened and tired and hungry, as he was, yet at moments like this she seemed forged of steel, like a statue of some warrior heroine of the struggle. Themba opened the serrated blade on the Leatherman and started to saw through the tough skin where the tail joined the main part of the body. It was hard work and blood welled up over his hand.

'*Ewww.*'

Well, perhaps not quite the warrior woman. He carried on with the grisly work. He had seen men in the village cleaning slaughtered animals. Sometimes the beasts they had killed were buck, taken illegally from the national park and other game farms. Themba had grown up thinking this was perfectly acceptable, and that most animals provided food of some kind or another.

Since his time as a rhino guard, however, he had come to realise that wild animals had a greater value to man than merely the taste of their meat, or the use of their skins.

He hated the fact that they had killed the creature he had just butchered. No one he knew liked crocodiles, but Mike had taught him that everything had a part to play in the environment, that an ecosystem was about balance and acceptance that everything was there for a reason. 'Even vultures?' Themba had joked.

Mike had smiled at him, one of the rare times, because even though Themba thought they might be friends Mike was never truly a happy man and rarely smiled. 'Especially vultures.'

Themba called Mike 'Inqe', the vulture, not to his face, but in his own mind. He had once thought of the bird as ugly and evil, a scavenger that lived on death, but Mike had taught him that without the vulture there would be disease and more death in the veldt. The vulture travelled great distances, as Mike did, in the course of its important work, and it could see very far. The *inyangas* used the myth that vultures could even see into the future as an excuse to peddle their heads, and while Themba did not believe that, he had believed in Mike's vision for the future: that one day, with hard work, Themba could end up like him, working in the bush, helping to conserve wildlife, and that he would not end up dead in a gunfight or locked up in prison.

Yes, Themba thought as he dragged the crocodile's tail back to the river and rinsed away the blood – quickly, in case another was drawn by the scent of the swirling redness – he had believed in Mike's prophecy of the future.

But not any more.

*

Nia saw the flashing blue lights of the white police double cab *bakkie* ahead. She scanned for powerlines and other obstacles, but saw that the cops had picked a good, open space for her to land – by the side of the tar road from Nyalazi Gate to Mpila Camp. She brought the helicopter down.

A woman in uniform strode towards her as Nia shut down. She climbed out of the R44. The woman extended a hand and Nia shook it.

'Sergeant Catherine Munro,' the policewoman said, blonde hair peeking out from below her cap.

'Nia Carras.'

'Lindiwe, my partner, has taken Suzanne Fessey north of here. They're setting up a second roadblock, checking all cars crossing or using the access road between iMfolozi in the south and Hluhluwe in the north. Suzanne's gone so she can identify her baby. You're familiar with the park and the road?'

Nia nodded; she was. 'Good idea.'

'We know what we're doing, but before the missing kids reach the access road they have to cross this road first. We've set up in the open, as you can see, so that they can see us from a long way off. We want them to surrender peacefully to us,' Sergeant Munro said. 'This way, please.'

The woman led Nia towards the police *bakkie*, around which stood three men. The trio straightened as she approached them and Nia nodded to them.

'This is Captain Swanepoel,' Catherine said. 'He's a detective.'

Nia shook hands with the man. He had white hair that almost looked bleached and blue eyes. He gave a curt nod and smiled. 'We're pleased you can join in the search.'

'Sure,' said Nia. 'Anything to help find a missing kid.'

'I'll fly with you, if that's OK with you,' said the captain, 'and the sergeant will head our ground team, with my two other men.'

Swanepoel pointed to his colleagues, one black and one brown, both in plain clothes.

'My radio's playing up,' said Sergeant Munro, 'so I'll keep in contact with Captain Swanepoel via cell phone.'

Nia shrugged. 'Sure, fine by me. You'll let me know if you hear from Mike Dunn, right?'

Catherine nodded. 'Of course.'

As the sergeant turned Nia noticed a purplish stain on the collar of her uniform. 'Hey, what happened to your shirt there?'

Sergeant Munro reached up and touched her collar, then looked back. 'Oh, I attended a car accident this morning. One of the victims was badly hurt. All part of the job, you know.'

Nia nodded. She had seen more than her fair share of car crashes from the air and like all South Africans knew only too well that her country had a terrible road toll. It was odd, however, that the policewoman would have blood on the back of her uniform, and not the front. Sergeant Munro was quite pretty, Nia thought, though she looked like she had been in a few scrapes. Her face would have been almost perfect if it wasn't for the scar across her left upper cheek.

'OK, can we get airborne, please?' the captain said. 'I don't want to seem pushy, but there are young people at risk somewhere out there in the bush.'

'Right,' Nia said.

They walked to the helicopter and Catherine went to her police truck. Swanepoel was striding ahead of her and already getting up into the chopper.

'I'll give you a quick safety briefing,' she said, climbing in beside him.

'I've been in plenty of helicopters,' he replied.

He *was* pushy. 'Well, you haven't been in mine, and I'm required by my employers to give you a briefing.'

'Very well.'

She noted his impatience and cared nothing for it. Delaying their take-off by a minute would make no difference. Nia went through her briefing, ignoring the captain's rolled eyeballs, handed him a set of headphones, then she started the aircraft.

While Nia was going through her checks she felt her phone vibrate in the pocket of her flight suit. She pulled it out and saw Mike Dunn's name on it. Normally she might have ignored a call at this point, as she needed to concentrate on her pre take-off procedures, but she had been worried when Mike hadn't called her. She glanced at Swanepoel, whose raised eyebrows seemed to ask, *What now?*

Nia answered the call, which only she could hear. 'Hi, I was worried,' she said by way of greeting.

Mike's voice came through her headphones. 'Nia, I called your base. Are you up in Zululand already?'

'I am.'

'Are you alone?'

She glanced left again and saw the captain drumming his fingers on his trouser leg. 'No.'

'Don't let on it's me you're talking to.'

'OK.' She wondered what was going on. Above the background noise of her own engine warming up she thought it sounded like Mike was driving, as he was talking loudly over the sound of another machine.

'Did you meet this Sergeant Munro person you mentioned in your message to me?'

Swanepoel was holding his wristwatch up to her now, tapping the glass. She held up a hand to him. 'I did.'

'Nia, the people I'm with, some Americans, security people, contacted Mtubatuba police station. They confirmed what I thought, that there is no Sergeant Munro there. They've been trying to contact Lindiwe Khumalo by radio and phone and there's no answer from her. Something's very wrong. Can you get some-where to talk alone?'

'Not really, no.' She felt her heart beat faster and a chill spread through her body.

'OK. Sergeant Munro – was she blonde, about five-five, blue eyes, with a scar on her left cheek?'

'Yes. How did you . . .?'

'Nia, shit. Listen to me. Get away from whoever you're with.'

'I'll try. Give me a second.'

Nia leaned forward and made a show of touching a couple of gauges. She switched the headset control from her phone to the intercom, so that she could now talk to the man next to her.

'We've got a problem,' she said into her microphone.

'You can say that again. We need to get airborne and find those kids. Now.'

'We're not going anywhere. I've got a problem with my engine temperature.' She could see, even as she spoke the words, his eyes scanning the gauges, looking for the warning sign. She ought to have thought of something cleverer, but she was also fighting a rising tide of panic.

'I can't see anything wrong,' he said into his mike. 'You'd better not be . . .'

Nia flicked back to the phone channel, cutting the man off.

'Nia, hello, are you there?' Mike was saying. 'That woman; she's really Suzanne Fessey, the one whose child is missing. She's no innocent victim of crime, though, she's . . .'

The feed to Nia's headset went dead as Swanepoel pulled the phone cord out of the socket.

Nia pulled off her headphones. 'Hey, what do you think you're doing? We've got an engine problem here. Evacuate, evacuate, evacuate!'

The man didn't move. He also took off his headset and looked at her with his pale, creepy eyes.

'I said, get out of my helicopter, I'm shutting down.'

He shook his head. 'I'm not going anywhere. You're going to take off now and we're going to fly over the national park.'

Nia started to reach into her pocket to pull her iPhone out.

Swanepoel's hand went into his open jacket. Nia was stopped by the cold, hard steel of the barrel of a pistol, which the man pressed painfully into the side of her head. 'Fly.'

Chapter 15

Jed Banks drove as fast as he could, weaving through the Durban traffic.

Across the road from the giant Moses Mabhida Stadium, built for the FIFA World Cup, he turned into Isaiah Ntshangase Road and stopped at the gates to the headquarters of the Natal Mounted Rifles.

Mike knew the depot well; he had spent part of his national service there. The NMR, as they were also known, was an army reserve unit of the South African National Defence Force. An impressive collection of battle tanks dating from the Second World War to the Border War in Angola were arrayed around the parade ground. Two men in uniform asked Jed for ID; one was a South African soldier in kevlar helmet and body armour, carrying an R5. It wasn't normal to see a trooper in full battle kit on the gate, but what was even more out of the ordinary was the US Marine standing next to him in camouflage fatigues and a similar suit of armour, and carrying an M4 assault rifle.

The American nodded to Jed and told the South African

soldier to let them pass. Mike noted the scowl on the face of the African, whose authority had just been usurped by a foreigner, but that display was nothing compared to what awaited them on the parade ground ahead.

Mike would have felt bothered for his countrymen about the way the Americans seemed to be riding roughshod over their hosts but he, like Jed and Franklin, was in too much of a hurry to care about protocol.

A grey MH-60 Sea Hawk helicopter decked out in the stars and markings of the US Navy squatted malevolently in the car park. More American and South African military personnel shifted aluminium trunks from the chopper into the NMR headquarters. The building itself, like the tanks around it, dated from another era; it had once been the terminal building for Durban's original airport which was long gone.

'This is the command centre for the operation to find the people who assassinated our ambassador,' Jed said as they quickly got out of the car and strode across the parade ground.

'Looks more like the foothold of an invasion,' Mike replied dryly.

Jed looked at him, unsmiling. 'We don't mess around when someone kills one of our own.'

The Sea Hawk's engine was whining to life and the blades began turning as the crewman, attached to the helicopter by an umbilical communications cord, motioned for them to move forward and take a seat in the back.

Once inside the helicopter, the crewman, who had also climbed aboard, slid a green vinyl dive bag across the floor to Jed. The crewman then took up position behind a swivel-mounted machine gun and they lifted off.

Jed unzipped the bag, took out a Heckler and Koch MP5 submachine gun and passed a second to Franklin.

'What about me?' Mike yelled over the noise of the engine.

Jed reached into the pocket of his jacket and drew out the nine-millimetre pistol he had taken from Mike. He handed it to him. 'We'll handle things on the ground. You hang back.'

'You're it?' Mike asked. 'Where's the rest of the cavalry?'

'This chopper's from the visiting destroyer in Durban harbour. There's a SEAL team – Navy special forces – inbound, as well as FBI investigators on their way from the States and people from half a dozen other agencies. However, the South Africans are sensitive about the US military charging around their country. We've only got clearance to fly this helicopter on "familiarisation" flights, so for now, yes, we're "it".'

Mike had no intention of getting involved in a gunfight, but he did feel a knot in his stomach. He was worried for Nia. He felt responsible for her being drawn into this situation. The fact that the call he had made to her on the way to the base had been cut off so abruptly filled him with dread. It must have shown on his face, because Jed reached over and grabbed Mike's shoulder. 'She'll be OK.'

Mike nodded. He didn't know why the American would think he needed that kind of reassurance. Franklin and Jed had grilled him enough to know that he had no personal connection to Nia – at least not formally – but the truth was that she was there because of him.

'You'll have to guide the pilot in when we get closer,' Jed said to him.

Mike nodded. 'OK. But can't you track Nia's chopper?'

'We're trying to.' Jed made his way between the armed men to the two pilots and put on a spare headset. He leaned back to Mike a minute later.

'Air traffic control at Richards Bay hasn't heard from her.'

'Does that mean she hasn't taken off?'

'Maybe,' Jed said.

Mike found himself warming to the CIA man. 'I'm surprised

you can even pronounce "Hluhluwe", not many tourists know the "hl" is pronounced like the double "L" in Welsh names.'

'I'm not a tourist any more. I've worked in Africa since 2005,' he said. 'My daughter from my first marriage was working as a lion researcher in Zimbabwe and that's what brought me here. I ended up back in the States, but not for long. I met my second wife in Africa and she also loves it here.'

'What does your wife do?' Mike asked, out of courtesy.

'She teaches, at an international school near where we live.'

'Which country?' Mike asked.

'That's classified.' Jed laughed. 'Our son's eleven. His mom teaches him, which is kind of cool and kind of weird.'

Mike smiled. He wondered what it might be like to start over, to try and do better with a marriage and a family than he'd done the first time. 'You look like you're proud of both of them.'

'I am,' Jed said. 'I truly am.'

Mike saw that Jed meant it. 'What part did Suzanne Fessey play in the assassination of your politician?'

Jed seemed to consider the question, shouted over the engine noise. 'Maybe a lot, maybe nothing, but the fact she'd packed up her house in Hillcrest and that she was on the run, apparently without her husband, means we think it's maybe a lot.'

'Who's her husband?'

'Now that, my friend,' said Jed, 'is definitely classified, although I can tell you he is missing, believed obliterated.'

Mike looked out the window of the Sea Hawk. The US ambassador to South Africa, he thought, would have been a relatively easy target, by American standards, for a suicide bomber. He'd read somewhere that she liked to get out and about, and South Africa would not have been considered as dangerous for US diplomats as, say, Kenya or other parts of East and North Africa. Below him the rich greens of his homeland flashed by. He longed to be out in the bush, searching for vulture nests.

'What are you thinking?' Jed asked him.

Mike thought about the question. 'That I'd rather spend time with vultures than people.'

Jed nodded. 'Any day. Do you have a favourite?'

Mike was a little taken aback by the question. 'The lappet-faced.'

'The can-opener.'

'You know your vultures?' Mike said, unable to hide his surprise.

'The lappet-faced is the largest of the vultures; he has the biggest beak and opens up the carcass for the rest of the birds to feed. My daughter taught me that.'

There it was again, Mike noted, the sense of pride Jed had for his daughter. Mike had let his own family down and Jed's wholesomeness, despite his work, almost irked him. 'Well, she was right.'

Mike was always happy to talk about vultures, but the co-pilot of the Sea Hawk looked over his shoulder at that point and beckoned to him. Mike stood and gripped the back of the pilots' seats. The man who had beckoned him forward handed him a headset.

'Afternoon, mister,' said the co-pilot. 'I sincerely hope you know where we're going, because I've never been here and I have no idea.'

Mike looked through the cockpit windscreen and soon got his bearings. The Somkhele mine was ahead of them and off to the left. 'It's not far from here,' he said into the microphone attached to the headset.

'Hold on,' said the pilot. 'Got 'em on radar. She's airborne, over the southern half of the park.'

Mike didn't know whether to feel relieved or more worried. If Nia was flying that could mean that all was fine and she was working with bona fide local police officers or, as Jed had theorised, she had been kidnapped by possible terrorists and forced to take off despite Mike's warning.

'Can you call her?' he asked the pilot.

The pilot turned back briefly to look at Jed, who was also on a headset.

''Fraid not,' Jed said. 'We don't want to tip off whoever is in the chopper with Miss Carras that we're tailing them.'

'I understand,' Mike said.

'How far?' Jed asked the pilot.

Mike was staring through the cockpit windscreen and he recognised the border of the park below, where the land changed from beaten, overgrazed farmland to the rolling grassy hills and acacias of iMfolozi.

'About ten klicks,' said the pilot.

'Get in a little closer, but stay out of visual range,' Jed said. 'Track them by radar and let's see if they start losing altitude. That'll tell us if they've found the kids.'

'Are the South African police in on this as well?' Mike asked over the intercom. 'Have you got local ground support?'

'They're on their way. The local cops are worried about your Sergeant Khumalo,' Jed said. 'Our people at the Natal Mounted Rifles have a South African Police Service liaison officer feeding us information. But for now it's just us, and we're going to catch these people.'

'You still haven't said exactly who "these people" are.'

'All you need to know is that they're the bad guys and we're the good guys,' Jed said.

Mike shook his head exasperatedly. He knew life was never that cut and dried.

'Besides,' Jed added, 'it's their ground element I'm interested in. That's where we'll find Suzanne Fessey and the people she's working with.'

'There's a road coming up ahead,' said the pilot.

'That's the road to Mpila Camp,' Mike said.

'Also leads to the Nyalazi Gate, right?' Jed asked.

Mike nodded.

'Those kids have an AK-47. They might just shoot their way out,' Franklin said.

'We're not talking about Bonnie and Clyde here,' Mike said. 'Anyway, I thought you were more interested in finding Suzanne Fessey and her crew than the runaway kids.'

'We find Suzanne's baby before we find her, then that will give us leverage over her,' Jed said.

Mike had formed the opinion that, for a spy, Jed was a decent enough guy, but a remark like that reminded Mike of who he was dealing with; or, rather, who had taken him into de facto custody and along for the ride.

*

Nia was flying with no headset on. It felt unnatural not to have contact with the outside world, but the man with the pistol was wary of her sending a distress call. He had the gun pointed at her, only glancing away every now and then to scan the veldt below.

She was working a grid pattern, at his instruction. He had a cell phone in his left hand and was using it periodically to check in with the people on the ground.

Nia was desperately trying to think of some way to fool the man, or to sabotage his attempts to find the children. When she had tried slowly increasing her airspeed, to make it harder to search, he had put the barrel to her head again and told her to slow down to her normal cruising speed.

When she began climbing, he tapped the altimeter. 'Do you think I'm stupid?'

'I don't think you're stupid enough to shoot me in the head while I'm flying,' she had replied.

'I don't have to shoot you in the head.' Nia had started when he'd rested the tip of his pistol between her legs. He moved the barrel from the apex of her legs slowly down over the seat until the weapon was pointed at the floor of the helicopter. Nia had screamed when he pulled the trigger.

It had taken all her willpower to regain her self-control after that moment. The man had mocked her with his grin, sitting back in his seat, but the neat round hole in the floor, which she glanced at again now, reminded her that she was dealing with a cruel man with brains.

'Are you going to kill me, when this is over, when you have what you want?' she asked him.

He shrugged. 'Probably not – at least not if you help us, and you don't try anything foolish like you did before. The South African police will have our names and our photos by now. You can't hurt me, but I can most certainly hurt you. If you want to fly your helicopter into the ground, that is your prerogative; some may call you a heroine for taking me with you, but you won't stop us all. The others are in two cars, and they'll be smart enough to park away from each other, so you couldn't kill all of us even if you tried.'

Nia hadn't, in fact, thought of flying her helicopter into a carload of whatever these people were, but she was creepily intrigued at how the man beside her was mulling over the various options of a planned suicide.

'We're just trying to rescue a child,' he continued as he searched the ground below.

'Then why in God's name didn't you just leave it up to the real police?'

'You ask too many questions. Just fly, find the kids, and we'll go and you'll live.'

So Nia flew, scanning the bush below for the trio of missing young people. If she did see them and the man didn't then she would give no sign of having located them. Whoever they were and for whatever reason they had taken the infant, Nia had the distinct feeling that they would die a horrible death.

She glanced at the man with the gun and he smiled back at her. As much as she wanted to believe him, she knew he would kill her as soon as he was finished with her.

*

Lerato watched Themba cooking the crocodile tail while she nursed the baby in the shade of a tree. Mercifully the infant was sleeping.

She had felt quite proud of herself, killing the crocodile, and now she found that something as simple as the smell of cooking meat could lift her spirits a little. She told herself they would be out of this mess soon. But the boy she had trusted would be out of her life too. She could still barely believe that Themba was the kind of man who held up people and stole their cars.

Themba looked to the sky. 'Listen.'

'Shush, you'll wake the baby.'

'Quick.' Themba kicked dirt over the fire. 'We must hide.'

'You're ruining the meat,' Lerato said. 'You've got sand all over it.' As if on cue, the baby woke and started crying. 'Now see what you've done.'

He ignored her and pointed to the sky. 'Helicopter.'

He had made the fire under a stout Natal mahogany tree; the leafy foliage protected them from the sun and would filter the smoke, making it harder to see from the air, but if the chopper flew directly over them, a sharp-eyed pilot would spot them.

Lerato set the crying baby down in the grass. She'd had enough. 'I'm going to run out there and wave at it. They're probably searching for us.'

'Wait,' Themba said. 'Be quiet.'

Lerato was taken aback at the tone in his voice, but she sullenly complied.

Themba fetched the binoculars and focused on the dark speck against the clear blue sky. 'It's the same one as yesterday, the red car-tracker.'

'They've got the car, so they're looking for us.' Lerato started to move out of the shade of the tree.

Themba chased after her and caught her by the arm.

'Hey, let go of me.'

'Come back under cover. *Yes*, they are looking for us, but it's not their job.'

Lerato wriggled in his grip. 'The police might be using their helicopter to come find us.'

'It could be those men who tried to kill us, Lerato. They're not with the police. They're murderers.'

'You don't *know* that, Themba. They might just be the uncles of the child or friends of the mom or whatever. You're not making sense.'

Themba looked stricken. 'Lerato, please listen. There is something else going on here. Most moms don't have hand grenades, AK-47s and rhino horns in their cars. These people are bad. They're criminals.'

'We are the ones acting like criminals. *You're* a criminal, Themba.'

The helicopter was almost overhead. Themba let go of Lerato's arm and raised the binoculars to his eyes again. Lerato saw that the aircraft was coming right towards them, and it was low. Through the branches and leaves above she could make out the pilot, the same woman as the day before. There was a man in the passenger seat next to the woman and all Lerato registered of the man was a shock of bright white hair.

She didn't try to hide her anger. 'OK, Themba, what are we going to do?'

'We're moving.'

Lerato was smart enough to know she wouldn't last long in the bush by herself, but she hated the sound of those two words.

*

177

Nia saw the glint of sunlight reflected off glass winking at her through the foliage of the mahogany tree that flashed below her skids.

The odds of there being something man-made under a tree this far from any access or game-viewing road were astronomical. Using her peripheral vision she checked the fair-haired man. He gave no indication of having seen anything.

Nia looked around her, and memorised the spot.

Ahead of her she saw the black tar of the road from Mpila Camp to Nyalazi Gate. A dozen or more vehicles were stopped and at first Nia thought it was a typical national parks' traffic jam, with tourists queued up to see a lion or a leopard. Then she saw the police *bakkie* parked to one side of the road.

'Make a left turn when we get to the road, then head south again,' the man said to her.

*

'Breaking right,' the US Navy Sea Hawk pilot said into the intercom, as he turned that way.

Mike gripped the seat back in front of him. The evasive manoeuvre was to stop the people in Nia's Robinson from seeing them.

'I'm going to orbit off to the east for a bit, then pick them up again.'

As they circled back around Mike saw the queue of traffic. 'That's unusual.'

'Police roadblock?' Jed asked.

'Yes. Unusual because Mtubatuba police didn't say anything about a roadblock in the game reserve.'

Mike took his phone out of his pocket. He had a signal. From his contacts he selected the number of the section ranger for the area north of the access road into Hluhluwe.

Chapter 16

Themba came to the brow of a hill and dropped down on his belly. Lerato eased herself down too, the baby asleep on her back in his wrap, and wriggled up until she was beside Themba.

'Police!'

'Shush,' said Themba. 'Keep your voice down.'

Lerato frowned. 'Why on earth should I? We agreed that if we saw any cops we'd give ourselves up, so what are we waiting for?'

Themba took out his binoculars. 'It's unusual to have a roadblock here in the park.'

'So what? Who cares? It just means we won't have to walk any more. I've got blisters all over my feet and this baby is breaking my back.'

Themba ignored her complaining and focused on the officers below. There was a white woman in blue police uniform leaning into the window of a Mitsubishi Pajero four-wheel drive. A man in civilian clothes walked around the vehicle, inspecting it from the outside, while another man in plain clothes sat in the driver's seat of a police *bakkie*. Something wasn't right about the scene. The policewoman leaned back and waved the vehicle on.

'Let's go,' said Lerato.

Themba held up a hand. 'Wait.'

'What's the problem?' The frustration was clear in Lerato's voice.

'Those men in civilian clothes could be detectives.'

'And?'

'And there's only one officer, the woman, in uniform. The cops normally work in pairs.'

'I won't ask how you know so much about police procedure.'

'Don't,' Themba agreed. He focused in on the man in the police vehicle but it was hard to make out their features through the windscreen, which glinted with reflected sunlight. 'They must be looking for someone in particular. Maybe even us.'

'Yes,' Lerato exhaled. 'Maybe even *us*. Maybe they want to help us? Maybe they're worried sick about this bundle of wee and pooh on my back.'

Themba wrinkled his nose. It was true, the baby needed changing, and the half a dozen disposable nappies they had salvaged from the Fortuner had run out. The child needed to be cleaned, fed again and, somehow, have its diaper changed. That would happen if they gave themselves up to the police officers below. He would be arrested, Lerato would be questioned, but if they allowed him a phone call, he could call Mike Dunn. Everything would be sorted out.

'It will be fine,' Lerato said, reading the hopeful wishes in his mind, but still he wasn't sure. The down on the back of his neck rose.

Below them, a new model Land Rover Discovery towing a caravan pulled to a halt behind the Pajero. The policewoman waved the SUV closer and the Discovery driver crept forward a few metres until the officer was abreast of him.

Lerato pushed herself slowly upright.

'What are you doing?'

'I'm going down there. If you're coming, Themba, then come. If not, I won't tell them where you are. I'll say we parted company and I went off on my own, which is exactly what I'm doing right now. You're kidding yourself if you think we can last any longer out here in the wilds with a tiny child.'

'Wait.'

She ignored him, brushed the dirt off her front and set off down the hill. Thorn trees shielded her from view from the people below, but she would soon break into the cleared area on the verge of the main road. The vegetation was kept down on the sides so that motorists would have ample warning of game crossing.

Themba heard the drone of a helicopter and instinctively burrowed closer into the ground. They were coming for him; he was sure of it. He peeked above the stems of grass in front of him and looked around. There it was, low on the horizon and heading straight for the roadblock. It would pass right over him.

He raised his binoculars and focused on the aircraft, then inhaled sharply. This was not the same sort of small helicopter that had been chasing the stolen Fortuner; this was a much bigger machine, painted a dull, menacing grey. It reminded him of the logo of the KwaZulu-Natal Sharks Board, a fearful-looking great white coming at him head-on. On one side he saw something sticking out, and when he steadied his hands he saw that it was a machine gun. A crewman in a bulbous helmet had his torso out in the slipstream. The gun was raised to the horizontal, at the ready. *Are they coming to kill me?*

'Lerato!'

She didn't hear him, so he risked calling louder. Lerato stopped and turned. He pointed up in the air with a finger and she shielded her eyes with a hand and looked up. Just as he had hunkered down, Lerato's first impulse was to drop to her knees, fearing the oncoming war machine.

Themba transferred his binoculars back to the roadblock and picked up movement. One of the men was getting out of the parked police *bakkie*, the policewoman beckoning to him and pointing to the caravan behind the Discovery. The driver, an elderly man with grey hair, opened his door and went to the caravan. Themba could see that the man had been told by the policewoman to open the door of the caravan. He sorted through his keys to find the right one as the man from the *bakkie* took up a position behind him. Themba focused his binoculars on the younger man and drew a breath.

'What's happening?' Lerato called from where she was crouching.

'That man down there, behind the caravan, he's one of the men who shot at us.'

'Oh my God.'

'They're not police, Lerato.'

A shadow eclipsed the sun for a second as something zoomed over them. The big grey helicopter slowed, circling the vehicles below. A voice boomed down from the aircraft.

'Citizens below, move away from your vehicles and place your hands in the air. Do not run. Do not panic.'

Themba picked up the American accent from the slightly distorted voice from above. The old man by the caravan had his key in the door, but had taken his hand off it and looked upwards when the voice sounded. The man behind him shoved him in the back. Themba wanted to run down the hill and yell to the old man to get away, but he felt rooted to the earth, paralysed with fear.

'What are we going to do, Themba?' Lerato wailed. 'I'm scared. Are they the police? The army?'

Themba saw the black star with two bars on either side of the helicopter's tail. These were not South Africans, clearly. The crewman in the big helmet was pointing his machine gun down at the ground. Themba gripped the AK-47. He had no intention of picking a fight with this giant aerial beast, and wondered if he should toss his rifle away, in case the gunner above caught sight of him and opened fire.

'*Move away from your vehicles, put your hands in the air*,' the disembodied, God-like voice called from the heavens.

A woman got out of the passenger side of the Discovery and darted towards the caravan door. The man, her husband, shook the other man off his shoulder and ran to his wife and hugged her. The man who had shot at Themba reached under his jacket and brought out an R5 assault rifle.

The couple from the Discovery looked up at the helicopter, then walked a few metres away from their vehicle and put up their empty hands. The policewoman called and waved to the man she had dispatched and he ran to her. She looked up as well, waving to the circling helicopter.

'*Ma'am, put your hands in the air. Draw your service pistol and toss it on the road where we can see it*,' said the American voice.

The helicopter was still moving in a slow circuit. Themba switched his gaze from it to the people on the ground. As the chopper passed over the parked police *bakkie* and the Discovery, its tail rotor and rear now to them, the second alleged policeman got out and ran to the rear of the truck. Themba saw that he was undoing the vinyl cover of the *bakkie*'s load area. The helicopter settled into a hover as the policewoman and the other man waved to it, distracting the crew.

'*Police officers, please put your weapons on the road, where we can see them*,' said the voice.

The elderly couple had backed away further, about twenty metres from their four-by-four and caravan. They stood, necks craned, watching the helicopter.

Lerato had retraced her steps and was kneeling next to Themba, who was now up on his knees. He shifted the binoculars back to the police *bakkie*. 'The other man is getting something out of the back.'

'What is it?' Lerato said.

Themba saw the long tubular object that the man was hefting up onto his shoulder. 'No!'

'What?'

'It's an RPG,' Themba said as he got to his feet. 'Anti-tank weapon. He's going to shoot them.'

'Who?'

Themba started to run down the hill.

'Wait for me,' Lerato called.

'Stay back,' he yelled to her, not even turning. Themba waved his arms in the air. 'Hey, hey, down here!'

The elderly couple looked Themba's way, hearing his frantic screams above the drone of the helicopter's engines. Someone aboard the chopper must have seen him too, because the nose of the machine started turning in his direction.

'Behind you!' Themba pointed furiously towards the *bakkie*. There was no way the people on board could hear him. Themba saw the crewman turn his machine gun towards him and suddenly realised he was still carrying the AK-47. *They're definitely going to kill me.* He tossed the rifle into the grass.

'*You down there, Themba Nyathi, stay where you are,*' the voice said, and Themba was shocked that they knew his name.

He kept running, though, waving and pointing to the rear of the helicopter. He stopped, thought for a second, then turned back and ran to where he had discarded the AK-47. He picked it up.

'*Themba Nyathi, drop the weapon or we will open fire. I repeat . . .*'

Themba's heart was pounding so hard the sound of rushing blood deafened him. He brought the rifle up, swung and took aim in the general direction of the police truck.

Themba pulled the trigger and sent a wild burst of 7.62-millimetre rounds towards the man with the RPG-7 launcher. Puffs of dust and stray stalks of grass seemed to erupt around him as the machine gunner on board the helicopter started firing at him. 'No!' Too late, he realised he'd done the wrong thing. All eyes on the helicopter were focused on him now, and not on the real danger.

From across the road below the hill came a *whoosh*, and Themba watched a trail of dirty white smoke streak across the clear blue Zululand sky. A second later came a clap of thunder and Themba's upturned face caught the heat of the black and red fireball that erupted from the helicopter. Its tail all but sheared off, the helicopter started to spin under its main rotors. A blaring siren replaced the robotic voice and Themba ran as more bullets, this time from ground level, started whizzing through the air around him like angry high-speed wasps.

Themba saw the old white couple, the woman shrieking hysterically, run for their Discovery. The helicopter, which had been almost directly above him when the RPG man had fired, was coming down.

'Run!' Themba called to Lerato. 'The caravan!'

*

'Brace, brace, brace,' ordered the pilot over the internal loud-speaker on board the Sea Hawk.

Mike Dunn put his head between his legs and clasped his hands together underneath them. Jed Banks, he noted, was firing his MP5 out the open hatchway. Mike glanced up and, as the chopper spun, caught a glimpse of the blonde woman in the police uniform running towards the parked vehicles. There was no sign of Themba, who Mike had positively identified to the Americans.

The machine gunner, too, was still looking for targets.

'Don't shoot the boy!' Mike yelled.

There was a tortured screech from the rear of the Sea Hawk as something else sheared off and the pilot seemed to lose what little control he had in the auto rotate. The helicopter yawed sickeningly over onto its side. Mike's last vision was of the ground rushing up outside the open cargo door.

The rotor blades hit the earth first, sheering off in different directions, and then the fuselage crashed into the grassland. Mike's body whiplashed, and his head hit the wall behind him which, though padded, still managed to stun him.

He came to and looked around the interior of the helicopter. Jed was leaning over someone.

'Franklin,' said Jed. 'He's alive, help me.'

Mike undid his seatbelt and crawled to Jed.

'He's unconscious,' Jed said. He searched around the cabin and found the dive bag from which he and Franklin had taken their weapons. Jed fished out a grenade the size and shape of a drink can. 'This is smoke. Get ready to deplane.'

Mike crawled to the crewman who had been firing the machine gun. Brave, though foolhardy, the man had stayed standing, firing his gun as the helicopter crashed. His head was twisted at an unnatural angle. Mike felt for a pulse, but there was none. 'Must have broken his neck.'

'Sons of bitches.' Jed pulled the pin and tossed the grenade out. A swirling wall of red smoke rose up, obscuring the blue of the sky.

Mike clambered over the body and helped Jed lift the unconscious Franklin up to the edge of the cargo compartment. On a count of three from Jed they hoisted him over the edge then scrambled up and out themselves.

Mike heard gunfire in the smoke, but realised it was Jed laying down some cover. 'Stay down,' Jed said.

Mike flattened himself into the grass, which was just as well as a burst of gunfire stitched four holes in the fuselage about thirty centimetres above his head.

'Leopard-crawl,' Jed said, not too loud. Mike followed his voice and they each grabbed Franklin under an arm and, awkwardly, dragged him with them.

The smoke was spoiling the aim of the bogus police officers, but Mike could hear shouting. Soon the cloud would lift and they would be exposed.

'Pilots?' Mike asked.

'Heading there now.'

They crawled to the cockpit, leaving Franklin in a dip in the ground, which would cover him from view of their enemies. The smoke was thinning. Mike saw a man across the road, standing by the parked cars. 'Jed, down!'

A noise like a rushing train was followed by a smoke trail as a second rocket-propelled grenade scythed through the air between Jed and Mike. The two men flattened themselves on the ground as the projectile slammed into the cockpit of the downed Sea Hawk. The grenade detonated and fire mushroomed.

'If they were still alive, they're finished now,' Jed said. 'Run!'

*

Themba had run down the hill, away from the falling, spinning helicopter, and had felt the impact of the crash reverberate through his feet. Lerato had been right behind him and Themba had motioned her to the rear of the caravan.

As gunfire burst around them and a second RPG round slammed into the helicopter, Themba made his way to the side of the caravan and, finding the door unlocked, grabbed Lerato's forearm. She struggled, the weight of the baby on her back making it harder for her to get inside.

The engine of the Discovery roared to life. Themba saw that the elderly white couple had made it back to their car during the chaos. The Discovery lurched forward, and the caravan with it.

'Themba, hurry!'

Themba ran after the caravan, pushing himself into the fastest sprint of his life. Ahead there was another long burst of gunfire and the Discovery weaved hard to the right. The caravan slewed and rocked and for a moment Themba feared it might roll over, but the evasive manoeuvre slowed the van enough for Themba to catch up.

Lerato hung half out the door, her arm extended. 'Take my hand!'

'Take the rifle.' Themba hurled the AK-47 and Lerato just managed to catch it, almost fumbling it in the process. She tossed the rifle inside. Themba's legs pumped as fast as they could and his heart hurt with the effort of keeping up. The Discovery started to accelerate again now that the caravan had stabilised. Themba reached out and felt Lerato's fingers grip him as he leapt. She pulled and he scrambled and for an instant he thought his arm would be wrenched from its socket, but she managed to haul him into the doorway and he landed on the floor inside with a painful thud.

Lerato reached over him and slammed the door shut then moved to the front of the caravan. She undid the wrap and laid the baby, screaming from the noise and movement, on a couch. She stacked pillows around him to try and stop him from moving. Chest heaving, Themba hauled himself to his knees and peeked through the closed blind on the rear window. The woman in the police uniform and the two men were all firing at two other men in the grass beyond the burning wreck of the helicopter. Themba saw the woman pointing at the departing caravan and yelling something to the men. Then the trio began getting into the police *bakkie*, the woman at the wheel. Moments later they took off, coming down the road behind the caravan. The two men from the helicopter were on their feet now and ran into the middle of the road, firing after the police vehicle. 'Help me,' Themba said.

Themba unfastened the lock on one side of the long rectangular window. Lerato went to the other side and unlocked it as well. Themba pushed the window out, locking it in the up position, then retrieved the AK-47 from the floor of the van.

'Get down,' he yelled at Lerato.

She lowered herself beneath the window as three rounds zinged through the inside of the caravan. The man in the front passenger seat of the *bakkie* was firing at them with a pistol.

Themba popped his head up and fired a burst of rounds at the *bakkie*. He had the satisfaction of seeing the gunman and the driver duck their heads as their windscreen shattered, but the truck kept coming. In fact, the gap between them closed as the woman accelerated.

Lerato was peeking through the window. 'Hurry, they're catching us.' The child was screaming.

The man with the pistol fired again and Lerato retreated deeper into the caravan and lay on a bunk bed, moving some of the pillows and covering the child with her body, Themba marvelled at her courage. He must be brave, too. Ignoring the incoming fire he stood, braced himself with his legs apart and fired a long burst, emptying his magazine, into the engine bay of the *bakkie*.

Bullets glanced off the bonnet, scarring the white paintwork back to bare metal, but Themba had also hit something vital. Steam jetted like a geyser from either the radiator or a punctured hose. The driver slewed to try and get out of Themba's line of fire, and the *bakkie* started dropping further back.

The caravan lurched as the Discovery took a left turn, hard and fast, and Themba had to reach out a hand to steady himself on the kitchenette counter. 'They're falling behind!'

'Where are we going?' Lerato asked.

Themba checked the countryside around them. 'Heading north. We've crossed underneath the main access road that divides iMfolozi from Hluhluwe; that means he's crossed into Hluhluwe instead of going into the outside world via the Nyalazi Gate.'

'Is that smart?' Lerato asked.

Themba thought about it. 'He could drive much faster once he's out of the national park, but he also might be more vulnerable to attack. I guess he feels safer staying inside a game reserve, where there will be rangers, hopefully, responding to what happened.'

'What exactly did happen just then?'

'I don't know,' Themba said, honestly. 'But it's clear they weren't real police officers you were about to surrender to. They just shot down an American military helicopter.'

Lerato closed her eyes, and when Themba looked at her more closely he saw the tears start to stream. 'What are we going to do, Themba? Who are these people and why are they still trying to kill us?'

He staggered the length of the rocking caravan – the driver might still be in the game reserve, but he was far exceeding the fifty kilometre per hour speed limit as he negotiated the winding road – and sat down on the bunk bed beside Lerato. She had the child in her arms, pressed to her breast, and was rocking him. Themba put his arms around both of them and felt Lerato's tears soak through his shirt onto the skin of his chest.

She looked up at him with red-rimmed eyes. 'I need to contact my father, Themba.'

'We should be able to use the electricity points in the caravan. If we're in luck they might even have an iPhone charger in here somewhere. I'll have a look in the drawers, see what I can find.'

'We have to get to him.'

'I'll get you to him as soon as I can,' Themba promised. 'At least we're safe for the moment, Lerato.'

She looked into his eyes. 'Themba . . .'

'Yes?'

She eased herself away from his embrace. 'I was thinking before, after I found out about your past, that I couldn't trust you. I wanted us to give ourselves up to those people, but you were right to be cautious; they are bad people.'

'Yes.' Hearing her words gave him no comfort.

She wiped her eyes. 'Tell me I can trust you, that you'll get us out of this, alive.'

'I will get you and the baby home safe.' *Or I will die trying.*

Chapter 17

Egil Paulsen's phone rang. He kept his pistol aimed at Nia Carras while he took the call.

'The Americans are on to us,' Suzanne said into the phone.

'It was only a matter of time,' Egil replied.

'We just took out a US Navy helicopter. Three men survived, one wounded, all in civilian clothes.'

'CIA?'

'Two of them, at least. One's dressed like a safari guide, no body armour like the other two. We're following the two youngsters and my baby. They turned north, probably heading to Hilltop Camp. You know it?'

Egil had stayed in Hluhluwe's main rest camp as a child, as Suzanne probably had. 'Yes. What sort of vehicle?'

'Land Rover Discovery, towing a caravan. The kids are in the caravan. They managed to climb aboard before we could get to them.'

'You should have no problem catching up to a Land Rover and a caravan.'

'The boy with the AK took a lucky shot. We're losing radiator coolant in the police car, and speed. I think we're about to overheat any second now.'

Nothing had gone according to plan since the killing of the American ambassador, Egil mused. 'Get another vehicle then.'

'That's our plan: as soon as we see one we'll hijack it. You take the BMW if you need it; it's too far for us to go back for it and the Americans will be waiting for us.'

'All right,' he said. He had stashed the car he had stolen from Dlamini in the bush near the fake roadblock.

He admired her. She was ruthless and tough. Egil thought about his options. He could get the woman pilot, Nia, to chase down the Land Rover and caravan, land, block the road, and he could kill the occupants and take back the child, but the boy in the caravan was still armed with an AK-47, and had shown he knew how to use it. Also, there were the three men who Suzanne and the others had failed to finish off. If they did manage to call for more American reinforcements then he and Suzanne would fail at their mission and none of them would get out of South Africa alive.

He made his decision. 'I'll take care of the survivors at the crash site and get the BMW and find you afterwards. If the people with the caravan are staying in the park they can only drive so fast.'

He ended the call and turned to Nia. 'Turn around and fly back to where the roadblock was.'

'Was?' said Nia. 'Did you friends get bored and leave, or did the cops come and shoot them all?'

'Don't get smart with me.' He watched her. She was scared, of course – this was the second time in two days she'd had a gun trained on her – but she and her boyfriend had killed one of his men. She would have nothing to smile about when he was finished with her, but for now he needed her helicopter.

They flew over the undulating countryside and Egil got his bearings, seeing the wide tar road running left to right up ahead.

The pall of smoke clearly indicated the resting spot of the Sea Hawk.

'Circle the crash site.'

'Whatever you say,' the woman said over the engine noise, her tone resentful.

Egil looked ahead and to the side as she entered her orbit, but kept his eyes on the woman as well. 'Don't try anything stupid.'

He surveyed the scene. The Sea Hawk was still ablaze but it worried him that the Americans had mobilised and located them so quickly. He wondered if the pilot had radioed a mayday; probably.

A man walked into the middle of the road, waving his hands above his head. Egil instinctively leaned back in his seat, not wanting the man on the ground to get too good a look at him.

'Scared?' the woman asked him.

He glared at her in reply and held up the pistol, resting the barrel against her temple again. She licked her lips; he liked her fear. It was almost arousing; no, it *was* arousing.

'What do you want me to do?'

'Land, but not close to him, in case it's a trap.'

'We wouldn't want that now, would we?' she said.

He would enjoy killing her. 'There are supposed to be three of them, one lying wounded. I see only one.'

The burning Sea Hawk had started a grass fire and the wind was blowing west, taking the blaze along the edge of the road. 'I have to land upwind, the smoke's too thick past the chopper.'

'Hover across the road from him.'

Nia nodded. She brought the R44 around until the nose was facing the waving man. Egil noted that the man's hands were empty and he could see no sign of a weapon in the short grass around him; that didn't mean he was unarmed, though. He could have shot the man from the air, but he needed to account for both of the mobile survivors. The third man had to be somewhere, perhaps lying wounded in the shade of a tree, perhaps even dead by now, but either way, Egil needed to make sure.

The pilot settled into a hover, as instructed. Egil adjusted his sports jacket so that it was over his pistol. 'Touch down, but be ready to lift off on my command. Don't alert this man in any way. I'm simply going to ask him where my colleagues went. If you try anything I'll shoot him in the head. Understood?'

She looked past him, to the waving man, and nodded.

Egil used his free hand to wave back, motioning the man to come to them. The man gave a thumbs-up, lowered his head and ran across the road. He was the one Suzanne had mentioned who was dressed in safari clothes. Perhaps the wounded man was not too badly hurt and the others had gone off in pursuit of Suzanne, Bilal and Djuma on foot, or had commandeered a passing vehicle.

The helicopter set down and the man ran to Egil's side. 'Is it safe to shut down?' Egil asked.

'It's safe,' the man yelled back to him over the engine noise. 'Hi,' the man called to the pilot. She glanced across at him.

'I'm in charge of this aircraft,' Egil said hurriedly. 'I'm Captain Swanepoel, South African Police Service.' He didn't want the man and the woman communicating.

*

'Yeah, and I'm Nelson Mandela,' Mike Dunn called back. He saw the momentary confusion, then realisation dawn in the man's face. Nia had all but ignored him, and he'd guessed better than to use her name.

Mike recognised the man in the co-pilot's seat immediately. It was the same person who had been at the Mona market, when the alleged rhino horn deal went bad. The recognition was mutual.

Mike had bought Jed a few seconds, but no more. In his peripheral vision he saw movement in the grass below the helicopter. Mike had experienced a heart-stopping moment, as Jed must have, when it looked like Nia was going to land right on top of the small depression where Jed had hidden. Mike had scraped dirt and dead branches over him.

Jed was on his feet now, moving at a crouch.

The white-haired man lifted his gun hand clear of his jacket and pointed his pistol at Mike. 'Don't move. Where is the other man?'

Nia looked at Mike, eyes wide, but Mike gave a small shake of his head.

Jed stood up, out of the white-haired man's line of sight, raised his MP5 and put two aimed rounds through the skin of the helicopter. His position meant that the bullets punched through the aluminium fuselage, then through the back of the co-pilot's seat. The man's body jerked forward against the restraints of his safety harness.

Nia, startled by the gunshots, instinctively raised the collective and the helicopter reared upwards. Mike waved at her to put the chopper down again.

Jed tossed Mike his pistol and Mike caught it. The two men shielded their eyes against the sun. 'You got him, I saw him take two hits,' Mike said.

Jed nodded. 'So why isn't the pilot bringing the chopper down?'

'I don't know; she saw me,' Mike said. 'She knows it's safe down here.'

The R44 swung around in a low orbit and as the passenger side came into full view again Mike and Jed both saw the arm sticking out the open door. The man started firing at them.

'Goddammit,' Jed said as they both ran to try and get under the chopper and out of the gunman's line of sight. 'He must be wearing body armour.'

'You can't open up on him, you might hit Nia.'

'Well she's going to be dead soon if we don't get him.'

*

Just the act of firing his pistol seemed to be causing her passenger and captor pain, Nia saw. He'd clearly been hit by one, maybe two bullets, but she could see no blood on his chest or anywhere else. His drew his breaths in ragged, painful drags.

'Around again,' the man coughed.

Nia saw the two men below. There was no way she was going to line up her helicopter to give this madman a chance to kill Mike or the other guy. She thought about what the man had said to her about committing suicide.

The man was checking himself out. He tried to run his hands behind his back, but couldn't reach where he wanted because he was still strapped in. He unsnapped his inertia harness and tried again to move his hand to the centre of his back.

Nia saw her chance. The man was momentarily distracted and the door on his side was still open. She knew he was going to shoot her if she didn't do what he asked, of that she was sure, and he would have her land somewhere before she bled to death. She turned away from Mike and the other man.

The man stopped fiddling behind his back and looked at her. 'Hey, what are you doing?'

'Killing you.'

*

'What the hell's she doing?' Jed asked.

Mike stood next to the CIA man, in the open. They had watched Nia fly away from them.

The helicopter climbed to about three hundred feet off the ground and banked into a tight left turn. Mike could see the passenger's side door hanging open and a man frantically reaching to close it. Next, the aircraft's engine note changed, stuttering to a quiet growl as Nia levelled out.

'She's cut power,' Jed said.

'What the hell for?'

The nose of the chopper came up a little and Nia then turned hard to the right. From below they glimpsed the man thrown outwards by the centrifugal force of the turn, clutching at the doorframe. The helicopter began to drop, its blades whining in a crescendo.

'She's doing an auto rotation – crashing deliberately,' Jed said.

Mike shielded his eyes. 'No!'

As the helicopter approached the ground the nose came up, sharply, and it looked to Mike that the tail rotor was about to spear into the earth. Just before it struck, however, Nia levelled out in what looked like a sickening drop. The protesting rotor blades were slowing and bending upwards now.

Mike started running towards the chopper as it smashed into the ground. As soon as it hit the aircraft began sliding forward on its skids. Then, as the toe of one skid dug into the ground the machine started to tip. Rotor blades chopped then sheared off the grass, helping to slow the forward movement. The helicopter's tail dropped, but just as Mike thought it might settle upright it rolled violently to the left. As he closed in on the crash scene he saw the man thrown from the still open door and the aircraft settle hard on its side in a cloud of dust.

The man stood up from the long grass, about twenty metres from the crash, and staggered away from them, deeper into the bush.

Jed fired at the man, but he was at the extreme range of the short-barrelled MP5 and was now hidden in the trees.

Mike ran to the crashed helicopter while Jed charged into the thornbushes into which Paulsen had disappeared. Mike steeled himself for what he might find. The engine was smoking, and as he came closer he saw Nia, motionless, hanging in her safety harness.

'Nia? Can you hear me?' There was no reply.

Mike tore away a section of cracked Perspex and fought his way awkwardly into the cramped cockpit. He found the release for Nia's safety harness and she dropped into his arms. He could smell fuel and hear it sizzling on the hot engine. He extricated himself from the tangled mess and jogged away from the wreckage, carrying the unconscious pilot. He heard the *whoosh* and *thump* as the chopper's fuel tanks exploded then a wall of scorching air knocked him forward onto his knees. Nia's fall had been cushioned by the long dry grass.

He cradled her head in his lap and wiped sticky blood off her face. He saw that she'd been cut on her forehead. 'Nia? Nia?'

She moved her head and blinked, trying to focus on him.

'Are you OK?' he asked.

She winced. 'What do you think? I've cracked a rib, I think. Not nice when I breathe in, but I'll live. Serves me right for crashing my own helicopter.'

'It's a bloody miracle you're alive,' Mike said. He felt anger well up inside him. 'What were you *thinking*?'

She frowned. 'I was thinking of saving your bloody life. That guy on board wanted me to swing around so he could cap you.'

Mike was still fuming. 'You could have killed yourself.'

'Well, he was about to shoot me in any case, so I didn't have much of a choice. It was my call and I bloody well took it.'

They both looked up at the sound of a motor vehicle engine starting up and revving hard.

'He's getting away!' Jed called.

'Stay down,' Mike ordered Nia, pleased that she was too dazed to refuse. Mike got to his feet and saw a sleek new black BMW emerge from the trees a hundred metres down the road and bounce over the cleared grass verge onto the tar road. Jed came running out, gun up. He fired a long burst at the car.

Mike took aim at the vehicle as well, but the white-haired man had floored the accelerator and was disappearing around a bend.

'Shit.' Jed lowered his MP5 and walked over to him. 'We just can't catch a break.'

'That guy,' Mike said, panting. 'I saw him yesterday. He's a dealer in rhino horn.'

Jed nodded. 'That's only half of it. His name's Egil Paulsen, he's a South African-born foreign fighter who served in Syria with IS. Now he runs a cell that crosses between Mozambique and here. He's linked to Suzanne Fessey . . . She's one of them as well.'

Nia had managed to stand and came to them as well, holding her side. Mike took out his phone and searched his contacts for the local section ranger. He tried dialling. 'No signal.'

Jed walked away, breathing deeply to control his anger, and at Mike's urging Nia sank down into the grass to rest. Mike watched as Jed went back to the still-burning wreckage of the Sea Hawk. He was heartened, at least, to see Franklin Washington get to his knees and stand as Jed approached him. The two Americans hugged.

The survivors took stock of their injuries, losses and their situation, then Mike suggested they start walking towards Nyalazi Gate, he and Jed supporting the groggy but now conscious Franklin between them. After fifteen minutes of slow progress, Mike heard a vehicle engine and, nerves raw, turned and held up his gun. He kept it trained on the white *bakkie* until it got closer to him and he saw with relief that it was a national parks vehicle with four armed rangers in the back.

Laying Franklin down, Jed and Mike met the vehicle, and Jed held his weapon up over his head. Mike knew the ranger driving the vehicle and spoke to him in Zulu. The men in the back, at first on guard given the devastation they had passed behind them, lowered their weapons.

'What a mess,' the ranger at the wheel said.

'Get the *okes* at Nyalazi Gate to stop a black BMW. Driver's armed and extremely dangerous,' Mike said to the man without preamble.

The ranger nodded and got on his radio.

'Let's get to the gate, we can call the police from there,' the ranger said to them once he got off the radio.

'Roger that,' Jed said. Nia, Jed and Mike climbed up into the rear cargo area of the truck and between them helped Franklin to clamber in and lie down. With the armed rangers sitting around them, Mike and Jed stood, leaning on the roof, guns ready as the driver accelerated down the road. Behind them in the distance was smoke from the burning remains of the Sea Hawk.

As the driver accelerated, Mike introduced Nia to Jed and Franklin and explained that Sergeant Munro was really Suzanne Fessey.

'So, she, these other people, they're the ones who killed your ambassador?' Nia asked Jed.

Jed glanced to Mike, then back to Nia. 'No point trying to be coy now. Yes, we believe Suzanne Fessey's husband was the suicide bomber who killed the ambassador. Egil Paulsen, who was in the chopper with you, heads a cell in Mozambique that works with or is perhaps under command of Fessey and her late husband. Franklin here's been tracking them – I just happened to be down at our embassy in Pretoria when all this blew up so I'm kind of playing catch up. Franklin knows more than me.' They looked to him.

Franklin winced, holding his ribs. 'That about covers it. Fessey, Paulsen and his crew run a side line trading in rhino horn, which helps fund their radical cause. They're like an IS splinter group. You know all you need to know about them now; they're dangerous and they're on the run and Suzanne wants her baby back.'

'Why?' Mike asked.

''Cos she's his mom,' Franklin said.

Mike looked to Jed, who shrugged. Jed either didn't know any more, or couldn't say. As much as he had warmed to Jed he was feeling less and less confident in the CIA and the United States government. 'Where's the Marine Corps? The SEAL teams? The army and the air force now?'

'We're it,' Jed said. 'South Africa doesn't want a US invasion, so we're relying on your police service now, and ourselves.'

Jed turned to look back, his thick fair hair catching the slipstream created by the speeding Toyota. He pinched the bridge of his nose with his thumb and forefinger, then took a breath to compose himself. He turned around to face forward again and took out his cell phone. Mike glanced at the screen and saw that they were once again receiving a signal. Jed immediately started making calls.

The United States of America had been humbled in South Africa. A senior diplomat had been killed and the people responsible were leaving a trail of bodies through Zululand. Jed and his compatriots had been bested this time, but looking at the CIA man's stone-set face and cold blue eyes Mike had the feeling that the terrorists had made the mistake of prodding a sleeping lion.

The beast was about to wake, but America had been defeated by rag-tag guerrilla fighters and terrorists in the past.

The ranger in the front cab leaned out of the front passenger window and called to Jed. 'News from the gate, and it's not good.'

'What's happening?' Jed asked.

'Paulsen's just been at the gate. He smashed through a barrier, guns blazing. A female ranger was hit, though it doesn't sound too serious. They called the police, but they didn't make it in time.'

'Shit.'

Mike knew that whatever was going to happen next it was a good idea for him and other innocent bystanders, such as Nia, to be out of it. He was relieved Nia was still alive and that she had survived the foolhardy but courageous stunt she had pulled with her helicopter.

Yet, as he scanned the road and horizon in front of them he thought of a young Zulu boy and two other minors who had also been dragged into this war. Could he really leave Themba and the girl with him to the jackals who were after him?

He wanted to believe Jed and Franklin and the South African Police Service could defeat the terrorists and rescue the children alive. Themba had tried to warn the Americans about the impending rocket attack on the helicopter, and had fired at the pseudo police officers, yet the gunner on the Sea Hawk had still opened fire on them. This man Paulsen and the others would kill Themba and the girl to get the baby back.

Mike had the terrible thought that if he did walk away now, as he very well should, more innocents would die. He knew this part of Africa better than any of them and he knew the parks, where Themba would most likely continue to seek refuge, as well as any ranger.

He thought of the blood-soaked earth under the body of another boy long ago and knew he could not turn away.

Chapter 18

Themba and Lerato had made themselves as comfortable as they could in the bullet-riddled caravan. Wind rushed in through the shattered rear window, but the teenagers sat close together on the double bed, with the baby, asleep again at last, between them.

Lerato had her elbows on her knees, her head in her hands. She looked up, her eyes red from crying. They had found a phone charger and power point in the van, and while Lerato's phone was now working she could not get through to her father. Her calls kept going through to voicemail. 'Themba, I don't know who to trust now.'

Themba felt the same way. His satisfaction at seeing the truck that was following them grind to a halt, its engine cooked, had been short-lived. He knew it would not take the people coming after them long to find a replacement ride.

'We have to turn ourselves in at the next stop,' she said.

He sagged. 'I can understand that.' Themba wondered if this day would end with him in a police cell.

Lerato stroked the baby's soft downy hair. 'I wonder what will happen to him?'

Themba shrugged. 'We don't know if those people are after the baby as well as the rhino horn. The way they were shooting at us, it was almost as if they didn't care if they killed him in the process.'

Lerato looked to him. 'Themba, toss the rhino horn out of the caravan. You don't want to have to explain to the police or national parks people how you got it.'

It was a tempting proposition. He was going to have a hard enough time explaining how he'd come into contact with Joseph again, and why he'd been wielding an AK-47, let alone recounting how he'd found millions of rands' worth of rhino horn and then run off with it. 'I can't just throw it away. It's evidence of a crime,' he said heavily.

'Yes, but not a crime you committed. You could go to prison for a very long time if they pin rhino horn smuggling on you.'

Themba was getting angry again. He punched the aluminium wall of the caravan. 'I have done nothing wrong.'

Lerato reached over and put a hand on his arm. 'I know that and you know that, and I'll tell the police you did nothing wrong, but your background will arouse suspicion. It won't be easy.'

Her touch calmed him. 'I feel sometimes that no matter how hard I try I can never escape my past.'

'You've done a lot already to change your life, Themba. Your friend, what's his name, the vulture man, he will speak for you.'

Themba thought of Mike. 'Can I use your phone to call him?'

'Of course you can.'

Themba felt the caravan begin to climb a steep incline, and he peeked out the broken window again.

'We're here, Hilltop Camp. Get the baby and be ready to jump out; I'll call Mike when we get clear.'

Themba shouldered their bags and opened the door of the caravan. They were slowing to a stop in the car park. Hilltop was the largest rest camp in Hluhluwe Game Reserve.

'Quickly,' he said, jumping down before the four-by-four halted. Themba knew they needed to get away before the old people got out of the vehicle, saw them, and raised the alarm. If they were going to turn themselves in, he didn't want it to be with a couple of freaked-out old people chasing them.

Themba strode alongside the van door and held up his arms. 'Pass me the baby,' he said quietly.

Lerato handed the child down to him just as the caravan came to a halt. Then she jumped down too and followed Themba as he darted around an open-sided Land Cruiser game-viewing vehicle that was parked next to them. They crouched behind the safari truck while the elderly couple got out of the Discovery.

'I'm going to the toilet,' the woman said.

'Be quick,' said her husband. He had his cell phone out and made a call. 'Hello, police? *Ja*, I want to report a terrible crime.'

A two-way radio hissed and crackled to life from inside the open vehicle they were hiding behind. 'Greg, it's Dirk, over,' a voice said from the tinny speaker somewhere in the Land Cruiser.

'Go, Dirk,' said the other voice. 'What's happening in your part of the park?'

Lerato started to stand, eager to move away, but Themba put a hand on her arm. The elderly man was telling the police about the crashed helicopter and the people following them, while the two safari guides continued their radio conversation.

'Sure, Greg, it's hectic here, *bru*. We just picked up some tourists, a Dutch couple, in the middle of the bush. They said some crazy cop lady on foot with a couple of detectives just commandeered their vehicle, man. They're heading for Hilltop now, chasing some dudes.'

'No way.'

'Yes way, *bru*. These cops sounded like, crazy. I don't know if they were for real. I radioed Hilltop to ask them to check them when they get there – they're in a blue Polo.'

Lerato grabbed his arm again and whispered fiercely, 'Themba, let's go, we'll find someone who will look after us.'

Themba peeked around the Land Cruiser. He had left the AK-47 in the van, deliberately, as he couldn't be seen strolling around Hilltop Camp with a gun. He felt naked, vulnerable, now without the rifle. 'You heard the radio – that woman and the men, they've got another car. They're coming for us.'

Themba unzipped his backpack and took out the binoculars he had found in the stolen Fortuner. He straightened and started moving around the vehicle, keeping out of sight.

'Themba, let's find someone to give ourselves up to.'

'Wait, first I must check the valley to see if it's safe.'

'Why?'

'You've seen what these people are capable of, Lerato. They'll blow this camp up, start shooting people until they get us. I don't want more blood on my hands. We have to get away from them.'

Lerato sighed, but Themba jogged off towards the reception building. He made it to a spot where he had a clear view of the approach to Hilltop Camp. He used the binoculars and scanned right to left, as Mike had taught him. Panning in the opposite direction to which one read a book, Mike said, meant one focused more and picked up little details that might otherwise be glossed over.

Lerato was behind him. She gave a short, sharp cry.

Themba looked back, his heart beating fast, but saw that she had been startled by a Samango monkey. The cheeky, blue-grey primate raised his bushy eyebrows up and down. Themba went back to checking.

Themba was confused. He wanted the sanctuary of authority to enfold him, but perhaps it was his past, his life so far, that made him realise that sometimes you had to rely on yourself, on your instincts. He saw the rolling hills of the Zulu king's hunting lands laid out before him like a rumpled green and khaki duvet tossed casually over a giant's bed. This was where he came from and this was where he would return. They needed more time, to stay a step ahead of their pursuers, and Themba knew he could only do that if they stayed in the bush. They would emerge when he was ready, somewhere Mike could find him first. Mike would understand he had done nothing wrong, no one else would.

Then Themba saw movement on the road, and re-focused the binoculars. It was a blue car. It wound its way up the snaking hill towards the camp, but stopped about half a kilometre away.

Someone got out of the car, in contravention of the park's rules. Themba saw the blue of the uniform and the brief flash of blonde hair. One of the men got out as well, and they set off, moving uphill, parallel to the road.

They were moving like soldiers advancing on the enemy, with one staying put and giving cover while the other darted forward, just as Mike had taught him to move on anti-poaching patrols. They knew what they were doing.

Themba knew then that whatever he did, the people following them would not stop until he, Lerato and the baby were dead or in their custody. The people chasing them had forced his hand; there was no time to alert the authorities now.

'What's happening?' Lerato asked.

'She is coming for us. They are leaving their new car, parked, so as not to arouse suspicion in case the rangers here have been notified. The woman and one of the men are coming first, on foot, to look for us.'

Behind them, in the car park, the elderly couple were back in their Discovery and had started the engine. Themba looked at Lerato.

She shook her head emphatically. 'No.'

'Yes, it is our only chance.'

'No, Themba, our only chance is to wait here for my father to come and get me. He *has* to return my calls soon.'

Themba looked at his cheap wristwatch. 'He should have been here two hours ago. I know how he cares for you and worries about you. Do you think he would have been this late if there was no problem? Lerato, we have to keep moving. If those people find you they will kill you.'

She looked back to the Discovery, which was trundling out of the car park towards the gate, bullet-holed caravan in tow. It pulled up at a stop sign, at an intersection about fifty metres from them.

'I'm going,' he said, but paused.

'I'm not.'

Themba looked to the vehicle. The couple had stopped to pore over a map book.

'Hurry, they're not looking.'

He darted across the road, keeping an eye on the wing mirror extensions on the four-by-four in case the woman in the passenger seat caught sight of them. He opened the caravan door, which was still unlocked. This was meant to be, he thought. Themba motioned to Lerato to come to him.

Beginning to feel desperate, Themba nodded his head and waved to her. She looked down into the valley again and Themba followed her gaze. A bend in the road shielded them from view, but Themba knew it wouldn't be long before their pursuers spotted them.

Lerato seemed to hesitate a moment longer then took a deep breath and ran, the child clutched tight to her breast. Awash with relief, Themba ushered her up and into the caravan. They were moving again. Running.

Chapter 19

Nia checked herself out of the Netcare Hospital in Umhlanga Rocks Drive and called Banger.

'Howzit, you've called Angus Greiner. I'm busy catching bad guys or watching the rugby. At the tone, do your thing.'

'It's me, I've been in hospital. Very long story. I'm OK, but I'd like to see you,' she said, then ended the call.

She'd been taken back to Umhlanga from the park in an ambulance. Nia had left two messages for him, not telling him about the crash in case he freaked, but she had been desperately hoping he would call back. It had been hours since her first call.

She waited fifteen minutes, her anger building, sitting on a park bench in her bloodstained flight suit, a bandage around her head. She tried Banger again but when the call went through to voicemail once more she dialled her tracker, John Buttenshaw, instead.

'Nia, my God, are you all right?' John said as soon as she mentioned where she was. She told him she was fine. 'I'll be there in ten minutes.'

John got there in eight and she eased her body, sore but nothing broken, into the front seat of his battered Ford Bantam *bakkie*.

Its rear side panel was dented from the fender bender John had been in on the previous morning. She told him of her eventful day and John fired a dozen questions at her, most of which she couldn't answer.

'Sheesh, Banger will want to *moer* those guys who did all this to you,' he said of the white-haired man and the other terrorists.

'He's not even picking up my calls right now. Is he out on a job?'

'We haven't had any call-outs today,' John said as he drove the short distance to Nia's apartment block. 'Want me to come up with you? I could make tea, or chicken soup.'

'I'll be fine.' She leaned over and gave him a peck on the cheek. 'Thank you, John, you're a real friend.'

'Only a pleasure. Call me if you need anything. It's no trouble at all.'

'Will do.'

Nia got out of the Ford and went into the building. She took the lift to her floor and the musty, salt-air smell from the carpet was comforting for a change, rather than annoying. It was good to be home. As much as she cared about the fate of the missing kids and the general state of mayhem that had descended on her homeland, right now she needed to lie down, and maybe have a mojito if she could be bothered fixing one. Perhaps a straight vodka would be better.

The lift doors opened and Nia went to her door. As she put her key in the lock she heard a noise, like someone yelling. She wondered if Banger was home and had the television on. But if he was, why hadn't he answered her call?

Nia opened the door and walked in. The balcony sliding doors were open, filling the lounge room with sunlight and a balmy, salty Indian Ocean breeze. Banger's blue uniform trousers and his gun belt were on the floor. That wasn't unusual; she was always picking up after him.

But then she heard the noise again.

Nia felt her chest tighten, but smiled as another explanation came to mind. She went to the master bedroom, hoping she'd catch him sitting in bed with the laptop on, watching porn. As she came to the doorway she saw a flash of movement. It was a reflection in the full-length mirror.

Framed in the glass were the wide eyes of a dark-haired girl on the bed. The girl was bouncing up and down on a naked Banger, facing away from him, towards the mirror. He had his hands on her hips and was thrusting and grunting. The girl screamed and said something in a language other than English, Italian perhaps.

'What, babe?' Banger said to the girl.

Nia walked into the room, stepping over a shirt, and, peeking around the girl, her boyfriend saw her in the mirror. The girl jumped off him and off the bed. She scrambled on the carpet, snatching up the pieces of her bikini and a wrap. Banger grabbed a sheet and held it up. Nia processed the scene. She felt goose-bumps cover her body, her blood suddenly ice cold.

'Get out.'

He held a free hand out to her. 'Babe, I can explain. I'm sorry. It meant nothing.'

'Don't you dare call me "babe".'

The girl spat something in Italian and Nia stepped aside as the other woman brushed past her, muttering something more as she tied on her bikini top. Nia heard the door slam behind her.

'Nia –'

'Shut up. Get out.'

'No, wait. I don't want that, I –'

'I don't care what you want.' She turned and walked back into the lounge, stopping to pick up the shirt and then his trousers and underpants. She went out onto the balcony and, feeling the weight of the utility belt and thinking about passers-by on the promenade that ran along Umhlanga Rocks beach, she took his nine-millimetre pistol from its holster and slipped it into one of the zippered pockets of her flight suit.

'No,' she heard Banger say behind her. 'Be reasonable. Let's talk.'

There was nothing to talk about. She threw his clothes over the railing and they fluttered as they fell.

She turned and walked past him into the bedroom. She opened the drawer that was his, took his remaining clothes in her arms and marched back into the lounge room.

'Don't be silly.' He reached for her.

'Touch me and I'll call the police.' He backed away from her and she went outside and threw the rest of his clothes into space. 'Get out,' she said again without looking at him.

'Nia, please . . .'

'Out.'

She did look back as she heard the door open, and saw that he had grabbed a towel to cover himself. He closed the door behind him.

Nia sat down on the couch and put her head in her hands. She wondered if Banger had also been having sex with this slut yesterday, when she needed him and couldn't get hold of him. The thought made her sick. Her phone rang.

'Yes.'

'Nia, howzit, it's Mike Dunn. How are you?'

How am I? 'What do you want?' She realised she sounded rude but didn't much care.

'I wanted to make sure you were all right.'

Nia swallowed hard and felt her lower lip start to tremble. She'd nearly been killed by a maniac and had crashed her own helicopter to try and kill her passenger. And Banger had fucked another woman in *their* bed. 'All right?'

'Yes. Are you still at the hospital? I was worried about you.'

She felt the tears stinging the corners of her eyes and wiped them away. 'I'm . . . I'm fine.'

'You don't sound it.'

She sniffed. *Damn Banger.* 'I'm all right. I'm out of hospital. What's happening up in the park? Have they found the kids?'

'No. That's partly why I'm calling. The Americans have arrived, in force, and they're flying all over the place in another military chopper trying to find the kids and the bad guys, but they don't know where to look. There were reports of Suzanne Fessey and two men heading to Hilltop, but they haven't been found.'

Nia thought about going to Virginia and signing out another helicopter, though she hadn't even thought about how she would tell her boss that she'd deliberately crashed the Robinson. Also, their other chopper would be on standby for car tracking, or out on a job. 'The parks people will have their airspace tightly controlled. Plus, the Americans might just shoot me out of the sky.'

'I wasn't thinking about you flying up here.'

'What, then?'

'I don't know who else I can turn to right now, or who else I could bring up to speed in a hurry about what's going on up here.'

Nia felt lethargic from shock, exhaustion and the couple of painkillers she'd taken. However, when she looked around her empty flat she decided she would rather be anywhere else than here right now. 'What do you want me to do?'

'I need someone to pick up my Land Rover from Suzanne Fessey's house.'

Nia sighed. 'I don't know.'

'It's all right,' he replied quickly. 'I'll find someone else. I know you must be hurting.'

His words, not at all meant to be unkind, scratched her. 'I'm not fucking hurting.'

'Hey, sorry.'

'Where's your vehicle?'

He explained where Fessey's house was and Nia felt hatred for the woman, criminal or terrorist or whatever she was, who had set them all on this deadly course. In her mind's eye she saw the burning, twisted carcass of the Sea Hawk again, the dead crew members. Her country was in a virtual state of war and she was angry. But the worry she felt for those three children was even greater. She wanted to finish this business as much as Mike did.

'I left the keys in the exhaust pipe when the Americans took me away to their chopper. Also, the Americans – CIA, FBI, Secret Service, whoever's running the operation now – want to talk to you and your friend the security guy. They need you to look at mug shots of terrorists.'

'I don't know where he is.'

'Well, what's his phone number? I'll pass it on to them.'

She didn't want to think about Banger. 'I'll go get your truck. See you in a few hours.' She ended the call and went out.

*

Themba leaned out of the caravan's broken window and looked for road signs. The Discovery slowed and started to turn to the right. Themba saw an Engen garage with a Wimpy on the corner. He leaned back inside. 'We've turned off the N2 to Mkhuze.'

'They're going to stay in the town, do you think?' Lerato asked.

'Nothing much here,' he replied. 'They're old, white and have a caravan. I think they're going to the Mkhuze Game Reserve. It's one of the few in this area that has camping sites. The other is Ithala, and their camping ground is at the end of a rough four-by-four trail.'

'You know a lot about national parks.'

He sat down on the bed and retrieved the last of the sandwich he had made on the move, from the caravan's cupboards and fridge. 'It was going to be my life.'

215

She reached out and put a hand on his. 'It still can be.'

He doubted it, but let it drop. 'Thanks for being brave,' he said to her.

She shrugged. 'I don't feel brave. I just want to be home and I want to know if my dad is all right. It's really weird that he hasn't called me.' Lerato had tried to reach her father several more times, but to no avail.

He squeezed her hand now. 'I'll make sure I get you back to him safely. It's been crazy these last couple of days. He could have been caught up in a police roadblock or something.'

'Can we give ourselves up when we get to Mkhuze?'

'We have to. We'll be clear of the people following us by then.' Themba had kept watch all the way from Hilltop and there had been no sign of the blue Polo so far.

She took his hand again. 'Good, I'm pleased.'

The van slewed as they rolled through bends and over a series of hills. Dust ballooned up from the gravel road and in through the broken window, making them cough. Lerato did her best to cover the child's face. It was late afternoon, turning to early evening and getting cold so she wrapped him around her front and zipped the fleece jacket she had taken from the Fortuner up over his little body. She looked out the window.

'The houses look poor here.'

'There's not a lot of employment here and there is a problem with people sneaking into the national park and setting snares to catch bush meat. They see the park as a source of income for others – for the government – but they feel they don't get enough from living near it.'

'How do you know all this stuff?' she asked.

'I learned about it on my rhino guard course. The parks board is trying to find more ways for people to benefit from living near wildlife.'

'How is that possible?'

216

'I was going to be proof of it, until all this happened,' he said.

Abruptly, the dust settled and the road became smoother.

'We're inside the park now, through the perimeter gate,' Themba said.

Lerato's eyes widened. 'Serious? They leave the road as gravel on the outside and tar it inside the park? No wonder the local people are resentful.'

'Yes. We will be at the boom gate soon, where the people will pay entrance fees, and the camping ground is next to that. We must be ready to move.'

'Why don't we give ourselves up at the gate?'

It was a good question, he had to admit, but something inside him was not sure about surrendering just yet. He thought up an answer. 'There will only be a junior person there; they will not know what to do with us. We could be there for hours and there will be nowhere to feed or change the baby, or for us to sleep if we are stuck here tonight.'

'Then we will turn ourselves in at the camping ground, right, Themba?'

'Yes. Let the old people get in first and we will sneak out of the van and find someone quietly. This couple have been through too much today.'

'So have we!'

They waited with their packs by the rear window of the van, ready to jump out in case some nosy security guard, alerted by the day's events, decided to search inside. As it was, they moved through uneventfully after a few minutes.

Themba felt Lerato's body pressed closed to him in the dark as they pulled into the camping ground. Once inside, the elderly couple did a couple of circuits of the camp, looking for a good spot to park. 'Get ready,' he whispered.

'But we're surrendering.'

'Just in case.'

Finally, the Discovery stopped. All that was left of the sun was a red glow through the dust in the western sky – the couple had only just made the dusk curfew.

As the car stopped Themba opened the caravan door. He didn't want the couple to see them; if he was going to give himself up it would be to a national parks official. He stepped down and motioned for Lerato to follow. At that second the passenger's side door of the Discovery opened and the elderly woman alighted. She pointed and said something that Themba didn't catch, then he noticed she was gesturing to the ablutions block. She took a few quick steps away then turned back when her husband called out something to her. As she turned her head she saw Themba and screamed.

He put his hands up. 'It's all right.'

The woman, though, leapt back into the cab of the four-by-four.

'Quickly,' Themba said to Lerato, who stepped down.

Themba walked slowly towards the car. As he did so he heard the engine start again. The woman's hand appeared out of the passenger side window and in it was a small-calibre pistol. She should have declared it at the boom gate and had it secured in a sealed security bag but no doubt after the day's events the couple probably wanted to have their handgun handy.

'No!' he yelled.

The car and caravan pulled away just as Lerato's feet hit the ground. There was the crack of a gunshot as the woman fired blindly, pointing backwards, and Lerato screamed.

'Run,' Themba said. He ushered Lerato and the baby in front of him and ran after them towards the tree line at the edge of the camp. He heard two more shots behind him and felt a bullet whiz past his left ear. He tensed as he ran, waiting for the impact, and a small part of his mind wondered what it would be like. At least he was between the woman with the gun and Lerato.

When they reached the trees Themba paused. The shooting

had stopped and the engine noise from the vehicle was fading as the couple drove back out the gate of the camping ground.

'Oh God, Themba, what will we do now? Everyone's trying to kill us! Why did she have to shoot at us?'

Themba caught his breath. 'Think what they saw today, what they went through. There were people shooting at them as well as us. They must have thought we were those same people.'

The camping ground was empty; it was outside school holidays. They walked around the stands and Lerato took the baby into the ablutions block and gave him a bath and changed him as best she could.

Themba stuck his head through the door of the ladies' room. 'Have a shower, if you like. You can leave the baby with me.'

'Thanks, I think I will. I feel awful,' Lerato said. She brought the baby, freshly clean and smelling of hand soap, and passed it to Themba.

He sat on the *stoep*, waiting for someone to come. If there was an attendant working at the camping ground then he or she hadn't come looking for them. Perhaps, he mused, they had run at the sound of gunfire, or hitched a lift with the elderly couple.

Themba nursed the infant, enjoying its warmth against his chest. He, too, needed a wash. He wondered who would come, armed parks rangers or police. Themba shivered; it could be the blonde woman and her male accomplices who showed up first.

Carrying the baby, he went for a walk and found an information board with a map of Mkhuze Game Reserve pinned to it behind glass. He had been here before, but he didn't know the park intimately. Putting the baby down on the grass, he looked around for a rock, found one, and hefted it. Funny, he thought, how he had transitioned from a one-time car thief to someone who now felt as if he was committing a mortal sin by breaking a window to steal a map that might save his life and the lives of two innocents. He smashed the glass and took down the map.

Mkhuze was home to some dangerous species of wildlife, including the elusive leopard and the irascible black rhino. Also, the bush here was different from where they had just been, in the Hluhluwe–iMfolozi Park. There it was open grassland sliced with deep, dark, dangerous river valley. Here in Mkhuze, however, the red soil nourished thick, dense undergrowth. The black rhino loved these thickets of thorn and the leopard had plenty of trees in which to hoist its kills at night and savour cool breezes by day.

Keeping a watchful eye on the baby, Themba scanned the map. The other distinctive feature of Mkhuze was its plethora of hides, well-constructed viewing areas overlooking waterholes and the big Nsumo Pan. These would be good places to hole up overnight and they would be safe, dry and relatively warm. They would have to be out before first light, though, when early-rising tourists or an attendant might arrive to view game or clean up.

Themba heard a car's engine and saw the sweep of headlights coming up the access road to the camping ground. He stood, scooping up the baby, and darted into the ladies' room.

Lerato was out of the shower and doing up her blouse. 'Themba!' She turned her back to him.

'Sorry, but there's someone coming. We need to get out of here.'

'Just let me get dressed.'

'No, I mean, hurry. Grab your clothes.'

She snatched up her things, clearly annoyed, and followed him out. The baby had fallen asleep. Hefting him up on one hip, Themba took Lerato's hand and ran back to the trees where they had been hiding. Looking back, Themba saw it was not one vehicle but two, a black, low-slung sedan followed by a national parks *bakkie*. In the back of the truck were four armed rangers.

The sedan stopped and a door opened. A man got out, but Themba couldn't see him clearly as he was silhouetted in the headlights.

The rangers jumped down out of their truck and fanned out, looking around them. A man in a national parks uniform got out of the front of the truck and joined the first man in front of his sedan.

'This is where the gunshots were reported,' the ranger said.

The *bakkie*'s lights were shining on the car now, and Themba saw it was a late model BMW sedan.

The solo man walked away from his car, into the cone of light cast by a lamppost in the camping ground. He had striking white hair, the same as the man in the helicopter that had been searching for them in iMfolozi.

Themba felt Lerato's hand clutch hard at his arm. 'The number plate,' she said, 'that's my dad's car.'

Chapter 20

Mike and Nia drove through the night. She had collected him at the Nyalazi Gate to Hluhluwe–iMfolozi Park and he had driven from there.

Mike had spent a frustrating afternoon at the gate, on the periphery of the action. Jed's South African police liaison contact in Durban had arranged for the CIA men to ride along in a South African police vehicle, but there had been no room for Mike. In the gate office he had monitored the progress of the search as best he could by listening in on the national parks' radio system. It was in desperation that he'd asked Nia to fetch his truck, rather than hitchhiking back to Durban.

He felt bad, now, dragging her back into this nightmare, but at the same time pleased he was back in the hunt. No sooner had he taken over the wheel than she had fallen asleep in the passenger seat of the Defender. She was cut and bruised, and while he had seen her injuries and helped attend to them at the scene of her helicopter crash, he could see as soon as he looked into her eyes that she was carrying more wounds than just the physical ones.

Mike had wondered if it was a delayed reaction, a deeper level of shock seeping into her. He glanced at her now. Occasionally she jerked in her sleep, as if having a bad dream. She had been what he had come to know as her normal feisty self when she had walked away from her crash, but the woman who had greeted him at the Nyalazi Gate had looked more than tired or battered: she'd looked sad.

He had thought, for a moment, as she got out of his Land Rover and greeted him, that she'd been almost about to cry. Again, it was an understandable reaction, but when he had thanked her for collecting his car and asked if there was anything she needed, she had fobbed him off with a curt, 'Sleep.'

Her whole body was racked by a spasm, as though she'd imagined falling over in a dream, and she sat upright in the passenger seat. 'Where . . .'

'We're on the way to Mkhuze. Not far now.'

'OK,' she said.

'There were reports of shots fired in the camping ground there, and the gate attendant reported seeing a shot-up caravan being towed by a Discovery. I called Jed while I was waiting for you and he's waiting for another helicopter. The South African police seem to be trying to keep him out of the action.'

'Great,' Nia said, 'more gunfire.'

'There are rangers out looking for the kids. Hopefully we'll have them soon. You looked like you were having a bad dream.'

She peered out of the side window, then back at him. 'It was no dream. It was reality.'

'What was?'

She shook her head. 'Nothing. None of your business, anyway.'

'OK.'

He drove on. She was fully awake now, but silent. Her phone beeped and she looked at a message, then tapped the screen. 'I'm forwarding Angus Greiner's contact details to you.'

Mike felt his phone vibrate in his pocket as the message came through. He recalled that the cocky young security guard, her boyfriend, had introduced himself by his nickname, Banger, and that Nia had used that name when referring to him as well. He wondered what had changed.

'He must be worried about you,' he probed.

'Huh.' She flicked her head and brushed a persistent strand of black hair out of her eye.

'Fight?'

She stared at him until he looked back to the road ahead. 'I get it, none of my business.'

'Exactly.' She yawned and rubbed her face. 'You're old to be a wildlife researcher.'

'Thank you.'

She smiled again. 'I'm just stating a fact. Have you always worked with vultures, like, since varsity?'

He normally avoided talking about his past, for example when research students from overseas started asking questions around the campfire, over drinks. But he was pleased Nia was at least talking, and he wanted to know more about her, so it was only fair.

'No. Like most guys my age I went into the army after school. I was born in Rhodesia – Zimbabwe – but my parents moved south in the seventies so I did my national service in the South African Army.'

'Were you in the war?'

He nodded. 'Yes, in South West Africa, Namibia. I did seven years in military intelligence, on the border, in the Caprivi Strip.'

'I thought you guys only had to do a couple of years of something. My parents went overseas, to Australia. I was a baby.'

'But you came back?'

'I was born here. I'm African, but hey, I am asking the questions here.'

He lifted one hand off the wheel in a gesture of submission.

'OK, OK. We could elect to serve longer, fulltime, and therefore avoid having to go back year after year to do our annual call-ups. The work was interesting.'

'Did you kill anyone?'

'Most people are too polite to ask that question.'

'That's not a category I fit into.'

He could see that. 'No. Not then, anyway.'

'Ooh, more mystery. You killed people later? What were you, a mercenary or something before you became a fulltime twitcher?'

'I was disillusioned, that's what I was. There were people all around me in the army making money out of the illegal trade in wildlife. The defence force was a party to the slaughter of rhino and elephants in Angola and parts of Namibia, and shipping out the horn and ivory in military convoys.'

Nia swivelled in her seat and rested her arm on the console box between them. It looked like she wanted a diversion from whatever was on her mind. He really didn't like talking about this part of his life, but he didn't want to see her go back to staring out the side window, looking like she was about to cry. 'What did you do about it?'

'You're assuming I did anything at all.'

'You don't strike me as the sort of man who'd turn his back or put his head in the sand if he came across people doing the wrong thing. Nor are you the sort who'd be cheating.'

The last comment was strange, and he wondered where it came from, but he drew a breath and told his story.

'I tried to raise awareness of the illegal trade through official channels, but it was covered up. Senior officers promised investigations, but they either never happened or they were whitewashes. In frustration, I went to the press, but because everything was censored in those days nothing really changed. All that happened was that I got a name as a troublemaker.'

'Did you get in trouble?'

'I was passed over for promotion. I was never going to progress far, but speaking out put the brakes on any career I might have had in the army. I didn't care, as by that time I'd had enough and I'd lost faith in what we were fighting for.'

'What did you do after the army?'

'I joined the Natal Parks Board and worked in conservation and eventually I went to university and studied zoology. I did my PhD in birds of prey – martial eagles. It could have been a dream job, but it turned into a nightmare.'

'I'm intrigued.'

Her eyes widened with anticipatory glee. Those eyes were, he saw as he allowed himself to be distracted from the road for another instant, quite beautiful, almond shaped, with dark pupils. 'I wanted to do more than just research or study birds and wildlife. I wanted to stop the trade in endangered animals. I joined the investigations branch of the parks board.'

'Like wildlife cops?'

'Pretty much,' he said. 'Rhinos and elephants were still in desperate trouble, mainly outside South Africa at the time, in the neighbouring countries, which were becoming independent, though in some cases still in a mess.'

'But what could you do about it from inside apartheid South Africa?'

'Have you ever heard of Operation Lock?'

She shook her head. She would have been a toddler at the time, he realised.

'Prince Bernhard of the Netherlands came to Africa in 1987 and was appalled at the plight of our wildlife. He was the head of what's now known as the World Wide Fund for Nature, the old WWF, but he wanted to do more. He bankrolled a secret program to target poaching gangs in Africa and in the countries where the rhino horn and elephant ivory were destined for – Operation Lock. The WWF denied any involvement.

'A mercenary firm made up of ex Special Air Service operatives was recruited to do a lot of the dirty work. They also engaged some local South Africans who knew how the wildlife trade worked on the ground.'

'You?'

'Yes, I was one of them.' The events of those two years rolled through his mind as he stared ahead at the road.

'And?'

She wasn't going to let up now that he had opened the door on his past. 'It was a war, but this time I ended up on the front line. I began by gathering intelligence, running a network of informers, but after a while I was spending more and more time in the field, going undercover and posing as a rhino horn seller. I felt like I was finally achieving something, but our methods . . .'

Nia didn't say anything now. He drew a breath, then continued. 'Our methods weren't always legal. At the time I justified my actions by telling myself that what we were doing was saving animals from extinction.'

'Everyone knows it's a dirty business, poaching, and there's no shortage of people on Facebook every day calling for poachers to be shot on sight, like they do in Zimbabwe, or have their testicles cut off and so forth.'

He'd seen what she was talking about. He used Facebook and Twitter to keep his organisation's supporters up to date with his vulture research, but too much of the commentary on social media was driven by armchair conservationists who didn't really know what they were talking about. It was one thing to call for poachers in national parks to be shot on sight – and he wasn't against that – but it was another thing to be the one pulling the trigger.

'What are you thinking about? You've got a faraway look in your eyes. Are you OK?'

He blinked, and focused again on the road. He couldn't look at her as he spoke in a soft monotone. 'Operation Lock was canned – the press found out about it and wild rumours started circulating that we were working for South African intelligence, trying to destabilise African countries. That was nonsense, but we were out of business. I wanted to do more, to stop poaching, so I moved back to my home country, now Zimbabwe, and got a job in anti-poaching on privately owned land near Gonarezhou National Park in the southeast. There was a war going on there, with animals being slaughtered and I wanted to take the lessons I'd learned in Operation Lock and apply them there. I started running a network of informers again. One of my assets – a person, I mean – delivered some good intelligence on a poaching gang in Mozambique, across the border from Gonarezhou. I was part of a covert team that crossed into Mozambique, illegally. My man was a Shangaan schoolteacher, and a poaching syndicate operated from his village. They were his neighbours, and he taught some of their children.'

'What happened?'

'My team went in and, using information from the schoolteacher – Abraham was his name – we ambushed the poaching gang and took them out.'

'Killed them.'

He swallowed. 'All four of them. They were armed with a couple of AK-47s, tomahawks to cut off rhino horns, knives.'

'Did they fire on you first?'

'No.'

'Two guns, you said.'

He nodded. 'We set an ambush. The poachers were moving right to left, along a track in front of us. I was on the right of the line. The guys with the AKs were in the front, and when they had gone past our guys to the left we opened fire. There was so much noise, and light from the muzzle flashes, all you did was look for a target and fire. When it was done we got up and checked them.'

In his nightmares he saw the bodies, riddled with holes, he and his men standing over them, photographing them.

'Go on,' she said, filling the void.

'The two on the right, the ones in front of me and my partner, were just kids, sixteen and eighteen as it turned out. The youngest was at the end of the line, where I was firing. I killed a child, Nia, an unarmed teenager.'

'You weren't to know in the dark that the other two didn't have guns. Besides, if the Zimbabwean national parks guys had come across them in Gonarezhou they would have done the same thing. It's happening in South Africa's national parks all the time these days.'

He'd used the same justifications himself many times over the years. Mike clung to the steering wheel as if it were a lifeline.

'That wasn't the only time I was involved in a contact,' he said, 'but it's the dead eyes of that sixteen-year-old boy that will stay with me forever.'

'Did you stop your undercover operations after that?'

'No.' That shamed him as well. The remorse had come later, delayed, in the form of nightmares. He'd always been a drinker, but had sought more and more refuge in whisky to try and self-medicate. At the time, he had felt elated, the adrenaline high of participating in and surviving combat.

'You did good work, Mike. Hard, dirty work, but you said it yourself, it's a war, this fight against poachers, and the guys on the other side have no qualms about killing. How did you end up back in South Africa?'

'Eventually I had to leave Zimbabwe. A local politician had me in his sights after I killed a poacher relative of his. I came back down south and went back to work with the parks board, in game capture. I tried to put the killings behind me. I married a lovely girl I knew from school, Tracy, and we had a beautiful daughter, but I couldn't let go of the past. I drank too much, had too many nightmares. I was unsettled and spent too much time away from Tracy and Debbie. I lost my job thanks to affirmative action, like a lot of people, but I lost my family because I pushed them out of my life. Tracy tried to help me, but I kept running away to the bush to try and heal myself. In the end it didn't work and she found someone else.'

'Wow, I'm sorry to hear that. How did you get into your current job?'

'An old friend working for the NGO bumped into me in a bar and offered me a job.' The man had probably save his life. 'I found that working in the field, alone but with a purpose instead of just hiding, was what I needed to get my head right again.'

'What happened to the schoolteacher? Abraham, was it?'

Mike took another deep breath. He wanted to lie to her, or tell her it wasn't his fault.

'Mike?'

He felt the nausea rising up in him, the stinging pricks of tears threatening to surface. He didn't want to cry in front of Nia. 'They cut Abraham's head off.'

'What? Who did?'

'No arrests were ever made, but the word was that it was the two brothers of one of the poachers, uncles of the dead sixteen-year-old.' He looked to her, quickly, then back to the road after he saw the shock on her face. 'We killed a father and son, and their relatives hacked off Abraham's head with a machete.'

'My God, that's horrible. Who would do such a thing?'

'The same sort of person who would shoot a sixteen-year-old in cold blood.'

She had no reply to that. He should never have told her. What was done was done, and he was stupid to have thought that talking to a virtual stranger about it would be of any help. If he'd wanted to open up to her to get her talking, perhaps

230

build some rapport with her, the opposite seemed to have just happened.

Nia stayed silent as he drove on through the night.

'That's what this is all about, isn't it? A lost boy,' she said eventually.

*

Themba looked for the Southern Cross in the stars and worked out that they were still heading east, deeper into Mkhuze Game Reserve, away from the campsite and the eMshopi entrance gate.

He could tell Lerato felt deflated, and it wasn't just from the trauma of the day and the exhaustion of picking her way through the dense bush. She also looked like someone who had lost all hope.

'We have to keep moving,' Themba said gently.

Lerato started to cry and that set the baby off. Themba went to her and wrapped his arms around both of them. 'Please don't cry.'

'I can't help it. I'm worried about my dad and I'm terrified, Themba. I can't go on. I just want this to end. Maybe there's some rational explanation why that guy's driving my dad's car.' Lerato kept sobbing. 'Or maybe he killed my father.'

Themba held her tighter. He was scared too, and clinging to her helped.

A wood owl made its *who, who, who are you* call and Themba checked the stars again. He broke away from Lerato and took out his torch and checked the map. The kwaMalibaba hide was closest to them, but it would be logical for searchers to check it. If they carried on a few more kilometres, heading east, they would reach the tar road that ran south from the main Mantuma Camp. The ground rose up to the Lebombo lookout and the climb would be hard on Lerato, but after that they could descend to the kuMasinga hide. It would be a safe place for them to sleep, and there were toilets.

After two hours Themba was feeling like every step was the hardest physical action he'd taken in his life. Lerato offered to take the baby back from him. She, too, was slowing down, but she insisted. They made it to the tar road and Themba turned left. His plan was to walk north until they came to the Lebombo viewing point then carry on a further thousand paces. From there, if he turned right, once more heading east and downhill, he calculated they would eventually cross the access road that led to kuMasinga. There were no helicopters in the air, and no sounds of vehicles driving up and down the road. No tourists would be out at this time of night, but there might be national parks rangers on patrol after hours.

Lerato's spirits and energy levels seemed to lift a little as they walked on the smooth tar road.

'You'll like this place, the hide we're going to,' Themba said.

'Are you sure about that?'

Themba gave a little laugh at her sarcasm – at least she could still make a joke. 'I've seen white rhino there, kudu, baboons, all sorts of animals.'

'Are all rhinos dangerous, like the one that charged us?' she sniffed.

'Not the white ones, so much,' he replied.

'I didn't know they were different colours,' Lerato said.

'They're not.' He stopped and they rested a moment. 'They have different-shaped mouths, which is one way to tell them apart, but Mike told me another. The black rhino is like a black woman; her calf, her baby, walks behind her, similar to the way a Zulu woman carries her child on her back, and like you carry the baby. The white rhino's baby moves in front of her, like a white woman pushing a pram.'

Lerato gave a small laugh. 'Speaking of babies on backs, this one is killing me. I don't know how my mother coped with me. I was a little fatty.'

'You're not fat.'

'No, but I was when I was a baby. You should see pictures of me.'

He smiled. He had no photos of himself as a child; his family had been too poor to own a camera or have pictures made.

'Hey, I need a toilet break.' She undid the knotted wrap and Themba picked up the sleeping baby and held him in his arms, looking down at its now peaceful face.

'Don't go far,' he said.

'Oh, don't worry, I won't. I'm too scared. You watch the baby, in case he wakes – you know how much he likes to explore.'

Themba gently rocked the baby in his arms and turned his back to give Lerato more privacy. He heard the rustle of dry leaves and branches as she made her way behind a thicket.

'I think I'm hallucinating,' she said from the bushes.

He resisted the urge to look around. 'What do you mean?'

'I'm so hungry I think I'm going crazy; I'm smelling things.'

'Like what?' he asked.

'It's the funniest thing. I can smell hot buttered popcorn. Is that weird or what?'

Themba shook his head. 'You're . . .' He was about to tell Lerato that she was right, she was going crazy, when something Mike had told him, in a lecture, came back to him. 'Lerato, are you decent?'

'No, not yet, and don't you come over here. I'm not sharing my popcorn with you for anything. I'm not imagining it, I can really smell it now.'

Themba turned. He had to get her away from here. He looked at the AK-47, which he'd put on the ground when they'd stopped. To pick it up and use it he would have to put the baby down on the ground. Fear paralysed him. 'Hurry.'

'OK, keep your pants on,' Lerato said. 'I've got mine on now.'

Themba eyed the rifle. He set the sleeping baby down on the dry grass and snatched up the AK. He turned and ran to where

Lerato had disappeared into the bush. She had gone even further than he thought, to avoid embarrassment, he guessed.

He saw the branches move in front of him and Lerato appeared, wide-eyed at the sight of him holding up the assault rifle.

'What's wrong? What did you do with the baby?'

He ignored her questions. He sniffed the air and caught the unmistakable odour.

'You smell the popcorn, right?'

He put the index finger of his left hand to his lips and whispered: 'Hurry, the baby's back there. We have to get out of here, quickly.'

'What is it? What's that popcorn smell?'

'It's . . .' The rasping sound, like a saw cutting wood, silenced both of them.

Themba spun on his heel and felt Lerato press her body into his back. He saw the movement in the grass, the silhouette low, sleek and dappled.

'Leopard.'

'Oh my God,' Lerato said.

'Hush.'

Mike Dunn had amused and surprised his group of student rhino guards when he'd given them a lecture on the most elusive of predators, the leopard. Glands on their rump, he said, excreted a scent that smelled like hot buttered popcorn. By rubbing against a tree or bush a male leopard used the scent to mark its territory.

'The baby,' Lerato hissed.

Themba drew a deep breath. 'Stay here.'

He started to walk back to where he'd left the baby and it felt like his feet were encased in lumps of cement. His heart was beating like a shebeen's bass speakers. Themba gripped the AK-47's pistol grip and stock so hard it hurt his fingers. He heard movement behind him.

'I told you to stay back there.'

'I told you to look after the baby,' she hissed back to him. 'You know how he crawls away.'

Themba heard another growl and froze. It was warning him to stay back, not to approach. Mike had explained that the big cats would give warnings and it was a stupid man who ignored them.

'Stay here.'

'No.'

He exhaled. She was so stubborn. He took a step forward, then another, and brushed a thorny branch away with the barrel of the rifle. Themba remembered the compact torch he'd taken from the Fortuner. He took it out from his pocket with his left hand and flicked it on.

Themba cast the beam ahead as he walked slowly closer. He saw movement, then two yellow eyes burned from the darkness. He stopped.

Lerato screamed. 'It's got the baby.'

Themba played the beam down. The leopard was standing over the infant, which had woken up and now started to cry. The leopard lowered its head and sniffed the wailing being. Trying to still his shaking hands, Themba held both the torch and the stock of the rifle in his left hand and raised the rifle. He took aim.

'Shoot it,' Lerato said.

They were still twenty metres from the cat, at night, and its head was low as it continued to inspect the strange creature in front of it. Themba was worried he would hit the child. He raised the barrel, aiming just above the leopard, flicked the selector to automatic and pulled the trigger.

A burst of five rounds erupted from the barrel, which, true to form, pulled high and to the right as Themba fired. The baby gave a violent start at the noise and began to shriek, and the leopard turned in a single bound and raced away into the dark.

Lerato ran past Themba to the baby and scooped it up, holding it close to her chest. Tears rolled down her cheeks and she muffled the infant's cries with her breasts. Themba jogged to them and wrapped his arms around both of them.

'Take me home, Themba, please take us home,' Lerato sobbed.

He wanted, more than anything else in the world, to make this nightmare end. Themba knew, however, that the loud fusillade would have alerted anyone following them to their position.

And so, he realised with an almost crippling despair, they had to keep running.

Chapter 21

Nia and Mike drove through Mkhuze Game Reserve, scanning the bush on either side of the road for movement.

So far they had seen genet and civet cats, a fat python sluggishly sliding across the road, nyala and a quick glimpse of a white rhino, but no sign of the fugitive youngsters.

When they arrived at Mkhuze Mike had been put through to the park warden via the gate guard's radio. They had learned that there were already rangers out looking for Themba and Lerato and the missing baby. There was a police detective with them as well, apparently. The warden had given permission for Mike and Nia to join the search and to drive around in the dark, which was forbidden for regular visitors to the park. Mike told Nia that he knew Mkhuze well, as he regularly came to the park to count vulture nests and check for eggs and chicks.

Nia felt bad, on reflection, about the way she had spoken to Mike. 'I'm sorry for what I said, the way I acted, earlier.'

He shrugged off her apology, eyes still scanning the bush. 'It's none of my business and I didn't mean to pry into your personal life.'

'You just caught me at a bad time. I found out today my boyfriend, Angus, has been cheating on me.'

He looked to her. 'I'm sorry.'

She smiled, but it didn't last. 'He is a jerk. But then, I've been thinking about it. I can be very demanding. I'm always correcting him, other people. He complains about me being too critical.'

'Is that enough of a reason to sleep with someone else?'

She sagged in the seat. 'I know. I mean, I thought we – well, I thought we were getting on OK.'

What she was really thinking about was their sex life. He was good in bed, and a beautiful specimen of a man, but lately she'd found herself wanting more from him, more conversation. When they had time off together he would sit in front of the television watching rugby, or golf, or cricket, and they would go for hours not talking to each other. As nice as the other night had been, she had once more been left to take care of her own pleasure after he'd fallen asleep. That wasn't a first. She realised, if she was honest with herself, that there had been signs for some time that their relationship would not last forever.

She didn't always want to talk, but at other times she longed for someone she could converse with about politics or religion or even helicopters. She had always been a tomboy growing up, but she also loved the ballet. She'd taken Banger once and he'd made snide jokes about the male dancers. She'd been red-faced by the end of the performance, embarrassed by his behaviour and angry. Nia had never suggested they go together again.

'You seem very bright,' Mike said, then looked away, out the window, as if regretting the remark.

'I read a lot. I went to university, studied law, because that's what my parents wanted, but by the time I graduated I realised there was no way I wanted to be a lawyer. I'd started flying for fun and I loved that more than anything else in the world.'

'You'd make more money as a lawyer.'

'Says the man with the PhD who works for a wildlife charity. I'm guessing you could make more money as a lecturer.'

He looked back at her and it was his turn to smile. 'I don't like classrooms.'

'I'd feel the same way about a courtroom, or an office.'

'Are you going to keep flying forever?'

She shrugged. 'Forever's a long time. I'm enjoying life for now. Part of me thinks it would be nice to settle down with someone and have a couple of kids.'

'But part of you dreads it.'

She was surprised. 'Hey, how did you know that?'

'I like being out in the bush by myself, not wondering if someone at home is missing me, or being faithful.'

'Like one of your birds?'

'Oh, they're far more settled and domesticated than I am.'

She laughed. He was a nice guy, and quite handsome, in a rugged, rough sort of way. He needed a new haircut, and khaki didn't suit his colouring, though she guessed neutral tones were needed for walking in the bush.

She had been with a man much older than herself, once. Roger had been a client, a wealthy merchant banker from Johannesburg. He'd flown to Durban and arranged for a chartered helicopter to take him to a friend's fiftieth birthday party on a golf estate on the north coast. He was only in the province for a day so his time was short, although his cash clearly wasn't. On the twenty-minute flight he had flirted with Nia and told her, straight out, that he thought she was beautiful. She had laughed off his advances but throughout the party, as Nia had sat in the shade of a tree by her helicopter, waiting to fly him back again, he had used the contact number she'd given him to send her SMSs from his phone.

Roger was funny and smart as well as flirty, and she had replied, teasing him about his age. He was also fifty, and she had been just twenty-eight at the time.

On the flight home, very tipsy, he had told her that he hadn't meant any offence. She had laughed and they had talked about their families – he'd said he was divorced – and their shared loves, flying and, surprisingly, the ballet.

'Any man would be lucky to have you as a girlfriend,' Mike said, breaking into her thoughts.

Nia decided to confide something of what she'd been thinking. 'Before Angus I was going out with a banker from Johannesburg. He used to fly down to Durban to see me. I liked him a lot. He was much older than me.'

'And much more married.'

'How did you guess?' she asked.

'You dumped him for a security guard.'

She leaned over and punched him in the arm. 'Don't be a snob, penniless wildlife dude.'

'Ow!'

'Maybe I dumped him because he was an old man, though probably younger than you.'

He looked to her. 'Don't be ageist.'

'Nah, you're right. I didn't leave him because he was old – my dad's actually twenty years older than my mom – I left him because he was married. He lied to me. I flew up to Johannesburg one time, to surprise him, made an appointment to see him using a fake name, and when I showed up at the investment bank at Melrose Arch he was kissing his wife goodbye on the street outside; they'd just come back from lunch.'

'Ouch.'

'Yip, double ouch.'

Suddenly Mike pulled over and turned off the engine.

'What is it?' Nia asked. She hadn't seen anything.

He held up a hand. 'Sounded like a burst of gunfire.'

'I couldn't hear anything over the noise of this Land Rover's engine.'

Mike put a finger to his lips, then opened his door and got out. He stood, mouth open, and looked around into the darkness. Nia got out and joined him.

Mike got back into the Land Rover and turned on his satellite navigation device. Nia returned to the passenger seat. 'Pass me the map, please.'

'Sure.'

When the sat nav picked up signal he used it to work out his exact location, then cross-referenced it with the map of Mkhuze Game Reserve. Nia watched as he ran his finger in a line from the camping ground, where the park warden said the fugitive children had been reported by the couple with the caravan, through their current location on the road.

'He's heading to kuMasinga.'

'That sounds familiar. But I've only been to this park a couple of times.' Nia had last been there with her parents a few years ago when they had returned to South Africa on a holiday to spend time with her.

'It's the most popular viewing hide in the park.'

'Oh, right, the one on the stilts that hangs over the waterhole.' She remembered glimpsing a black rhino there, the first she'd ever seen.

'Yes, that's the one. I'll radio headquarters.'

'They're going there for shelter?' Nia asked.

'I'd say so; it's a good place for them to spend the night, and safer than sleeping in the bush, but they'd need to be clear of the place by shortly after dawn, when the first tourists on morning game drives make a beeline for the hide.'

'You said this Themba was a car thief before he went straight?' Mike nodded.

'Might be a good place for him to find a new set of wheels, once the tourists are in the hide.'

'Good thinking. People often leave their vehicles unlocked at places like that. Let's go.'

Nia felt the adrenaline pulsing through her veins as Mike took off, at speed. The excitement of the chase dispelled her tiredness, and the ache in her head and ribs had dulled to a throb.

Mike took his phone out of his pocket and handed it to Nia. 'Could you please call the park warden? His name's Jonas. His number's the last one I dialled. Tell him where we're heading.'

She did as he asked and relayed Jonas's message, that he would send his patrol, accompanied by the police detective coordinating the search, to the hide. 'Jonas says it sounds like we're closer, so he told you to be careful, as we'll probably get there first. He's asking if you want to wait for back-up.'

'Tell him no thanks,' Mike said, focusing on the road ahead as he sped through the park. The risk of them hitting a nocturnal animal was high. 'I know the kid and I want to approach him first if we find him.'

'OK.' Nia relayed the message and ended the call.

They headed north, then made a tight turn back to the south-east when they were almost at the main Mantuma rest camp. The Land Rover roared through the night and Mike had to brake hard to miss a spotted hyena. 'I hate driving this fast after dark in the bush.'

She gripped the dashboard in front of her. She'd done some crazy low-level flying sometimes, pursuing car thieves, but she thought this was perhaps scarier. Nia loved the thrill of the chase. It was the same in the relationships she'd had in her life; she'd been most interested, most stimulated in the early court-ship stages.

She was intrigued by Mike Dunn. He was university educated, but he'd turned his back on academia and teaching and spent his life living on a pittance in the bush. She admired his passion, if not his business sense. Still, she mused, opportunities for a middle-aged white zoologist in South Africa would be pretty limited. He was doing what he loved for the love of it and not for money, and in that respect, despite their age difference, they were very much alike.

'You should stay in the car when we get to the hide.'

'No. I'm coming with you.'

'Themba knows me, but he's armed and he'll be jumpy. He's been on the run a while now and he'll be tired, confused. Just stay behind me.'

'I've got a gun.'

'I thought you said you didn't carry a weapon?'

'I don't, usually. It's my ex-boyfriend's. I threw his uniform off the balcony of my apartment and I didn't want some tourist below getting brained by his pistol.'

Mike smiled, then returned his concentration to the road. 'I wouldn't want to get on your bad side.'

'Then don't tell me what to do. You owe me, going to fetch your vehicle then coming all the way back up here. I'm as involved in getting these kids back as you are.'

Nia took Banger's pistol out of the pocket of her flight suit. She knew enough about firearms to be able to remove the magazine, clear the breach and then reload it. The action was smooth. Banger was a gun nut and cleaned his weapon every day. She felt a twinge of sadness, followed by anger.

'We're nearly there,' Mike said.

She cradled the pistol in her lap and felt a chilly shot of fear mix with the adrenaline.

Mike took the turnoff to the kuMasinga hide car park. He drove to the end of the access road, switched off the engine and they both got out. Mike stood there, his rifle in his hands, cocked his head and listened. A hyena gave its eerie whooping call somewhere in the dark.

'Stay behind me,' he said quietly. 'Kids with AKs aside, there could be leopard drinking at the waterhole at this time of night.'

'Don't run, right?'

Mike nodded. They set off, Nia following close behind him. She cocked the pistol and was careful to keep it pointed down. She had walked in the bush before, but never at night. No one in their right mind did this. She felt the downy hair on her arms stand on end.

The moon was full and bright, a poacher's moon, people called it. Mike moved off the track that led through the bush to the hide, stopped and studied the ground in front of him.

'Someone crossed the track here,' he said quietly.

'So?'

'People don't walk through the bush here, they stick to the pathway. This person's come from the left, through the trees and crossed over. Looks like a woman or a girl's shoe.'

Nia gripped the pistol tighter in her hand and Mike moved slowly through the bush. 'Can you see any more tracks?'

'He was careful. He would have jumped across the track, but she left half a footprint. They're here.'

Mike retraced his steps to the pathway and, rifle raised and at the ready, moved forward again. 'Themba! It's Mike, Mike Dunn. Come out. You're not in trouble.'

Past Mike's broad shoulders Nia could see the wooden structure of the hide. Beyond and on either side of it moonlight glittered on the still, steely-coloured water. A baboon barked a warning call somewhere.

Mike stopped abruptly and Nia started as a bark echoed out and a form flashed across the pathway. Nia's heart pounded as she watched the little brown bushbuck hop away. Mike resumed walking. 'Themba?'

They approached the entry to the structure. Nia checked her pistol.

Mike's boots clacked as he stepped onto the timber walkway. He lowered his rifle and she could see that the hide was empty. Mike's shoes now clanged on a steel grid that formed part of the floor.

'Themba,' he called again, louder this time, 'it's Mike Dunn. If you're around here, please let me know. I've come to get you out of this.'

'Mr Mike?'

Nia looked around. She didn't know where the voice had come from, but Mike looked down, between his feet. Nia went to him and also stared down.

There, ankle-deep in mud and staring up at them through the steel grid, were the faces of the three missing children.

*

Egil Paulsen studied the map of Mkhuze Game Reserve by the dim interior light in the cab of the warden's *bakkie*.

Dlamini's BMW was getting low on fuel, so he had left it at the camping ground and elected to ride with Jonas, the park warden.

The warden was driving, having received a call from Mike Dunn that they had found the three missing children, and that Dunn had taken them peacefully into custody. Dunn had confiscated an AK-47 and a bag of rhino horn. The warden was on his way with Egil, who was still masquerading as Detective Swanepoel, and four armed rangers in the back of the truck.

Egil had made conversation with the warden, trying to learn more about this man, Dunn. To his surprise, Egil learned that Dunn was a vulture researcher who fancied himself something of a wildlife cop. The warden's brother-in-law, a retired ranger named Solly, had told him on the phone that day how Mike and he had been involved in a shootout at the Mona market. Egil had nodded, agreeing that it had indeed been a crazy couple of days in KwaZulu-Natal, while inside he had felt a surge of excitement that he would again come face to face with the man who had set up an ambush for him at the site of the helicopter crash.

Egil had tried, unsuccessfully, to persuade the warden that he didn't need so many armed men, and that perhaps they should be allowed to return to their quarters for the night since Mike Dunn had found the children. Unfortunately the warden had insisted on bringing along his posse of rangers.

From a pocket of his jacket Egil took out a silencer. When they turned off onto the access road to the kuMasinga hide, Egil judged that the time was right. He took his Glock from his holster and cocked it.

The warden showed no concern until he pulled up at the hide's car park, near a white Defender emblazoned with vulture research signs, and saw that Egil was screwing the silencer onto the barrel of the pistol. 'What do you need that for?'

Egil raised the pistol and pointed it between the warden's eyes. 'Sadly, this.'

The slam of the slide and the muffled but still audible report of the shot was lost in the noise of the *bakkie*'s springs creaking as the armed rangers climbed out of the back of the Toyota.

Egil got out of the passenger's side. 'The warden's making a call. Get yourselves ready. I need a quick piss.'

Two of the men laughed, but all four turned their backs to him as they checked their weapons. Egil used their respect for his privacy to put the first two men down quickly, a close-range shot in the back of each of their skulls. The third turned and Egil shot him between the eyes.

The fourth was quicker, smarter than his colleagues and, perhaps falling back on something he'd been taught in training, he dropped to his knee to make himself a smaller target. He was barely five metres from Egil, but the sudden move was enough to add a split second to Egil's aim.

As Egil pulled the trigger the field ranger's rifle was coming up, the barrel pointing his way. Egil fired twice, a double tap. The first round caught the ranger in the chest, but before the second went into his open mouth the man was able to pull his trigger and an unsilenced shot shattered the calm.

Egil was also already moving to the right so the bullet missed him, but it would have alerted Dunn and the children. Egil stepped over the dead man.

He cursed. He had lost the element of surprise. He reached into the warden's *bakkie*, took the keys from the ignition and pocketed them. The only other vehicle in the car park was the white Land Rover Defender he'd seen when they'd driven in, the stretched version with the double cab. He went to it and saw that it was locked, no keys. He fired a shot through the driver's door window, then used a stout stick to smash out the shattered glass. He reached inside, popped the bonnet, then opened up the engine bay and put a bullet into the injector fuel pump.

With the Land Rover disabled he jogged down the pathway to the hide. 'Mr Dunn? Mike Dunn? This is the South African police,' Egil said, disguising his voice with a heavy Afrikaans accent. 'There's nothing to be alarmed about, one of the rangers just had an accidental discharge with his rifle. We're coming to rescue the missing children.'

There was no answer. Egil unscrewed the warm silencer from his pistol and pocketed it – the suppression device would look suspicious to a man who knew firearms.

He was so close to getting the child back. He wondered where Suzanne and the others were, and hoped the Americans or the real South African police had not captured them. For all their talk of disavowing torture he knew the CIA would be able to break one of the group. He had to get the baby and get out of the country. It would not be easy, but nothing about this mission was ever going to be that. The Americans had been bloodied and they would be angry.

'Mike Dunn, I'm coming to you and I'm armed.'

There was no reply.

Egil slowed as he saw the outline of the wooden game-viewing hide. He raised his pistol and its barrel followed the sweep of his eyes as he checked the bush on either side of him. He wished he had taken a green bush hat from one of the field rangers he had killed to cover his white hair. It was a mistake, but he could not go back now. Time was crucial.

Looking down he saw fresh tracks, two sets, one big, the other smaller. Dunn was not alone, and it looked like he had a woman with him.

Egil stepped softly onto the wooden walkway, but nonetheless his footsteps echoed. He walked into the hide and heard the note of his footfall change from rubber on wood to the soft clang of metal. There was no one in the hide. He looked down through the metal grating, which had been placed to allow visitors to view hippos, crocodiles and other creatures below.

There was nothing.

Chapter 22

J ed Banks and Franklin Washington stayed behind in the officers' mess of the Natal Mounted Rifles, in Durban, after the meeting of a rapidly growing team of South African and American law enforcement, government and military officials broke up.

With them, not long off a chartered jet flight from Nairobi, Kenya, was the head of the CIA's Africa station, Jed's boss, Chris Mitchell.

Jed was smarting from being pulled back from the search, but the South Africans were getting their collective act together to keep a tighter rein on the Americans in their country. Also, Chris wanted to talk through strategy with him, and Franklin had needed to be bandaged up. He had cracked some ribs and suffered a couple of lacerations, but he was still in the game.

The briefing had heard that a blue Volkswagen Polo stolen by the fugitive Suzanne Fessey and two accomplices had been recovered near Hilltop Camp in Hluhluwe–iMfolozi Park, but Fessey and her men were still in the wind.

'What's your take, Jed?' Chris asked now.

'Suzanne Fessey is a mom,' Jed said, stating what many in the room had probably been thinking, 'but she's also a hardened terrorist and a committed jihadi. I can understand a woman going to the ends of the earth to get her child back, but not the rest of her cell.'

'I would have expected them to cut and run at the first sight of us,' Franklin weighed in. 'I mean, it's all very well for her people to help the woman try and get her kid, but is it worth them taking on a Sea Hawk helicopter in broad daylight? And what do a bunch of jihadis care about a half-white kid in any case?' he added.

'Those kids have got something else the terrorists want,' Jed said.

He looked at Chris. With his wavy grey hair, round spectacles and softly spoken manner he looked more like a kindly old grandfather than America's top spy in Africa. Chris was a Cold War warrior who'd stayed on to fight America's new enemies. Africa had started as a backwater in the war on terror, but now home-grown terrorist groups such as Boko Haram and Al-Shabaab were almost as much a household name as al-Qaeda and ISIS. They were all now very much on the front line.

Chris nodded. 'We're now certain Suzanne Fessey was the so-called White Witch.'

Jed and Franklin had been discussing Fessey's possible role in global terrorism since they had been partnered, at Chris's orders, shortly after the bomb blast in Durban.

The nickname applied to a mysterious white woman rumoured to have been caught on surveillance video at Osama bin Laden's hideout in Pakistan, just days before the mission that killed him. The witch was also thought to be an accomplice in three suicide bombing attacks in Kenya since bin Laden's death. Suzanne Fessey had been hiding, underground, here in Durban in between missions for at least two years.

'We now believe,' Chris continued, 'that rather than being an accomplice, Fessey was actually the mastermind behind the African attacks, including this latest one. As you know, the man who assassinated the ambassador by blowing himself up was her husband, a half-Nigerian undercover Boko Haram man, Omar Farhat.'

'Where does the baby fit into all this?' Jed asked. Suzanne Fessey had kissed her husband goodbye and sent him off on his mission to blow himself up. Why, then, was she willing to risk her life and the lives of the rest of her cell to get back her child? Mother's instinct alone?

'The terrorist cell working with or in support of Fessey has a new target: those three children or, more specifically, something they have. I don't believe it's just about her child,' Chris said.

'Money?' Franklin asked.

'Always a strong motivator,' said Chris. 'Fessey and her people are hardline, ideologically motivated killers, but like all terrorist groups they need cash to wage war. It seems Fessey was on her way out of the country and she was going to start a new life, or a new operation. She may have had her stash of cash or valuables in her car. We've had cases before of terrorists trading in wildlife products to finance their operations.'

'Rhino horn?' Jed asked.

'Could be,' Chris replied. 'That stuff's worth more than gold or cocaine and it's easily transportable.'

'They're risking a hell of a lot to get back some rhino horn, even if it is worth a lot,' Franklin said to Chris.

'Suzanne could have been taking some horn with her that she could sell for travel expenses – we suspect she was heading for Mozambique and from there somewhere further on. But that could be just petty cash. Suzanne's late husband, Omar Farhat, was not some Boko Haram bush fighter. He was the son of a wealthy Nigerian oil family and converted from Christianity to

Islam when he was at university in Paris. He studied accountancy and we know from his records he was top of his class, with a genius IQ.'

'Money man?' Jed asked.

'Yes,' said Chris.

'He doesn't fit the profile of a suicide bomber. He's too smart, not some dumb kid with his head stuffed full of hatred and promises. Maybe something or someone forced his hand.'

'Well what we do know,' Chris said, 'is that he was one of the youngest members of Osama's inner circle in the old days of al-Qaeda, even though he was only in his late twenties at the time. We believe he and Suzanne secretly married in Pakistan in 2011, just before we got bin Laden. Both of them vanished.'

'So Omar knew where al-Qaeda stashed its cash?' Franklin asked.

'Yes, a lot of it at least, maybe enough to set up an African franchise based out of South Africa,' said Chris. 'Also, and this is of more concern than one-man suicide bombings, Langley's been getting reports of European-looking Muslims going shopping in Russia, and there have been a few suspicious Ivans visiting Africa lately; former military people we suspect of being in the arms trade. The current thinking is that someone in one of the al-Qaeda spin-offs is putting together another spectacular, maybe even shopping for a Soviet-era portable suitcase nuke.'

Jed stroked his beard. It was the West's biggest fear that somehow extremists might get hold of a nuclear device. 'That would require serious money.'

'Yes, and Omar would have known how to get it and, more importantly, where to hide it. We need to get hold of everything those South African teenagers took from Suzanne Fessey's car before she does. We need them, and we need the baby. This is a matter of national security. Those kids can't get away from us.'

'How did Suzanne Fessey get away with living here for so

long?' Jed asked. 'Seems like we know a lot about her, and can connect her to other bombings. What have the South African security people been up to?'

'Good questions, Jed,' Chris said. 'It would be easy for me to tell you that they're just incompetent, but we think there are other issues in play here.'

'Such as?'

'On the face of it they've told us that they can't get anything on Fessey, that she's either innocent – meaning we were wrong about her – or too good at covering her movements and actions. Our suspicion, however, is that there are elements in the South African security service who were happy to let Suzanne and Omar do their own thing.'

'That's a big call,' Jed said.

Chris nodded. 'There are, we understand, elements in the service and military who believe South Africa needs to be doing more to fight Islamic extremism on the continent, but the government's been sympathetic to parts of the Middle East we don't see as friends.'

'You mean the hardliners in South Africa *want* something to blow up, literally, here?' Jed asked.

Chris looked him in the eyes. 'Or someone.'

Jed knew a lot of dirty stuff happened in the intelligence world, but would the intelligence people here in South Africa really allow a foreign ambassador to be assassinated on their home soil in order to galvanise their government to join the international fight against terrorism?

Jed's phone vibrated in his pocket. He took it out and looked at the screen. 'Excuse me,' he said to Chris. 'I really need to get this.'

Chris looked mildly annoyed, but nodded. Jed walked out of the officers' mess and down a flight of stairs.

'Banks, it's Mike Dunn.'

Jed had already recognised the number. 'Where are you?'

'I'm . . . Game Reserve. The two . . . baby are with me. Come . . . '

'Mike, you're breaking up. Say again, where are you?' There was static then nothing. 'Mike, say again, what is your location, are you at Mkhuze?' That was where the missing children had last been spotted.

The call dropped out and Jed tried redialling, but got a recorded message saying the caller he was trying was not available or out of range. 'Shit.'

Jed tried twice more then went back upstairs to the officers' mess. 'Dunn, the man Franklin and I picked up at Suzanne Fessey's house, seems to have found the kids. I lost contact with him before I could find out where they are. They could be in Mkhuze Game Reserve.'

'Get on it, Jed,' Chris said. 'Keep trying and see if the South Africans can trace where that call came from. Then let's get the hell out of here.'

'To where?' Jed asked.

'Mkhuze, for a start. There's no word that the South African police have picked the kids up so maybe we can get to them first. I've got authorisation for another helicopter and permission from the South Africans to "assist" in the search.'

*

Nia carried the baby, clutched close to her chest, and ran after Mike as he cleared a path through the thick, thorn-studded bush.

Behind her was the girl, Lerato, who despite being relieved at not having to carry the child, was huffing and puffing. Nia looked back. 'Come on, catch up.'

'I'm *trying*. I've been running for days.'

Themba, who was bringing up the rear, turned his back to her. 'Climb up, I'll give you a lift.'

'No.'

Mike stopped. 'Do as Themba says, Lerato. We can't stop.'

Lerato swallowed her dignity and jumped up on Themba's back. Nia wondered if Themba carrying Lerato – even though she was slim – would be any faster. Themba, however, easily kept pace as Mike charged ahead again.

They had all hidden in the bushes when they'd heard the noise of the approaching car engine. As soon as the man claiming to be a policeman called out, Nia had put her hand on Mike's arm. 'That's him, the man who hijacked my helicopter.'

'Egil Paulsen.'

Mike had wanted to go after him, to confront him, but Nia had quickly talked him out of it. 'He's ruthless, Mike, you know that. Unless you're prepared to line up and shoot him in the head as soon as you see him, we have to run.'

'I might not rule that option out if we do see him coming after us,' Mike had said grimly.

Mike led them north, parallel to the tar road, close enough to hear and stop any passing national parks vehicle. He set a hard pace, but not so fast as to let Nia or the youngsters lag behind him. He'd told Themba to keep an eye out behind them, but it was hard work for him, having to stop and turn around with Lerato on his back.

'I'll be the rear guard,' Nia said, dropping back. Mike gave her a look, but she stared him down. She had the baby on one hip and Banger's pistol in her right hand. She was still fatigued from her earlier trauma, but the thought of what might happen if Paulsen caught them – especially her – kept her legs pumping and her senses alert.

As it was the middle of the night there was no tourist traffic. Nia could only hope that more national parks people, or legitimate police, responded to the call that must have gone out that the children had been found in Mkhuze Game Reserve. She also wondered what had happened to the other terrorists, whether they had been caught or if they, too, were still searching for their quarry.

The baby grizzled. Nia put her pistol back in the pocket of her flight suit. The child started to cry in earnest and she pressed his little face to her chest, rocking him as she strode through the bush. She rubbed the back of his neck, soothing him, but as her fingers moved over the soft warm skin she felt a lump.

The first thing Nia thought of was a tick. They were annoying creatures and easily picked up in the bush. They could cause tick bite fever, which was a horrible condition. Nia had had it as a child and recalled the terrible pain.

Nia moved the baby from her breast and held him out. She had to slow to a walk so as not to trip and drop him. Mike looked back, as he periodically did to check on them.

'What is it?'

'I don't know, but the baby's got a really hard lump in the back of his neck. I'm worried it might be a tick.'

'Take a five-minute break, everyone. Themba, put Lerato down. Drop back about fifty metres behind us and come running if you hear anything – and I mean anything – following us.'

Mike came to Nia and pulled a small torch from his pocket. He turned it on and, shielding the light with his left hand, directed the beam at the baby's neck.

'Look, there's a little wound here, like a puncture mark, but it doesn't look like a tick bite,' said Nia.

'Nor a spider bite,' Mike said. 'Let me feel it.' Mike ran his fingers over the skin then pinched the spot where Nia had felt the lump. He rolled it between his fingers. The baby gave a little cry. 'Sorry, little one.'

She looked at Mike's face. He squinted his eyes, thinking. 'No.'

'What were you thinking?'

'It's hard, like a foreign object.'

Nia fondled the infant's skin again. 'Yes, it's not like a pimple or a bite or anything, is it? What could it be?'

Lerato, who had sat down on the ground, looked up. 'Don't look at me, I don't know anything about babies.'

'You think I do? You've had two more days' experience at being a parent than I have. Mike, what do you think this thing is?'

He shook his head. 'I almost can't believe it, but it feels like a microchip.'

'A what?' Nia was incredulous. 'My old cat had one of those. They put it in with a big bloody needle.'

Mike gently felt the child's skin again. 'A syringe, but yes, it would have hurt. As well as using microchips in domestic animals, to record their owners' phone numbers and address, we use them in wildlife conservation, in rhino horns and in other animals to identify them.'

'Who would do such a thing to a baby, though, and why?' Lerato asked.

Nia thought about it. 'Information. If this is a microchip then there's something important on it, something someone took extreme measures to hide.'

'Yes,' Mike said. 'The Americans told me the baby's mother's possibly a terrorist; she would know that if she was caught in South Africa, or crossing a border, the authorities would go through all of her possessions with a fine-toothed comb. If she's got data to protect she couldn't put it on a USB stick, and the security services seem to be able to hack everyone's emails and online accounts these days. She'd be strip-searched, but a baby . . .'

'No one would subject a baby to that kind of search,' Nia said, finishing Mike's thought. 'What type of people *are* they?'

'We've seen that for ourselves.'

He was right. Nia shuddered. She was about to ask Mike how they would find out what was on the microchip when they all turned at the sound of breaking branches. Themba burst into their clearing.

'It's Paulsen,' he wheezed, catching his breath, his voice low and urgent. 'He is coming. Listen.'

Nia cocked her head. 'Engine.'

'He's driving a national parks *bakkie*, very slowly.'

'Did he see you?' Mike asked.

Themba shook his head.

Mike had tried calling the warden's phone, but it had just rung out. He feared that Egil Paulsen had killed Jonas, and if that was the case it meant he had also killed all the men the warden had brought with them. That might explain the shot they had heard as they'd left the hide.

'I'll call the police,' Mike said to the others, 'tell them what we know, and that Paulsen is here in Mkhuze masquerading as a police officer, but it's going to be hard to explain to whoever answers the phone.'

'We need to act now,' Nia said.

'We must stop this man,' Themba said.

Nia looked to the boy. Two days earlier she'd thought he was trying to kill her. The impression she had of him had changed. He seemed bright, fearless and mature beyond his years. She saw, too, from the way he looked at Mike that he respected the older man. He waited for Mike to answer, but the researcher was mulling things over.

'Mike?' she prompted him. She knew enough about his past now to have an idea what was going through his mind.

Mike looked to her and then to Themba and Lerato in turn. 'Themba's right, we need to stop this monster.'

Nia waited for his eyes to return to hers, which they did. 'Kill him, you mean.'

'Yes.'

Chapter 23

Paulsen drove with his left hand on the wheel and used his right to swing a hand-held spotlight he had found in the national parks vehicle. He shone it left to right, over the cab of the truck and back again.

He scanned the bush as he cruised slowly along. Several times he picked out the twin glow of animals' eyes between thickets.

Egil was banking on his quarry making a mistake, or at least the next move. It was about three kilometres from kuMasinga hide to Mantuma Camp, and his plan was to be there waiting for them at the camp if he didn't find them in the bush first.

He calculated that the fugitives could not have reached this far yet, so he made a U-turn and retraced his route, illuminating the bush on either side of the road with the spotlight. A couple of kilometres down the road he turned again and retraced his route once more.

Paulsen swung the light up ahead and put his foot on the brake. There, on the left-hand side of the road, was something white. He was sure there had been nothing man-made, no piece of litter dropped by a careless tourist, when he had passed here twice before. He stopped the *bakkie* fifty metres short of the object, turned the lights off and got out, taking the keys with him. He let his eyes adjust to the moonlight. In the belt of his trousers was his pistol and in his hands he carried a slain ranger's 7.62-millimetre R1 rifle. In the bulky pockets of his pants were two more magazines of ammunition, taken from the rest of the team.

He brought the rifle up and cut left into the bush. He advanced slowly, every sense on the alert.

Off to his right he saw the object in the bush on the side of the road. He could tell, now, that it was an item of clothing; it looked like a T-shirt that had snagged on a thorn-covered branch. As he moved forward he looked down and saw freshly broken branches, the pale bark shining in the moonlight. From the direction of the breaks he could tell that his quarry had walked from his left to right, across the road.

Paulsen turned right and started following the track.

No, he thought to himself. This was not right. Just as he began to turn, gunfire erupted around him.

He ran a few steps to the right then dived to the ground and crawled as fast as he could. Barbed thorns hooked his clothes and raked the skin on his cheeks, but he ignored the pain. Leaves shredded by bullets fell on his head.

'Aim low,' a man's voice called amid the firing.

Paulsen flattened himself and felt a round cleave the air just above his spine.

There were two guns firing, by the sound of it: an AK-47, its distinctive *pop-pop-pop* signalling short bursts, and the slower, deeper repetition of a heavy-calibre hunting rifle, bolt action.

Paulsen leopard-crawled, the R1 cradled in the crook of his arms, until he reached the comparative safety of a stout tree. The solid trunk would stop any bullet. He curled himself around, took up the prone firing position, flicked the selector on his rifle to automatic and squeezed off three rounds.

'Down!'

He had made them cease fire for a second. Paulsen jumped up and ran, keeping the tree more or less between him and the road. When he reached the tarmac he saw a figure dart from the national parks *bakkie* into the bush on the side of the road he had just come from. He raised the R1 and fired two quick rounds, but it was a snap shot at a running target and he doubted he hit anything.

A split second later a plume of black greasy smoke and orange flames blossomed from the back of the *bakkie*. He remembered now the jerry can of fuel lying in the back tray. With a *whoosh* of heat and an explosive *whoomp* the truck was consumed with fire.

Another weapon opened up, smaller calibre, a pistol, and a bullet flew past his face, dangerously close. It had come from the direction of the burning *bakkie*, but from the other side of the road. He was being bracketed. The AK fired again, a speculative burst.

Paulsen fired three rounds towards where the pistol shot had come from, but then had to swing and fire again as the AK-47 and hunting rifle tried to find him. His phone vibrated in his shirt pocket. Ducking down, he took it out and read the WhatsApp message.

He was at a disadvantage. His assailants would all be in cover and here he was on the edge of the road, ducking and weaving. He crawled to a tree and thought through his options. Arrayed against him was a man, a woman, and two teenagers. Three of them were armed.

'I surrender,' he yelled, then stood up.

Paulsen waited, bracing his body for the impact of a bullet. If he was Dunn, or even the woman pilot, he would have killed him without a second thought. But these people were not killers. He walked into the middle of the road, his hands up and the R1 held high above his head. 'I'm putting the rifle down.'

'Do it,' a man's voice said.

Slowly he lowered the rifle and placed it on the ground.

'Handgun.'

Paulsen slid his pistol from his belt and, holding it by the trigger guard, placed it down next to the rifle.

'Kick them aside.'

Dunn wasn't taking chances, or, to be more accurate, he was doing his best to minimise the risk. Paulsen smiled inwardly and gave both weapons a swift kick so that they clattered and slid all the way to the gravel verge of the tar road.

He closed his fingers into fists, feeling the tip of the stiletto strapped to the inside of his right forearm. He would slash Dunn's throat and use his gun to take out the boy first, then the woman.

'Stay where you are. Put your hands on your head. I'm coming out.'

Paulsen complied and waited. He blinked as a beam of light from a torch lit up his face. He heard branches moving from a different direction, to his left, and looked that way.

Dunn emerged from the bush and stood at the edge of the tree line. He raised his rifle to his shoulder and took aim.

'No need for that, I'm giving myself up,' Paulsen said.

'Shut up.'

'Hey, I'm coming to you, OK?' He took a step.

'Don't move. You take another step and I'll put a bullet through your chest.'

'Centre mass, not the head. Good thinking.'

'Good training.'

'You want me to be afraid of you?'

'The only reason I haven't shot you yet is because when the Americans get hold of you they'll break you and the information you give them might save some lives. You've killed enough people, Paulsen. You deserve a bullet.'

'Ah, so you know my name? You're a South African but now

you're the lackey of the Americans, the Great Satan. They don't care about our country, our Africa.'

'I'm not on your side.'

'You know nothing of my side. All I was trying to do was rescue a kidnapped child and bring it back to its mother.'

'Another terrorist.'

'I can see the Americans have filled your head with lies. What woman wouldn't do everything in her power to get her child back?' Paulsen needed to get closer to Dunn, near enough to kill him, quickly. He took a step towards the man.

The gunshot echoed around the hills of Mkhuze and Paulsen felt the hot rush of air past his left cheek. He stopped.

'At this range a head shot is just as easy as centre mass,' Dunn said to him from the shadows. 'Lie down on your belly and put your hands back behind your head.'

'You're not taking any chances, are you?'

'No.'

Paulsen got down on his hands and knees, then prostrated himself. He put his hands behind his head and from the corner of his eye saw Dunn circle around. He heard the man's footsteps on the road behind him. He was close.

'There's no need to be so worried. I'm sure you've got the boy somewhere close by covering me with his AK-47. I wouldn't be surprised if that wildcat of a helicopter pilot doesn't have a gun as well. The warden told me you had a woman with you and I can only assume it's her.'

'Everyone is safely away from here. It's just you and me now. No witnesses.'

'Should I be scared?'

'You don't strike me as the kind who scares easily.'

Dunn was right. Paulsen wondered if Dunn really was alone. It would make sense for the children to keep moving through the bush. Once he killed Dunn he would have to track them, though this time he would be prepared for an ambush. He had underestimated these fugitives' ability to fight back, as opposed to simply fleeing like startled prey. He would not make the same mistake again.

'What's on the microchip?'

Paulsen bit back the curse. 'What microchip?'

'The one that you or some other sick fucker, or the baby's mother, inserted into the back of his neck, as if he were a dog.'

Dunn worked with wildlife; he would know a microchip when he felt one. There was no reason to continue playing dumb, Paulsen reasoned. What he needed to do was kill Dunn and the others before one of them passed on this information to the Americans.

'You think I'm going to tell you?'

'I think the Americans probably know.'

'It's nothing to you, the information on the chip. Give the baby to me – the chip is all I want. The Americans will kill the baby, kill anyone who knows about that chip.'

'Bullshit,' Mike said. 'Americans don't kill babies.'

Paulsen nodded. 'Usually their soft hearts get in the way, or if they kill children in battle they call it "collateral damage". They are weak. But trust me, they will kill that child if they have to in order to get that chip. You, the teenagers who are on the run, the woman, are expendable to them. They don't want to take the risk of you leaking information to the media. They're weak, but they're at war. You will be collateral damage to them, like the innocent victims of some indiscriminate bombing campaign.'

Dunn shook his head. 'I'm not buying it, and there's no way I'm handing over a child to you after what you've done, the people you've killed.'

'This is not your war.'

'You're right about that, and it's not South Africa's. As far as I'm concerned, you, and the Americans, anyone who wants to bring this shit to my country can go to hell. We've got enough problems of our own here. Tell me, what was your deal with Bandile Dlamini? You were supposed to sell him some rhino horn, yes?'

'Yes. I'd heard that despite his holier than thou comments in the media he was actually a big player in the illegal wildlife trade.'

'You've just admitted to a crime that could see you put away for years in a South African prison.'

'I'm being honest with you,' Paulsen said. 'I don't have any rhino horn, but I took Dlamini's money. Tell the cops, see if I care. Give the child to me or, if you don't trust me with it, cut the chip out of the back of its neck with your Leatherman. The child will scream, but it will live, as long as the Americans don't get hold of it first and exterminate it.'

'Even if I agreed to your sick request, what would I get in return?'

'I have no need to kill you, or the woman, or the others if I get that microchip. I will let you live.'

Dunn scoffed. 'I'm the one pointing the gun at the back of your head and you're the one lying face down on the ground. I know what you look like, your name.'

'So do the Americans, and they haven't been able to catch me yet.'

'You're one man; they're an army.'

Paulsen said nothing. Instead he turned his face abruptly and let his cheek drop to the tarmac of the road. At the same time he dropped his arms to his side, careful to keep his right wrist downwards. The back of his neck was covered in blood. 'I'm . . . I think you hit me. The shock . . . didn't feel it.' He closed his eyes and let his body go limp.

The position Dunn had made Egil adopt had helped him with his plan. Before he surrendered he had slipped the sheath from the knife strapped to the inside of his right forearm. Unseen by his captor, Egil had been slowly pressing the needle-like point of the blade into his wrist. As they talked he had let the blood pool on the back of his neck, creating the impression of a wound.

He lay there and heard Dunn change position behind him. Dunn nudged him in the ribs with the toe of his boot, but Paulsen had been prepared for this, and gave no reflexive response.

Paulsen had no way of knowing if there was enough blood on his neck to be convincing, but he was counting on Dunn to do what he was sure he would. He heard the rustle of the other man's clothing, the soft thud of the rubberised stock of the hunting rifle being placed on the ground. He willed himself to lie still, just a couple of seconds longer.

'Hey,' Dunn said. 'Are you awake?'

Paulsen didn't move. He felt Dunn's fingers touch his neck, searching for a pulse. It was his cue to strike.

Paulsen rolled and folded his hand back, exposing the bloodied point of his stiletto. He rammed it up towards Dunn's throat but the other man was also quick, already ducking to one side. As he moved, Dunn tried to bring his rifle up and Paulsen's dagger *pinged* on the blue steel of the barrel.

Dunn fell backwards, and Paulsen was up, on his knees. He dived on Dunn, preventing the man from bringing his rifle to bear. Dunn dropped the weapon and reached for Paulsen's right arm, but Egil twisted his wrist, slicing Dunn's palm.

Dunn drew back his hand and Egil sprang to his feet. He lashed out with a kick that caught Dunn under the chin and sent him sprawling backwards. Dunn recovered quickly and, one-handed, raised his rifle and pulled the trigger. The shot boomed, but Egil was already rolling and the bullet missed him, although it was another near-miss.

Egil closed on the other man and kicked again, knocking the rifle from Dunn's hands as he tried to work the bolt to chamber another round. He punched the researcher with his left fist and heard the satisfying crack on the man's skull. If the blow hadn't knocked him out, it had dazed Dunn. Egil felt the fight go out of him. He drew back his right hand again, bared the blade, and knew that with Dunn out of the way he would easily be able to catch the young ones and that arrogant helicopter pilot, kill them, slice open the baby and –

Chapter 24

'**M**ike,' Nia said. 'Mike, can you hear me?' She slapped his cheek again.

Mike opened his eyes and tried to focus on her.

'Thank God. It's all right, you're alive, but you're bleeding.'

'Paulsen?' He looked around him.

Nia glanced towards the body and Mike winced in pain as he turned his head to follow the direction of her eyes. Nia swallowed back the bile that was rising again in her throat. 'I shot him.'

'I thought . . .'

'I know, I know, you told me to go with the kids for my safety, but I also told you I don't like following orders. It's just as well I stayed behind. I've seen that man in action, remember.'

'Thanks.' He grimaced again as he felt the back of his head.

'You're bleeding there as well as on your palm, but head wounds always bleed a lot. I don't think it's too bad, unless you've got concussion.'

'It's all right,' he said, 'I know where I am. Where are the others?'

'Themba said he knew the way to the Nsumo. He's heading there now, with Lerato and the baby. They're safe, Mike.'

'I'm not so sure about that.'

'I know the baby's mother and the others are still out there, but surely we can make it to safety before they find us here.'

'Paulsen might have got a message to them about where we were, here in Mkhuze,' Mike said, 'but I'm also worried about the Americans, what they'll do if they get to the kids first.'

'What do you mean?' Mike told her about the conversation he'd had with Paulsen. It seemed incredible, that whatever was on the microchip was sensitive enough that the Americans might kill three children – and possibly them as well – to cover up its existence.

'I know it sounds far-fetched. And Paulsen had every reason to lie to me, to try and get me to drop my guard,' Mike said.

Nia nodded. 'True, but the lengths that everyone – the Americans and the terrorists – are going to in order to get hold of this baby are crazy. I'm worried about them now. Are you going to contact the Americans to tell them where we all are?'

Mike fingered the back of his head again. 'I'm not sure. You know what I'm thinking?'

She looked into his eyes. 'I do. You want to find out what's on that microchip before we hand the baby over.'

'It's crazy.'

'It sure is. Let's do it.'

'But we have to get out of here first, take the kids somewhere safe. The only problem is how.' Mike got to his feet.

'I've sorted out our transport,' Nia said. 'I didn't know how bad you were hurt or how we could get out of here quickly in case the woman and the others come, so I've organised an evacuation chopper. My friend John's on the way.' She looked down at the man she had just killed. 'What about him?'

'Who cares?'

*

Themba carried the baby on his back and the AK-47 at the ready. Lerato was close behind him, one hiking pack on her back, the other across the front of her body.

Themba was pleased that Lerato had found a new sense of purpose. They were moving fast, so perhaps she was conserving her breath. The infant, amazingly, was sleeping. He thought of the foreign object that had been inserted into his little neck; Themba was no stranger to the concept of cruelty to children, but this seemed particularly sickening to him. He thought of Nandi again, and his vow to her. If he ever had children he would protect them with his life.

Mike had told him to swing around to the south, towards the big Nsumo Pan.

'If I don't get Paulsen, the white-haired man, he will assume you are heading to Mantuma Camp,' Mike had said before setting his ambush. 'Go to Nsumo instead; you remember we went there? You can hide in the ablutions block, get yourselves and the baby cleaned up. I'll come for you.'

It was a long walk to Nsumo Pan, about thirteen kilometres, but Themba had followed the orders and was making good time, using the road. They would melt into the bush at the first sound of a vehicle engine. Mike had also ordered Nia to come with them, but she had ignored his command as soon as Mike had left them.

In the distance he heard a gunshot, then another one soon after.

'Wait,' said Lerato. 'Should we go back and check on them?'

Themba looked over his shoulder at her and shook his head. 'Keep going. He was clear in his instructions.'

'All right. I'm trusting you, Themba.'

More than an hour later they were still trudging towards Nsumo. Themba didn't know if he would be able to keep Lerato's trust and though she was trying to be stoic, he knew that she, like him, was thinking the worst. After the gunshots Themba had expected Mike and Nia to come find them at any time. He heard a noise, stopped, raised his hand, and cocked his head.

'What is it?' Lerato asked.

'An aircraft, another helicopter, I think. Move into the bushes.'

They heard the rotors, away in the distance, but when Themba looked up through the trees he could see no search light, no winking navigation lights. *That's fine*, he thought, *if I can't see them, then they can't see me.*

*

'Two individuals, wait, three. One has a baby on its back. They're moving south,' said the pilot through the Sea Hawk's intercom system. 'About four hundred metres to the west of us.'

The helicopter had been overflying Mkuze Game Reserve searching the bush with its FLIR – forward-looking infrared camera. They'd caught an unexpected break.

'Roger that,' Jed said into the boom microphone. This was the second Navy chopper he'd been on and they were all of them in a heightened state of alert after the disaster of the first flight in pursuit of the targets. There were only two Sea Hawks on board the warship berthed at Durban, and now one of them was gone, but Jed knew that a mini invasion force of more choppers, US Navy SEALs and CIA officers were on their way to South Africa by air at this very moment. For now it was just Jed, Franklin and Chris Mitchell on board.

Jed knew that Chris, despite his age, was ambitious. Chris wanted to catch these fugitives and find out what, if anything, they were carrying in addition to the baby before the South Africans or any other US Government agency could beat him to it. For now the reality was that Jed, Franklin and Chris were the tip of America's spear.

'They've gone to ground,' said Chris. He was watching the

glowing images of the runaway kids on the screen of the FLIR. 'Let's not spook them. We'll deploy a klick to the south.'

'Understood,' said Franklin.

The pilot circled around to the south. 'Five minutes,' he said.

Jed and Franklin checked and cocked their MP5s. They were each carrying half a dozen spare magazines. It might have just been three kids, but they weren't taking any chances. Fessey, Paulsen and the other terrorists were unaccounted for.

'One minute,' Chris said over the intercom.

Jed took off his headset. The crewmen on either side of the Sea Hawk slid open the cargo doors and Jed and Franklin waited in the open hatches. Jed flashed back to his time in Afghanistan. He'd nearly been killed a couple of times and never thought he'd be going into action like this again in his lifetime. But the war he'd left for after September 11, 2001, had never really ended.

The pilot flared the nose of the big bird, and as it settled on its wheels Jed and Franklin jumped out. In an instant the Sea Hawk was gone and around him was the quiet of the African bush, the silence broken only by the *chirp* of a tiny Scops owl.

Jed and Franklin took up positions close to the verge on either side of the road. When the kids came towards them – the FLIR had shown them using the road so he assumed they would continue to do so – Jed would show himself to them first. He didn't want them being harmed. They would get whatever it was the bad guys were after, and they would do it without spilling more blood.

Jed watched the road. Visibility was good, thanks to the moonlight.

'Jed,' Chris's voice said into the earpiece of the tactical radio Jed carried.

'Go, Chris.'

'We've got a problem. Pilot says one of his engines is red-lining. We've got to put down so the crew can check it out. You and Franklin are on your own for now.'

'Roger that,' Jed said into the radio. He snapped his fingers and Franklin looked over at him. In a low voice he relayed the message.

'At this rate the US Navy's going to run out of helicopters,' Franklin said.

*

Themba strode ahead, the baby still on his back, and Lerato half jogged to keep pace with his long steps.

'Slow down,' she hissed.

He couldn't blame her for getting annoyed. He, too, was feeling the effects of fatigue, but he couldn't let them slow down. As he walked his foot crunched on a twig. He looked down.

Strewn on the road were several more small branches in a line across his path. From the positioning it almost looked like the dead leaves and twigs had been blown across the road, but that, too, was unusual, because there wasn't a breath of wind, and hadn't been all day. He bent and took a closer look at the branches and leaves – they did not look like they had been chewed and discarded by elephant or other game.

He slowed his pace and raised the AK-47.

'At last,' Lerato huffed.

'Shush.'

'Themba!' a voice called from ahead. A tall man with a beard and fair hair, though not white like the one who had been chasing them, walked out onto the road. He had his hands raised, though in one of them was a short-barrelled machine gun. 'My name is Jed Banks, I'm with the American Government. Please don't shoot.'

'Into the bush,' Themba said to Lerato.

She hesitated, unwilling to leave his side as Themba brought his rifle up to his shoulder.

'He's going to shoot!' another voice called from the opposite side of the road to where the first American was standing.

Themba started to lower his weapon. He heard one shot, then two, and felt something punch him in the shoulder. He staggered backwards, then darted to the side, towards the trees. Lerato screamed. Themba's only thought was that he should try to stay upright; if he fell backwards he would crush the baby. He heard the clatter of an engine above and behind him and the next instant he was bathed in light.

This, he thought, was the moment in which he would die. He wondered if the light above him was from heaven, a beam to transport his soul upwards. He suddenly felt light-headed. 'I love you, Lerato.'

'What? Don't be stupid. Are you all right?' She had her arm around him and the baby, supporting them.

He could see two men on the road now in the distance. One was a black man, wearing khaki cargo pants and a safari shirt. He was raising a submachine gun. The man fired again, but the fair-haired man who had first appeared on the road put his hand on the man's weapon and forced it down.

The light flooded them and Themba looked up. It wasn't the afterlife calling him, it was a helicopter, and through the open door of the rear compartment he could see Mike Dunn waving to them, motioning them to come closer. Themba took one step, then another, then crumpled to his knees.

*

Mike jumped down out of the Bell Jet Ranger. He ran to Themba.

'He's been shot,' Lerato said.

Nia came to them – Mike had known it would have been pointless to tell her to stay in the chopper. With Lerato's help she unwrapped the baby from Themba's back; it was a miracle the child hadn't been hit as well. As it was, he was screaming his little head off.

Mike got an arm around Themba and led him to the helicopter. 'Who was shooting at you?'

'Americans,' Themba mumbled.

Past the helicopter Mike could see Jed Banks and his partner, Franklin, heading their way. Franklin had an MP5 in one hand and was running his left hand across his neck, motioning for the pilot to cut his engine.

It had been a tense wait for John in the helicopter but, from what Nia had told Mike, John had pushed the Jet Ranger to its limits to cover the more than 300 kilometres to Mkhuze as fast as possible.

'They tried to kill Themba,' Lerato said to Mike.

Mike looked to Nia, who nodded. 'We're South African citizens, Mike, all of us. There's no reason for us to surrender ourselves to the CIA.'

They helped Themba up into the chopper. 'We need to get a dressing on that wound.'

Nia climbed into the co-pilot's seat and put on a headset. Mike could see she was talking to John, perhaps trying to explain why two men in khaki were walking up the road side by side, pointing their MP5 carbines at them.

Mike pressed a dressing onto the wound on Themba's shoulder and had Themba hold it there while he wrapped a bandage around him. Glancing through the front window, Mike could see that Franklin was taking deliberate aim at them. The American fired a burst of rounds.

'Holy shit, what do we do?' John yelled through the intercom.

Nia jabbed a finger skywards. 'Go!'

Lerato kept a close watch on Themba as they flew. Mike put on a headset.

'Where to?' John asked them.

'I have a good friend who's a veterinarian,' Mike said. 'He's got a small farm inland from Umhlanga Ridge. Can you take us there?'

'Sure,' John replied on the intercom. 'I'm not supposed to be flying the company's chopper in any case, so it doesn't matter where I land it.'

'The Americans will alert the South African police; they'll put pressure on them to find you, to ask you questions,' Mike said. 'We need some time.'

'I'm sure I won't be able to remember where I dropped you. At least not for a few days.'

'That should do it,' Mike said.

'Themba needs a doctor,' Nia said.

'My friend, Dr Boyd Qualtrough, used to work in Botswana as a vet. He had a side line treating humans, illegally. The local hospital near where he had his practice was understaffed and poorly equipped. He stitched me up one time after a buffalo gored me.'

'OK,' Nia replied. 'Is he discreet?'

'Judging by the number of affairs he's had with married women, he's very discreet.'

John flew low and fast through the night, hugging the Indian Ocean coastline. Just north of Umhlanga Rocks he turned west, inland, and Mike guided him over the hills, to Dr Boyd Qualtrough's farm.

They circled the main building, a whitewashed single-storey house with a green corrugated iron roof. In a fenced yard below Mike could see a zebra. Boyd, he could see, was still collecting orphaned or unwanted wildlife, probably without permits if he was still up to his old tricks.

'There's an empty field up ahead,' John said. 'I'll put down there.'

When they landed John kept the engines turning as Nia leaned over and kissed him on the cheek and Mike walked around to the pilot's side and shook his hand and thanked him. When they were sure Boyd was around – a light came on inside the house and a bare-chested man walked out – Mike and Nia helped Themba and Lerato down and John took off.

Nia carried the wriggling child in her arms.

'What the hell?' Boyd began, walking across the grass to them on bare feet. He carried a shotgun in his hands. 'Mike Dunn. Quite an entry, boy, almost as dramatic as the last time I saved your life.'

Mike and Boyd hugged. 'Boyd, it's good to see you, but we're in the *kak*, big time. This is Themba. He's taken a nine-mill bullet to the shoulder. I need you to work on him.'

'Okey dokey.' Boyd nodded to Nia. 'Ma'am.'

'Howzit, I'm Nia and this is Lerato. We'd really appreciate your help, Dr Qualtrough,' Nia said.

'Never been able to refuse a pretty face, ma'am. Lerato. Come on in and let's have a look at young Themba here.'

Boyd led the way through his house, picking up a T-shirt from the sofa and shrugging it on as he walked. 'Excuse the mess. The maid only comes once a week, and that's tomorrow. I'm in between domestic goddesses at the moment.'

Mike noted the open bottle of bourbon on the coffee table, the overflowing ashtray and the American football game on the television. Beside the whisky was a half-eaten Debonairs pizza.

Boyd opened the door on an adjoining two-car garage that had been converted into his clinic. There was an operating table, lights, a digital x-ray machine, racks of drugs and cabinets with other medical supplies. A cat miaowed from a cage on the wall and a grey-headed parrot called, 'Hello.'

Boyd's hair had thinned a little since Mike had last seen him, just before Boyd had been kicked out of Botswana for mouthing off about crime and poaching. Mike wasn't sure what else the vet may have done to get the government offside, but it had been enough.

Mike and Nia helped Themba up onto the table.

'There's a bathroom out back, if you need it,' Boyd said to Lerato. 'I think from a certain odour I'm detecting that your baby might need changing.'

'He's not my baby,' Lerato said, 'but if I could get a hand towel or something that would be great.'

'I'll help, Lerato,' Nia said.

'It's OK,' Lerato said to Nia, 'you stay and watch over Themba.'

Boyd washed his hands, put on rubber gloves and laid out an array of surgical instruments, gauzes and dressings. He cut away the bandage and lifted the dressing from Themba's gunshot wound.

'Can you wiggle your fingers, then make a fist for me, Themba?'

Themba winced, but was able to do as the vet had asked. 'It hurts.'

'I'm not surprised.' Boyd drew up a syringe. 'You were lucky, Themba, the bullet missed your vital organs and there doesn't seem to be too much damage. I'm going to give you an anaesthetic for the pain and we'll get that slug out of you.'

'You're a real doctor?'

'Well, none of my patients ever complained, at least not the four-legged ones.' He looked to Nia. 'Want to scrub in? Old Bird Man here nearly passed out last time I stitched him up.'

Mike grimaced. 'It's true. I don't like watching this kind of stuff.'

'I'm happy to,' Nia said. She went to the sink and washed her hands and put on a pair of gloves.

Relieved, Mike stepped back to the wall of the home surgery and looked away as Boyd injected Themba.

'How long have you been in Africa?' Nia asked.

Mike had heard Boyd's story, which he related to Nia. At fifty-five he'd had a midlife crisis and left his wife, not for another woman but for a new continent. Boyd had, somewhat ironically given his profession, been a big game hunter. He'd travelled to Africa a dozen or more times to shoot antelope and buffalo and like many foreigners had become addicted to the place. When his marriage had gone sour he'd sold his lucrative practice in Florida, cashed in his share of the business and his home and moved to Botswana.

'I worked as a voluntary wildlife vet there,' Boyd told Nia as he waited for the anaesthetic to take effect on Themba and had her apply a compress to the wound to staunch the flow of blood. 'The Botswana Government even made me an honorary ranger for a time, but I'm an opinionated, loud-mouthed, arrogant SOB and the locals didn't take kindly to me telling it like it was, and how I thought it should be.'

'You seem quite meek and mild to me,' Nia said as she swapped the pads on Themba's wound, 'not at all like most Americans I've met.'

Boyd laughed. 'You got yourself a pistol here, Mikey boy.'

'She's not mine,' Mike said, at the precise moment that Nia confirmed, 'I'm not his.'

'Snap. Well, you two would make a hell of a power couple, except Nia here's a better nurse. Just saying. Time to operate.' Boyd held out a hand. 'Nurse, scalpel.'

Nia frowned, but found the knife.

What Boyd hadn't mentioned to Nia, not that he would, was that his health had been deteriorating. Mike knew Boyd had been suffering from pancreatitis but his condition seemed to have worsened since the last time he had seen him. He had lost a good deal of weight.

'Just a minute, Boyd,' Mike said.

'What is it?'

'Do you microchip dogs and cats?'

Boyd looked at him, eyebrows raised. 'I do. I'm going out backwards here, people don't have enough money to look after their pets, but some of them spring for a microchip with their phone numbers on it. Why?'

'I need a reader.'

'Should I ask what for?'

'No.'

'OK, well, you help yourself – the reader's in the steel cabinet over there in the corner, and if you don't mind I'll take the bullet out of our young friend here. Sit tight, Themba. Won't take a minute.'

Mike went to the cupboard, pleased to be away from the sight of Boyd cutting Themba's skin and delving into the gunshot wound. He found the reading device, turned it over in his hands a couple of times, and located the on–off switch.

He left the makeshift operating room and went back into the house. He found Lerato in the bathroom, where she was patting the baby dry and dressing him.

Lerato looked up at him. 'He's all better now. It's amazing how strong he is, for someone so little.'

'Kids are tough. You and Themba are tough.'

'How is he?'

'He's in good hands with Boyd.'

'That man looks like an old drunk.'

'His heart's in the right place. I need to check the baby.'

She pointed to the reading device. 'With that?'

Mike nodded.

'He's not something in a supermarket with a barcode, you know.'

'I know, Lerato. He's a tiny human being who doesn't deserve to be mixed up in this *kak* any more than you and Themba do, or Nia and me for that matter, but we've got him and we need to know why people are prepared to kill for whatever has been put inside him.'

'OK. But let me hold him.'

Lerato picked up the baby, cradling him, and slid down his T-shirt so that the soft skin on the back of his neck was visible. Mike pointed the reading device at it and pulled the trigger. The reader bleeped.

Mike looked at the screen.

280

'What is it?' Lerato asked, rocking the child gently.

'Numbers. A long one, starting with the letters "CH", and a shorter one, six digits.' Mike wondered if he should write them down, but then had a better idea. He took out his phone, selected contacts and added two new names, old girlfriends he hadn't seen for years. He split the numbers on the reader into two, each the length of cell phone numbers, and added '+27', the international dialling code for South Africa, in front of them.

'What do they mean?'

'I don't know,' Mike said, honestly. 'Let's go through and check on Themba.'

They went to the garage operating theatre where Boyd was finishing off, with Nia snipping the last suture.

'Good work,' Boyd said to Nia.

'Thank you, Doctor. That was fascinating.'

Themba was conscious, but his eyelids were heavy.

'How's he doing?' Mike asked.

'He'll live, but he's lost a lot of blood. I'm going to rig up a saline drip for him. He needs to rest for a few hours.'

'Boyd, thank you, but we need to get moving again,' Mike said.

'Well I say this young man needs to rest a few hours.'

'I'm beat as well, Mike, and so is Lerato,' Nia said.

'I've got three guest bedrooms,' Boyd said. 'Won't take but a minute to make them up.'

Mike looked to Nia, who nodded. 'OK, thanks, but we've got to find a way to get moving first thing tomorrow.'

Nia said, 'I've got my car at Umhlanga.'

'You can take my *bakkie*,' Boyd offered. 'It's only a single cab in any case. The kids'll be safe here with me until you get back.'

Mike looked to Lerato.

'I'm sick of moving,' she said. 'I just want to sleep indoors. I'll take care of the baby.'

'All right,' Mike said.

Boyd reheated some leftover lasagne for them and Mike, Nia and Lerato ate, too numbed to converse over dinner.

Mike and Nia helped Boyd make up the beds. The spare rooms and the linen smelled musty, as if they were rarely used. While they were making Lerato's bed Boyd winced and stood, placing his hand on his belly.

'You OK?' Mike asked.

Boyd gave a small shake of his head. 'It's the pancreas. Nothing's worked. I'm on the way out, it's cancer, buddy.'

'Boyd, I'm so sorry.'

He shrugged. 'Hell, I've had a pretty good time of it, the last shitty year notwithstanding. I always figured I'd die in Africa, but I hoped it would be in different circumstances.'

'Is there anything you can do?'

'My doctor told me to give up the booze and cigars, but what's the point in that? Moderation's for monks.'

'Thanks for this. You haven't even asked what it's all about,' Mike said.

'Well, you're a friend in need and I won't ever forget how you came and visited me in prison in Botswana before I was deported, how you brought me food and stuff to read.'

'That was the least I could do for you. I'm just sorry things didn't work out for you there.'

'TIA, buddy.'

Their situation couldn't just be written off as 'this is Africa', Mike thought. It was far worse than that.

Lerato wanted to keep the baby with her, so Boyd put her in a room with two single beds and pushed the baby's close to her. Lerato rolled some towels to prop around the baby and keep him from falling out of the bed. Mike and Nia said goodnight to the girl and went out into the corridor.

'I'll leave you to it,' Boyd said, and while Nia was looking away Boyd gave Mike a wink.

Mike would have laughed if he hadn't been so exhausted. Still, he lingered in the hallway when he and Nia reached their rooms, which were opposite each other.

'Well, goodnight,' he said.

She stood there, with her hand on the door knob, also waiting. 'Yes, goodnight. It's been quite a couple of days.'

'Yes, it has.' He couldn't think of anything else to say. However, he had an overwhelming desire to be with her, not sexually, but just close to her. He wondered if he was just feeling protective.

'I'll be OK, you know,' she said.

She was prickly and forthright, but her words didn't sound like a recrimination. 'I know that. But sometimes it's good to know we've got somebody else looking out for us.'

Nia smiled. 'I'll look out for you. Are you OK?'

Boyd had cleaned and bandaged the cut on Mike's hand after he had finished operating on Themba, and the pain from the lump on the back of Mike's head had been downgraded to a dull throb. Mike sensed, however, that Nia was asking him about more than his physical injuries. 'I should have shot Egil Paulsen on sight. That way we could have all got away quicker, before the Americans arrived.'

She reached out and put a hand on his forearm. 'You couldn't kill a man in cold blood, not after what happened to you when you were younger. You weren't to know Paulsen was going to try something.'

'No, but I should have guessed he would. Thank you for saving my life,' he said.

'It was a pleasure. I'm glad I killed him, he was evil, but I wouldn't have executed him if he hadn't tried anything. Don't beat yourself up for being a good guy, Mike Dunn. There are damn few of you around. Trust me, I know.'

Mike looked into Nia's eyes. She moved, slightly, leaning closer to him. Mike's phone rang. 'Sorry.' He took it out of his pocket and showed Nia the screen. It was Jed Banks.

'Jed.'

'Mike.'

'You got a trace on me, Jed? If so I'm hanging up.'

'You need to work on your tradecraft, buddy. This is the digital age. If I had a trace on you I'd have you already. No, I'm stuck in Mkhuze goddamned national park waiting for these Navy squids to fix their helicopter. Where are you?'

'Um, pass, Jed. Your pal shot at us.'

'Well, he gets trigger-happy around AK-47s. I know how he feels. Tell us where you are and we'll bring you in, to safety,' Jed said.

'This isn't the Wild West, Jed, it's South Africa. We'll look after ourselves for a while, thanks. In the meantime, why don't you mobilise America's military might to catch the people who are trying to kill these kids?'

There was a pause on the end of the line. 'You've hit a nerve there, Mike. This investigation's been a clusterfuck from the beginning. For Pete's sake, a US ambassador's been killed and we can't get our shit together. Work with us, not against us.'

Mike rubbed his eyes. He was tired. 'We're safe for now, but if the bad guys find us you'll be the first person I call, Jed.'

'We're still looking for you all, Mike.'

'Good luck with that.'

PART 3

nqe and his partner watched their chick expectantly. He had grown from a tiny ball of fluff into an increasingly stronger young male.

He had been hopping about in the nest for some time now and the moment had come for him to take his first flight.

The chick flapped its wings and jumped to the edge of the nest. Its parents beat their massive wings and took flight. There would be no room for the three of them here.

Inqe circled the leadwood tree slowly and at low level. Such was his size that he needed the benefit of a warm thermal rising from the earth to assist him to take off properly. The chick might fare better, with his lighter size, but for now, Inqe had to touch down on a branch and watch.

The chick looked too gangly, too uncoordinated to ever make it into the air, but with another hop he had left the safety of the nest. His wings flapped madly and for a moment it looked like he might collide with a sharp branch, but in the next he was flying.

They were not safe yet, not the chick, not Inqe, not their species, but there was hope.

Chapter 25

Mike held Banger's pistol up and at the ready as Nia unlocked and opened the door of her apartment. She would have thought the scene laughable if she hadn't seen what the terrorists were capable of.

They had driven to Umhlanga Rocks in Boyd's *bakkie*. The vet turned human doctor had checked on Themba in the morning, once they were all awake, and reported that the boy's shoulder was still bleeding. He wanted to put another couple of stitches in him and this would take time. Also, he wanted Themba to rest a little longer.

Nia and Mike had been reluctant to leave the three children, but as Boyd had pointed out, his vehicle could only take two, three at a pinch, in the cab.

Her additional worry, right now, was that the Americans might be here waiting for her, just as they had ambushed Mike at Suzanne Fessey's place. They knew her name, so it wouldn't take them or the South African police more than a few minutes to find her address. Mike brushed past her and moved through her flat, gun still up, then announced, 'All clear.'

She resented the way he took over, but she also reasoned that it was good to have him with her.

Nia went into her bedroom, took a backpack down from the top of her wardrobe and filled it with clothes, toiletries and her South African and Australian passports. She went to the kitchen and filled the available space with some tinned fruit and three cans of tuna.

Her head throbbed and she felt the fatigue start to overtake her. She put a hand out to steady herself on the kitchen bench. 'I think I need to lie down.'

'Not here,' he said.

'I understand. Do you think the kids are safe with Boyd?'

'For the time being, but we all need somewhere else to hide up and rest.'

'We can't keep running,' she said. 'But we need to hide.'

'My place is too risky; if it's not being watched already it will be soon and they'll be checking this flat out soon enough as well,' Mike said. 'We can go back to Boyd's, but I'd really like to get the kids out of there this evening.'

'We could get a couple of hotel rooms,' she replied.

'Good idea. Got something in mind?'

Nia went to her balcony, opened the doors and walked outside. Mike walked out and stood beside her. She pointed down the beachfront.

'You're kidding, right?' he said.

'My parents gave me one of their credit cards. It's only for use in absolute emergencies. I think this qualifies.'

'Well, if you're sure,' he said.

'I am.'

They took the lift to the basement of the apartment block and got into her car. When the garage doors opened she drove out and paused on the edge of the road, checking up and down for possible surveillance vehicles. A few minutes later they drove into the car park of the most famous hotel in Umhlanga Rocks, the Oyster Box.

'You know, I've lived in Durban all my life and I've never been into this place – mostly because I could never afford to even eat here,' Mike said.

'It's my treat,' Nia said. The security guard at the boom gate saluted and pointed them towards the hotel's entrance. They parked and a porter in a colonial-style uniform and pith helmet came up to them. Nia opened the boot and the man took her backpack. 'My parents used to come and stay here every year when I was at school. They were from Joburg but they loved it here in Umhlanga. They bought the apartment I'm living in five years ago.'

'Clearly they could afford it.'

'My parents didn't have a lot of money when they left South Africa, but they had good business sense. They bought a sleeping bag manufacturing company in Australia and worked hard.'

Nia asked the woman on reception if there were two rooms free and she confirmed that there were two adjoining sea view suites available. 'I'll take both.'

The Oyster Box was old-fashioned in its feel and decor, down to its black and white chequerboard tiled floor; even the maids' uniforms looked like they hadn't changed since the 1930s. Nia thought the place was much the same as when she first visited, and its service was still impeccable. A porter escorted them to the rooms and showed them into the first suite. He opened French doors that led onto a strip of green lawn with two sunbeds. Just beyond the grass was the sparkling Indian Ocean and the red and white striped lighthouse.

'Would you like to see the other room, sir?' the porter asked.

'No, it's fine,' Nia told the man. 'Just leave the key.'

Mike tipped the porter, who left them. '*Lekker* view.'

'It is,' she said. 'I never get tired of it. About the rooms . . .'

'Yes?'

'Don't think me a wimp, please, but I just don't want to be on my own right now, OK?'

'I understand.' Mike called Boyd on his cell phone and walked outside to talk. He kept her in sight while he spoke.

'What's the news?' Nia asked when he came back in.

'He's given Themba a sedative, but the new stitches seem to be holding. He says Themba can't be moved for another six to eight hours, after dark. He says Lerato's going full teenager and is still asleep. The baby's fine.'

'They're as safe there as anywhere else. Let me check on John.' Nia called Buttenshaw, who assured her he was safe and sound and no one, not even the US Government, had yet got around to asking if it was him who had flown them out of Mkhuze the night before, or where the fugitives were hiding. Nia relayed the news to Mike.

'That's good,' he said. 'I think we should get back to Boyd's soon, though.'

'OK, but first I'm going to have a shower and get into some clean clothes. I'm offending even myself.'

Mike took a bottle of water from one of the bedside tables and sat on the chair outside, with the French doors open. It was sunny and warm and tourists were making their way to the hotel swimming pool, and down the steps in front of their room, to the left, to the beach below. Watching them, Nia wished she could be living their carefree life at the moment.

Before she closed the door she stole a glance at Mike's broad back. He reclined in the chair and clasped his hands behind his head. There were those nice forearms again, she thought, tanned and muscular. He still sported a full head of thick hair.

Nia went into the bathroom, turned on the water and stripped out of her flight suit and underwear. She stepped into the shower and luxuriated in the feeling of shampooing and soaping herself.

She thought about the way Mike had looked at her the night before, when they had both paused at the doors of their respective rooms. They were both too tired for anything to have happened, but she had sort of understood what he had said, about people needing someone to look out for them, or watch over them.

Nia had liked that feeling, but in her mind it was over with Banger and that made her want to feel like she didn't need anyone, least of all a man, in her life. She had been very independent ever since she was a child, but Banger had still hurt her. Nia was sad and angry and the fact that Mike Dunn seemed like a decent guy with a sensitive side was mildly annoying. She was ready to dislike all men, at least for a while, and here he was just trying to do the right thing by everyone.

She closed her eyes as she let the hard, hot water pummel her skin and rinse her clean. For a moment she wondered what it would be like to feel those big hands on her body, to touch him, and feel his skin against hers. She was sure that she would miss Banger's touch, his texture, more than the sex. It was ironic that despite her self-admitted prickliness and her feminist leanings she lived for the sensation of touch, a man's fingertips on her, and the feel of his skin.

Nia finished washing, got out of the shower and dried herself. There were plenty of towels so she wrapped one in a turban around her wet hair. When she went back into the room she could see Mike sprawled in the outside chair, asleep.

She walked as quietly as she could to her bag and took out some fresh clothes, but something must have stirred him as he looked over his shoulder at her.

'Sorry to wake you.'

'No problem,' he said. 'I think I'll shower as well.'

'OK, I'll get dressed here in the room, you help yourself to the shower.'

He got up out of the chair and walked inside. As he passed her she could see he was trying not to look at her bare legs, or the skin above the top of her towel. He was quaint, a gentleman, averting his eyes. She liked that.

Nia was tired and her head still throbbed. The thought of even getting dressed seemed almost too much to contemplate. Instead, she lay down on top of the bed, still wrapped in her towel. The softness of the duvet and the mountain of pillows was like a sedative. She closed her eyes and let her exhaustion overwhelm her.

She woke to the sound of a bottle being opened.

'Sorry,' Mike said. 'Sparkling water.'

'I'm a light sleeper at the best of times,' she said.

'I'll go out on the balcony. I wouldn't mind a snooze myself.'

She looked out the French doors. 'It's hot out there. Come, lie on the bed. No hanky-panky, though, and I promise to keep my hands off you.' Nia saw the momentary indecision in his eyes. 'It's all right.'

'It does look tempting. I could go to the other room, of course.'

She patted the bed beside her. 'Like I said, I don't want to be alone right now.'

He came to the bed, sat on the mattress and eased himself down. He lay on his back and closed his eyes, his hands folded across his belly. Within a couple of minutes he was snoring softly.

Nia closed her eyes. Sleep didn't come as easy the second time and she wondered if it was because there was a strange man lying next to her. She didn't feel vulnerable in Mike's presence, more the opposite. She felt safe with him nearby, not threatened, but all the same her nerves felt on edge now.

Again, though, her body got the better of her, and she must have drifted off because the next thing she knew she was opening her eyes and Mike was coming back from the bathroom.

'The curse of old age,' he said to her, when he saw her looking at him.

She blinked a couple of times. 'You should get your prostate checked.'

He gave a short laugh. 'You're not backward in coming forward, are you?'

'Sorry, discretion has never been a strong point.'

He held up his hands. 'It's OK. I've had the check, and the blood test. I've had a few friends with that problem.'

'Good – that you're OK, I mean.'

He looked down at her. She felt embarrassed, now that the first thing that had come into her head was something so personal, so intimate. It was not the sort of thing virtual strangers discussed with each other. On the other hand, they had just both been sleeping in the same bed.

'Are you still tired?'

She nodded. 'I am. I didn't think I'd get to sleep, but I did.'

'You were snoring.'

'Impossible,' she said. 'I don't snore.'

He laughed again.

'What's so funny?'

'You sounded like a warthog.'

Nia reached behind her head, grabbed a pillow and threw it at him. Mike ducked.

'Sorry.'

'*Pah*,' she said. 'I still maintain I don't snore.'

Mike looked at his watch. 'We've got a few hours still before we can go pick up the kids.'

Nia let herself sag back into the bed. 'You know what I'd really like now?'

'What?'

'A drink. I don't drink too much booze, but I'd love a gin and tonic.'

Mike got up and went to the minibar. 'Coming right up. I won't join you, though. I want to keep a clear head.'

'This one's for medicinal purposes.'

He took the miniature bottle of gin and small can of tonic from the fridge and poured them into a glass over ice he took from a bucket on the bar. There was pre-sliced lemon on a saucer and he added a wedge. It seemed decadent, somehow wrong, given the situation, but when he passed her the glass and she took her first sip she closed her eyes in bliss.

'Good?'

'Very.'

He sat down on the bed again and sighed.

'Still tired?'

He nodded.

'Lie down, rest while you can.'

He lay back, resting his head on the pile of pillows, then looked to her. 'You're very brave, you know.'

She shrugged and took another sip. 'Your young friend Themba is brave. A little silly, but also brave.'

He nodded. 'I'm sorry you had to get involved in all this.'

'It's just one of those things.'

'Your boyfriend's an idiot.'

She snorted some gin and tonic up her nose, coughed, then laughed. 'Thank you, I know.' He passed her a serviette and she wiped herself. 'You don't know me, though.'

'No, but the little I do know of you tells me that any man should count himself lucky to have you.'

'No one has ever *had* me, except in the Biblical sense.'

He held up his hands again. 'Sorry.'

'It's OK. And thanks, I get what you mean. I kind of needed to hear that as well, after what happened.'

Mike rolled onto his side and propped himself up on one elbow. 'What were you doing with a guy like him?'

Again, she felt her hackles rise. 'He was hot.'

'But he's below your station.'

'Below my *station*? Are we back in the nineteenth century?'

'You are too smart for him.'

'So I need someone smarter than me, is that what you're saying?'

He shook his head. 'An equal, I think.'

'What if that doesn't exist?'

'Well, a close second then.' Mike did something totally unexpected. He reached out his hand towards her and her heart started pounding madly as she felt the back of his fingertips brush her cheek.

'What are you doing?'

'I don't know.'

He didn't remove his hand, instead he gently stroked her skin. She felt like she was getting a million tiny static electricity shocks as his fingers moved across her, but it was not unpleasant.

'Mike . . .'

'Nia . . .'

Mike reached out a hand and took her chin lightly in his fingers. He gently rubbed his thumb across her lips. 'You're gorgeous.'

She swallowed, hard, her heart pounding.

Then he leaned over to her and kissed her. She was amazed. Her first thought was how soft his lips were. The rest of him looked weather-beaten, tanned, but his lips were like a girl's. Nia opened her mouth. She wanted more of him, wanted to erase the memory of Banger, and to explore someone new again. She'd come so close to death, more than once in the last couple of days, and had killed a man, and now she realised she needed to feel alive again.

Mike trailed the backs of his fingertips over her chest, over the top of her breast above the towel. He carried on, not urgent or insistent and she was content, for now, just kissing him. He was very good at it – Banger had been a bit of a slobberer.

Nia thought briefly of the three kids, but the touch of his fingers on her thigh, below the hem of the towel, banished them.

She rolled onto her side, met his increasingly firmer kisses with her own hunger, and thrilled herself a little by crooking her knee and raising her leg.

She felt his fingers move between her legs now, not zeroing in on her, but rather stroking the soft skin on the inside of her thighs. He would run a finger up to the top of her leg, barely brushing her lips, then back down again. She began to breathe faster. She wanted him to touch her more.

He moved his mouth from hers, kissing her cheek, then the side of her neck. He lingered at her collarbone, dainty and protruding ever so slightly too much, and kissed it. She crooked her head and took his earlobe in her mouth, gently sucking it. He moaned a little. She smiled to herself.

Mike broke free and his lips traced tiny steps down to the white fluffy towel. He used his free hand to undo the loose knot and then she was bare to him. At the same time as his lips and tongue found the first of her nipples his finger trailed along to her clitoris. She could tell, under his touch, that it was swollen. He slowly stroked her between her legs as he gently sucked. She felt herself swell in his mouth and the intensely pleasurable sensation seemed to have a direct line from her nipple to her pussy.

Nia wanted him all over her body, wanted to touch him, to kiss him everywhere at once. She reached for him, and felt his hardness through his pants. She fumbled with the buckle of his belt, his zipper. He moved away a little and helped her, then got to his knees on the bed as she undid him. His penis sprang free of his underpants and she admired the girth of it.

'Lie back,' she said to him. Two could play at this game. She could see her grin mirrored in his. He did as commanded.

Nia turned and straddled him, and took him inside her mouth. As she concentrated on the feel of him, incredibly soft yet very hard, she felt his tongue find her. He traced a line between her swollen lips to her clitoris and, as he'd done with his fingers, traced a path around it.

Nia moaned as she positioned herself so he could have more of her, all of her. Her arousal grew, but she knew she needed him inside her. When she moved off him and lay down he came to her, holding himself up above her, looking down at her. He smiled and lowered his face to her and kissed her again. Then he moved from her, got off the bed and went to his pants and took out his wallet.

'Are you sure?' he asked her as he took the foil-wrapped packet out.

'No. But make love to me anyway, Mike.'

Chapter 26

Mike Dunn woke and was confused. The sky outside was pink but he didn't think it was possible he had slept through the night. Plus, the sun would be coming up over the ocean and it should have been brighter.

And then there was Nia.

He rolled over and looked at her. She was lying on her back, her glorious chest gently rising and falling as she slept. It would be a pity to wake her.

Mike laid his head down on his pillow. It was still damp from his sweat. They had made love twice – fortunately she'd been as prepared as he had been. He hadn't known he had it in him, and she was insatiable. He checked his watch. They had slept an hour, maybe two.

He replayed their time together in his mind. The first time was fast, both of them eager, and he'd kissed and sucked her nipples afterwards as she'd brought herself to orgasm. She'd been embarrassed that it had taken her a long time but he'd reassured her that he loved being there for her, with her, when she came.

The next time was slower, more tender.

Now that he looked at her, saw her comparative youth, he wondered what had just happened. Was it simply survivors' sex? he wondered. She was on the rebound as well, so perhaps he was just part of her own personal healing process, a way of getting over Banger. It was the day after her break-up, but she didn't strike him as the promiscuous type. She did, however, clearly like sex.

For him, it had been a taste of a forgotten paradise, feeling her body under him and above him, marvelling at her slender arms, her muscled bottom. Her skin was soft and smooth, young, unlike his own.

He swung his legs off the bed and sat up, running his hand through his hair. He reached for his pants on the floor and took his phone from the pocket. While he scrolled through his recent calls to find Boyd's number he felt the touch of her hand on his back.

Mike looked over his shoulder.

Nia smiled up at him. 'Hello.'

'Hi.'

'What time is it?'

'Time for us to go collect the kids.'

'We sound like an old married couple.'

'Not quite.'

'No.' She left her hand there, her palm small, warm, soft on his spine. 'Thank you.'

'My pleasure. Thank you.'

She lowered her hand. 'Mike . . .'

He stood, picked up a towel and wrapped it around him. 'It's OK. You don't need to say anything. Besides, I need to call Boyd.'

He went to the French doors, opened them and went outside and sat on a sun bed. He dialled Boyd's number.

'Mike?'

'How are they? Everything OK?'

'Themba's looking better,' Boyd said. 'The bleeding's stopped. Physically he's looking a little stronger. I'd like to keep him overnight, but I know you want to get going.'

'I've found somewhere safe, you don't need to know where, but he'll be resting up soon after we collect him.'

'Need to know basis only, huh? I like that. Very James Bond. OK, you on your way?' Boyd said.

'I'll be with you in less than an hour.'

'Roger that. All good here, buddy.'

Mike ended the call and walked back inside. Nia was sitting up in the bed, the sheet pulled up, covering her breasts.

'Don't turn your back on me and walk out when I'm about to say something to you.'

Her tone annoyed him. 'Don't tell me what to do. We're not married, you know.'

'Why are you treating me this way?' she asked.

'I get it,' he said. 'You were going to tell me that this was a one-off. I'm too old for you, Nia. In any case, we have to go get these kids.'

'You have no idea what I was about to say.'

He looked at her. She glared back at him, her green eyes unblinking. She pursed her lips.

'Well?' he asked.

'The truth is that I don't know what I was about to say. What happened before was, well, to tell you the truth it was pretty fucking wonderful, but I just don't know . . .'

'It's OK. It's no big deal.'

'Don't say that.'

'Sorry,' he said.

He remembered fights with his wife; sometimes they hadn't even begun as fights, but it had seemed that every word he said, no matter how carefully thought out, had been wrong. He felt like he was in one of those situations now. 'I'm going to shower. I'll be ready to leave in ten.'

Mike walked past her, shook his head, and got under the water.

*

Boyd Qualtrough sat on the *stoep* of his house with a pump action shotgun resting across his knees. He was in a swinging chair, the kind that would have looked more at home in his house in Florida than here in Africa, but he liked it. There was a fine African sunset brewing and he took a moment to savour it.

He reached down and picked up his glass of bourbon and Coke and took a sip. It was his first of the day; he needed to make sure he had his wits about him until Mike arrived to pick up the youngsters.

He took the binoculars he'd placed on the seat next to him, raised them to his eyes and focused.

'Lerato?' he called.

The Zulu girl – she would be a head-turning beauty as she matured – came out to him. 'Yes, Dr Boyd?'

'Do you know how to drive?'

'My dad's been teaching me.'

'Ever driven a quad bike?'

'Um, once, on holidays, at the beach.'

'Come with me.'

Boyd led her back to the room where Themba was resting. His eyes were much brighter as they entered. Boyd set his shotgun against the wall, checked the saline drip and saw it was almost finished. He pulled out the cannula from Themba's arm and put a sticky plaster over it. 'You've got to go now, son. There's a car pulled up down by my gate and three people just got out. One of them's a lady cop.'

Themba and Lerato looked at each other. 'No,' the girl said.

Boyd nodded. 'Looks like it could be the folks who are after you. Mike told me about the woman. The baby's mom, right?'

Lerato sighed. 'She's crazy, Dr Boyd, they all are. Part of me wants to just give her the baby and hope she'll leave us alone.'

'You've seen her, you've seen what she and her kind have done. You know she's not just gonna leave you be, don't you, girl?'

Lerato sniffed.

'Come with us, Dr Boyd.'

'Mike took my truck. The only other transport I've got is my quad bike, and there's no way we're all going to fit on that.'

Boyd helped Themba get out of bed and with Lerato's assistance they dressed him in a fresh shirt Boyd had taken from the closet, and the boy's dirty, torn school pants. 'You'll need some new duds when you get to safety.'

Lerato went to her room and came back with the baby. He was clean and fed with a small hand towel pinned around him as a nappy. He seemed content enough and gurgled as she bounced him gently on her hip. 'Please don't leave us alone, Dr Boyd.'

'Hush.'

He took up his shotgun and led them out the back of the farmhouse. The zebra foal he'd been caring for brayed, sensing the tension. 'Hush, now, boy, ain't nothing to worry about.'

They went to the carport. Boyd showed Lerato how to start the quad and turned the key for her. 'Throttle and brake are here, it's easy. Climb aboard.'

Lerato got on the driver's seat and Boyd set the baby down on the grass and helped Themba onto the back. When the boy was seated Boyd lifted the child and placed him between the two teenagers.

'Lerato, a friend of mine, Pete Nairn, farms on the other side of the valley. Head down to the stream, and where you see those two tall trees, there's a rocky drift where you can cross. Water's not deep this time of year. I'll call Mike and tell him where you're headed. Touch base with him when you get to Pete. Tell Pete you're the favour that he owes Boyd.'

Boyd had saved Pete's favourite dog, stitching him up after a leopard had savaged him, but Pete was having a bad year farming and couldn't afford to pay the bill. So many of Boyd's patients were in similar situations. Pete said he owed Boyd a favour and Boyd had told him he'd call in a big one someday.

'Go, now.'

'I'm scared, Dr Boyd,' Lerato said. 'If those people come they'll kill you.'

'Don't worry about me, young lady. I'll just stay here and keep an eye on things and once I know you're safely away, I'll give those bad guys the slip. Now go on, get. On your way.'

The quad bike lurched and Themba had to wrap his good arm around Lerato to make sure he didn't fall off backwards.

Boyd turned, went back to the house and stopped first in his bedroom. He went to his closet and took out a pair of hand-tooled vintage cowboy boots that he'd bought as a graduation present to himself when he'd finished veterinary college.

He sat down on the bed, shook off his sandals and pulled on his boots. Boyd stood, picked up his shotgun by the sliding stock and flicked his hand, chambering a shell. From his closet he also took his .375-calibre hunting rifle, with telescopic sights. Also in the cupboard was a small safe; he opened it, took out a Smith & Wesson .44 revolver, and stuck it in the waistband of his pants. His phone rang and he looked at the screen.

'Howdy, Mike.' Boyd walked down the corridor of his home, his boot heels clicking slowly, rhythmically, on the floorboards. He hadn't been here long, but he liked the place. He was pleased he'd bought it before moving to Botswana. It was one of the few sensible decisions he'd made in his life. He took a deep breath, through his nose, imprinting the house's smell on his senses – wood, floor polish, cigar smoke.

'Boyd, howzit.'

He walked out through the front door onto the *stoep* and set the guns down. 'Could be better. I got company coming up the drive, moving tactically, covering each other as they advance. Two men and a woman. I've sent the kids to the property behind me. Pete's place. You know it?'

'I do. We're on our way. Get out of the house, Boyd, go with them.'

'Shortage of wheels, my friend, and on that note, just so you know, your bad guys have found themselves a new ride, white Toyota Land Cruiser Prado.'

'Call the police, Boyd.'

'I'll do that, directly, but I wanted to give the kids time to get away.'

'Boyd, run.'

'I don't do running at my age. See you soon, Mike.' Boyd ended the call and took his hunting rifle. He knelt on the timber decking and rested the barrel on a carved wooden handrail. He traversed left to right and saw the form of a man running, bent at the waist, behind a hedgerow. He allowed for the man's speed, and possibly the fact that he wasn't a terrorist and just a madman running concealed, and took aim. Boyd fired.

He knew the bullet wouldn't hit, but it had the effect he had desired. Through the leaves of the hedge he saw the man drop to the ground. He scanned the countryside. Boyd saw a flash of blue, the woman in uniform, disappear into some long grass. She had gone to ground.

'Good.'

He had slowed their advance on him, they would be more cautious now, but he had also just signalled that he had seen them and knew who they were.

'Come on, come out,' he willed them.

Another man was up, but he had turned away from the farm-house and was running. Boyd tracked him, keeping the cross hairs of the scope on the man's back as he headed to the parked

Land Cruiser. Boyd was sorely tempted, given what he knew of these people and what they had done, to shoot the man through the back. He even half squeezed the trigger, but something stayed his hand. The man ducked behind the white four-by-four and dropped out of view.

Boyd saw movement in the grass. It was the woman. She was up and running and he could see she was aiming to get around behind his house. He could see now that she was carrying an R5 and he had to stop her before she saw the fleeing kids. He fired, but it was a snap shot, and he saw the bullet kick up dust in front of her. She did stop though and take cover behind the trunk of a big Natal mahogany. She opened up on him.

Bullets smacked into the timber frame of his *stoep* and shattered a window. Boyd dropped to his belly behind a planter box. The flowers in it had died shortly after his most recent girlfriend had left him.

He poked his head up and was answered with another burst of automatic fire. A man was running towards him, but before Boyd could draw a bead on him the man was behind an old cement water trough.

Boyd bided his time. He reckoned he would take at least one or two of them with him, and that would give the youngsters enough time. He looked to the Land Cruiser, where the third person had gone. He saw the missing man now, standing up straight, bracing himself against the vehicle. The object in his hand was long, and pointed at the end.

'Crap!' Boyd got up just before he heard the bang and the *whoosh* and saw the trail of white smoke as the rocket-propelled grenade left the RPG-7 launcher. Bullets tore into his house around him as he made for the door to get inside.

The grenade exploded behind him, on the *stoep*, and the shockwave of the blast knocked him over and propelled him across the lounge room floor. His head smacked into a doorframe.

Smoke filled the house, and as Boyd rolled onto his back he felt multiple stabs of pain. He'd been peppered either with shrapnel or debris from bits of his own home. He looked around him. He had dropped his rifle and the shotgun was outside somewhere, probably blown away by the grenade blast.

Boyd tried to stand but his legs would not function.

He rolled to one side and saw the blood pooling on the floor. He reached down but when he pinched each of his legs in turn he felt nothing. He didn't want to die, certainly not a long painful death from cancer, but now that he was staring it in the face he tried to be a man about it. He said a quick prayer, thanked God for the love he'd known and apologised for the pain he'd caused.

There were voices outside, speaking a language he didn't understand. He thought it sounded like Arabic. Boyd took his phone out of his pocket, dialled Mike Dunn and set it down beside him.

From his belt he took his revolver. He heard footsteps, fast as they took the stairs then slower as they reached the front deck. Boyd judged where the target would be, raised the heavy pistol, and fired. The pistol bucked twice in his hand and the heavy slugs smashed through the front timber wall of the house. He heard a yelp.

'Hit at least one of them,' he said aloud, in case Mike was listening.

A burst of automatic fire smashed what was left of the front windows and stitched a long line of holes above Boyd's head. Splinters and plaster rained down on him.

Boyd rolled over onto his belly, grabbed the phone and used his elbows to drag his paralysed body further inside, to the kitchen. He heard voices behind him. He reached the oven and pulled its door open.

'Boyd?' he heard Mike's voice on the phone. 'We're close.'

'Go to Pete's and hush now. Just listen. They're coming for me. I'm finished, Mike. Been good knowing you, pal.'

'Boyd . . .'

'Quiet.' He hoped Mike would be able to hear what was going on, but no one who entered would hear him speaking.

'Dr Qualtrough,' the woman called from out the front of his house. 'We don't want to hurt you.'

'Bit darned late for that,' he croaked back. 'How'd you find me? The pilot?'

'Let's just say Mr Buttenshaw won't be flying again for some time. Perhaps never. It's good you're still alive, though. We'll get you medical attention.'

Boyd scoffed to himself. 'All right, I know when I'm outgunned. Come on in.'

'Throw out your firearms,' she called back to him.

'Rifle and shotgun are on the *stoep*. This *pistola*'s all I got left.' He tossed his Smith & Wesson through the door. He heard footsteps as someone retrieved the pistol. The woman said something in Arabic.

The barrel of an R5, followed by a brief glimpse of a face, peeked around the doorframe. Boyd had his hands up. The man came out from cover, rifle in his shoulder. Boyd saw the blood soaking his shirt.

'You're the one I winged. How's the woman?'

'I'm fine, Dr Qualtrough,' she called from the other room.

She was too canny to show herself or come into the room until she knew it was safe. The man was a solid-looking brute, cannon fodder, he guessed. 'I ain't so fine.'

The man spoke in their language, and Boyd guessed he was giving her an assessment.

'That's right, my legs are gone. Your guy's seen the blood trail on the floor. Come on in, darling, I can't hurt you.'

'Where are the children? That's my baby they have with them. All I want is to find him and take him home with me. After that I'll be done.'

'I don't know why you need to kill so many people to do that. If you were legit, you'd leave it to the police.' Boyd said nothing about the microchip in the baby's neck. He didn't want to let on that Mike and Nia had found it. He looked up at the thug with the gun, who watched him with dark, unfeeling eyes. The man blinked.

'Your boy here isn't looking so good. I can take a look at him if you like. Come on in and take the gun from him. You can cover me while I patch him up. I'll have to do it sitting down, though.'

'Enough bullshit, Dr Qualtrough. Save me some time, and your life. Tell me where they've gone and I'll be on my way.'

'How about you bite me, missy.'

The woman gave a command in Arabic. The man aimed, pulled the trigger and a bullet slammed into Boyd's left shoulder. The blow didn't hurt right away. Boyd coughed. 'Hard ass, hey?'

'Doctor, you don't know the half of it. We can do this slowly and painfully, or quickly and mercifully.'

'I ain't going to talk.'

'Everyone talks. Always.'

The next shot went into his groin. Boyd screamed more in shock than pain. He was dead below the waist in any case and soon he would be dead, full stop. 'You're not coming in here, are you?'

There was a pause. 'What's that smell?' she asked from the other room.

'You got me, Suzanne,' he said, using her name for the first time.

'You know who I am. You know there's only one way this can end, Dr Qualtrough.'

'Yep,' he said.

The man looked down the open sights of his R5.

'Djuma, get out of there!' the woman yelled. The man glanced over his shoulder.

Boyd lifted his right hand and reached into the breast pocket of his bush shirt. As he pulled his Zippo lighter out of his pocket the man, Djuma, looked back at him and fired twice.

The bullets shattered his forearm and wrist, but Boyd had just enough strength left in his dying body to rotate the wheel. The spark leapt from the flint and Boyd tossed the ignited lighter towards the open door of his gas oven.

Boyd's house exploded.

Chapter 27

Themba heard a loud thump and walked around to the front of Pete's farmhouse. He saw a black and orange fireball roll up into the blue sky from Boyd's house.

Lerato came to his side, the baby on her hip. 'What was that?'

'The doctor, Boyd, he is dead.'

Lerato sniffed. 'This has to end.'

'Come, back to the car.'

Pete the farmer was not at home; his house was closed and locked. They had found an old Mercedes parked in a carport at the rear, and Themba had been searching for a spare key in the places he knew people most often hid them, to no avail, when they had heard the explosion.

They went back around to the carport. It seemed Pete had been doing some work at some stage on the Mercedes, as there was a tool box sitting on the concrete slab. Themba took out a screwdriver and a pair of pliers, then looked around him, on the ground.

He found half a house brick, picked it up and smashed in the window of the front passenger's side door. Lerato winced at the sound and the baby began to cry.

He opened the door and climbed in then, painfully, stretched across and unlocked the driver's side. 'Get in, and put the baby in the back.'

Lerato bundled him in the wrap and lay him on the seat. She did her best to restrain him with a seatbelt but he was already wriggling, trying to get out of his confinement. 'What are we going to do; we don't have a key.'

'I can't do this with one hand.' He handed her the screwdriver and the pliers.

'What am I supposed to do with these?'

Themba felt his head spin, and knew it was the loss of blood. He forced himself to concentrate. 'Put the screwdriver into the gap in the panel under the dashboard and push it down.'

Lerato tentatively probed the join in the fascia. Themba reached over, gasping in pain, and rammed the screwdriver home. 'Push down, as hard as you can.' The lower panel snapped away from its securing screws. 'Now pull out all those wires.'

He saw the three bundles in her hand, one for the lights and indicators on one side of the steering column, another for the window wipers and washer, and the third, most important, that led to the battery, the ignition switch and the starter motor.

Themba reached across, biting down against the pain of yet more movement, and touched the relevant wires. 'These two are for the battery. Pull them out and strip a couple of centimetres of insulation from each end.'

'What?'

'Use the pliers, cut a little bit and pull off the plastic stuff.'

'OK.'

Themba looked out the car window. Smoke was still billowing over Boyd's place. Dogs were barking somewhere and further away Boyd's zebra was braying. Lerato looked up at the sound of a gunshot. 'Hurry,' Themba urged.

She went back to her work, and after a couple of attempts the metal wires at the end of each cable shone bright.

'Now twist them together.' As the wires connected the dashboard instruments flashed on, off, then on again. They had power. 'Good.'

'What next?'

'You have to strip the starter wire,' he tapped it, 'but be careful, it's live now that we've connected the battery.'

Lerato cut into the insulation, but the metal of the tool hit the wires within and it sparked. She shrieked and dropped the pliers. 'Ouch!'

'It won't kill you,' he said, in frustration.

'No, but it *hurt*, Themba.'

'A bullet will hurt much more, trust me, I know.'

She looked at him, wiped her eyes and picked up the wire again. Being more careful, she gently nicked the insulation and pulled it free.

'Great work,' he said.

'And now?'

'Another scary bit. You have to touch the bare end of that wire to the battery wires. It will spark, but hopefully the car will start.'

Lerato drew a deep breath, then tentatively touched the two ends of bare copper together.

'Aah!' The wires sparked and the starter buzzed. The engine almost caught, but Lerato dropped the cables. 'I can't.'

'You can.' He reached over to her and grabbed one of her hands with his good one. 'You can do anything, Lerato. I think I love you.'

She looked at him and blinked. 'You do?'

He nodded.

She picked up the wires again, took a deep breath, closed her eyes and touched the bare ends together. Sparks flew and the engine turned over and caught.

'Push the accelerator, rev it!'

Lerato looked down and pressed her foot hard to the floor. The old diesel engine coughed a couple of puffs of black smoke then roared. Lerato looked down between them. 'This car is automatic, but where's the gear stick on this thing?'

'On the column.' Themba touched it and Lerato peered through the steering wheel, selected reverse and accelerated. They leapt backwards out of the carport and she turned and braked. 'Hurry.'

'I am hurrying. I'm trying to find "D", for Drive.'

'Hassan!' a high-pitched voice called. They looked around.

The baby pulled himself to his feet on the back seat and was staring out the back window.

Themba saw the woman with the blonde hair. Her police uniform looked blackened in places and her face was smudged. She held a pistol loose by her side. She called the name again and the baby screamed.

'It's his mother,' Themba said.

Lerato looked to him. She had found the right gear. 'What do we do?'

As crazy as all of this had been, the child belonged to this woman. 'Maybe we should just leave him.'

The woman was walking towards them, and as her strides quickened to a jog she brought up her pistol to the ready position.

'She won't shoot at us with her baby standing there looking out. She can't take the risk.'

They both kept watch, heads craned, looking over their shoulders, not knowing what to do. About fifty metres short of them the woman stopped. The baby waved his little fists at his mother and squealed excitedly.

'Get out of the car and put your hands up, both of you,' the woman called.

Themba and Lerato looked at each other again. 'She's going to shoot us as soon as we get out,' Lerato said.

He knew she was right. Themba leaned between the two front

seats and reached for the handle of the rear door on Lerato's side.

'Are you going to push him out?' she asked.

He hated the thought of the child ending up with this madwoman, even if she was his mother. 'I won't stand by and let you get hurt, Lerato. You mean too much to me.'

Lerato glanced in the rear view mirror. 'She's walking, coming closer!'

Themba hooked a finger around the door handle and just as he was about to pull it open the rear window shattered into a thousand glittering fragments and cascaded down over the child, Hassan.

*

Nia drove them both in her Golf, so fast that Mike had a hand braced on the dashboard in front of him. The rev counter was red-lining as she changed gear, and she hit one-eighty.

Mike pointed through the windscreen. 'Smoke, over Boyd's farmhouse.'

'I see it. Where's the turnoff to his neighbour's place?'

'Up ahead. Left, one hundred metres.'

Nia drifted into the turn, geared down and was just about to accelerate up the driveway when an old model white Mercedes sedan came around the bend in front of her. She jinked left, braked hard and skidded to a halt in the grass.

'It's them,' Mike said.

The Mercedes bumped and juddered up to them. 'Rear tyre's shredded.'

They got out and Nia drew Banger's pistol. Mike ran to the other car.

'The woman, she's here,' Lerato shrieked. 'She tried to kill us – and her own baby.'

'Get in the Golf,' Nia said. She raised the gun and cupped her left hand under her right, as Banger had taught her. 'Get them inside, Mike.'

Mike scooped up the baby from the back seat. The child was screaming and crying, and Mike passed him to Lerato, who was sliding into the cramped rear of the little Volkswagen. Mike then went to Themba, who looked unsteady on his feet, and, wrapping an arm around him, led him to Nia's car.

Nia glimpsed movement on the other side of a hedge that lined the road halfway up to Boyd's neighbour's house. She squeezed the trigger and the pistol jumped twice in her hands.

'Let's go,' Mike said.

Nia fired again, and as she got into the driver's seat she heard gunshots. Something clanged into her car. She planted her foot and dropped the clutch. The Golf fish-tailed on the grass and she aimed for the front gate. In her mirror she saw the woman firing at her, but they were more than a hundred metres from her, at extreme range. All the same she heard another bullet strike.

'Everyone all right?' Mike asked into the back.

Over the noise of the baby's crying Themba said, 'Yes.'

Nia didn't take her eyes off the road at the speed she was attaining. 'Lerato?'

'She's fine,' Mike said.

Nia risked another glance in the mirror and saw that the girl had her face buried in the baby's chest, as she alternately kissed the infant and sobbed.

Nia ran a hand through her short hair. 'Where to? Back to the hotel?'

Mike rubbed his chin, thinking. 'No.'

'Why not?' she asked.

'I could hear Boyd's conversation over the phone before he died. They knew John Buttenshaw flew us, and it sounded like they got to him.'

'Oh no,' Nia drew a sharp breath. Her heart almost stopped with fear for John and the thought they had brought harm to him. 'How did they know?'

'I don't know. Maybe someone's tracing our phone conversations, yours and mine. Could be a cop feeding information to Suzanne. If so, they'll know I was at the Oyster Box. We need to change direction, head north.'

'Fly or drive?'

'Drive. Everyone, the Americans, the cops, the bad guys, if there are any still alive other than Suzanne Fessey, knows where you work.'

Nia nodded. 'OK, so where in the north are we headed?'

'Zimbabwe.'

Nia raised her eyebrows. 'Seriously?'

Mike looked to the kids in the back again. 'I take it neither of you have passports?'

'No,' Themba said.

Lerato sniffed. 'Me either. My dad was about to get me one.' Mentioning her father's name seemed to bring on another wave of crying.

'That's fine, we'll work around it.' Mike turned to Nia. 'You want me to drive?'

'No, you sleep. I'll go around Swaziland so we don't have to cross any borders; I'll wake you in few hours when we get to the N4, and you can drive from there.'

Mike took out his phone and started tapping the keyboard on the screen.

'Who are you messaging?'

'Banks, the CIA guy.'

'You're not telling him where we're going?'

Mike shook his head. 'I'm letting him know where Suzanne is right now – I told him I would. However, I doubt she'll still be there by the time the Americans arrive. Banks will tell the cops as well.' He pressed send.

When the message was gone Mike searched his contacts on his phone, selected one and held the phone to his ear.

'Who are you calling now?' Nia asked.

'A friend of mine in Zimbabwe. Last call, in case we're being traced.'

'Who is it?' she asked.

'A guy called Shane Castle. He's a one-man army, and he's got some heavily armed friends.'

*

Just after dawn they reached Phalaborwa, a mining town and the site of an entrance to the Kruger National Park, about halfway up the reserve's western boundary. Nia opened her eyes, blinked a couple of times, yawned and checked her watch as they pulled up outside the town's Spur restaurant.

'Get out and take a break,' Mike suggested. 'I'll go in and get takeaway, that way people won't remember us. We're a pretty memorable crew.'

They gave him orders for toasted sandwiches, chips, Cokes and coffees. Mike went in and ordered the food, then he waited outside the restaurant, keeping an eye on the car while the others were stretching their legs. He went back inside, collected the order and brought it out to them.

'We should shop, get some food for the road,' Mike said. 'There's a Spar just before the Kruger gate. We'll load up there and drive through the park.'

'Aren't we better off staying on the main road?' Nia asked.

She seemed to like to challenge everything. He tried not to resent it, reasoning that it was just the way she was: strong, independent, questioning. 'The Americans will convince the South African police to set up roadblocks on the N1 and other roads heading north, once they work out we haven't gone to Durban.'

'And they won't expect us to be tootling slowly through the Kruger Park.'

He nodded as he pulled up at the gate office.

'Clever.'

Her saying that pleased him. He'd been thinking about her. When he had received Boyd's call for help, Mike had felt guilty that he and Nia had been having sex while the children were facing danger. Even worse was the sickening feeling in the pit of his stomach when he had heard the explosion on Boyd's phone and seen the pall of smoke still rising from the veterinarian's home.

Now he felt numb. He wondered if Nia was also feeling as mixed up as he was. Their flight from danger had been all consuming, the rush to get away sucking out all other feelings from his mind and body. He'd felt a moment of victory, turning the tables on Paulsen in Mkhuze, but then Mike had almost died. Nia had saved him.

They ate their toasted sandwiches and takeaway chips standing around the car, then climbed back into the Golf. On impulse Mike reached over to Nia and squeezed her hand. She returned the gesture and, just for an instant, he felt warmth in his heart. She let go of him. 'We should go.'

He drove towards the national park and turned right into the car park of the Kruger Park Spar supermarket. 'We need fuel,' he said.

'You go across the road to the service station,' Nia said, pointing to the garage, 'and Lerato and I will shop.'

'Yes, ma'am,' Mike said.

He drove to the garage, and while the attendant filled the tank he and Themba got out and leaned against the car.

'I'm sorry you had to get involved with this, Mr Mike,' Themba said.

'You can call me just Mike, after what we've all been through.' Mike looked through the window into the car. The baby was asleep on the back seat. Mike fixed Themba with a stare. 'Tell me you did nothing wrong.'

Themba blinked twice. 'It was all going fine, too fine. I was doing well at school, I was getting to know Lerato, I was getting good marks. It couldn't last.'

'What couldn't?'

'I'm cursed, Mr . . . Mike. I am a criminal. I get what I deserve.'

Mike took hold of his arm. 'You're not. I saw something in you, Themba. You're a victim of circumstances.'

Themba looked at the ground. 'You once told me I couldn't use that as an excuse.'

'You told me in the car what happened, how Joseph forced you to help him at gunpoint. I couldn't foresee something like that, but it's an excuse. Themba, listen to me, I need you to be a man, for the girls, for all of us. You've proved that you can do that, but I need you to stay strong.'

Themba looked up and Mike held out his hand. They shook and Mike drew Themba to him, holding him close. The service station attendant hovered nearby, so Mike let Themba go, ignored the man's puzzled look, and paid for the fuel.

It was less than a kilometre to the entry gate to the Kruger National Park. When they reached it, Mike got out and went towards the reception office. A security guard, yawning from the early hour, intercepted him and handed him a form and Mike took it back to the car.

'We need everyone's names and ID numbers.'

'Is that wise?' Nia asked.

Mike was tired, like the guard. She was right. He had an idea. 'Let's all pretend we're foreigners. Pick a name and a country, not African, and make up a passport number. We'll pay the overseas rate; the parks people won't bother asking for passports if we're paying the maximum entry fee to Kruger. If they ask I'll tell them we left our passports at our hotel.'

They filled out the form and Mike took it to the office, where the man behind the desk tapped the names into his computer.

Mike looked out the window. There was a police officer checking a car leaving the park; the man glanced at him and went back to his task. Police checks were not uncommon at the Kruger Park gates due to rhino poaching in the park.

Mike paid the entry fee in cash, not wanting to leave a paper trail that the Americans or South African police might pick up on. He knew the Kruger Park was the busiest of all of South Africa's national parks, even outside of school holidays. 'Do you have any accommodation in the park between here and Punda Maria?'

The man tapped his computer keyboard and ran his finger down the screen. '*Eish*, we are always very full. I only have a three-bedroom bungalow at Shimuwini. It's a bushveld camp, and has no shop or Eskom electricity.'

Mike would have liked to travel further, but Themba needed more bed rest and the others were tired. 'I'll take it.'

He paid, went back to the car, got in and started up. They drove to the boom gate, where a national parks security officer checked their permit and asked if they had any firearms. Mike laughed off the question. 'Of course not.'

The police officer who had been working the exit lane was ambling across to the entry point. Mike gave the man a friendly wave and the officer made no move to stop them.

Mike entered the park and accelerated to fifty kilometres per hour, the maximum speed on tar roads. Eight kilometres in he turned left onto the H1-4 and headed northeast.

'What's the camp where we're staying?' Nia asked.

'Shimuwini. Nice place. It's a bushveld camp in the north of the park, one of the smaller camps in Kruger. It's a line of bungalows overlooking a river, no camping ground, no shop, no restaurant.'

'Will we be safe there?'

All he could do was shrug.

The countryside on the drive to the Shimuwini camp was characterised by a seemingly endless wall of mopane trees. Now, at the end of dry season, their butterfly-shaped leaves were red-gold, but in the summer they would be bright green. Elephant loved the tree and even when the landscape was ravaged by fires, started by the lightning storms that were the curtain-raiser to the wet summer, the big pachyderms still devoured the burnt trunks, savouring the caramelised red sap that oozed from the bark and cooked in the flames.

Fifty-five minutes later they turned onto a gravel access road reserved for guests staying at Shimuwini camp. Once at their destination they presented their paperwork at the office and were given directions to their bungalow, the last on their right as they looked out over the Letaba River.

'It's beautiful,' Nia said, pausing to admire the view before they unpacked the car.

Themba stood next to Lerato, who cradled Hassan, as they now knew him, in the crook of her left arm. She used her right hand to wipe away a tear. Nia went to the girl and put her arm around her.

Mike stood slightly behind the group and looked at them, one by one. It was odd, he thought. They were almost like a family. The thought made him sad. He had lost his own because of his work and his inability to confront the traumas of his early life. He had shut himself off from Tracy and Debbie for too long. Now he found himself, once again, responsible for others, and the thought scared him.

'What are you thinking?'

He saw that Nia had left Themba and Lerato, who were standing so close to each other their arms were touching, and had dropped back to be next to him.

'I'm thinking we need to get these kids as far away from harm as possible, as fast as possible.'

Nia nodded.

She was shorter than him, and her head was tilted back, looking up at him. Lerato and Themba had their backs to them.

He crooked a finger under her chin and she looked into his eyes. He kissed her, on the lips.

'Thank you,' she said.

'For what?'

'For looking after us.'

'I don't know where we're going, what we're going to do,' he said.

She hugged him. 'We'll work it out together.'

Chapter 28

Suzanne pushed the buzzer on the intercom by the gate at the entrance to the housing complex in Pinetown. 'Mrs Dunn, it's Sergeant Brooks.'

'OK, come in.'

The electronic lock on the gate clicked and it rolled open. Suzanne drove the stolen white Corolla inside and past manicured lawns and bright flower beds until she came to number three. The woman opened the front door and came out to meet her.

She was attractive, well groomed, with long dark hair which she brushed away from her eyes. Suzanne had readied herself for the meeting with Dunn's ex-wife. She needed to keep up this disguise as a police officer a little longer so she had bought some new cheap clothes from a Pep store, found a laundromat and washed and dried Sergeant Khumalo's filthy, blood-stained uniform. She had showered at a gym whose chain she still had membership for, changed into the clean uniform and fixed her hair as best she could.

'Sergeant, I'm Tracy Zietsch. Dunn was my first husband's name. I remarried. Is everything all right? Is Mike hurt?'

Suzanne heard the genuine concern in her voice, perhaps a residue of love in the query. 'To tell you the truth, we're not sure, Mrs Zietsch.'

'Oh my goodness, come in. Please call me Tracy.'

Tracy led Suzanne down a hall and into the lounge room, where she gestured for Suzanne to take a seat.

'Lovely house you have here. Is Mr Zietsch home?' Suzanne asked.

'My husband's away, visiting his mother in Namibia. He's from there originally. She's not well.'

'Sorry to hear that.'

'Sergeant, what is this all about?'

'Mr Dunn was helping us with some enquiries; he happened to be on the scene during a pursuit of a stolen car. He was later involved in the hunt for three missing people, two teenagers and child. You may have read about it or seen it on TV?'

'Oh, yes. Something about a shootout in the game reserves, first iMfolozi, then Mkhuze, after the American ambassador was killed. I was just watching it live on TV. The American president was saying he wants to send the FBI and their military into South Africa to find the people who did it, but our silly government is saying we don't need help. No offence to the police.'

Suzanne nodded. 'No problem. But, yes, that's the situation. He wasn't part of the official search team, but . . .'

'But Mike couldn't have stayed out of it if he knew there were young people in trouble. He was involved in mentoring young men who'd gone off the rails.'

Suzanne took the late Sergeant Khumalo's notebook and a pen out of her breast pocket and took some notes for effect.

'Are you in regular touch with your ex-husband, Tracy?'

'My daughter, Debbie, keeps in regular contact with him on Facebook. I find out from her where he is.'

Suzanne made a note. 'Tracy, do you know your ex-husband's movements over the next week or two?'

'Not specifically, no. It's hard, he moves around so much with his work, checking on vultures, attending meetings. He travels all over Africa.'

'How does he travel?'

'A mix. He has that horrible beloved old Land Rover of his, takes commercial flights sometimes, and if it's somewhere remote he might take a charter aircraft, if the charity he works for approves the budget.'

'I see.' Suzanne tapped her pen against her lips. 'Does he have a favourite place that he travels to for his research work? Perhaps somewhere remote where he has lots of friends?'

'Outside of South Africa, that could be anywhere south of the Sahara Desert. You should see his Facebook page, he has friends in wild places all over – Namibia, Zambia, Zimbabwe, Mozambique.'

'Can I put that question another way?'

'Of course? Would you like tea?'

'That would be lovely, thanks,' Suzanne said. She got up and followed Tracy into the adjoining kitchen. When Tracy had put the kettle on and taken down two mugs and a jar of teabags, Suzanne continued. 'If your ex-husband wanted to get away, to drop out for a while, get away from it all, to take a well-earned break, where do you think he might go?'

Tracy regarded her. Her Facebook profile said she was an advocate, and while Suzanne had Googled the firm she worked for and had seen that Tracy specialised in property rather than criminal law, she clearly had a brain. 'What are you trying to say, Sergeant?'

'Please, call me Jane.'

'Are you implying Mike's on the run?'

Suzanne shrugged. 'Honestly, Tracy, we don't know. The young people he's following, they're armed and dangerous.'

'You're not making sense,' Tracy said. She held the boiled kettle in her hand, but refrained from pouring. 'One minute you're implying Mike's on the run, hiding, the next that he might have been hurt. What's going on here?'

Suzanne put her hands on her hips, her right resting on Khumalo's Z88 service pistol.

Tracy put down the kettle. 'On second thoughts, I don't know how I can be of further assistance.'

'Did Mike ever mention a young man by the name of Themba Nyathi?'

The sudden change of tack seemed to throw Tracy. She ran a hand through her hair. 'Um, I'm not sure.'

'He was a car thief.'

'Oh, yes, I remember, he did mention him a couple of times. His latest "cause". Themba was a student on one of the courses Mike runs for disaffected young people. They're training to be rhino security guards, future rangers, that sort of thing.'

'He's the one who is on the loose. He's gone back to his old ways. He stole the car with the little baby in it, and has now kidnapped the child. They're the ones on the run.'

Tracy put a hand to her mouth. 'Oh, dear. I'm sorry, Sergeant, Jane, for the way I reacted earlier. Mike's always been a sucker for a sad story – at least, he has been since early on in our marriage.'

'Well, if he thinks this boy Themba is innocent, he's wrong. You would have read that he tried to shoot down a civilian helicopter, and we suspect him of being involved in the downing of that American military chopper that crashed in the iMfolozi Game Reserve.'

Tracy shook her head. 'Mike,' she said softly, 'what have you done?'

Suzanne reached out and put a hand on the other woman's arm. 'Don't be too hard on him. Some people just want to see the good in others; they can't help it if they miss the signals.'

Suzanne noticed Tracy's eyes go to the tattoo on the inside of her right arm.

'Is that a birthday, 30 January 2016?'

'Um, yes,' Suzanne said. 'My son.'

'That's a coincidence, my daughter Debbie's is the same day, though quite a few years ago.' Tracy took a phone out of the back pocket of her jeans. 'Debbie's far more interested in Mike's work than I am. She wants to study zoology or veterinary science at varsity when she graduates; follow in his footsteps, as it were. I'll see if she knows where he might be headed.'

'Thank you.'

Tracy poured two cups of tea and they sat in the kitchen, sipping. Suzanne looked around, noted the pictures of a girl with braces on the refrigerator. Suzanne wondered what life would be like if your main priority was raising your child to adulthood. She looked out the window to hide the look in her eyes from the other woman.

Tracy's phone beeped. She picked it up, read the screen, and nodded. 'Yes, I should have thought of that.'

'What's that?'

'I think I know where Mike may be headed. Debbie's just reminded me.'

*

Nia opened her eyes, saw the ceiling fan above her slowly turning and wondered for a moment where she was.

She looked from side to side and then saw Mike, lying on his back next to her, snoring softly. It all came back to her. She was fully clothed, but Mike had stripped off his shirt before falling asleep after the long night's driving and the trip through Kruger.

There were three rooms in the bungalow. They'd put Lerato and the baby in one room, Themba in his own, and Mike and Nia shared the third.

Nia remembered their lovemaking in the Oyster Box Hotel. What she wouldn't give to be back there now, she thought, perhaps with a bottle of champagne in an ice bucket next to the bed. She sat up, yawned and reached for her phone on the bedside table. The screen said it was just after four in the afternoon. By her calculation she had slept for a little over four hours.

Mike must have sensed her movement. He opened his eyes and looked her way. 'What time is it?'

She told him. 'You were snoring.'

'I don't snore.'

'Yes, you do,' Nia said.

'My ex-wife used to lie like you do.'

She smiled. 'Do you think we're safe here?'

He shrugged. 'As safe as anywhere else. We can't move any further today in any case; there's no accommodation further north so we'll have to wait until first light tomorrow and then leave the park.'

Nia swung her bare feet off the bed and stood. 'I'm going to check on the kids.'

'Yes, dear.'

She wagged a finger at him and went out into the small lounge and dining area. Themba was in the kitchen, by the stove. 'Hi, Nia. I've just boiled some water. Would you like tea?'

She nodded. 'Please.' He was a contradiction: a polite, seemingly intelligent young man who had once been a car thief. 'Where's Lerato?'

'She's bathing the baby. They're both fine.'

Nia added milk to the cup that Themba poured and they both went out of the bungalow onto the *stoep*. The Letaba River glittered in front of them, beyond a manicured, watered lawn.

Themba blew on his tea. 'It is beautiful here.'

'It is.'

'Can I ask you a question, Nia?'

'Sure.'

'Do you, I mean, are you . . .'

'What?'

'You and Mike, do you like each other?'

Nia gave a small laugh. 'We're friends, I guess, and I like him.'

'OK.'

She sipped her tea. A hippopotamus honked from somewhere down river, mocking Themba's serious face. 'What's on your mind, Themba?'

'Nothing.'

'There is. Is it about you and Lerato?'

He glanced from the river to her, then back in the direction of the hippo.

'Are you in love with her?'

He looked to her again and nodded. 'I think so. But I don't know if she likes me.'

Nia gave a sympathetic smile. 'Well, after what you've put her through the last few days . . .'

'Please, Nia, you know I meant none of this, and I didn't mean to threaten you when you were hovering over me in your helicopter. I was scared.'

Nia reached out and put her hand on his arm. 'I know, I didn't mean to tease. You're young, Themba, and so is Lerato.'

'But that doesn't mean I can't love her.'

'No, you're right. You're both nearly adults. Tell her you're sorry for what she's had to go through, and that you think she's done a great job with the baby. Ask her if you can still be friends.'

He mulled over her words. 'You think that will be enough?'

'It will show her you care.' Nia looked away, out at the river. She couldn't get over how serenely beautiful it was.

Themba nodded, and seemed to take the advice on board. 'I'll go and check on her now.'

'You do that.'

Mike came outside, buttoning his shirt. Instead of a cup of tea he'd taken a beer from the fridge, one of the sixpack they'd rationed to themselves. In his other hand he carried a folded brown blanket he had liberated from the bungalow. He raised the bottle in salute to her.

'A little early to be celebrating?'

He took a drink from the green Windhoek Lager bottle. 'Not much else we can do.'

'What's the blanket for?'

'Picnic.'

He walked past her, towards the fence that separated the camp's grounds from the river, and laid the blanket out in the shade of a tree. Nia followed and, balancing her teacup, sat down cross-legged beside him. She looked over her shoulder and saw that Themba and Lerato were sitting on chairs outside the bungalow, and the girl was feeding the baby. She wondered if Themba had plucked up the courage to follow her advice. 'It's beautiful here, so peaceful.'

'I love the north of Kruger.' He took another sip. 'It's the quietest part of the park, a good place to get away from it all.'

'We can't, though, can we?' she asked.

Mike looked out at the river, rolled the dewy bottle in his fingers, picked at the label. 'I don't know if we're doing the right thing, Nia, but I'm worried for those kids.'

'I've been thinking about the microchip. It was just numbers that you found when you scanned it, right?'

'Yes.'

'Could it be a bank account?'

Mike took a drink. 'Yes, but I've got no idea how we would find where it might be. It looks too long for a normal South African bank account number.'

'I've got an idea how we might find out.'

He set down the bottle, now empty, on the blanket and looked at her. He raised his eyebrows.

'You remember I told you about the old rich guy I was seeing, the banker who was married?'

'Yes. You think he might be able to help?'

'It's worth a try. Can you give me the number?'

He unbuttoned the left breast pocket of his khaki bush shirt, took out his phone and scrolled through his contacts. 'Here it is, in two contacts. I listed the first half as Carla's phone number and the second as the end of Helen's, but ignore the "+27"s at the beginning. The first number on the chip actually starts with the letters CH – one of the reasons I picked Carla and Helen – and the second number on the chip is the last six digits of Helen's number.'

'Carla and Helen?'

'Old girlfriends.' He winked.

'TMI,' Nia said.

'What if the police are tracking your phone?' he asked.

'I've thought of that.'

Nia took Mike's phone, got up off the blanket and walked to the left along the grassy lawn, towards the timber bird hide. Just before the hide was a big tree. Under it was a park bench.

One of the camp attendants, a man in national parks green, was sitting on the bench, holding his phone up and at arm's length from his mouth. He was talking on speaker. Nia had seen someone else doing this when they had first arrived and, after enquiring at the office where they checked in, learned that the big tree was about the only spot in the camp where there was a phone signal. Even there it was weak, and the woman at the check-in desk had advised her to hold her phone up in the air, as the man was doing now.

When the man was finished his call Nia asked him if she could borrow his phone, as she was out of credit.

'I'm not sure,' the man said.

'I'll give you five hundred rand for one, maybe two calls.'

'Sure?'

'Serious,' she said and pulled the cash from her pocket.

The man grinned and handed her his phone and moved away out of earshot, counting his money.

She sat where he had been, her bum on the back rest of the park bench, and held the phone up, waving it around until she got a three-bar signal. The first number she called was directory assistance, and she asked for the number of Roger Green in Rosebank, Johannesburg. The number was sent to her a few seconds later.

Nia held up a finger to the man, who was watching her. 'One more call.'

She dialled, hoping that Roger was home – it was a Sunday after all – and that she didn't get his wife. She was in luck.

'Hello?'

'Roger, it's Nia Carras, the helicopter pilot, from Durban. I'm not sure if you remember me.'

He lowered his voice to a terse whisper immediately. 'What are you doing calling me at home?'

'I need help.'

'I'm hanging up.'

'Please, Roger, it's important, life and death even.'

There was a pause on the end of the line. 'I'm not going to give you money, if that's what you want.'

She was annoyed that he thought she might be trying some amateurish blackmailing scheme, but then she reflected that they hardly knew each other. 'Relax, Roger, I don't want your money, I just need some help. It's important, life and death, for what it's worth.'

'What is it?'

'I've got two numbers, Roger, which I think might be for a bank account. The first one's very long, with two letters at the start, and the second has only six digits. If I read it to you, can you take it down and see if you can make any sense of it?'

The line was quiet again while he thought. 'Is this legal? I'm not sure I can help.'

'Don't be a wimp, Roger. Look, if you had any genuine feelings for me then I would hope that you might help me with this. It really is very important. People are willing to kill for this number. A child's life is at risk because of it.'

'Sounds like this isn't a joke. OK, what's the first number, the one with the letters?'

Nia checked the screen of Mike's phone and read him the first number.

'OK, got it. I can't talk long,' he whispered.

'Wife nearby?'

'Do you want to mock me or do you want the information?' he said, still in a hushed voice.

'Sorry,' Nia said.

'It's an IBAN, an international bank account number. It's Swiss – you can tell that from the letters "C" and "H" at the start. The other digits identify the bank and the account.'

Nia smiled. They were right, it was a foreign account. 'Can you tell me where in Switzerland the bank is, and its name?'

'I'll check online and SMS you the name and address.'

'Can anybody access an account like this?'

'The Swiss are famous for their discretion, as you probably know. They don't put people through the hoops when it comes to accessing the account, but as well as the number there is always some other form of identification needed, of course.'

'What sort of identification?'

'A password, or another number.'

'Like a PIN?'

'Yes, pretty much the same system, only it would be more complex than a four-digit PIN. It could be the other number you have there – six digits would be too short for another account number.'

'Is it like a normal account? I mean, could I log on to the internet to check what's in it?'

Roger gave a small laugh. 'No. With all this cloak and dagger and life and death stuff you mentioned I'm guessing this is a numbered account, the most private kind. I'm assuming it contains money that someone wants to hide?'

'Looks like it,' Nia said.

'Criminals and even semi-legit businesspeople who want to avoid paying tax use these accounts because there's no paper trail or electronic records that police can access. Typically these accounts are based on personal contact. You could call the bank and try giving them the passcode number and see what they say, but they're usually not even keen on telephone exchanges. I'll include a contact number in my message to you once I look up the bank and its address.'

'Roger, thank you for this. I can't tell you how important it is to me.'

'Important enough to have a drink with me next time you're in Johannesburg or I'm in Durban on business?'

She had to smile. 'You're incorrigible.'

'You don't know the half of it.'

'Thank you, Roger, and goodbye.'

'Nia . . .'

She was in a hurry to get back to Mike, but Roger's tone had softened. 'Yes?'

'I'm sorry, I should have told you my situation.'

'It wouldn't have changed anything, but yes, you should have.'

'Bye.'

Nia ended the call. She waited on the bench, keeping the phone in signal range for a little longer. The phone beeped and vibrated.

Roger's message said: *Grunelius Bank, Geneva*, followed by a phone number and address.

'Switzerland,' she said to herself as she walked back to the bungalow.

Chapter 29

Jed, Franklin and Chris Mitchell pored over a map of southern Africa in the officers' mess of the Natal Mounted Rifles in Durban.

Chris Mitchell traced a line from Mkhuze Game Reserve northwards. 'We would have picked them up if they'd tried to cross into Swaziland or Mozambique at any of the recognised border crossings.'

Jed stroked his beard. 'That frontier's as porous as a mosquito net, boss.'

Chris nodded. 'Agreed, but we know the kid, Themba, is wounded, and they'll all be tired.'

They had missed Suzanne Fessey at Dr Boyd Qualtrough's farm, and the South African police had found a white Toyota Land Cruiser burned out on a side road off the N2 north of Umhlanga Rocks a few hours ago. The colour and model matched that of a vehicle that several eyewitnesses had seen leaving Qualtrough's place. Egil Paulsen, meanwhile, had been found dead in Mkhuze Game Reserve.

The American presence in South Africa was ramping up by

the hour. Communications experts from the warship in the harbour had come ashore and installed a bank of computers in the mess. The picture of a white-bearded, ruddy-faced man was on a widescreen plasma television that had just been mounted on the wall. 'Qualtrough, another American citizen,' Jed said. 'His death just makes this an even bigger story for the folks back at home, as if the loss of the ambassador and her secret service guys wasn't enough.'

'What do we know about Qualtrough?' Chris asked. He'd been on a conference call to the US for the past hour and they were bringing him up to speed as well as trying to deduce where the fugitives might be headed.

'Good friends with Dunn, judging by their Facebook pages,' Jed said.

'Damn,' Chris said. 'Fessey is ahead of us and we can't catch three kids and a female chopper pilot?'

They all looked to each other. Tempers were fraying.

'All right,' Chris said. 'Let's move on, but to where, I don't know. What we do know is that thanks to the late Dr Qualtrough, Fessey is down to one sidekick. She's in a new vehicle, though we don't know the make and model, and Dunn, Carras and the kids are in the wind somewhere in Africa.'

Jed's phone rang. It was a liaison officer in the South African Police Service. He took notes then ended the call. 'More news, and it's good,' he said to Franklin and Chris. 'An eagle-eyed police officer at the Kruger National Park's Phalaborwa gate called his superiors after he got the South African equivalent of an all-points bulletin about our targets. He saw a white man and woman in a car with two black teenagers and a baby checking into the park. Didn't think to question them further at the time, but realised who they were once he got the alert.'

'At least someone's doing their job. Do we know where they were headed?' Chris asked.

Jed went to the map pinned to the wall and located the green strip that marked the national park. 'A place called Shimuwini. I know it; I took my wife and youngest there last year. It's a bush-veld camp, quiet place in the north of the park.'

'They're headed north,' Chris said. 'Zimbabwe?'

'Or maybe Mozambique,' Jed ventured. 'At the north of Kruger there's a place called Crooks' Corner on the Limpopo River where South Africa, Mozambique and Zimbabwe all meet. Ivory poachers used to hop from one country to another to escape prosecution.'

Chris nodded.

'The South African police are putting up roadblocks on the way to the Beitbridge border crossing into Zimbabwe and the entry points to Botswana to the west, in case they head that way. They've also alerted their people at the Giryondo and Pafuri crossings into Mozambique from Kruger.'

Jed studied the map. 'They're too conspicuous to keep travel-ling as a group, and Dunn will guess that the borders will be closed. Besides, the teenagers wouldn't be carrying passports. They're going to cross illegally, on foot, through the bush. We've got to get them before they leave the Kruger Park.'

Chris looked at him. 'Then get on your way. And don't come back empty-handed.'

*

Mike ran the backs of his fingers lightly down Nia's spine. She rolled over.

'Sorry I woke you,' he said.

'No, I was already up. I'm too wired. What time is it?'

'Four am,' he said.

They'd had sundowner drinks by the river, the kids with Coca Cola. Afterwards Mike had *braai*ed steaks and Nia had made a salad. It was a deceptively relaxing evening. When Themba and

Lerato had gone to their rooms Mike and Nia had sat up for a while, discussing their next move.

Eventually, she had looked him in the eye, taken his big hand in hers, stood, and led him to their bedroom. Mike had pushed the two single beds together and they had made love, slowly, then fallen asleep.

It was still dark outside. 'Do you want to go back to sleep?' he asked.

'No. I want you.'

She reached for him and drew her to him, hugging him with a strength he found surprising. He squeezed her back. 'I want you, too.' He kissed her cheek and then her lips.

Nia relaxed her embrace then put a palm on his chest and motioned for him to move onto his back. She climbed on him, straddling his body, and eased herself down. Mike looked up at her, quietly and silently in awe of her beauty and the feel of her body. She felt almost weightless on him as she moved, slowly at first, gradually increasing the tempo.

'You're not going to have a heart attack on me, are you?'

'Not if you keep doing all the work.'

'Huh!' She bent forward and kissed him. He arched his back, sliding even deeper into her.

They made love silently, so as not to disturb the children. Nia rode him harder, faster, and when he felt himself getting closer he put his hands on her hips, slowing her to a stop. He pulled her to his chest and rolled on top of her. He started to move inside her again, slowly, looking into her eyes. He could feel her respond, opening herself up to him, so he could go even deeper inside her. Moving faster, he felt himself swell. She smiled at him then pulled him towards her and kissed him, hard, and he came inside her.

They dropped back into the sheets, exhausted, and kissed.

A minute later the alarm on his phone went off. He sighed, kissed Nia again then went to the shower. She joined him and scrubbed his back. He soaped her, but this was not the time for more sex. They had to be ready to go as soon as the camp gates opened, which at this time of year, early October, was five thirty.

Nia made toast and coffee for all of them. Lerato fed the baby with food they had bought on the road and Themba helped Mike pack the car for the trip.

The sky was turning pink as the attendant Nia had borrowed the phone from opened the gate for them. They headed north.

They saw elephant and a big herd of three hundred or more buffalo, but Mike kept his speed steady at the maximum, fifty kilometres per hour. They were not here to sightsee.

They stopped in at Shingwedzi Camp for a toilet break and to stretch their legs. Nia bought more coffee and Cokes from the camp shop and then Mike hustled them back into the car and they set off again. The day was warming – it was always hotter this far north in the park – and Mike kept his speed up. Eventually, several hours after they had set off, they reached the turnoff to the road to Crooks' Corner.

Mike drove Nia's little hatchback slowly down a dirt road that was signposted on a cairn with a red and white no entry sign until the track petered out. 'Let's get some branches and cover the car.'

When they had finished camouflaging the Golf, Mike shouldered the heaviest pack. Nia carried the baby on her back, in a wrap that Lerato tied for her. Lerato took the pack with food in it.

Mike led the way, his rifle up and across his body, his senses alert for game, especially lonely old buffalos, and guided them through a shade forest of fever trees that gave way to a line of thick bush growing on the edge of the flood plain. They emerged to find the wide, open, sandy expanse of the Limpopo riverbed. A fish eagle called its haunting cry and Mike raised a hand to shield his eyes from the glare as he found it in the sky.

'Looks quiet.'

'The river's a lot narrower than I thought it would be,' Nia said.

The water flowed along the bank on the Zimbabwean side, a couple of hundred metres across from where they stood. 'Let's go,' Mike said.

They trudged through the thick sand of the riverbed, sweating in the sun without the benefit of trees above them. Lerato stumbled, but was able to get back to her feet without assistance. Mike continually scanned left and right. The biggest risk for them here was that a military or national parks anti-poaching patrol might appear. On the other side of the river the first swathe of land was designated for hunting, so there was also the chance they might bump into a shooting party.

There was no fence on either side of the river that marked the border between South Africa and Zimbabwe. Hundreds of thousands of illegal immigrants crossed the Limpopo from Zimbabwe every year, some of them through the national park.

They came to the water's edge and Mike strode on, not bothering to take his boots off. The river here was only about twenty metres wide, and no deeper than his knees. The others, seeing it was safe, followed him. A hundred metres to his right, where the river widened, he saw the silhouette of a crocodile, but the water was clear and cool where they crossed and Mike could see there was no danger, at least not from reptiles.

'Welcome to Zimbabwe,' he said to Nia as he held out his hand and helped her scramble up the steep sandy bank.

Once they were all up Mike led them deeper into the new country. There had been fires here and the landscape was blackened. In places fallen tree trunks still smoked.

'It's like a wasteland.'

'In places like this, on the edge of national parks, poachers sometimes deliberately set fires at the end of the dry season,' Mike said.

'Doesn't that scare the animals away?' Nia asked.

'The small stuff, what's left of it on this side of the border, will take flight, but when the first rains of summer come the fresh green grass shoots are too much for the buffalo, impala and other grazers on the Kruger side of the river to resist.'

'Bastards.'

They trudged on. The sun was up and the remnant heat from the fire and the lack of shade added to their discomfort. They were all sweating and making hard work of their walk in the sand. They came to a dry riverbed and Mike called a rest break under a tree that had escaped the worst of the blaze.

Lerato gave the baby a drink.

'How's the little guy holding up?' Mike asked.

Lerato looked up at him. 'He's hot and tired, like the rest of us, but he's a good baby.'

'I know he is. And you're a good carer.'

They set off again and Mike kept an eye on the sky for heli-copters or search planes. All he saw was a pair of white-backed vultures, lazily circling, trying to catch a thermal to help lift their heavy bodies skywards. Some people might have worried at such a sight, but these were his birds, his totem, and it pleased him to see them.

After forty-five minutes of trudging they came to a road, which had probably been where the fire was set. On the other side the bush was unburned: long, dry golden grass studded with thorny acacias. They sat down again in the shade.

'What now?' Nia asked.

'To our east,' Mike pointed, 'is the Mozambican border. To the west, if we follow the road and hook around to the right, we'll come to some Shangaan villages. We could walk northeast, through what's known as the Sengwe Corridor, but it's a long hike through the bush. We'll start running into big game, espe-cially elephant, and they're nervous and sometimes aggressive here – they've been hunted and poached for decades. I say we wait for a lift.'

'Are there many cars here?' Themba asked. 'It looks quiet.'

'There are smugglers, sneaking goods into Zimbabwe from Mozambique to avoid customs duty, and bringing people to the border where they can cross illegally into South Africa. I'm counting on flagging down someone who won't ask too many questions.'

They sat in the grass, resting, and Nia edged her hand closer to his. Mike covered it with his own. It was good to have her by his side, though he had trouble imagining what a future with her might look like.

Themba had been lying down, near Lerato, but now he sat bolt upright. 'I hear an engine.'

Mike cocked his head. Themba's young ears were better than his. 'I hear it now.' He stood and moved closer to the road, shielding his eyes from the sun's glare with his hand. A couple of hundred metres to the east the road made a bend. He saw the dark green bulk of a truck emerge. Mike dropped. 'Everyone down! It's the Zimbabwean Army.'

They all lay in the grass and Mike, who was closest to the road, held his breath as he peered through the yellow stalks in front of him. Half a dozen soldiers dozed in the open rear of the truck and the driver leaned lazily on his steering wheel. As the truck passed them Mike saw a big sign stuck on the back of the vehicle. In bold red lettering on a white background, below a skull and crossbones, were the words, *Danger, land mines in this area. Do not walk.*

Once the truck had passed out of sight they all sat up. 'Hey,' Nia said, 'did you see *that*?'

'Don't worry,' Mike reassured her, 'this area's clear. They're concentrating their work up and down the Mozambican border, which was heavily mined during Zimbabwe's war of independence.' Mike stood. 'I'm going to walk up the road a bit, see if I can see anyone.'

Just as he set off they heard another vehicle coming. Mike dropped to a crouch, but got to his feet again when he saw a battered Isuzu *bakkie* heading their way, a cloud of black diesel smoke in its wake. Mike flagged the man down.

'*Avuxeni*,' Mike said to the driver.

'*Ayeh imjani.*'

'*Kona*,' Mike said, completing the greeting, telling the man he was well. He switched to English. 'Please, can you take my friends and me?'

'Where do you wish to go?'

'Do you know Fish Eagle Lodge?'

The driver rubbed the grey stubble on his chin. 'I do, but it is far. I can take you there, for a price.'

'I have money,' Nia said.

Lerato took Hassan into the front passenger seat and the rest of them climbed in the back, Themba lying down on an old, haphazardly folded tarpaulin and Nia taking a seat next to Mike. He put his arm around her. It was good to be moving, with the warm breeze on their faces. 'You're not worried the children will see us?'

He laughed. 'It's good to have something to joke about. I think they've probably guessed.'

Nia leaned over and whispered in his ear, 'Themba loves Lerato.'

'Shouldn't you be passing me a note to tell me that?'

She punched him lightly on the shoulder. 'Think we can risk a kiss?'

Mike looked theatrically over his shoulder at the back of Lerato's head in the cab, then gave a small nod. Nia rolled into him and kissed him hard on the lips. As he savoured the feel and taste of her mouth he glanced to the side and saw that Themba had opened his eyes. The youngster winked at him, then went back to pretending to be asleep.

When they broke apart, Nia rested her head on his shoulder and Mike closed his eyes. When he opened them again he saw a speck against the blue sky. He put his hand gently on Nia's and she looked up at him.

'What's wrong?'

'Chopper.'

She looked to where he was pointing. 'It's over Kruger, heading parallel to the river. Shit, it's an American Sea Hawk again.'

'Themba!'

The lad was already following their gaze.

'Unroll that tarp. We've got to cover ourselves.'

Nia took the end of the tarpaulin from Themba, and with Mike helping they shook out the green sheet and laid it over themselves. The road they were on veered right, away from the Limpopo River.

Mike peeked out from under the cover. 'They're not crossing the river. Even the Americans have to respect international airspace, and they won't be welcome here in Zimbabwe.'

'I sure hope not,' Nia said, though she didn't sound convinced.

Chapter 30

Suzanne Fessey took the turnoff to Johannesburg's O. R. Tambo International Airport. It had been a six-hour drive from Durban. She felt invigorated despite her lack of sleep.

Bilal, the last surviving member of the team that was supposed to have met her at the Mozambican border and escorted her north to Tanzania, dozed with his head against the passenger-side window.

Dunn's ex-wife had given her the lead she needed to catch up, or even overtake the fugitives. She had decided to let the woman live; if she had killed Tracy then Dunn would have found out and known she was closing in on him. The risk was that Mike Dunn might call her, or the real South African police might pay her a visit, but Suzanne balanced that thought with the fact that Dunn had not called her so far, so he was unlikely to ask her for help from Zimbabwe.

Bilal stirred as she parked her latest stolen car, a Chevrolet Aveo, in the high-rise car park.

'Stay here,' Suzanne said to Bilal. 'I'll go buy our tickets and come back for you. I'm going to change my appearance and then you can do the same, separately from me. The authorities will be looking for a couple.'

Bilal nodded. He was a foot-soldier, used to following orders. If he objected to being commanded by a woman, as some men did, he gave no sign of it.

Suzanne headed to the left luggage office and presented a dog-eared, crumpled ticket to the grey-haired attendant.

He checked the card. 'Ah, but this bag has been here a long time.'

'I've been busy.'

'You've been travelling in our beautiful country?'

Suzanne looked at her wristwatch then at the man. 'Please, I'm in a hurry, my flight leaves very soon. It's a small black wheelie bag.'

The man checked the ticket again and turned and shuffled slowly into the storeroom behind him. Suzanne drummed her fingers on the counter top while she waited. A few minutes later the man returned with her dusty bag.

'It took me a while to find it. Sorry for the wait.'

'No problem.'

The man worked out the cost and Suzanne paid in cash.

'Would you like a receipt?'

'No, thanks, I must rush.'

Suzanne walked through the terminal to the nearest toilets. She had stopped at the shopping mall at Pietermaritzburg, outside of Durban on the road to Johannesburg, and bought herself jeans, a couple of T-shirts and some flat shoes. She had ditched her police uniform in a rubbish bin.

She let herself into a disabled bathroom and locked the door. Then she unlocked the padlock on the bag with the tiny key on her key ring and unzipped it. Inside was an Irish passport in the name of Mary O'Sullivan with her picture on the identity page, though her hair was black. Also in the bag were another change

349

of clothes, underwear, a hand towel, a leather purse containing five thousand US dollars and twenty thousand rand in cash, and a counterfeit credit card also in her assumed name.

There was also a zip-up toiletry bag. From it Suzanne took a bottle of hair dye and a small plastic contact lenses case. She draped the hand towel around her shoulders, ran some water in the hand basin and set about dying her hair.

When she was done she rinsed her hair then opened the contact lenses case and changed the colour of her eyes from blue to brown. She stepped back a pace and regarded her new self in the mirror. She wetted a paper towel and wiped black dye from her hairline, then nodded to herself and threw the bottle in the bin. She let herself out and went into the terminal.

She made her way through Terminal A, where international departures was located, and found the British Airways office. She greeted the woman in blue behind the counter. 'Do you have any seats available on the next flight to Zimbabwe, please?'

'Harare, ma'am?'

'Yes, please.'

Her red-painted nails clattered on her computer keyboard. 'Only two seats left, ma'am, but they're both in business class. Would that be fine?'

'Yes, no problem, I'll take one.'

'OK, ma'am, I'll make the booking. Will you be paying by card?'

'Cash.'

'Fine.'

The woman processed the ticket. It was expensive, but money meant nothing to Suzanne. All that motivated her was getting to her child, and the microchip in Hassan's little body.

Suzanne looked around her, ever watchful, expecting at any minute to see a posse of armed police or CIA operatives in plain clothes. She had been trained to fight through tiredness and exhaustion and to draw sustenance from her mission. She tried not to think about the personal losses she had suffered. Her husband had died for the cause and he was in paradise. She loved their son, but she saw him as a warrior as well. His path may very well be martyrdom, but she hoped he would live.

'Are you all right, ma'am?' the woman asked from behind the counter.

Suzanne felt the wetness and wiped her eyes, blinking. 'Death in the family.'

'My deepest condolences,' said the woman. 'Is that why you're going to Zimbabwe?'

Suzanne felt a surge of strength energise her and banish her tears. 'Yes, that is why I am going to Zimbabwe.'

'Shame. I'm so sorry.'

Suzanne nodded her thanks and left. She walked back out to the car park, trailing her wheelie bag. Bilal was leaning against a pillar, reading a discarded newspaper. He looked up as she came nearer and she indicated for him to meet her at the car.

When they were reunited she bent and unzipped her bag. 'Get in the car.'

He did as ordered and took the passenger scat. From the bag Suzanne took out the Tokarev pistol with a silencer attached. After a quick check to make sure no one was in view or close enough to hear the muffled report, she opened the driver's door and shot Bilal twice in the head.

Chapter 31

The Sea Hawk helicopter's pilot touched down on a gravel access road not far from Crooks' Corner in the northeast of the Kruger park.

Jed and Franklin got out and Jed headed towards the South African national parks section ranger responsible for this part of the reserve; the man had guided them into the landing zone by radio. Franklin went to the edge of a grove of almost luminous green fever trees, sat down in the shade, and began stripping and cleaning his MP5.

Jed and the ranger shook hands. 'Our forward command post in Durban is now receiving a live satellite feed from over Zimbabwe. As soon as we know where that *bakkie* with the fugitives on board is headed we'll be leaving here.'

'You're going to cross into Zimbabwe?' the ranger asked.

Jed winked. 'I didn't say that. We could see the people we're looking for in the back of a truck hiding under a tarpaulin with a FLIR camera on the chopper and we've got a bead on them now. We're watching where they're headed to and when we get the go from our government, well . . .'

'OK, then I won't ask any more questions.'

Jed clapped him on the arm. 'Probably a good idea.'

Jed walked over to Franklin and sat down in the grass beside him. The other man continued cleaning and oiling his weapon.

'We need to talk,' Jed said after a while.

Franklin began reassembling the machine pistol. 'About what?'

'I know you can't talk about where you were before this.'

Franklin racked the cocking handle backwards and forwards, testing the slick action.

'It was Syria, right?'

Franklin looked through the sights, aimed at a tree and pulled the trigger. The hammer clacked on the empty chamber. 'You said yourself, you know I can't tell you that.'

'You know more than you're letting on, more than Chris knows, or more than he's giving up.'

Franklin set the gun down, took up the magazine and started thumbing out the bullets into his floppy bush hat, which he had set, upside down, on the ground.

'You're Muslim.'

Franklin glanced at him. 'Says who?'

'I saw you praying, discreetly, closing your eyes and facing Mecca yesterday.'

'Last time I checked it wasn't a crime.'

Jed tried another tack. 'Paulsen's dead. Tell me about him.'

'What makes you think I knew him?'

'Only reason you're here is because you know these people. You don't know Africa, that's why I'm here. Chris didn't partner us up just because we both happened to be in South Africa at the same time. Was Paulsen a true believer?'

The other man paused in his work. 'True as they come. There's no one so zealous as a convert.'

Jed nodded. 'I get that. I guess he was the right man for this job

353

because he blended in, being white South African and all, but he sure must have stuck out in Syria.'

'They called him Hamza al Sabah, "the ghost", in Syria. Firstly, because he was as white as a ghost with his blond hair and complexion, and secondly because he sent plenty of nonbelievers to their graves. He was ruthless.'

'More so than anyone else in ISIS?'

Franklin seemed to ponder the question. 'Yes. He went through a lot to get to the front line. Naturally, with his looks and background, plenty of the *Daesh* guys thought he was a plant.'

'Sounds like you were there.'

'You know better than to ask questions, Jed.'

Jed let it lie.

Franklin loaded the rest of the magazine then slotted it back into the MP5. 'Yep, Egil was different. He killed to prove he was a true believer. Soldiers, civilians, women, kids. They put a parade of captives in front of him and he never flinched, though he sweated plenty – beheading thirty people is damn hard work.' Franklin looked off into the distance, towards the Limpopo. 'Don't know if a true undercover agent could have done what they made him do, to prove himself.'

Jed didn't have to say any more. If Franklin had been undercover in Syria he might have been through similar tests to Paulsen. Jed could see from the haunted look in his eyes that he, too, must have done some things he would never want to reveal. It accounted, perhaps, for the cold-blooded way he had opened up on the kids with little provocation in Mkhuze Game Reserve.

'We don't work like them, remember?' Jed said.

Franklin looked back at him, his cold, dark eyes empty. 'Don't we? You heard Chris. The Company doesn't care if we kill that baby to get hold of it, search it, find out what it's carrying or what its mother was hiding.'

354

Jed hated to admit it to himself, but Franklin was right. The stakes were high in this chase, maybe too high for him. He'd seen his fair share of killing, righteous and otherwise, in a couple of tours in Afghanistan, and some action on the African continent. He wondered if he was going soft in his old age, or whether having a family a second time around had simply reset his moral compass to normal.

'I trust Dunn,' Jed said. 'I think he'll deliver the kids, the baby and the teenagers to us, once he knows they're safe, both from us and from ISIS. I think he'll reach out to us.'

Franklin put his handkerchief away and his bush hat back on his head. 'You could be right, Jed, but if Suzanne Fessey gets to them first, it's game over. If we can't get her the next best thing is to get her kid.'

For the first time in a very long time in his life, Jed Banks felt a shiver run down his back, as though he'd just encountered something evil afresh. 'Tell me about her.'

Franklin shook his head, slowly. 'Paulsen killed like a machine. Suzanne's not like that. She's a monster.'

*

The driver of the *bakkie* took Mike, Nia and the children into Gonarezhou National Park through the southern entrance.

It was a wild place, largely devoid of tourists, particularly in the south. They startled a small herd of zebra and every now and then passed a lone bull elephant.

They crossed the Runde River, driving through the shallow water, then followed the road east until they saw the magnificent Chilojo Cliffs.

'They're beautiful, Mike,' Nia said. She'd heard of this national park, famous for its towering, sheer red rock formations, but this was the first time she had been here. The countryside was very different from KwaZulu-Natal, brown instead of green, sparse instead of lush, rocky instead of fertile. However, it was stunning in its own wild way.

'It's normally a place of great peace for me,' he said, 'which is odd.'

'Why odd?' He turned away from her, looking out at the cliffs. She suddenly realised the meaning of his words. 'Was it here that it happened, that the boy was . . .?'

'That I killed the boy, yes. Near here, just across the border in Mozambique.'

Nia saw Themba look up and over at Mike. They had folded the tarpaulin after they had lost sight of the helicopter. Nia caught his glance and gave a slight shake of her head. Themba seemed to understand, and lay his head back on the tarpaulin, once more pretending to sleep.

'I came here,' Mike went on, 'to these cliffs, after it happened. I camped out here for three days by myself, not moving. I drank. A lot. I would sit in the riverbed each evening as the sun was going down. I took a cooler box of beers, Scotch, whatever was left, and sat here, listening to the lions calling, half hoping they might take me. I still come here, when I'm down.'

Nia saw him screw his eyes and his fists tight. She reached out and felt his arm shake with the torment still pent up inside him. He blinked a couple of times. 'It's OK, Mike.'

He looked at her, eyes red. 'It's not.'

'It is. You were in a war, a victim of that conflict. It was an accident, what happened.'

'That's what I told myself.'

'It's the truth.'

He wiped his eyes with the back of his hand. 'Yes, right.'

Mike slumped down into the back of the truck and closed his eyes. Nia tried to doze, but the road was too bumpy, the view too magnificent to sleep. She saw eland, waterbuck and reedbuck, which gave a squeaky alarm call when they were startled by the truck full of people.

At last they came to the other side of the park, on the Save River. They stopped briefly at a thatch-roofed hut where a Zimbabwe Parks and Wildlife ranger checked their entry paperwork. The driver continued along the sand road and took a turn to the right. The riverbank fell away to the left, a sheer drop to the sandy bed below. Nia grabbed the metal side wall of the *bakkie* as the truck slewed around a tight turn to the left.

For a second she thought they might slide or roll over, but the driver gunned the engine and the momentum of the downhill run carried them through the sand and into the river. The first channel seemed quite deep and water fantailed on either side of them as he ploughed on. They came up onto the wide, sandy middle section of the bed and the driver revved the engine hard to maintain their momentum.

When they reached the channel on the other side of the river the surface underneath was studded with large rocks worn smooth by the water. The driver slowed so as not to damage his suspension. Nia saw birds on either side: a pair of tall, elegant black and white saddle-billed storks with yellow spots on their bills; a pied kingfisher which hovered above the river's sparkling surface then dove straight down in search of a fish, spearing the water; and in the shallows a black crake, which was wading and making a loud honking call that belied its tiny size.

Clear of the river they climbed the other bank and took a dirt road for a few kilometres through bushland until they came to a turnoff, to the left, to Fish Eagle Lodge. The driver took them through the boom gate and then up a steep paved driveway to the main lodge, where he deposited them at the entrance. They offloaded themselves and their baggage, grateful to stretch their legs and put an end to their 'African massage', as bumpy roads were often called. Mike thanked the driver and Nia paid him with a folded wad of rand.

The quiet around them had a soothing effect on them all. As they approached the entrance to the main building, a young woman welcomed them to the lodge, introducing herself as Cassandra, the manager. Another woman handed around a platter of cold towels. Nia wiped her face and hands and the back of her neck.

'Is David here?' Mike asked Cassandra.

'He's coming now.' She pointed ahead as she led them out onto the terrace that overlooked the Save River.

David Stowell was part owner and resident general manager of the lodge, Mike had told Nia. He had white hair and a bushy Father Christmas beard that contrasted with the dark mahogany of his mottled skin.

'Mike!'

Mike introduced David to Nia and the teenagers. If David thought it odd that Mike had arrived with a rather bedraggled and multiracial entourage he gave no sign of it.

'Welcome,' he said.

Mike and David went into a huddle and Nia moved to the railing of the deck. Themba and Lerato, who carried the baby, joined her. Nia heard Mike asking David if he could use the lodge's phone and the two went into the manager's office.

'Wow,' Lerato said.

The river looked cool and inviting, but on the far side they could see three large crocodiles. The reptiles were a reminder, not that they needed it, that danger lurked even in a seeming paradise. A trail of round, crater-like holes pitted the sand beneath the river's surface: the tracks of a hippo that had been active the night before, Nia imagined.

After a few minutes Mike broke from David and came to them. 'There's a self-catering camp here that's vacant. We can stay there for now.'

'For now?' Themba asked.

'We don't know how long it will be safe for us to stay here,' Mike said. 'But we have planning to do.'

Cassandra came back to them. 'I can get our camp attendant, Stanley, to take you to the camp now, if you like.'

Mike thanked her. 'Themba, Lerato, please take the baby and go find a room – or rooms – that you'd like to stay in. I just need a minute with Nia.'

The youngsters left with Stanley, who helped carry their bags.

When they were alone, Mike turned to Nia. 'We need to talk,' he said.

'Sounds ominous.'

'It is. Suzanne Fessey knows where we are.'

Nia felt a familiar shiver of dread rack her body. 'How?'

'David just told me that my ex-wife, Tracy, rang him, asking if I was here. David said no, but Tracy asked him to get me to call if I showed up. She said she was worried about me and that the police were looking for me.'

'And did you call her?' Nia asked.

Mike nodded. 'Just now, from David's office. I got a description of the female police officer who interviewed Tracy. It was Suzanne.'

'My God, Mike, Tracy's lucky to still be alive.'

'I told her to get Debbie, my daughter, and to leave town. They've gone to stay with friends in Port Alfred. It's not Tracy's fault; she was just trying to help. However, she was suspicious enough of Suzanne, in hindsight, to try and tip me off.'

Nia slumped down onto one of the deckchairs and Mike lowered himself into the chair opposite her. 'What do you think?'

Nia felt the sense of relaxation escape from her body, like she'd been punctured. 'When are we going to stop running, Mike? Will we ever be truly safe anywhere?'

He ran a hand through his hair. 'Not while Suzanne Fessey is still on the loose and while the CIA is trying to track down both her and us. We've awoken a sleeping giant, Nia, running from the Americans. It won't take them long to use every resource at their disposal – men, aircraft, satellites, drones – to find us. Our time is limited.'

'What do you suggest?' she asked.

'What do *you* suggest? You track people for a living. I monitor vultures.'

Nia liked that he wanted her opinion, and she sensed it wasn't for show or to curry favour. She thought about their situation. 'Suzanne Fessey and her crew were prepared to destroy Boyd's farmhouse with rocket-propelled grenades to get back her child, but that doesn't reassure me that she cares for the baby's safety.'

'So,' Mike followed her train of thought, 'that would indicate she's more interested in retrieving the microchip.'

'What kind of mother thinks like that?' Her question was rhetorical, so she carried on. 'If the microchip number *is* a bank account, which seems likely, then she's after the money. We could just give the child to her, or leave him somewhere where she could find him.'

Mike nodded, slowly. 'We could. Do you want to do that?'

Nia thought about it. 'She's a criminal, a murderer, and she deserves to face justice, in South Africa and wherever else she's committed her crimes. Also, even if she has feelings for her baby, what kind of life would we be condemning him to?'

'My thoughts, too,' Mike said.

'The Americans are behaving almost as recklessly. Nobody cares about this child except us. Can we remove the microchip from the baby?'

'Microchips are easy to implant,' Mike said, 'but they're damned hard to remove. I looked into this with vultures. When I first heard about the technology I thought we could maybe re-use the chip if a bird died and we retrieved it. It turns out it's a difficult procedure, even on a dead bird. The chips are hard to locate – they move around under the skin away from where they're first inserted – and scar tissue forms around them where they come to rest, so it's not as simple as, say, making a small incision. The baby would have to be anaesthetised and it would take a plastic surgeon to dig around and get it out and, more importantly, repair the damage done under the skin as well as stitching him back up.'

'So, if Suzanne or the Americans get the baby, dead or alive, they're going to be able to read what's on the chip. We can't give up, though,' Nia said. 'If Suzanne or the other terrorists get the information they could access the bank account and use it to fund some terrible attack, like maybe another 9–11.'

'We could just hand the baby over to the Americans. I can call Jed Banks, and we can give ourselves over to them – with no guns this time,' Mike said.

It was a tempting proposition, Nia thought. If the Americans had the baby then Suzanne would have no reason to come after them. Or would she? She might have already deduced that they had read the information on the chip.

Mike appeared to have had the same thought. 'Suzanne would probably still try and get the information from us. Damn.'

'Damn what?' Nia asked.

'If Suzanne checked Boyd's operating theatre, and I'm sure she would have, then she would have seen that the microchip reader was lying around after I'd used it. I should have put it away.'

'Don't beat yourself up,' she said. 'Suzanne's outsmarted everyone so far.'

Mike leaned towards her, his elbows on his knees. 'The interesting thing is that unless Suzanne is just a grieving mother trying to get her kid back – and her recklessness with his safety seems to contradict that – then she mustn't know the numbers on the chip.'

'That could mean she's not in the loop,' Nia reasoned, 'or that this was something that only just recently happened. The puncture wound from where the chip was inserted hasn't healed yet.'

'Either way, she now needs the numbers.'

'And we have them,' Nia said. 'Question is, what do we do with them?'

'What do you think?' Mike asked.

She thought it through. The idea she had in mind was crazy, could never work, but they had to turn the tables on Suzanne. 'We go find the money.'

'Go to Switzerland? Crazy,' said Mike.

'Listen to me. I fly to Switzerland, check out the bank, go there and find out what's in the account. I've got the account number and what looks like the passcode number.'

'Call the bank,' Mike suggested. 'See if they'll tell you what's in the account.'

Nia shook her head. 'My friend Roger said that with these numbered accounts they don't do electronic or telephone banking or give out details that way. Think about it, Mike, if Suzanne knows I'm in Switzerland she'll know for sure we have the numbers and that it's too late for her. Roger told me that these Swiss banks are cracking down on criminals using their services, so if I go there, access the account and tell them the money belongs to terrorists, they can call in the police. If Suzanne knows we've locked up the money then there's no reason for her to keep chasing the kids and the baby, though I guess she'll want her child back eventually as well.'

Mike stood, his fists clenched by his sides. 'No, Nia. She might head to Switzerland herself if she knows you've gone there, and I won't allow you to be bait for her to follow. You can't just jump on a plane to Geneva!'

That made her mad. She got to her feet. 'You won't *allow* it? I know the numbers, I can do what I damn well want with them.'

'I'll go to Switzerland, then,' he said.

She put her fists on her hips. 'No.'

'Why not?'

'You need to stay here and look after these three kids of ours, that's why not,' she said.

'Ours?'

She grimaced. 'You know what I mean.' She changed the subject. 'What do we do about the Americans?'

'I share your misgivings about them, but I'd still rather Jed Banks found us than Suzanne.'

Nia nodded. 'Lesser of two evils. But the Americans want the baby – and presumably the money – as much as Suzanne. We're all still at risk. The money gives us leverage over all of them, and insurance.'

Mike continued to clench and unclench his fists by his side. 'I still don't like it, particularly if it draws them after you. I'd rather stash you and the kids somewhere else safe, maybe find a place in Harare, and go myself.'

'Three reasons why it has to be me, Mike.' She raised her thumb. 'One, there *is* nowhere that's really safe and at least you know the terrain here.'

She could see from the set of his mouth that he knew she was right.

'Two,' she raised her index finger, 'I've got the cash to buy a standby ticket. I might even use my parents' Amex card and go business class. Do you have that sort of money?'

He didn't return her smile. 'You know I don't.'

'Sorry, I don't mean to rub it in.' She raised a third finger. 'Three, I've got an Australian passport with me so I don't need to organise a visa in advance. I've been to Switzerland a couple of times on holiday with my folks. I can find my way around. I'll phone you from there and let you know how it's going.'

'You still need to get to Harare.'

'I've thought of that. Cassandra,' she called inside to the manager. The young woman came over to them. 'Do people sometimes fly in and out of this place?'

'Yes, we've got a light aircraft due in today.' Cassandra checked her wristwatch. 'It's due any time now.'

'Can I get on it?'

Cassandra seemed momentarily surprised. 'Well, um, sure. It'll be empty, so I'm sure we can find you a seat and work out a means of payment.'

Mike shook his head. 'I don't like this, Nia. You'll have to use your real name and passport number to book your international flights. The Americans will be monitoring that kind of stuff. They'll find you and they'll be waiting for you when you fly to Europe via Johannesburg. You won't get a direct flight from Harare to Switzerland.'

'I've thought of that too,' she said. 'I know people who've flown into and out of Zimbabwe before. I can get a flight to Nairobi and go from there. The Americans may be able to track me, but I won't make it easy for them by going via Joburg. Also, I'd like to see them try and pick me up in Switzerland without creating an international incident.'

'No,' Mike said.

Nia put her hands on her hips. 'Yes. If Suzanne does show up here, as we think she will, then try to find a way to parley with her. Tell her we'll give her the bloody numbers if she leaves Africa and guarantees your safety and that of the kids. I'll leave Switzerland and she can take her chances with the bank and the cops there.'

'It's still crazy. Also, Suzanne doesn't seem like the type to negotiate. She shoots first.'

Nia sighed. 'This whole thing is mad, Mike. If we get access to her money we get ahead of her, really in front of her, for the first time.'

They were at a stalemate. The sound of vehicle engines revving to climb the steep driveway to the lodge made them both turn.

An open Land Cruiser game viewer carrying a party of eight tourists pulled up at reception. As the guests were greeted by Cassandra a double-cab Land Rover Defender arrived as well.

The occupants of the second vehicle walked in, and they were a very different breed from the tourists.

There were three white men and two black; all wore green military-style field uniforms that were mottled black with sweat under the arms and across their broad chests. Their clothes were also coloured with dust and dirt; all carried a few days' worth of stubble and their hair was unwashed, spiked, matted. As they came closer Nia smelled them.

'Nia,' Mike said, gesturing to the man at the head of the phalanx, 'meet Shane Castle and Tim Penquitt. They run the anti-poaching operation in this part of Zimbabwe.'

They all shook hands. Cassandra politely interrupted them. 'Nia, if you want to get the flight out, then the vehicle that just brought the tourists can take you to the airstrip. The plane leaves in twenty minutes.'

'Excuse me,' Nia said to the new arrivals. She took Mike by the elbow.

'Don't do this,' he said.

'I have to, and you know it. Keep the kids safe, Mike. Trust me on this, and if you can't, then it doesn't matter. I'm my own person, I'm going.'

He put his hands on her shoulders and she felt small, but also safe, in his grip. 'I think that's one of the things I like about you.'

She took a deep breath. Her tough talk belied the fear that balled in her chest. She was worried that she was leaving him in grave danger. Nia looked up at him. 'I like a few things about you, too.'

Mike kissed her and she wrapped her arms around him.

'Be safe,' he whispered in her ear.

Chapter 32

Mike, Shane Castle and Tim Penquitt walked the perimeter of the self-contained satellite camp that David had recently established about a kilometre away from the main lodge, deep in the bush.

They were preparing for a battle and, on reflection, Mike now felt better that Nia had left. At least she would be out of the line of fire when Suzanne showed up.

Shane and Tim were well known to Mike. Tim was the older of the two, around sixty, Mike reckoned, and he had a justifiably fearsome reputation as a former member of the Selous Scouts, an integrated black and white unit of the Rhodesian Army, before the country gained independence and became Zimbabwe. The scouts had specialised in pseudo operations, with African soldiers loyal to the government and white men covered in black makeup masquerading as nationalist guerrillas, ambushing and disrupting the genuine revolutionaries' forces.

Shane stopped, rested the butt of his FN self-loading rifle on the ground and looked around him. 'Ja, this'll do,' he said, his accent a mix of Australian and Zimbabwean. Shane, Mike knew, had been born in what was then known as Rhodesia, before his parents had moved the family across the Indian Ocean to Australia. Now in his forties, Shane had served with the Australian SAS, the Special Air Service, in Afghanistan, and as a hired gun in Iraq.

Tim was in charge of the anti-poaching operations in the Save Valley Conservancy, on the border of Gonarezhou National Park, and often operated on the Fish Eagle Lodge property as well. Shane was something of a military consultant and it spoke volumes for his experience and intelligence that Tim, a hardened veteran himself, accepted the outsider's counsel. Jordan, Tim's son, one of the three younger men in the team, had his own military pedigree, having served in the British Army's Parachute Regiment in the bloody fighting in Afghanistan's Helmand Province before returning home to Zimbabwe to take a position in what had become the family business – hunting poachers. The remaining members of the team, Mike knew, were brothers. Oscar and Sylvester Mpofu were like family to the Penquitt boys. Tim liked it that way; family would never betray each other and would never leave a member stranded or wounded on the field of battle. The younger members were with the three fugitive children.

As well as seeing Tim and the rest of his team from time to time while doing his vulture monitoring, Mike and Tim had a shared past. They had served together on anti-poaching operations in this same area after Mike had left Operation Lock. Tim knew all about the young boy Mike had killed and knew well enough not to ever raise the matter.

'We'll set up a sentry post here,' Shane said for Mike's benefit. 'Good view out over the valley, towards Mozambique. That's where you think they'll come from?'

Mike shrugged. 'This woman, Fessey, could come from any direction. My guess, though, is that if she brings hired muscle they'll have to come in from across the Mozambican border.'

Tim chewed a blade of yellow grass. 'No shortage of guns over there.'

'Why didn't you take the baby and the other two kids to Harare?' Shane asked.

Mike looked at the two ex-soldiers. 'Because I want to end this, and for once I have the advantage: you two are here. Also, we're out in the bush. This woman's caused enough collateral damage.'

Shane gave a half-grin. 'That bad, hey?'

'You said she and her people deal in rhino horn?' Tim asked.

'Yes, that's right,' Mike said. 'We've found evidence they've been using the trade in horn out of KwaZulu-Natal's parks to help finance their terrorist network. I've got some of the horn here, young Themba found it in the woman's car. I can show you if you like.'

Tim shook his head. 'I trust you, Mike. All right, this makes them our enemy as well.'

Mike was curious. 'You wouldn't take them on simply because of what they've done in South Africa, and around the rest of the world. Like I told Shane on the phone, these people are part of ISIS; they're fanatics, the rhino horn is their way of part funding their operations.'

Tim gestured back towards the tented camp. 'My boy Jordan fought those people in Afghanistan. He said he didn't know who the bigger religious fanatics were: the Taliban and their supporters, or the Americans. I understand, in a strange way, killing for something like rhino horn. I don't believe it has any magical medicinal powers, just like I've never cared for diamonds, but these are commodities, things worth money, and people will fight to take and protect these things. It seems, in its way, somehow more understandable than a fight over gods.'

They were all silent a moment.

'Enough philosophy.' Shane clapped Tim on the shoulder. 'There are scared kids back in the camp whose lives are in danger and we've got the chance to take out a rhino horn trader. If these people can't get their horn in South Africa they'll just join the queue of people trying to rip it out of Zimbabwe. I'd say that's a fight worth taking on both counts.'

'Me too,' said Tim.

They walked to the safari tents that made up the fly camp, a term for a semi-portable encampment, and found Lerato and Themba eating.

'Sylvester and I fixed them some scoff, Dad,' Jordan said. 'Oscar's standing watch.'

Tim surveyed the setup. 'Good work, Jordie. Clean and check your weapons, all of you, and get some food for yourselves as well.'

'Mike?' Shane said, and beckoned to him with a nod to follow.

They went to Shane's Land Rover and Shane opened the door and flipped a lever to make the back of the driver's seat slump forward. He reached in and pulled out an assault rifle.

'R5.'

Mike took the weapon from him. 'I know it. Been a while since I handled one.'

Shane lowered his voice. 'Tim told me a little about your time together here back in the day, hunting poachers. He didn't give me details, but I know how the bad stuff can stay with a man. Are you good with this?'

Mike nodded.

'Jordan, Sylvester, Oscar,' Tim called. 'We need some firing positions here. There's fuck-all cover in this place.'

'I found somewhere, Dad,' Jordan said.

Mike and Shane walked over and joined the others. Jordan led them to the far right of the tents, where he showed them a deep hole, about three metres long, two wide and a metre and a half deep.

Tim put his hands on his hips. 'Bloody plunge pool.'

Mike smiled. Tim had said it as though he couldn't imagine how or why anyone would have need of a swimming pool out in the bush. He lived on a reserve where people paid up to a thousand dollars per person per night to dine on fine cuisine and view big game, while he, his son and his fellow rangers spent their nights patrolling, lying in ambush, and swatting mosquitos.

Shane moved away a short distance to where there was a pile of building materials, bags of cement, timber formwork and some corrugated sheeting. Gingerly, he lifted a sheet of metal with the tip of the barrel of his FN rifle. He jumped back a pace in obvious fright.

The others began laughing out loud.

'What is it?' Mike asked.

Tim wiped his eyes. 'Our big bad hero of the Australian SAS is scared of snakes.'

'It was just a lizard,' Shane said, 'thank fuck.'

'I've seen this man run at an armed poacher, firing from the hip, but show him a boomslang and he near shits himself,' Tim said.

The brief moment of mirth over, Tim marshalled his troops back to work. 'Right, lads. This is our strong point, last line of defence. Stack those cement bags around the edge and leave gaps for your rifles.'

Sylvester, Oscar and Jordan lay down their weapons within easy reach, stripped off their shirts and got to work. Mike, Shane and Tim went into a huddle.

Shane looked to him. 'Jordan and I know the sort of people we're dealing with, Mike. We're not leaving anything to chance.'

Themba approached them. 'Mike, Lerato and the baby are resting in one of the tents. How can I help?'

'Best if you stay with Lerato,' Mike said.

'But I would like a gun, as well.'

Mike looked to Shane. 'What do you think?'

'He's young,' Shane said.

'He knows how to handle an AK. He's a good student these days but he used to be a car thief,' Mike said.

Themba looked pained at the revelation.

'This is a fight we're getting ready for, mate, not an algebra lesson,' Shane said to Themba.

'I am a man.'

Shane looked him up and down. 'Getting close. You want a gun?'

Themba nodded.

'Go over to the Landy, and have a look in the back under that green tarpaulin.'

Mike and Shane watched as Themba walked to the truck.

'What's in the back?' Mike asked.

'We came to you straight from the bush. We had a contact last night.'

Mike walked slowly after Themba. If he hadn't known Themba's background, the horrors he had already seen in his short life, he would have been worried about what sort of test Shane was putting him to. Men like Shane and the Penquitts had lived through the horrors of war, and the fight to save the rhino was not much different.

Themba went to the back of the truck, reached over the side wall and lifted the green tarpaulin. Mike heard the buzz of disturbed flies and Themba took an involuntary step back and put his hand to his mouth.

'Two Mozambicans,' Shane said quietly. 'We killed them last night; they were tracking a rhino, and when we told them to drop their guns they opened fire on us. It was over quick.'

Themba straightened his body and seemed to compose himself. He went back to the side of the vehicle and once more lifted the cover. He bent over, reaching inside, and pulled out an AK-47. He came to Mike and Shane and, noticing blood on his fingers, transferred the rifle to his other hand while he wiped it off on his school pants. 'Do you have magazines?'

'In the Landy,' Shane said evenly, 'behind the seat. You'll find a stack of them, still loaded.'

'Thank you, sir,' Themba said.

'Tough kid,' Shane said to Mike.

'He is.'

'Sounds like he'll need to be.'

Mike walked to the vehicle. A cloud of disturbed flies still hovered above the bodies, not willing to stray too far from their new hosts. Some settled onto eyes, into nostrils, others returned to the bullet wounds. *I can do this*, Mike told himself. *These were men, not boys. They carried guns and would have killed the anti-poaching forces if given a chance.*

It's a war. It's combat. Get over yourself.

Shane was beside him. 'Mike? You OK?'

The trees around him were swirling and he saw pinpricks of light at the periphery of his vision. He smelled how the men, or one of them at least, had fouled himself. The bile rose in his throat. He closed his eyes, but saw the face of the sixteen-year-old he had shot. He'd had to load him onto a truck, after the killing was done. He heard the gunfire, the screams; they filled his head.

'Mike?' Themba echoed.

Mike staggered away from the truck, the dizziness taking over, amplifying the feeling of nausea. He stumbled to a tree and hugged its rough bark for support. The noise in his mind was deafening. There was another, animalistic sound all around him. After a few moments he realised that it was coming from him. Tears streamed from his eyes as he vomited.

He felt hands on him, heard the murmur of soothing voices through his own rage, but he didn't want them, didn't want their pity or their sympathy. He was weak, falling apart at a time when the children needed him to protect them, when Shane and the

Penquitts needed another gun. This was *not* the time to unravel. This was *not* the time to let this tide of sorrow and shit swamp over his head and drown him. He *had* to hold it together.

But he could not.

He should never have let Nia go, he realised. She would not be safe, there was nothing he could do to protect the children, or himself. They would all be dead soon, and it was all his fault. He had failed them all; he had damned them all because of the child he had killed all those years ago.

Mike was aware of the others around him, but he stood and stumbled towards the nearest tent. Inside he found a canvas basin and splashed water on his face. He looked at himself in the mirror, disgusted.

'Mike?'

He looked and saw Themba waiting by the opening. Mike sat down on a stretcher, his face in his hands.

'Mike,' Themba said again. 'You're a good man, Mike. Without you, I wouldn't be here today, I'd be in prison or, worse, dead.'

He couldn't look up at the boy, he was too ashamed. He felt the despair was shutting him down, as though it would cripple him, kill him. Any good he did was useless; he was damned, as sure as the rest of them were.

'Mike, listen to me, please. You came for me, for Lerato and the baby. You found us in Mkhuze. You didn't have to do that, you got me to your doctor friend.'

'And he's dead,' Mike sobbed.

Themba put a hand on his shoulder. 'He fought for us. He gave his life for us, Mike. You got us away from those people, from those crazy people. You could have just handed us to the police or the Americans and I'm worried what they would have done to us.'

Mike lifted his head and looked up at the boy. He had been a surly, angry criminal when Mike had met him, but now Themba was more of a man than he.

'We all need help, Mike. I do, my sister does, we all do. You taught me that. It's OK to reach out for help. You suggested once that you could find me someone to talk to, about my problems and my past, but I found that person. It was you.'

Mike drew a deep breath to try and still himself. He heard his own words, the ones Themba reminded him of, through the fog of his sorrow.

'Mike, there are good men here. They will protect us. You can stay here, rest. I will take care of you.'

He swallowed and felt the tears well again, but this time not from sorrow but from sheer pride in the person Themba had become. He wiped his eyes.

'Thank you.' Mike took another breath and looked at Themba, seeing a man where there had been a boy. He had made a difference with Themba, and now he owed it to him to ensure he could live the life they had both envisioned for him. Themba was right, he did need to reach out for help. He would look for it, but for now he had a job to do. 'I won't let you down, Themba.'

Mike stood. Themba came to him. They hugged.

*

Nia ran to catch her flight.

She had queued impatiently behind a posse of American big game hunters, their pastime and professions clear from their camouflage clothes and small talk about their dental patients back home. Once through immigration and customs she had sprinted.

The light aircraft from Fish Eagle Lodge had been delayed at its second stop, another safari lodge where the guests were late arriving. Nia had been petrified she would miss the flight that she had booked online from Cassandra's computer.

'Sorry I'm late,' she wheezed at the flight attendant.

The woman forced a smile. Nia was, after all, at the pointy end of the aircraft, the only seat still vacant when she had booked. 'No problem, Miss Carras, go right ahead.'

Once inside she averted her eyes from the accusatory stares of her fellow passengers and the captain announced the doors were 'at last' closed. Nia stowed the daypack she had bought in South Africa, her only luggage, in the bin overhead, then slumped into her seat.

A male attendant brought her a glass of champagne on a tray. 'Don't worry, we knew you were coming, we wouldn't have left without you.' He cast an eye over her filthy bush clothes. 'Looks like you really *have* been on safari.'

She took a gulp of the sparkling wine as she watched the safety briefing. Mike and the kids were not safe, not in the slightest. Nia had the awful feeling that she had betrayed them, that they needed her.

With Mike, after their brushes with death, she had felt the overwhelming need to be with him, to be close to him, and she realised now that she thought about it that making love with him had possibly been the logical extension of that. But she felt more, now that she was away from him. It was like a piece of her was missing, amputated, and she felt the phantom pain of that missing element in her heart. It was palpable; so much so that she wanted to cry.

Chapter 33

Suzanne Fessey surveyed her five men. They were not ideal, dressed as they were in an assortment of charity clothes and faded military fatigues, but they would do. They were hard men, veterans of Mozambique's civil war, rhino poachers.

She would have preferred to have kept Bilal alive and with her for longer, but, unlike her, he'd had no new identity stashed at Johannesburg airport. Still, for the sake of security and her mission, she would have had to dispose of Bilal eventually. Likewise, when these brigands had done their job they would not be left alive to talk about her.

Suzanne had trained herself to be adaptable and that was just as well, because a chain of misfortune had led her here to the Zimbabwean lowveld.

Egil had usually been based in Mozambique and had looked after their fundraising there, selling rhino horns on to a Vietnamese contact in that country's embassy in Maputo. However, the diplomat had been busted and the ambassador was making an example of him by sending him home.

Suzanne sourced rhino horn from local poachers in South Africa, who shot them in KwaZulu-Natal's game reserves. The horn came to Suzanne via a middle man, a devout Pakistani trader loyal to their cause. The poachers were always trying to squeeze more money out of the trader and had recently threatened to go to another buyer, Bandile Dlamini, who had put word out that he was in the market. Suzanne had passed on this intelligence to Egil who, through the Pakistani, had set up the meet with Dlamini in the Mtubatuba market.

Egil and his men had crossed into South Africa on the morning of the bombing with the intention of collecting the latest consignment of horn direct from Suzanne – she had sent the trader to paradise to cover her tracks. The plan had been that Egil would do the deal with Dlamini then catch up with her at the Muzi border crossing back into Mozambique. He and his men, armed with their rifles and RPG that had been cached in northern KwaZulu-Natal for some time, were also there to provide firepower in case something went wrong. Indeed, just about everything had gone wrong after her car had been hijacked.

'You have a weapon for me, Alberto?' she said in Afrikaans to the man who stood in front of the other three.

'*Ja.*' He unslung a green kitbag from his shoulder, unzipped it and took out an AK-47 and two spare magazines.

Suzanne inspected the rifle and worked the cocking handle backwards and forwards. The action was smooth. These men were unkempt, but weapons were the tools of their trade and they clearly cared for them more than for themselves. She nodded and Alberto gave her a broken-toothed grin.

'We're not going hunting for rhino,' she continued in Afrikaans. Alberto had worked on the mines in South Africa and he translated from that language to Portuguese for the benefit of his underlings.

'What, then?' His voice was gravelly.

'Men.'

Alberto raised his eyebrows. 'We are not murderers, but we are regularly fired upon by anti-poaching patrols. Sometimes they kill us, sometimes we kill them. I don't think you can pay us enough to murder in cold blood.'

'Oh, I think I can.' Suzanne unzipped her own bag and took out an envelope bulging with US one-hundred-dollar bills. She handed it to Alberto. 'That's the first half. The second half is when I get my baby back.'

'Baby?'

Suzanne outlined the mission. She had picked up a rental car at Harare Airport and parked and camouflaged it in the bush near Fish Eagle Lodge, then conducted her own reconnaissance on foot. None of the people she was looking for were visible at the lodge but at the outlying tented camp she had found Dunn, the two teenagers and Hassan. She had seen Lerato Dlamini walking around the camp with the baby in her arms, wrapped in a brightly printed cloth. Suzanne would have made straight for the girl if it hadn't been for the fact that she was being escorted on her little walk, while she rocked Hassan, by two armed men.

'There are five armed men in green uniforms, two black and three white. They look like anti-poaching operators,' she explained to Alberto.

The poacher scratched the stubble on his chin. 'One of the white men is old, grey hair, another much younger, the third in middle age.'

Suzanne nodded. 'You know them.'

'It is the Penquitts, father and son, and their dogs, the Mpofus. The other white man is an Australian, a former soldier. I take back what I said before. It will be a pleasure killing these men. They have killed too many friends of mine.'

'Whatever. There is another white man, about fifty, who will be armed as well, and a teenage Zulu boy and girl. The girl will be caring for my baby. I want no witnesses left alive, Alberto.'

'All right. We will do our best to ensure your child is not harmed.'

'Just do your job.'

Suzanne had made a mud map of the camp, a three-dimensional model using rocks for the tents and lines in the sand for the tracks around them. She used a stick as a pointer as she got back to the business of briefing her assassins. 'They have been making an improvised bunker, here,' she pointed to the trench she had etched in the dirt. 'This means that they know that I know they are here and that I am on my way.'

Alberto translated and squatted down on his haunches. 'I will position two of my men on the right flank, to lay down fire support, with extra ammunition, and to act as a diversion. You and I and the other two will then circle around.' He looked to one of his men, 'Eduardo, *granada de mão*.'

Eduardo reached into a canvas satchel he wore across his chest and pulled out two Russian-made hand grenades.

Alberto smiled. 'We sometimes put these under the carcasses of dead rhinos, to catch the anti-poaching bastards when they come to inspect the animals. These will take care of your bunker.'

'Good thinking,' Suzanne said. 'We will take up position, not too close, because the anti-poaching people look well trained. They may patrol around the camp. We will watch, though, and make sure no one leaves with my baby.'

'We attack at night, two in the morning, when some of them will be sleeping.'

'Agreed,' Suzanne said.

*

'Themba,' said Lerato, 'could you do something for me, please?'

Lerato and Themba sat in the rudimentary bunker, an assortment of blankets and pillows not quite making it comfortable nor warm enough. Themba was pleased that Hassan, at least, was somewhere safe. Oscar Mpofu stood and scanned the bush at the edge of the camp through a pair of night vision binoculars.

'Anything,' Themba said. He meant it.

'Will you hold me, please?'

He shifted closer to her and tentatively put an arm around her shoulders.

'Tighter.'

Oscar looked down and grinned. Themba replied with what he hoped was a stern look. Oscar shrugged and went back to his surveillance. Themba drew Lerato to him and she laid her head on his chest. Themba felt like he never wanted to let her go.

'I'm scared, but I feel safe with you, does that make sense?' she asked.

'You give me courage and strength, Lerato.'

She nodded and looked up at him.

Themba's heart was beating faster. He looked at her beautiful lips, her shining eyes, and moved his mouth to hers. Just as he was about to kiss her there was a shout from beyond the other side of the camp, and the gunfire began.

'Contact, wait out,' a voice said from the hand-held radio on Oscar's belt.

'What is it?' Themba said.

'Keep your heads down.' Oscar continued watching the bush ahead and in an arc in front of him. 'That was Shane. He and Tim were on a clearing patrol, to the east. They have found someone.'

There were more bursts of fire.

'Two enemy.' Shane's staticky voice was calm through the radio.

'You want the QRF?' said the younger white man, Jordan, through the radio. Jordan and Oscar's brother, Sylvester, were in the centre of the camp acting as the small contingent's quick reaction force, ready to rush to any part of the battle when they were needed. Mike had been roving around the camp checking on all of them. Themba hoped Mike would be OK after his earlier breakdown.

'Hold your position, son,' Tim Penquitt radioed.

There was shouting and more gunshots.

'He's running!' Shane Castle yelled, loud enough for them to hear from the far side of the camp.

There were two shots and then silence. A minute later Tim broadcast: 'Two dead enemy. Both have AKs and there's a span of magazines stacked here. Looks like this was the fire support team. QRF, stand by to move to Oscar. Jordie, you're in charge, for now, my boy. We've got one WIA.'

'Someone is wounded in action,' Oscar said to Themba.

'Shane's taken one in the leg,' Tim said over the radio. 'He'll live but he can't stand. I'm going to patch him and be with you just now.'

'Roger, Pops,' Jordan said.

'Be ready, you two,' Oscar said. 'What Tim is saying is that there are others, somewhere near here, who were getting ready to attack us while those other two men tried to divert our attention.'

Themba stood, his legs feeling a little weak, and pointed his AK-47 out towards the darkened bush.

'Stay down, boy,' Oscar said.

'Don't call me boy. I am a Zulu. My people are warriors.'

Oscar tutted. 'You have a woman to protect now. You should stay down.'

Themba was about to continue the argument when he detected movement in his peripheral vision. He turned. 'Oscar. There's someone in the trees.'

Oscar picked up his night vision binoculars again and swung them to where Themba was pointing. 'Grenade, get down!'

Themba saw the person's arm moving. A burst of automatic gunfire came their way as well. Oscar shoved him in the back and Themba fell down, on top of Lerato, who screamed.

Oscar dropped the binoculars and reached as though trying to catch something. He missed and a metal orb bounced and rolled into the trench between Oscar and Themba.

'Get it out of here!' said Oscar.

Themba tried to, but he was tangled with Lerato. Oscar pushed him aside again and grabbed the grenade. As he tossed it, backwards, over his shoulder, he dived forward, falling across Themba and Lerato, crushing them.

The grenade exploded and shrapnel rained down over them. Oscar screamed.

*

Mike hit the ground when he heard Oscar call out the warning about the hand grenade. A storm of dirt and rocks washed over him.

As soon as he'd heard on the radio that Shane and Tim had encountered the fire support team he'd left Jordan and Sylvester and started moving to the bunker. He heard the screams from the trench.

Mike got up on one knee and saw a slight figure moving through the tree line. It had to be Suzanne Fessey. He raised his rifle to his shoulder and fired, but the woman dropped too soon. Gunfire came his way. He was in open ground so he crawled as fast as he could towards the trench.

Two men were up and running from the trees towards the bunker. As they ran two rifles opened up from the darkness, laying down a hailstorm of fire. Mike made it to the edge of the trench and slid in, landing hard on the people inside.

'Oscar's hurt,' Lerato said.

Themba helped Mike to his feet. 'He saved us.'

'Get up, Themba, there are two of them coming this way.'

Mike raised his head, forcing himself to ignore the bullets whizzing around him, and opened fire with his R5. Themba's

AK-47 joined in with a near-deafening fusillade by Mike's right ear.

A bullet cleaved the air between Mike and Themba. 'Get down, Themba.'

'No.'

Behind them they heard a yell and Mike glanced around quickly to see Jordan Penquitt screaming a war cry as he ran across the open ground from the safari tents. He fired his R5 from the hip as he charged and Sylvester, behind him on one knee, covered him with fire.

Mike saw one of the enemy in front of him stagger and fall, but now all the other rifles from that side, three by the looks of it, were firing at Jordan.

'Crazy bastard's drawing their fire. Themba, aim at the muzzle flashes.'

Mike and Themba took careful aim and fired single shots. One of the opposing AK-47s stopped firing in the darkness, but Jordan cried out in pain and fell.

There was a momentary pause in the shooting. 'Keep watching, Themba,' Mike said, 'aimed shots when you see a target.'

Mike looked around and saw that Sylvester was running to Jordan. Mike remembered what Tim had said, about them all being like family. Sylvester raised his rifle and sprayed the bush with a full magazine of bullets, then dropped to his knees. He slung his weapon and heaved Jordan up onto his shoulders in a fireman's lift.

'Cover him, Themba,' Mike said. They both started firing and a couple of AK-47s answered in reply.

*

Suzanne crawled to a granite boulder before firing again. She knew her enemies would be aiming for where they had last seen muzzle flashes.

She took aim not at the bunker, where the firing was coming from, but at the man who had just picked up the wounded anti-poaching man from the ground. She drew a breath, then expelled half the air from her lungs. Suzanne held the pistol grip of the assault rifle, her finger curled around the trigger. She squeezed her whole hand, as if making a fist.

The African man carrying the white man pitched forward into the dust. Neither of them moved. The firing stopped.

'Suzanne Fessey,' a voice called out. 'It's Mike Dunn here. You know who I am, I'm sure.'

She cocked her head, listening. There were still a couple of anti-poaching guys unaccounted for. They could be sneaking up on her and Alberto while Dunn tried to distract her.

'We have your baby here, in the bunker. There has been enough killing.'

Suzanne changed firing positions, crawling to a leadwood tree, and took aim at the bunker. There would not be enough killing until she had that baby in her arms and found a microchip scanner, though where she might find one of those in the wilds of Zimbabwe she did not know.

'I'm coming out.'

You do that. Suzanne watched the edge of the trench, waiting for her shot.

'We have your money, Suzanne.'

She lowered the end of the barrel of her rifle a little. She felt a physical pain in her chest.

'It's true,' Dunn called. 'We felt the microchip in the baby's neck and scanned it at Boyd Qualtrough's surgery. We got the account number and the passcode number. Nia Carras is in Switzerland now. I just got an SMS from her. She's got access to the account if she wants it.'

'I don't believe you,' she called back.

Dunn crawled out of the bunker and stood. Hands up. 'You

haven't seen her in the camp, have you? I'm unarmed. Let's talk. We want to give you your baby back, let you go in peace.'

Suzanne's mind raced. Dunn could be bluffing, but on the other hand it was possible that he was telling the truth. Omar had told her, just before leaving on his mission to blow up the American ambassador, that he had taken Hassan to a friend, a veterinarian, the evening before. She'd believed him when he told her he had just taken the child out in its stroller for a long walk, to say goodbye to him. When she'd detected the sticky plaster on the back of Hassan's neck Omar had told her he had been bitten by a horsefly. It wasn't until she kissed Omar goodbye that he'd whispered in her ear, on the remote chance that their house was bugged, that he'd had a microchip implanted in Hassan's neck.

Omar had told her that he would find a way to leave her the account number and a clue to the password, and as they had discussed, she would receive the number and clue or be able to find it after his death and after she was out of South Africa and safe. If she was caught leaving the country the Americans would surely get the number and code out of her somehow. As tough as she was she knew everyone broke eventually.

The money, twenty million euros, had been specifically earmarked by the Sheik, Osama bin Laden, to purchase a nuclear device, should one ever actually come on the market. Omar had believed that they were tantalisingly close to a deal with the Russians, and that deal was still a possibility.

Omar had been worried, though. Not by the effects that a nuclear blast might have on the country they attacked, or the rest of the world, but rather that he might be detected and somehow arrested or assassinated by the Americans before he was able to detonate the device. Paulsen had received intelligence from a Russian former military man that a corrupt contact of his in the FSB had told him the CIA suspected Omar – no one else – of being in the market for a nuke.

Suzanne and Omar had discussed how they might both each make the ultimate sacrifice for their cause and go to paradise as martyrs. The visit by the American ambassador to Durban, so soon after the news that Omar may have been compromised, had seemed like a sign. Omar had left knowing his wife had the means to see through the deal to buy the ultimate weapon of terror.

'The account number and the passcode number were on the microchip,' Dunn said now. 'We've got all the information. Give up, Suzanne, you've lost.'

'Give me my child.'

'Put down your rifle, as I have, and I will bring the baby to you. Then you and whatever men you have left alive may leave.'

'I'm pointing a gun at you. What's to stop me shooting you right now?'

'I've got a man with a gun trained on you as well,' Mike said.

Suzanne looked to the bunker and saw the face of the teenage boy, Themba Nyathi, appear over the parapet. He had an AK trained on her. 'Ha! A child, not a man.'

'No, that young Zulu is a man,' came a voice from off to Suzanne's right. A tall man stepped from the bush, pointing an R5 at her. 'And I'm another man.'

She glanced at him. It was the older white Zimbabwean. She looked behind her; now was the time for Alberto to step out and even the odds.

'Looking for Alberto Flores?' the grey-haired man said.

Suzanne said nothing.

'I've been looking for him for a long time, and after what his gang have done tonight, and to the rhinos and elephants of my country for so long, it was only a pleasure for me to slit his throat just then. You're on your own now.'

Suzanne lowered her AK-47 and slowly put it down on the ground. Then, she reached into the pocket of her pants.

'Keep your hands where we can see them,' Dunn called. He had picked up his rifle again.

Suzanne ignored him as well as the old anti-poaching man who was striding towards her, rifle up and ready. From her pocket she pulled the hand grenade Alberto had given her.

'Want me to kill her?' the Zimbabwean called to Dunn.

Suzanne looked up and behind her at the phenomenal, endless natural theatre of the African sky at night. She had loved gazing up at the stars as a child. How had her life gone so horribly wrong?

The whine of the Sea Hawk's turbine engines washed over her and its big blades cleaved the air above. A spotlight fixed on her, blinding her.

'Suzanne Fessey, do not move. Drop your weapons or we will open fire,' came an American-accented voice from above.

Suzanne looked around her. The others had moved out of range. The two teenagers were scrambling out of the bunker, dragging a wounded man between them. Dunn was backing away, but keeping an eye on her.

'The baby. Where is he?' she yelled over the engine noise.

'In an orphanage, safe,' Dunn called. 'Lerato's been carrying around a doll wrapped in a blanket.'

Suzanne dropped the hand grenade beside her and smiled to herself as she watched the others run from her.

Chapter 34

'She gave up, just like that?' Nia asked, her voice clear in Mike's cell phone even though she was in Switzerland.

'I know, amazing, right?' he said. He was in an aircraft hangar at Air Force Base Makhado near Louis Trichardt in South Africa, not far across the border from Zimbabwe. It was hot inside, the day's heat trapped under the steel roof. The Sea Hawk sat on the tarmac outside the open sliding door. Inside was a South African National Defence Force Gripen jet fighter. 'She had a hand grenade and dropped it beside herself when she was cornered, but she hadn't even pulled the pin.'

'How is everyone?' said Nia.

'Themba's doing OK, even with his wound and all he's been through, and Lerato is in front of me, being hugged by her dad. The South African police brought him here. I misjudged him – he really was taking part in an undercover sting when I had him arrested at Mtubatuba. The serious and violent crimes squad detectives that were supposed to be there to arrest Paulsen got caught in Durban because of the bombing. He lost a lot of money but the police apparently found the cash on Paulsen's body.'

'I'm pleased Lerato's safe.'

'Me too.'

Mike gave Nia a rundown of the firefight in Zimbabwe and told her how the US Navy helicopter crew had taken the wounded anti-poaching operators, Shane Castle, Jordan Penquitt and Oscar Mpofu, to Chiredzi Hospital. Sylvester had been shot in the back, fatally through the heart, while he carried Jordan on his shoulders.

'Such brave men,' Nia said.

'Yes. Tim's looking after them.'

'Where's Suzanne?'

'The last I saw of her she had a hood on her head, cuffs on her wrists and Franklin Washington was escorting her to a black Chevrolet van with a couple of South African police detectives in tow. Jed's here with us. He wants to talk to you.'

Nia had already told him, as soon as she'd ascertained he was safe, that she'd had no luck at the bank. Mike had been bluffing when he told Suzanne that Nia had accessed the account. Suzanne had no idea of how early Nia had left Zimbabwe for Switzerland, but the fact was that it was three in the morning when the gunfight went down near Fish Eagle Lodge.

Nia had told him the banker she was dealing with at the bank in Geneva had confirmed the account number was valid, but the password, 828866, was not valid.

'What else can we do about the account?' Nia asked on the phone. 'I tried giving them the number in reverse, but that didn't work either. It's some other sort of code, I guess.'

Themba was finished with the police, evidently, because he wandered towards Mike and stopped a couple of metres away, waiting for him to finish the call. Mike held up a finger and Themba nodded that he was happy to wait. Jed, too, was hovering nearby, though out of earshot. '828866,' Mike said aloud. 'Assuming it's a code, then the repetition of numbers might help us.'

'I'm not a code breaker,' Nia said.

'Talk to Jed for now. He's not a bad guy,' Mike said.

'OK.'

Mike motioned for Jed to come over and handed him his phone. The CIA man walked away, apparently to avoid Mike overhearing. Mike didn't care; he was sure Nia would fill him in on what the American wanted. Themba, meanwhile, had moved off as well, to the side of the hangar. Outside a crew room was a whiteboard with flight schedules on it. An airman in camouflaged fatigues stood looking in interest as Themba wrote on the board with a pen the man had let him borrow. Mike walked over.

'What are you doing?'

'I wanted to help. I heard you talking about a number, a code. Those sorts of things interest me.'

Mike could tell from soon after he'd met Themba, then a surly criminal on probation, that he had an enquiring mind. As part of the rhino guard course Mike had set some challenges that he'd picked up during his own army training, and Themba had always been among the first to solve them. On the board he'd written the numbers one to nine, in three rows of three. He was busy writing letters under each digit. 'What are you doing?'

Themba glanced at him, over his shoulder, then went back to writing. 'I don't have a phone on me, but I'm writing out a cell phone keypad.'

'Why?'

'Look. You know those companies that get their own personalised phone numbers from the phone companies? They make the number out of the name of their firm, using the letters on a keypad.'

Mike folded his arms and nodded.

'Your number is 828866, right?'

Mike was impressed with his memory. Themba had only just overheard that number. 'Don't tell Jed or anyone else, OK?'

'I won't.' Themba finished writing and stepped back so Mike

could see the whiteboard. Themba reached out and tapped the numbers he'd written. 'Eight comes up three times, and under it, on a phone, see here, are the letters "T", "U" and "V".'

Mike rubbed his chin. 'So we try "T" first, maybe?'

'Yes. And if we look at the number that's also repeated, six, it could be "M", "N" or "O".'

'There are some words in English that have two of all of those letters, but if you supposed "T" was the letter designated by eight, then . . .'

Mike was tired, more exhausted than he'd been since his army days or when he was on patrol looking for poachers. Tracy was good at cryptic crosswords and sudoku, but he had never seemed to be able to apply his mind to such things. 'What?'

'Look here, the number one never has letters under it – I never worked out why – but under two, the other number in your code, the first letter is "A". "T", "A", "T", "T".'

Themba looked at him like a patient teacher waiting for a slow child to grasp something. 'Tattoo?'

'It's a word. Does that woman who was following us have a tattoo?' Themba asked.

'I don't know. The Americans might, but like I said, I want to keep this between us for now, OK?'

'I won't say anything.'

Mike had a second thought. 'Actually I do know someone else who spent some time with Suzanne.'

Jed had finished his call and was striding across the hangar to them. Themba picked up a felt eraser and rubbed his part of the schedule board clean.

Banks squared up to him. 'Mike, I know I've asked you nicely a couple of times, but you really need to tell me what was on that microchip.'

'I'm guessing Nia wouldn't tell you, either.'

'You're guessing right. What are y'all doing here with the board?'

'Homework,' Themba said. 'I've been out of school a few days.'

Jed shook his head. 'That money's not Nia's or yours.'

'Nor yours either, I would have thought,' Mike said.

'Nia could be in danger, Mike. The bank might have been under instructions to call someone if a person showed up and tried to access the account and failed. That sort of thing happens.'

Mike thought he was bluffing. 'Who are they going to call? Suzanne Fessey? Her husband Omar Farhat? Egil Paulsen? Osama bin Laden? They're all dead or incommunicado.'

'I represent the US Government, Mike.'

Mike put his fists on his hips. 'Yes, and I'm a South African.'

Jed ran a hand through his thick fair hair. 'OK. I told Nia that the US Government will probably offer a reward, perhaps a cut of whatever's in the bank account. I can't say that for sure, but our aim is to shut that account down, even if we can't get the money, so that it's not accessed by someone else for the use we think it was set aside for. That money was for something that history would remember forever, for all the wrong reasons.'

'A nuclear weapon?'

'Yes.'

Mike didn't want that either, but he did want to make sure the baby, Lerato, Themba – and Nia and himself – got out of this safely and didn't end up in a CIA interrogation facility in some country in America's debt.

'The baby's safe, right?' Jed prompted Mike.

'Yes.'

'Well, I trust y'all on that front. I understand your concerns, Mike, but I'm not going to torture this out of you.'

'I'm pretty sure you wouldn't, Jed, but how do I know what the rest of the CIA has planned for us? I'll tell you what, give Nia and me the night to think about this. I've got friends in the government, and so does Bandile Dlamini. I want some ironclad guarantees for the safety of the children and I want lawyers and senior people aware of what's going on.'

'A word in private, Mike?' Jed said. 'Excuse us, please, Themba.'

Themba moved away, heading to where Lerato sat on a bench next to her father. Mike was pleased he wasn't heading for that confrontation. 'What is it, Jed?'

Jed checked to make sure there was no one else in earshot. 'If you get the money, you and Nia will be targets. The terrorists will come looking for it, eventually. I can broker something. If you guys want to take a cut, I'm cool with that. No one knows how much is in there, anyway.'

Mike was annoyed. 'We're not criminals, Jed. We don't want to line our own pockets with terrorists' money.'

Jed raised his hands. 'OK, sorry. Just keep me in the loop, all right?'

'Give me some time.'

Jed looked him in the eye. 'I can hold off my boss, Chris Mitchell, 'til dawn, no longer.'

Mike got the message. Jed might be a good guy, but he worked with some bad ones.

*

Themba felt more scared than he had at any time since his cousin Joseph had forced him into the stolen Fortuner.

Bandile Dlamini had his arm around Lerato, holding her close to him. She had sobbed for a long time and Themba could see the big man's shirt front was damp. Her father kissed her on the top of the head and turned his head slowly in Themba's direction. Themba was reminded of the old male buffalo that had nearly killed him in Hluhluwe.

'What do you want?' Dlamini asked, drawing out each word.

Themba swallowed. 'To apologise, sir. I am very sorry for everything that happened to Lerato.'

Dlamini scowled. 'You are a criminal. If I so much as hear from a teacher that you have even spoken to my daughter I will have you arrested.'

'Father.' Lerato lifted her face from his chest and sniffed. 'Themba can't be blamed for what happened.'

'He was supposed to see you home safely.'

'And he did, Daddy,' she said.

Dlamini glared at him. 'If I had known you were a car thief, I would never have allowed you to escort Lerato.'

'He's not a thief, Daddy,' Lerato said. She grabbed her father's forearm.

Themba cleared his throat. 'I have something to ask.'

Dlamini raised his eyebrows. 'You have some temerity.'

Themba drew a breath. 'I would like permission to see Lerato, outside of school hours.'

'No.'

Lerato let go of her father and stood. She went to Themba and stood so close to him she was almost touching him. 'Themba, I would love to go out with you.' His worried face broke into a grin. 'Though perhaps not to a game reserve, at least not for some time.'

He laughed, and then got such a shock he thought he might faint when she reached out to him, put her arms around his neck and kissed him on the cheek.

*

Nia walked down the street from her hotel to the bank in Zurich. The buildings were three and four storeys high, painted in subdued colours.

It was sunny but cool enough for her to have needed to buy a coat. There wasn't a scrap of litter on the footpath or in the gutter and the people she passed were dressed neatly and conservatively, mostly in business attire.

She went to the door of the bank, which was located in a non-descript, modern stone building, and pushed the button on the intercom. Only a tiny plaque the size of a postcard advertised the bank's name, Grunelius. She'd felt foolish earlier, and as polite as the bank manager had been he'd been unable to hide his disapproving look of suspicion as she had fumbled her way through as many combinations of the passcode as she could think of.

'Miss Carras, how nice to see you again.' The man's eyes spoke otherwise as he let her into the building.

'I have the passcode,' she said.

He raised his eyebrows. 'Please, take a seat.'

Nia read the account number to him, as she had done yesterday, and his fingers were barely audible on the keyboard.

'The passcode is 30–1–16,' she said.

Mike had called her, in the night, and told her that he had spoken to his ex-wife, Tracy. He had remembered that Tracy had met Suzanne Fessey when Suzanne had been masquerading as a policewoman, and he'd asked Tracy whether she had noticed a visible tattoo of anything on the other woman. Tracy had told Mike that Suzanne had a date tattooed on the inside of her right arm, and that the two of them had discussed its significance. The day and month of the date, the birthday of Suzanne's son, were the same as their daughter Debbie's. Suzanne had explained that her son had been born in 2016.

The banker typed in the numbers and dashes, then looked at her over the top of the computer monitor. 'Here we are. How can I assist you?'

'Can I see the balance of the account?'

'Of course.'

The man swivelled the large monitor of his computer around so Nia could see it.

'*Eish*,' she said aloud.

Chapter 35

The next day Mike parked his rented car at Johannesburg's O. R. Tambo International Airport and walked through the undercover parking area to the terminal buildings and downstairs to Arrivals.

The hall was busy as always. Families were waiting for loved ones while safari operators and hire car drivers held signs with the names of arriving passengers. Two security guards in blue camouflage uniforms and matching berets patrolled past Mike as he took up a position and waited for Nia.

He checked his watch. It was 10.55. Nia had messaged him just after Swissair flight LX288 had landed, on time, at 10.25.

Long queue at immigration, was the next message he received from her.

All clear on this side, he replied.

'Mike.'

He turned around and realised he had messaged too soon to Nia. 'Jed.'

'I'm not here to grab Nia, if that's what you're wondering.'

Mike looked around the terminal for any other signs of

muscle power. 'The thought had come to mind.'

'I've got bad news, Mike,' Jed said. 'Suzanne Fessey is in the wind.'

Mike's chest tightened. 'She escaped?'

Jed nodded. 'Franklin didn't check in when he was supposed to, after leaving Louis Trichardt yesterday. Suzanne never arrived at Johannesburg's women's prison, where she was to be held in maximum custody until the US and South African governments worked out who was going to prosecute her, and what for.'

'Franklin?'

'There was him and two South African police officers in the SUV. The Chevvie was found burned out on a farm between Pretoria and Joburg. There were the bodies of three men on board and no Suzanne. Initial report is that all of the men were shot, and there was no sign of Franklin's pistol in the wreck. Somehow she got the jump on them.'

'While she's alive and on the loose Nia's at risk.'

'And so are you, Mike,' Jed said.

Mike looked around the Arrivals hall again. A pair of South African police officers, armed with R5s, moved through. He guessed the additional security was a result of the recent bombing. 'Do the South Africans know that Nia's on this flight?'

'No.' Jed lowered his voice. 'If your friend Nia hit the jackpot and emptied the terrorists' bank account then the South African customs or police people would seize any sizeable amount of undeclared cash. If Nia doesn't play ball with us, and collect her reward for her troubles, then I'm afraid I will call the airport police into play.'

Mike had no idea what, if anything, Nia had found, and she had been unwilling to talk about it over the phone in case he was being listened in on. 'I don't know if she found anything in the bank account.'

Jed looked him in the eyes. 'I know that, Mike.'

Mike smiled. He'd been right. They were both on the CIA's radar now, he and Nia, and with Suzanne out there again Jed would be thinking, perhaps hoping, that they might lure Suzanne into the open.

Mike's phone beeped again. Nia had cleared immigration and was on her way through.

*

Chris Mitchell pulled into a short-term parking bay in the pick-up zone outside the airport terminal but didn't turn off the engine of the hired Mercedes transit van.

He reached over and turned up the volume on the car radio. He'd heard the news on 5FM half an hour ago, but his two passengers in the back would have missed it. The timing was perfect.

'The President announced today that South Africa would stand shoulder to shoulder with the United States in the fight against terrorism on the African continent following the assassination of Ambassador Anita Rosenfeld in Durban. This radical shift in national policy was tentatively welcomed by the opposition Democratic Alliance.'

Chris turned off the radio and looked back at the man and woman in South African police uniforms.

'We're almost done here. Nia Carras will be coming into the Arrivals hall any minute now. Banks is there, as is Mike Dunn. You two good to go?'

'Affirmative, sir,' said Franklin Washington. He looked to the woman next to him.

'Yes, I'm ready,' Suzanne Fessey said. She took the Z88 pistol from the leather holster on her belt and cocked it. Franklin did likewise and the pair did a quick check of their equipment and radios.

It had been a shame about the two South African police officers that Franklin and Suzanne had killed in the Chevrolet, and the homeless man they had killed and burned in the truck to make it look like Franklin was dead. More troubling to Chris was the death of the Navy aircrew on the helicopter that Paulsen's men had brought down. Suzanne Fessey had told Chris she had not known that their cache of weapons included an RPG-7 anti-armour weapon.

Events had overtaken him there for a while, Chris mused, after Suzanne's car had been hijacked. The initial response, coordinated by Jed Banks, had been almost too efficient. Paulsen and his men did not know Suzanne had been turned by the CIA and they had brought down the Sea Hawk with deadly force, nearly killing Chris's man, Franklin Washington, in the process.

Franklin had done a masterful job, going undercover in Syria, and making contact with Omar Farhat and his wife, Suzanne Fessey. The couple had travelled there, covertly, a couple of times a year to talk strategy with their new masters. Over the past two years Franklin had turned Suzanne, who had become increasingly disenchanted with the way women were being treated in the ISIS-controlled caliphate.

Suzanne had always exerted a large degree of control over her accountant husband, in all matters other than finance. Omar was ideologically committed to the struggle and had a brilliant mind, but he was a nervous man, and was not physically strong. He'd kept the details of bin Laden's secret bank account to himself, but, with Suzanne's prompting, had decided the time was nigh for another spectacular attack, at the same or greater level as that of 9–11, to allow al-Qaeda and its allies to remind the west of their power.

Behind the scenes, Franklin had facilitated meetings between Suzanne and Omar and other CIA agents posing as Russian arms dealers with a suitcase nuke for sale. Suzanne had convinced

Omar the operation would be best planned from a country not on America's day-to-day surveillance radar – her homeland of South Africa.

In recent months Franklin, through feeding false information to Paulsen via Russian-speaking CIA operatives, had preyed on Omar's nervy nature and convinced him the Americans were getting wind of their quest for a nuke and that Omar was about to be exposed. Suzanne had talked of the two of them going out in a suicide attack on a worthy target rather than risk imminent capture. Omar had, as Suzanne predicted, suggested she should stay alive to raise their infant son, Hassan. The child hadn't been planned and while Suzanne hadn't wanted him she had some affection for him and he had proved useful in establishing their cover in South Africa as a happy couple.

As Omar had planned his own death, rather than risk capture and interrogation, he'd told Suzanne that he would leave her the number and passcode of the Swiss bank account that contained the money set aside by the Sheik to purchase a nuclear weapon. On the morning of his death Omar had told Suzanne about the microchip he'd had implanted in Hassan, and added that he had included on the chip a clue that she would understand to let her know the passcode.

If it had all gone to plan, which it hadn't, Franklin would have met Suzanne on the road to Mozambique, and when she'd rendezvoused with Paulsen and his men, Franklin and Suzanne would have assassinated them.

The operation to disrupt the extremists' plan to acquire a nuke was real and Chris Mitchell took solace in the fact that he was helping to prevent a catastrophe, but that was where the righteousness ended. When Suzanne had told Franklin how much money was in the Sheik's account, and Franklin relayed that to Chris, the three of them decided to split it three ways once Omar was gone.

Suzanne slid open the side door of the van.

'No more mistakes,' Chris said.

'Roger that, sir, we'll be back in five,' Franklin said.

*

Suzanne saw a young mother in the crowd, holding a newborn baby. She and Franklin had talked about having a baby, as part of their plan to start over.

They stayed on the far side of the crowd from where Banks and Dunn were waiting for the helicopter pilot.

'In position,' Franklin said into his radio microphone, giving Chris an update.

Suzanne watched the automatic sliding doors open and a trio of passengers arrive. Two were a couple, the third was Nia Carras.

'Standby,' Suzanne said into her radio. 'Target in sight.'

'Go,' Franklin said.

Suzanne reached into the satchel bag around her neck and pulled out a CS tear gas grenade. She pulled the pin and tossed it, high and far, to the other side of the Arrivals hall. At the same time, Franklin dropped another CS grenade by their feet. In the four seconds it took both to detonate Suzanne and Franklin had pulled out the gas masks from the pouches strapped to their right thighs and put them on.

Immediately scores of people began running for the exits, which were already blocked. Half a dozen people were on the floor screaming in pain from the debilitating gas and a few brave souls were staying to tend to them or help lift and carry them to safety. Others were coughing and crying from the effects.

Suzanne and Franklin ran fast, each heading straight for their target. Suzanne barrelled into Nia, who was retching and holding her hands to her eyes. 'Come with me, miss, I'm police, I'll get you out.'

Franklin had his arms spread wide and was pushing Mike Dunn and Jed Banks towards the exit, away from Nia. With his gas mask on and the other men's eyes clearly burning from gas, Suzanne was sure neither Jed nor Mike would recognise him.

Suzanne grabbed Nia by the forearm and half guided, half pushed her towards a set of escalators. Nia looked over her shoulder. 'Keep moving, you have to get out of here.'

As they made it to the escalator and started moving, Suzanne saw that Mike and Jed were trying to push back, so Franklin dropped another tear gas grenade. As it went off Dunn and Banks were forced to back off, spluttering.

Suzanne pushed Nia higher and higher and, glancing around, saw that Franklin was backing up the escalator behind them.

Franklin grabbed one of Nia's arms and Suzanne the other and they half dragged, half propelled Nia towards the exit. While the tear gas had filtered upstairs its effects were only just being felt there and the doors were not yet blocked. They ran out of the terminal.

*

Nia gulped in the warm fresh air, her eyes streaming so much she was barely able to see.

The tear gas had been brutal, and now everywhere on her body where there was moisture – her eyes, her mouth, even under her arms where she'd been sweating – stung like someone was injecting her with hundreds of tiny needles.

A big black van loomed in her vision and the smaller of the two police officers, a female, opened the side door. 'Get in.'

Nia wiped her eyes. She'd been more than happy to let the police officers lead her out of the terminal, but she had assumed there would be other innocent victims of the gas attack behind her. When she looked around she saw it was just the three of them. Panic seized her.

'No.'

The man in the police uniform grabbed her arm and dragged

her to the door. Nia screamed, but the woman came up behind her and grabbed her. The two of them dragged her into the van and slammed the door.

A man with wavy grey hair and spectacles turned to face her from the driver's seat. 'Miss Carras, my name is Chris Mitchell. I'm CIA. You're safe, believe me.' He held out an ID card with his picture on the left-hand side and the agency's logo of an eagle's head atop a shield with a compass rose.

'What about your other man, Jed?' she said.

'Banks is fine,' said Chris. 'He's meeting us later.' He turned to the other two. 'Get Miss Carras some water, please.'

The van started to move as Chris reversed. The male in the police uniform produced a litre bottle of water. 'Kneel on the floor and put your arms out. Try and keep your eyes open and I'll douse you with water. It'll take away the sting of the CS – the tear gas.'

Nia did as she was told and the man doused her with water. He was right, it immediately began to relieve the pain of the gas.

'Where are you taking me?'

'Safety,' Chris replied from the front without looking back.

*

Mike wiped his stinging eyes and tried to focus. Nia was nowhere to be seen and neither were the two police officers who had rammed him and brought Jed to his knees.

The downstairs exits were still clogged but Mike craned his head and looked up to the next floor of the airport, Departures. 'Jed, they've gone that way.'

The two of them ran for the escalator and took the stairs two at a time. They rushed to the doors and outside. 'CD,' Jed said.

'What?' Mike asked.

Jed pointed to a black Mercedes van that was speeding away. 'That vehicle's got Diplomatic Corps number plates. It's a Merc.

403

I think I've seen it before.' He took out his phone. 'Something else. That cop in the gas mask who pushed us aside, I got a look at his eyes. It was Franklin.'

'Shit.' Mike opened a bottle of water he'd bought at an airport kiosk and flushed his eyes with it. He did the same for Jed and poured it over the American, who blinked as he talked on the phone to a woman named Janey. Mike gathered she handled administration at the embassy. Jed ended the call.

'One of yours?' Mike asked.

'You got it. It's from the fleet. My boss signed it out this morning.'

'What's the CIA doing here, Jed?'

'I could say "beats me", but I'd be lying,' said Jed. Jed made another call. 'Janey, hi, it's Jed Banks again. Say, Chris said he was flying out today and I wanted to try and get on the same flight as him. I can't raise him on his cell phone. You don't happen to have his itinerary, do you?'

People were streaming around them and sirens heralded the imminent arrival of fire, ambulance and police vehicles.

'Mike, Mike Dunn, right?'

He turned. From the direction of the airport car park a young man jogged to him. He carried a bouquet of flowers and was dressed in jeans and a tight-fitting T-shirt. 'Banger?'

'*Ja*, Nia's, er, friend. Is she here, is she all right? A security guy just told me there was a gas attack inside.'

'No, she's missing, been taken,' Mike said. 'We're trying to get a lead on who may have her.'

Banger put his hands over his eyes. 'I called her mom and dad and they said she'd been to Switzerland and was flying in today. I can't believe it. I'm late. I could have saved her.'

'We were waiting for her and we couldn't get to her.'

'What can I do? I'll do anything. I've got a car.'

Jed came to them and Mike quickly introduced Banger. 'OK,' Jed said, 'I found out that Chris Mitchell, my superior in the CIA, *is* driving the embassy's black Mercedes van, and he's taking a US military flight from Wonderboom Airport at Pretoria.'

'That's less than an hour north of here,' Banger said. 'When did they leave?'

'Just now,' Mike said. 'Five minutes ago. Let's go.'

'Are you driving that Landy of yours?' Banger said.

'No, a rental, nothing fast.'

'I've got my Golf GTI. I'll scout ahead on the N1. We'll stay in touch on WhatsApp.'

They quickly exchanged numbers and Jed decided to stay with Mike, reasoning that if they caught up with Chris it would be good to have one man behind the wheel and the other with his hands free. The three men ran to the cars.

'Be cool if you catch them first, Banger,' Jed said as they jogged. 'Remember Nia's on board and the guy driving is a senior CIA officer.'

'If I catch them first I'll stick on them like glue, *bru*.'

Chapter 36

Nia was worried. The policeman and woman, still in gas masks, sat on either side of her. 'Where are you taking me?'

'Somewhere safe, like I said,' Chris, the CIA man said. 'But first, I need some information from you.'

Nia looked out the window. It seemed they were heading north, towards Pretoria. 'Like what?'

'Oh, I think you know. I need the account number and the password or code that was on the microchip in the baby.'

Nia shook her head. 'Not until I see Mike Dunn and have a lawyer or some independent witness present.'

Chris kept his eyes on the road. 'I was afraid you were going to say that. Let me be a little clearer. If you don't give me that information, you're going to regret it.'

'You threatening me, Mr Mitchell?'

'Nope, I'll leave the threats to my colleagues there in the back with you.'

The man and the woman each grabbed one of her wrists and when Nia struggled they pushed her forward so that her knees hit the floor of the van, then twisted her arms painfully behind her. The woman snapped cold metal handcuffs on her.

'What the fuck?'

'Shut up.' The woman slapped her face, hard enough to knock her sideways. The man pulled her up by her hair. Nia screamed.

'You can't do this to me.'

Chris drove on, at a steady speed, not breaking the limit, not looking back or into the rear view mirror. 'Carry on.'

'Give us the numbers,' the woman said, then pulled off her mask.

Nia took a good look at her face and saw the scar. 'Suzanne Fessey!'

'Clever girl,' Suzanne said. 'Too clever.' She slapped her again.

'You murdered so many people.'

Suzanne shrugged, then pulled out her pistol and put the tip of the barrel against Nia's temple. 'One more won't get me in too much more trouble then, will it?'

Nia felt like she might wet herself, but tried to control her fear. 'You won't kill me. You need the information I have.'

'True,' Suzanne said. 'I can beat it out of you, or we can go somewhere quiet where I can start shooting you. I'll start with your kneecaps first.'

The man took off his gas mask and Nia saw it was Jed Banks's partner, Franklin Washington.

'No shooting in the car just yet, please,' Chris said from the front. 'Franklin, help Suzanne convince Miss Carras the old-fashioned way.'

'Hold her down,' Franklin said to Suzanne.

Suzanne smiled then grabbed Nia's shoulders and pulled her towards her side of the seat. Franklin reached for a pouch on his belt and took out a folding knife. He flicked it open.

'No!'

'Oh, yes,' said the man.

Franklin punched her, with his other hand, hard enough to make her vision go blurry.

'Gag her,' the man said.

Suzanne pushed her pistol harder into Nia's head then took out a handkerchief and stuffed it in her mouth.

Nia was wide-eyed, desperately sucking air in through her nostrils. She shook her head violently from side to side.

Nia looked over her shoulder at Suzanne Fessey. She just grinned and tightened her grip around Nia's torso while digging the gun hard into her skin. Nia kicked and writhed and the man hit her again.

'Folks,' Chris Mitchell said, looking in the rear view mirror, 'I hate to break up the party before it begins, but we really should give Nia a chance to say something.'

Franklin paused, the point of the knife's blade was resting just below her right eye. Suzanne pulled the handkerchief from her mouth.

Nia gasped for air, drawing in a deep breath, then the numbers of the account tumbled from her. Chris held up a hand for her to stop, then took an iPhone out of his pocket and, in between keeping an eye on the traffic, selected the voice recording application. 'Once more for the microphone, please.'

Nia repeated the number.

'And the passcode or word?'

'It was numbers,' Nia said, 'but they spelled the word "tattoo", like when you assign letters to numbers on a phone keypad. Mike's ex-wife saw the tattoo on your arm and remembered the date of birth of your baby.'

Chris glanced back at Suzanne. 'What do you think?'

Suzanne nodded to him. 'That sounds like Omar. He liked the baby far more than I did.'

'What did you do with the money?' Chris asked.

'Nothing,' Nia said, 'it's still in the account. It's all yours. Please let me go. I won't say anything, I promise. I don't want the money.'

Chris looked in the mirror again. 'Fuck her.' Chris's phone rang. 'Gag her, Suzanne.'

Suzanne stuffed the handkerchief in her mouth again and Nia watched in horror, still kicking as much as she could, as the man closed the gap between him and her. She felt him touching her and tried to scream again.

'Jed,' Chris said into his phone. 'Oh, I'm just out for a little morning drive, then flying out of here . . . No, I can't tell you where . . . No, I'm not going to do that and you are to stand down, and that's a direct order, mister.'

Nia tried to scream louder so that Jed might hear her, but Suzanne clamped a hand over her mouth.

Chris ended the call and then Nia could feel the point of Franklin's knife, pushing against her.

'One moment, please,' Chris said.

Franklin backed off and Suzanne removed the gag again.

'Anything else you might have neglected to tell us, Nia? I suspect there's more. By the time my friend here is finished with you, you might wish you'd been more forthcoming, if there's more to your story. We'll keep you alive, by the way, until we've confirmed that the money is still in the account. If it isn't we'll progress from taking an eye or two to something even more painful until you tell us where it is. OK?'

Nia stilled herself. 'I moved the money into a new account.'

Chris held up his phone and pressed record again. 'That's more like it. Number and password, please.'

Nia gave him the numbers. She had never intended to keep the money for herself in any case.

'Good, thank you,' said Chris.

Chris came to a red light on the upward slope of a hill and stopped and applied the handbrake. Nia looked out the window, tears welling in her eyes. Soon she would be dead.

Suzanne looked to Franklin then moved the barrel of her pistol from Nia's head. She aimed it at the back of the driver's seat and pulled the trigger, twice. Chris Mitchell's body jerked against his seatbelt.

Nia screamed.

Franklin opened the sliding door, jumped out, shifted Chris to the passenger seat and climbed in behind the wheel. He released the handbrake and accelerated just as the light turned green.

Chapter 37

Mike's phone rang and he hit the phone icon on the satellite navigation system screen in his Land Rover. Banger's voice came through on speaker via bluetooth.

'Mike, I'm at Wonderboom. I'm in the car park and there's no sign of the van.'

'Shit,' Mike said. He was lagging behind Banger, as was to be expected. 'They should have easily been there by now.'

'We could try the South African police,' Jed said, 'but without some high-level diplomatic intervention they'd be unwilling to stop a vehicle with diplomatic registration plates. I don't know how else we can track them.'

'Track?' said Banger. 'Dudes, welcome to my world. Jed, all new vehicles in South Africa over a certain value have to have satellite tracking devices fitted to them in order to qualify for insurance policies. There's no way your embassy van wouldn't have a tracker on it. Can you call the embassy and find out what company you guys use?'

'Sure thing,' said Jed.

Mike continued on the N1 while Jed made a call on his

phone. When he hung up he used the screen on Mike's sat nav to call Banger.

'Howzit, Mike?'

'Banger, it's Jed here. The US embassy uses a company called Motor Track.'

'Yes! That's my company. I know some of the guys in Joburg. Jed, I need you to call Motor Track and report that van stolen. Leave the rest to me.' Banger gave them the emergency number then hung up.

Jed dialled the number and made up a story about the vehicle being stolen from the car park of Wonderboom Airport. Mike was about to turn off to the airport when the phone rang again.

'Banger here, guys. OK, a *bru* of mine in Joburg has a fix on your van. They've scrambled a chopper and the good news is the pilot owes me a favour. Their control room says your van is heading southwest on the N14. I think they're heading for Lanseria.'

'That's Johannesburg's second airport,' Mike said for Jed's benefit. 'They could have an international charter booked from there.'

Jed nodded. 'Banger, can you catch them?'

'Man, I'm doing one-eighty now. I'll catch them all right, now I know where I'm headed. You guys will be like a day behind me. The Motor Track guys use Bell Jet Rangers up here because the elevation's so much higher than Durban. They need bigger choppers than those little R44s that Nia flies to cut it in this thin air on the highveld. Andrew Barton's the pilot, and he's got room for you two in the back. I'll SMS you his contact details and you *okes* can tee up where to meet him.'

'Roger that,' said Jed. 'And thanks.'

*

Nia sat at one end of the bench seat in the back of the van, furthest from the door, and Suzanne sat at the other, covering her with her pistol.

Nia shuddered at the thought of what might have happened to her, but was even more afraid of what the couple planned next.

'We're taking you to a storage unit,' Suzanne said. 'I'm not going to kill you. We're going to tie you up and leave you there, no food or water I'm afraid, but if we get to Switzerland, use your new account number and passcode and find the money, then we'll make a call to the storage people and they'll come and get you. OK?'

Nia sniffed and gave a small nod. She wanted so much to believe that it might be the truth, that she might yet live.

'However, if the account number or passcode are wrong we'll make our way back here. It will take a little while, but you'll still be alive, starving and dehydrated, and Franklin will torture you until you give us the correct information. Worst case scenario, we can't come back to South Africa because the security's too hot so you will die of starvation and we'll still disappear.'

From the N14 they eventually turned onto the R512 which led to Lanseria Airport. The countryside here was still semi-rural and the traffic light. At a certain point, Franklin pulled over. He exited the vehicle, went around to the passenger side, and pulled out Chris Mitchell's body. Nia watched as he dragged the senior CIA man to a ditch then got back in.

'This is all about money, isn't it?' Nia asked.

Suzanne rocked her head from side to side. 'Yes and no. I spent enough time in Syria to know that I didn't want to live in an Islamic state any more, and Franklin spent enough time outside of America, doing his country's dirty work, to know he didn't want to call the Great Satan home. Neither of us wants the jihadis to get hold of a nuke. Of course, we also need some retirement money.'

The van was in the left lane and Nia saw a small car draw alongside them, on the right, keep pace with them for a second, then accelerate away. As it moved ahead of them she saw the distinctive Motor Track 'Eye in the sky' slogan on its rear. She caught a glimpse of the number plate: BANGBANG-ZN.

Nia bit her lower lip and her heart started to pound. Banger had bought an ex Motor Track Golf and hadn't yet got around to having the logos removed. Bighead that he was, he had found time to get some personalised number plates made.

She thought fast. She needed to distract Suzanne and Franklin. 'What about your baby, Hassan? Don't you care about him?'

Suzanne glared at her. 'It's none of your business.'

'Come on, you're his mom.'

'Shut up,' Suzanne said.

'I can't believe you're such a heartless bitch, Suzanne.'

Suzanne pointed her pistol between Nia's eyes. 'He's somewhere safe. That's good enough for me!'

'You're worse than an animal, Suzanne. At least a hyena or a vulture cares for her young.'

Franklin, who had been concentrating on driving, turned back to her. 'Shut the fuck up, bitch, or you're dead.'

'No, you are,' said Nia.

He looked back at her again. 'What the hell are you talking about?'

*

'He's distracted.' Banger's voice came through their headsets from the hands-free microphone in his car. 'Looking back. Time to giddy-up, amigos.'

'Don't mix your Western vernacular,' Jed said.

Banger laughed.

Mike had his pistol drawn and ready, as did Jed. Andrew Barton, the Motor Track helicopter pilot, had held position behind and above the Mercedes van while Banger overtook the vehicle and moved into position. Banger was now in front of the van.

'Slowing now,' Banger said, his voice calm and serious again.

'No other vehicles in sight,' said Mike. 'You sure you want to do it this way?'

'Affirmative,' said Banger.

Mike took a deep breath. They had discussed the options and Banger had argued that if the helicopter made itself known to the fleeing terrorists then they might kill Nia. For the same reason they had avoided contacting the South African police. Seeing an impromptu roadblock would also force their hand. They had to do this hard and fast.

'All clear?' Banger said.

Mike and Jed checked left and right out of the Jet Ranger and gave each other the thumbs-up. 'All clear, Banger,' Mike said. 'No traffic for a kilometre behind us.'

'Mike,' Banger said.

'Yes?'

'Do me a favour, *bru*, two in fact.'

'Sure.'

'Tell Nia I love her, even though I did fuck things up.'

'Don't be morbid. You've got an airbag and there's no one in front of you,' Mike said.

'I'm serious, dude.'

'OK,' Mike said, 'will do. What's the other favour?'

'Take care of her, man.'

'Cars coming up behind us,' Jed said. 'Now or never.'

'Remember, Nia's on the left side. *Adios*, amigos,' Banger said.

Mike watched as Banger bled off speed by lifting his foot off the accelerator. On this stretch of the R512 the road had narrowed to a single lane. When there was just fifty metres between the Golf and the Mercedes van behind it, the driver of the van switched on his right indicator, to overtake.

The Golf's tail-lights glowed bright red as Banger stood on the brakes and pulled on the handbrake and the van ploughed into him.

Banger held firm as his tyres blew out and sparks flew from the rims of his wheels. Andrew brought the Jet Ranger around to the left, trailing the vehicles which, locked together, skidded down the road. As they came to a halt Andrew dropped to a hover, a metre off the ground.

Jed and Mike already had the doors open and they jumped out. Jed went around the rear of the van, pistol up and ready, and headed towards the driver's door. Mike went to the left-hand side, where Banger had reported seeing Nia. The window on that side of the van shattered as two shots came his way. Mike dropped to the ground.

Mike moved backwards, to the rear of the van, hoping to get a clean shot from the rear.

'Mike, she's got a grenade!' Nia called, her words followed by a cry of pain.

A woman's hand reached out of the broken window and tossed out a hand grenade, which hit the ground with a metallic thud a couple of metres from the van. Mike moved behind the vehicle and ran. The explosion rocked the van and smoke washed over them.

Mike glanced around the right side of the Mercedes and saw that Jed had his gun up, pointing at the driver.

'Franklin, toss your gun out,' Jed called.

Franklin opened the door and staggered out from behind the inflated airbag. He carried a pistol in his right hand. Mike took aim at his broad back. He couldn't fire, though, in case he hit Jed, who was just beyond Franklin.

'Drop it, buddy,' Jed said. 'Let's talk.'

'OK.' Franklin held his gun arm out to the right, and just as it looked like he was going to drop it he turned his pistol on Jed and fired.

Jed returned fire, two shots, and Franklin's body jerked, but he didn't go down. Jed, on the other hand, dropped to one knee.

Mike didn't know if Franklin was wearing body armour, or if one or both of Jed's shots had been deflected by some of the police gear that Franklin still had on. Mike acted instinctively and fired a shot into the back of Franklin's head. He pitched forward, dead.

'I'll kill her,' Suzanne called from inside the van. 'Both of you back off, put your guns down. I'm coming out.'

Suzanne was holding Nia close to her, one arm around her neck and the pistol in her right hand held up under Nia's jaw. She eased Nia out first, and when her feet were on the ground Suzanne looked around her.

Mike had his pistol aimed at Suzanne. Jed was sitting, his gun also up, though his aim was wavering. He'd been hit somewhere in the chest or shoulder.

*

Banger used his Leatherman to puncture the airbag in his Golf. He crawled over the centre console of the little car to the passenger door, opened it, and slid out. He made his way on knees and elbows along the side of his car and halfway down the length of the Mercedes van.

He'd heard the grenade go off, and the firing. He pulled his Glock from the pancake holster on his belt and crawled under the chassis. He could see feet – Suzanne's and Nia's – and Jed Banks was sitting on the road, wounded, but holding up a gun. He also saw the body of a black man lying by the driver's side, no more than a metre from his face. Banger edged forward.

'Dunn, you're going to flag down the next car that passes,' Suzanne said.

Banger craned his neck and saw Mike Dunn's battered bush shoes at the rear of the van. He inched even further forward, thinking that if he could get close enough to Suzanne, he could maybe take a killer shot. The angle was difficult, though, and he had to be sure that if he shot her the bullet wouldn't go through her into Nia.

He looked right and then left again. Then Jed moved his head, just a fraction, and they locked eyes for a moment.

Jed spoke up. 'Suzanne, this is over for you. You're not going to get out of South Africa alive and get on a plane to Switzerland.'

'Shut up, and drop your gun.'

'Take me, Suzanne,' Mike Dunn said from the right. 'I've got the account number and the code.'

'I've already got that. It took surprisingly little effort,' Suzanne said. 'And in case you didn't know, your friend here moved the money into a new account and I've got that number as well. Toss your gun away, now, Dunn, to me, or I'll start shooting her, someplace where it will hurt, but which will still allow her to move.'

Suzanne took a step backwards, so that she was half leaning into the van's open doorway, as Dunn tossed his pistol to her. *Damn*, Banger, thought. Suzanne's move made it almost impossible for him to fire up at her.

From above he heard the chop of rotor blades. Andrew was coming back in the Jet Ranger. Angus heard the whine of the jet engine getting louder as the helicopter approached. Suzanne shuffled a pace to the side.

Banger looked over to Jed, who gave him the slightest of nods, then started to stand.

'Get down,' Suzanne yelled over the noise of the helicopter. Dust and dirt blasted them from the rotor wash.

Jed half stood, then, seeming to think better of it, dived to one side. Banger rolled out from under the van, the sound of his scrambling on the road covered by the helicopter's noise. He reached up and grabbed a startled Nia by the belt on her jeans.

Suzanne Fessey had moved her pistol from Nia's chin so that she could fire two shots at Jed. Banger hauled on Nia's belt and wrenched her from Suzanne's grasp.

'Run!' Banger yelled.

Lying on his back, Banger fired up at Suzanne, two shots. One went into her body armour, but the other seemed to go under her vest and up into her body. She pitched backwards into the van.

Banger was fit, strong, and fast. As he sprang to his feet, bringing his gun up at the same time, he saw Mike Dunn catching Nia and ushering her deeper into the dust cloud.

Suzanne Fessey was not as badly hurt as Banger hoped. From outside the van he saw her bring her pistol up and aim it at Nia's back. Banger did the only thing he could do – he dodged to the right, putting himself between Suzanne and Nia.

As the bullets from Suzanne's pistol smashed through his body Banger kept firing, until both of them went down.

Chapter 38

One year later

Mike put his hand on his hat to stop it blowing off as Nia flared the nose of her latest acquisition, a new Gazelle helicopter, and set down in an open grassy area near the lodge on the game farm Bandile Dlamini had recently purchased.

Mike opened the rear side door of the helicopter and Lerato stepped out, looking beautiful in a white off-the-shoulder wedding dress.

Next out was her father's girlfriend, a glamorous Eyewitness News reporter who had met Bandile while interviewing him in the aftermath of last year's terrible events. In her arms she carried a coffee-coloured toddler who was giggling with excitement from the helicopter ride. Harrison Dlamini, formerly Hassan Farhat, was now the ward of the wealthy former politician, a half-brother of sorts to Lerato.

Bandile himself was smiling widely as he climbed down and shook Mike's hand. 'So good to see you again, Michael, and in much better circumstances.'

'Indeed,' Mike said. 'You must be very proud.'

Bandile looked to Lerato. 'In the eyes of our culture Lerato and Themba are too young to be getting married, but their courtship was anything but traditional. By the way my former employee, who was selling the vulture heads without my knowledge on the day we met at the Mona market, has just been sentenced to a year in prison.'

Mike nodded. 'Could have been longer, but that's good news.'

'I agree.'

Lerato came to Mike and he kissed her on the cheek and took her hand. 'Good luck, Lerato.'

'After what I've been through, this will be a walk in the park.'

Bandile led his daughter, partner and son to a waiting Land Rover game viewer, driven by one of his safari guides.

Mike went to Nia and hugged and kissed her.

She laughed. 'Don't ruin my makeup, you know I hardly ever wear it.'

She took a step back from him and unzipped her one-piece black flight suit. The logo above the left pocket was the same as the one on the shiny new helicopter, that of the Endangered Species Organisation. ESO was a relatively new wildlife charity, set up in Australia some eleven months earlier. Nia's father was a board member.

Nia peeled off the flight suit and, with Mike holding one hand to steady her, stepped out of it. Underneath she was wearing a short, simple, sexy little black dress.

'Like a female James Bond,' Mike said.

'I've always wanted to do something like that,' she said, grinning. She reached into the helicopter and took out a pair of high heels.

He kissed her again. 'I love you,' he said.

They went to a second Land Rover, which took off immediately. The idea was that Mike and Nia would join the other guests first and take their seats while the bridal party followed slowly behind.

Mike and Nia got down off the game viewer after the short drive over rough ground. Themba was standing at the front, by the celebrant, looking very sharp and serious in a black dinner suit. His sister, Nandi, was in the front row on the groom's side, smiling broadly. She had been released from the care of the foster family and now lived with Themba. He caught sight of Mike and Nia and waved.

They waved back and eased past some seated guests to take two vacant chairs. At the end of the row, with a beautiful blonde holding his walking stick, was Angus Greiner. He smiled at them and Nia nodded to him. 'That's Banger's physical therapist,' Nia whispered to Mike. 'His rehabilitation's taking a long time, but he doesn't seem to be complaining.'

Mike chuckled in reply.

'Mike, Nia, how you doing?'

Mike turned at the sound of the American accent. Jed Banks was sitting behind them, wearing a blue blazer and khaki chinos.

'Jed,' Mike said as they shook hands, 'I didn't know you got an invite.'

'I'm a spy, right, who needs an invite?' He grinned. 'Seriously, I did get an invitation from the big man. We've talked a few times over the past year. You hear he might be running for politics again, on the other side this time?'

'I did read that,' Mike said.

Jed leaned closer to Mike. 'Official report's about to be released from Langley. The CIA's position is that Chris Mitchell and Franklin Washington were killed while trying to apprehend a wanted terrorist, Suzanne Fessey.'

'Official cover up, by the sound of it,' Mike said.

'It doesn't sit well with me, either,' Jed said.

'Was Suzanne ever really working for the CIA?' Mike asked.

Jed shrugged. 'The operation to stop the extremists getting a suitcase nuke was sanctioned. Franklin turned her, but at some point for the three of them, Franklin, Chris and Suzanne, it became all about the money. Chris had worked in Syria as well, prior to taking over in Africa. The word behind the scenes is that Chris had a gambling problem and big debts he was able to hide from the Company. Suzanne and Franklin were made for each other. Franklin's psych evaluations showed he was screwed up by the Middle East and some of the things he'd done there while undercover. They probably never intended to share the money with Chris. Phone records showed that Franklin was feeding information to Suzanne all the way through the chase, which is how she managed to stay a step ahead. She was going to use Paulsen and his guys to get her out of South Africa, but she was always going to waste all of them at some point to cover her tracks from the bad guys.'

'We thought the police or the CIA were tracing our phones,' Mike said.

Jed shook his head. 'Say, Nia, I guess you never remembered what happened to all that money, did you?'

Nia smiled. 'Like I said, Jed, the account was empty.'

Jed raised his eyebrows. 'Not like the piggy bank of the Endangered Species Organisation. They've been busy in this part of the world lately. A new helicopter for the company you're now a partner in; a university scholarship with all fees and accommodation covered for Themba and twenty other local kids who want to study environmental-related subjects.'

'They're a very generous organisation,' Mike said.

'Very,' Jed agreed. 'Even set you up with a vulture and birds of prey rehabilitation and education centre near Hluhluwe. You enjoying being the boss there?'

Mike adjusted his hat. 'Well, I do miss all the field work, but we're doing good work in the reserves and, more importantly, in the local schools and communities, educating people. That all costs money, and I have to keep an eye on the books.'

'I bet. I've been doing some more asking around and I see that your colleague, John Buttenshaw, Nia, has all the special care and wheelchair modifications that he needed for his home after being filled full of lead and left for dead by Suzanne and co.'

'What are you getting at, Jed?' Nia asked.

'Oh, nothing. We could have used that money for good, too, you know.'

'What's better, do you think, fighting wars or protecting the environment for the kids of tomorrow?' Nia asked.

'Well, as a father of two I think you can guess my answer. I just wanted to let you two know it's all over. You won't hear from me again.'

Mike reached out a hand again and Jed took it. 'Thanks, but we'll stay in touch, Jed. I need to send you an invitation to another wedding soon.'

Jed looked to Nia, who beamed back at him.

Mike stood, along with the rest of the guests. 'Here comes the bride.'

He looked up at the clear blue sky and far off he picked out the telltale swirl of specks. Inqe. It was a good sign.

Acknowledgements

With so many wildlife species in peril it's easy to overlook some of the smaller and less glamorous creatures (at least in some people's eyes) that are staring down the barrel of extinction.

I'm especially grateful to real-life 'vulture man' Andre Botha, manager of South Africa's Endangered Wildlife Trust Birds of Prey Programme, for suggesting I write a book which touched on the plight of vultures. The senseless killing of these magnificent birds, as described in this book, is happening now. It's a tragedy not just for the birds themselves, but for the wider natural environment which depends on them to keep the landscape healthy and habitable. Andre assisted with my early research and read and corrected the finished manuscript.

As always I'm indebted to many people who gave their time and knowledge to help me with researching and reviewing this story. I'll try not to forget anyone.

Annelien Oberholzer did an excellent job yet again of correcting not only my Afrikaans and other South Africanisms, but also several other errors. Sydney psychotherapist Charlotte

Stapf provided valuable feedback on the motivations of my characters and other aspects of the story. I'm grateful to former South African Defence Force sniper Fritz Rabe for his help with firearms matters; to Mike Reid for his time and his comments on helicopter flying; and Mike Furner and Tyler van der Merwe from JNC Helicopters, Virginia Airport, Durban, for information on car tracking.

My friends Peter and Alison Nairn showed me the sights of Durban several times; Warrant Officer Bobby Freeman, Regimental Sergeant Major of the Natal Mounted Rifles, gave me a tour of the regiment's impressive base (and even more impressive mess); Tema Matsebula provided valuable feedback on the manuscript; and Section Ranger Dennis Kelly from Hluhluwe–iMfolozi Park answered my many questions about poaching and the trade in illegal wildlife products. Thank you, all.

As with many of my previous books I've handed over the surprisingly tricky job of thinking up character names to a number of worthy charities and causes. The following people made donations to have names assigned to the cast of *Red Earth*: Mike Dunn, Chris Mitchell, Nicholas Duncan (on behalf of Nia Carras) and Suzanne Fessey, contributed to Painted Dog Conservation Inc; Annie Nolan (on behalf of Boyd Qualtrough), and Yvonne Buttenshaw (on behalf of John Buttenshaw) donated to Breaking the Brand (an Australian NGO focusing on the reduction of demand for rhino horn in Vietnam); and my former boss, Nick Greiner AM (on behalf of his grandson Angus 'Banger' Greiner), and Lisa Paulsen (on behalf of Egil Paulsen and Tracy Zietsch) made donations to causes close to their hearts. Jordan and Tim Penquitt are the sons of my friend Roger, who kept my morale up when we both served in Afghanistan.

Thirteen novels on my wonderful team of unpaid editors – my wife Nicola, mother Kathy, and mother-in-law Sheila – once again did an excellent job helping me to iron out timelines, correct inconsistencies and improve my characters. Thanks, too, to my other 'family' at Pan Macmillan Australia – Publishing Director Cate Paterson, Production Editor Danielle Walker, and copy editor Brianne Collins for their hard work, wise counsel, and their faith in me. Thanks, too, go to my agent, Isobel Dixon, and Pan Macmillan's affiliates in the United Kingdom and South Africa. I'm grateful to all of you for helping me live my dream.

I often use social media, not just to waste time, but to kick around ideas and get feedback from readers and friends. If you'd care to look for me on Facebook or Twitter you can find me as Tony Park Author, or via my website, www.tonypark.net. I'd love to hear from you.

Lastly, if you're still reading this, thank you. I couldn't do this without you.

MORE BESTSELLING FICTION FROM TONY PARK

An Empty Coast

A body. A cover-up. A buried secret.

Sonja Kurtz – former soldier, supposedly retired mercenary – is in Vietnam carrying out a personal revenge mission when her daughter sends a call for help. Emma, a student archaeologist on a dig at the edge of Namibia's Etosha National Park, has discovered a body dating back to the country's liberation war of the 1980s.

The remains of the airman, identified as former CIA agent Hudson Brand, are a key piece of a puzzle that will reveal the location of a modern-day buried treasure – a find people will kill for.

But Hudson Brand is very much alive, and he is on a quest to solve a decades-old mystery whose clues are entombed in an empty corner of the desert.

'Park writes with vigour and the story unfolds . . . with plenty of action . . . fascinating characters, interesting history and a real love of the country' CANBERRA TIMES

'Gripping action thrillers . . . never disappoints as a storyteller'
DAILY TELEGRAPH

The Hunter

Safari guide and private investigator Hudson Brand hunts people, not animals. He's on the trail of Linley Brown who's been named as the beneficiary of a life insurance policy.

Linley's friend, Kate, supposedly died in a fiery car accident in Zimbabwe, but Kate's sister wants to believe it is an elaborate fraud.

South African detective Sannie van Rensburg is also looking for Linley, as well as a serial killer who has been murdering prostitutes on Sannie's watch. Top of her list of suspects is Hudson Brand.

Sannie and Hudson cross paths and swords as they track the elusive Linley from South Africa and Zimbabwe to the wilds of Kenya's Masai Mara game reserve.

Tony Park's trademark storytelling prowess turns this hunt into a thrilling – and deadly – escapade through some of the most dangerous, yet beautiful, places on earth.

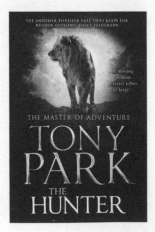

'Australian author Park, who spends much of his time living in South Africa, writes in the vein of Wilbur Smith and Bryce Courtenay, with a deep love for the African bush and wildlife.'
SUNDAY AGE

The Prey

Deep underground in the Eureka mine, South Africa's *zama zamas* illegally hunt for gold. King of this brutal underworld is Wellington Shumba – a man who rules his pirate miners through fear of torture and death.

Running Eureka's legitimate operation is former recce commando Cameron McMurtrie. When one of his engineers is taken hostage, Cameron does not hesitate to mastermind a dramatic rescue – and finish it off with a manhunt for Wellington. That is until corporate interference from the mine's Australia head office, in the shape of ambitious high-flyer Kylie Hamilton, gets in his way.

Doctor Hamilton is visiting South Africa supposedly to finalise a new mine on the border of the famed Kruger National Park, but instead she and Cameron are forced into a partnership to fend off an environmental war above ground, and a deadly battle with a ruthless killer below.

Cameron and Kylie have become Wellington's prey.

They must unite – their lives depend on it.

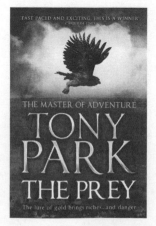

FAST PACED AND EXCITING. THIS IS A WINNER'
CANBERRA TIMES

THE MASTER OF ADVENTURE

TONY PARK

THE PREY

The lure of gold brings riches...and danger

Dark Heart

Atrocities from the past rise to the surface in this thrilling race to the death across Southern Africa.

Lawyer Mike Ioannou is dead after a hit and run in Thailand. A home invasion threatens the life of medico Richard Dunlop. In Johannesburg, a car jacker nearly kills photo journalist Liesl Nel.

Australian war crimes prosecutor Carmel Shang realises that all three victims are linked by a photograph that was clutched in the hand of a dying man in Rwanda nearly twenty years ago . . .

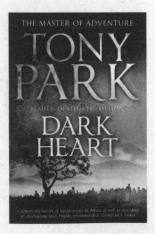

African Dawn

Three families share a history as complex and bloody as Zimbabwe itself.

Dedicated conservationists Paul and Philippa Bryant clash with the corrupt government minister, Emmerson Ngwenya. Twin brothers, ex-soldier Braedan and environmentalist Tate join the fight.

But when the brothers fall in love with the same woman, Natalie Bryant, their rivalry threatens to put the lives of all involved at risk.

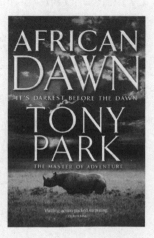

The Delta

After a failed assassination attempt on the president of Zimbabwe, ex-soldier turned mercenary Sonja Kurtz is on the run and heads for her only place of refuge, the Okavango Delta in the heart of Botswana. She's looking to rekindle a romance with her childhood sweetheart, safari camp manager Stirling Smith, and desperately wants a fresh start and to leave her perilous warrior lifestyle behind.

But Sonja discovers her beloved Delta is on the brink of destruction. She is recruited as an 'eco-commando' in a bid to halt a project that will destroy forever the Delta's fragile network of swamps and waterways.

Soon Sonja finds herself caught in a deadly web of intrigue involving Stirling, the handsome Martin Steele – her mercenary commander – and TV heart-throb and wildlife documentary presenter 'Coyote' Sam Chapman who blunders out of the bush in a reality show gone wrong.

Instead of escaping her violent past, Sonja is now surrounded by men who are relying on her killer instincts to save the day.

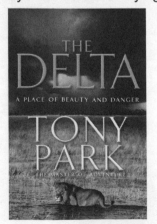

Where she came to find peace, she finds war . . . and it is not just the survival of the Delta that is at stake.

Ivory

Alex Tremain is a pirate in trouble.

The two women in his life – one of them his financial adviser, the other his diesel mechanic – have left him. He's facing a mounting tide of debts and his crew of modern-day buccaneers, a multi-national band of ex-military cut-throats, is getting restless.

They don't all share his dream of going legit, but what Alex really wants is to re-open the five-star resort hotel which once belonged to his Portuguese mother and English father on the Island of Dreams, off the coast of Mozambique.

A chance raid on a wildlife smuggling ship sets the Chinese triads after him and, to add to his woes, corporate lawyer Jane Humphries lands, literally, in his lap. Another woman is the last thing Captain Tremain needs right now – especially one whose lover is a ruthless shipping magnate backed up by a deadly bunch of contract killers.

Meanwhile Jane finds herself torn between the crooked but charming pirate and her coolly calculating millionaire boss, George Penfold. Both are passionate, and both are dangerous. What Alex really needs is one last big heist – something valuable enough to fulfil his dreams and set him and his men up for life.

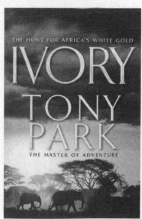

Silent Predator

In a luxury safari lodge in Kruger National Park, Detective Sergeant Tom Furey has just woken to a protection officer's worst nightmare. The government minister in his charge has been abducted.

Furey, and his local counterpart, Inspector Sannie van Rensburg, go against official orders and track the kidnappers to the coastal waters of Mozambique, and then north to the shores of Lake Malawi. Sannie can't resist becoming involved in Tom's mission, even risking her job to help him.

Africa is a land of danger as well as beauty, and soon lives are at risk. The hunt spirals into a fight to the death, and involves a crime beyond anyone's worst imaginings . . .

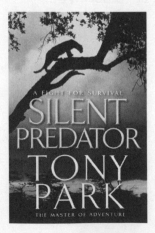

Safari

A volatile Zimbabwe and the jungles of the Democratic Republic of Congo are the battlefields for a deadly game of cat and mouse in Africa's wildlife wars.

Canadian researcher Michelle Parker jumps at the chance to visit the famed mountain gorillas, but she is wary of the man giving her this opportunity – professional big-game hunter Fletcher Reynolds.

Fletcher represents all Michelle has fought against – the slaughter of animals for material gain – but she finds herself increasingly drawn to his power and is reassured by his apparent support for the stamping out of poaching.

Into this mix steps ex-SAS officer Shane Castle. He has been recruited by Fletcher to spearhead the anti-poaching campaign. Shane is a man who has seen what bullets can do – to both human and animal – and he makes Michelle start to doubt the choices she has made . . .

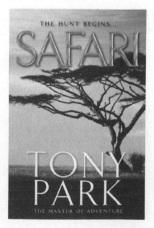

African Sky

Paul Bryant hasn't been able to get back in a plane since a fatal bombing mission over Germany. So, instead, the Squadron Leader is flying a desk at a pilot training school at Kumalo air base, Rhodesia.

Pip Lovejoy, a volunteer policewoman, is also trying to suppress painful memories. When Felicity Langham, a high-profile WAAF from the air base, is found raped and murdered, Pip and Bryant's paths cross.

Pip unearths a link between the Squadron Leader, the controversial heiress Catherine De Beers and the dead woman. What Pip thinks is a singular crime of passion soon escalates into a crisis that could change the course of the war.

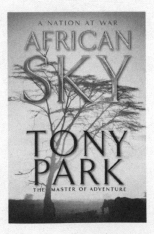